The *Paths* of the *Dead*

The Paths of the Dead

BOOK ONE OF THE VISCOUNT OF ADRILANKHA

STEVEN BRUST, P.J.F.

A TOM DOHERTY ASSOCIATES BOOK
NEW YORK

THE PATHS OF THE DEAD: BOOK ONE OF THE VISCOUNT OF ADRILANKHA

Copyright © 2002 by Steven Brust
"Publisher's Note" copyright © 2002 by Emma Bull
"Some Notes Toward Two Analyses of Auctorial Method and Voice" copyright © 2002 by Teresa Nielsen Hayden

Edited by Teresa Nielsen Hayden

A Tor Book
Published by Tom Doherty Associates, LLC
175 Fifth Avenue
New York, NY 10010

www.tor.com

Tor® is a registered trademark of Tom Doherty Associates, LLC.

ISBN: 0-312-86478-7

First Edition: December 2002

Printed in the United States of America

0 9 8 7 6 5 4 3 2 1

For Betsy

Acknowledgments

Thanks to David S. Cargo, with whom I consulted on the economics of feudal expansion, and Ilona Berry, who helped with geography. Thanks to Beki Oshiro, who did some great research for me. Thanks to Terry McGarry for outstanding copyediting. Without some timely remarks by Jason Jones, the books would have been worse by twelve inches or so.

As always, thanks to Robert Sloan, a k a Adrian Morgan, who did so much work on Dragaeran history and background.

Much thanks for heroic Scribblification to Pamela Dean, Will Shetterly, and Emma Bull (who also threw in the title).

It would, in addition, be manifestly unfair if I did not mention the various Dragaeran fan pages, most particularly Mark A. Mandel's Web site, *Cracks and Shards*, which, at this writing, is at: world.std.com/~main/Cracks-and-Shards/. I continually found myself using this site as a reference to avoid tripping over my own feet, especially with such matters as timing and geography. Thanks to this, most (or at least, many) of the inconsistencies between this book and my other works set on Dragaera were introduced maliciously, rather than by accident.

The Viscount of Adrilankha

BOOK ONE

The Paths of the Dead

Describing Certain Events Which Occurred
Between the 156th and the 247th Years
of the Interregnum

Submitted to the Imperial Library
By Springsign Manor
House of the Hawk
On this 3rd day the Month of the Athyra
Of the Year of the Vallista
Of the Turn of the Jhereg
Of the Phase of the Phoenix
Of the Reign of the Dragon
In the Cycle of the Phoenix
In the Great Cycle of the Dragon
Or, in the 179th Year
Of the Glorious Reign
Of the Empress Norathar the Second

By Sir Paarfi of Roundwood
House of the Hawk
(His Arms, Seal, Lineage Block)

Presented, as Always,
To Marchioness Poorborn
With Gratitude and Affection

Cast of Characters

Blackchapel and Castle Black
Morrolan — An Apprentice witch
Erik — A fool
Miska — A coachman
Arra — A Priestess
Teldra — An Issola
Fentor e'Mondaar — A Dragonlord
Fineol — A Vallista from Nacine
Oidwa — A Tsalmoth
Esteban — An Eastern witch

The Kanefthali Mountains
Skinter — A Count, afterward Duke
Marchioness of Habil — His cousin and strategist
Betraan e'Lanya — His tactician
Tsanaali — A lieutenant in Skinter's army
Izak — A general in Skinter's army
Brawre — A general in Skinter's army
Saakrew — An officer in Skinter's army
Udaar — An adviser and diplomatist
Hirtrinkneff — His assistant

The Society of the Porker Poker
Piro — The Viscount of Adrilankha
Lewchin — An Issola
Shant — A Dzurlord
Zivra — House unknown

Whitecrest and Environs
Daro — The Countess of Whitecrest
Khaavren — Her husband

CAST OF CHARACTERS

Lar —A lackey
Cook —A cook
Maid —A maid

Dzur Mountain and Environs
Kytraan —The son of an old friend
Sethra Lavode —The Enchantress of Dzur Mountain
Tukko —Sethra's servant
Sethra the Younger —Sethra's apprentice
The Necromancer —A demon
Tazendra —A Dzurlord wizard
Mica —Her lackey
The Sorceress in Green —A sorceress
Berigner —A general serving Sethra Lavode
Taasra —A brigadier serving under Berigner
Karla e'Baritt —A military engineer

Arylle and Environs
Aerich Temma —Duke of Arylle
Fawnd —His servant
Steward —His other servant

On the Road
Orlaan —A sorceress in training
Wadre —A brigand leader
Mora —His lieutenant
Grassfog —A bandit
Iatha —A bandit
Thong —A bandit
Ritt —A bandit
Belly —A bandit
Ryunac e'Terics —A lieutenant in Skinter's army
Magra e'Lanya —Ryunac's sergeant
Brimford —An Easterner and Warlock
Tsani —Grassfog's sister
Tevna —A pyrologist

Elde Island
Corthina Fi Dalcalda —King of Elde
Tresh —An exile

Nywak — Her servant
Gardimma — Imperial Ambassador to Elde

The Halls of Judgment
Barlen
Verra
Moranthë
Kéurana
Ordwynac
Nyssa
Kelchor
Trout
Tri'nagore

Miscellaneous Others
Sennya — Dzur Heir
Ibronka — Her daughter
Clari — Ibronka's maid
Röaanac — A Tiassa
Malypon — His wife
Röaanac — Their daughter
Haro — Their servant
Prince Tiawall — Hawk Heir
Ritsak — Lyorn Heir
Jami — A Teckla in Mistyvale County
Marel — Proprietor of a general store

In my two hundred years as publisher of Glorious Mountain Press, I have never seen such excitement over the publication of a book as there is in these offices over the novel you hold in your hands, *The Viscount of Adrilankha*.

Everyone here read Paarfi of Roundwood's *Five Hundred Years After*, of course. What novel in the last Cycle has been as wildly popular, as surprisingly successful, as that delectable tale of Lord Khaavren and his loyal friends and their role in the lurid events of Adron's Disaster? In hindsight, it's almost unthinkable that the book would not prove to be a popular fiction bestseller.

But *Five Hundred Years After* was meant to be a scholarly work in the form of an historical novel. It was published by the University press, and written in what some reviewers described as a "quaint" style (and what others, who are still being twitted for it by their peers, called "pure egocentric gas-bagging"). Certainly Paarfi's University editors had no notion what they'd midwifed.

Then, like some talking familiar out of an Eastern folktale, the novel ventured forth into the world and made friends for its scholar-author. It was the topic of conversation in every klava-house in Adrilankha. In salons and silk merchants' shops, on parade grounds and palace balconies, people of every House discussed the sword fights, the scheming . . . and, of course, the romance. Even literate Teckla sought out the book, identifying with the brave, clownish servant Mica and his sweetheart. Rumor has it that Lord Khaavren's admirers include high-ranking members of the Empress's court. (No names—that would be indiscreet—but a certain celebrated Dragonlord was seen with a copy peeking out from under his cloak!)

Paarfi of Roundwood was transformed from obscure historian to celebrity almost overnight. And what an elegant, gossip-worthy celebrity he makes! Who will ever forget his stunning appearance at the opening reception of the Imperial Academy of Fine Arts, where he dressed in white from hat to boots? "Artists," he declared, "are of no House and every House. I prefer to dress to suit the first proposition, as dressing to suit the second would be garish."

He became—and has remained—the must-have guest at every party. It is his arm that every rising young actress wishes to be seen on of an evening. That august poet, Ahadam of Hoodplain, has said of Paarfi, "He always buys the Wine. And he's a damn fine writer." What a testament to Paarfi's artistic accomplishments and his personal generosity!

The University press, far from delighting in and capitalizing on Paarfi's new notoriety, was taken aback. Anyone could have predicted that the gist of the University's mean-spirited notes and conversations would leak out. After all, what environment is so much a hotbed of gossip as an academic institution? The details of Paarfi's parting with the University have remained strictly private (as one would expect from such a gentlemanly and professional artist), but the rumors can't be wholly unfounded. An author who brings so much prestige and—let's not discount the material sphere—wealth to his publisher should certainly be rewarded by a few paltry perquisites and a quite humble increase of his royalties.

But that was not to be. Thus it was that when *The Viscount of Adrilankha* and its author sought a new publisher, Glorious Mountain was able to acquire them both, and the honor that comes with them, after lively competition with other worthy bookmen of the city. (All of us at Glorious Mountain extend deepest sympathies to Zerran and Bolis over the inexplicable flooding of their warehouse. It could not have come at a worse time for them, and we regretted the appearance of taking advantage of their misfortune.)

An author as popular as Paarfi of Roundwood has many obligations to his readers and admirers. He has been so much in demand for personal appearances, readings, lectures, and charity events that his writing time has been somewhat curtailed. But I'm sure none of his readers begrudge the extra decade it took him to complete this book, beyond our announced date of publication. Certainly we here in the editorial offices understood completely, and are sure our creditors will, as well.

Paarfi has begun work on the next volume of this landmark series, so we're sure there will be no similar delay with its appearance. Still, he makes time for other projects that enrich our culture. The Orb Theatre has commissioned him to adapt this very book for the stage, as a starring role for the great Valimer. Paarfi also lectures on writing at academies around the city, and especially provides encouragement to young women, whose voices are so underrepresented in our fiction.

Before *Five Hundred Years After*, few publishers would have acquired an historical novel, let alone competed for the privilege. Now historical novels are the rage, and even mediocre efforts are flying off the bookshop tables. What makes them so attractive to the sophisticated modern reader?

Nostalgia, says the cynical critic—and yes, there is something to what he says. Our world is fast-paced and obsessed with efficiency over grace. Teleportation flicks us from our door to our friends' without a chance for a happy survey of the landscape in between. Psychic communication robs us of the tactile pleasure of pen and paper, and the leisure to select the perfect phrase before we send our message to its intended recipient.

We face social upheaval that our ancestors were spared. We deal with Easterners, rebellious Teckla, and decidedly unchivalrous behavior in some of our most noble houses. How lovely it is to be transported, if only for a few hours, to a world where there is time for contemplation and elegance, and where the natural order is understood and secure!

But historical fiction isn't merely an escape from the present. It illuminates the things we have in common with the ancients. They, too, faced what were for them new sciences, new peoples, and new social situations. Their solutions to their problems might suggest our modern ones.

And of course, our uncertain times make us that much more fascinated with the cataclysm of Adron's Disaster, and the upheaval of the Interregnum. The great moral questions involved in those events are still alive, though in a different tunic. People who are uncomfortable discussing contemporary issues and personalities can instead examine events that seem safely in the past. By doing so, they come to terms with our sometimes painful present.

It would be coy not to at least touch on another reason for the success of *Five Hundred Years After*, specifically: scandal. I can't deny that I was eager to read a book that produced so much outcry from family members of certain historical figures who dispute Paarfi's interpretation of their ancestors' actions.

It's fitting that Paarfi of Roundwood should be the author to lead the rebirth of the historical novel. Paarfi's charming, slightly old-fashioned treatment of the elements of popular fiction—violence, sex, betrayal, humor—makes them easier to accept as part of history and as the stuff of contemporary life. The historian's well-verified facts don't offer the entertainments of character and language to draw the reader in. The deliberately shocking fiction of the "Truthful Art" school of popular modern novelists appeals only to those readers who already believe that life is shocking. Readers who seek diversion and pleasure in novels reject these novelists' insights along with their plots. Paarfi's approach to history and fiction has been called "dishonest" and "fantastical." But it is that very approach that enables him to make history, philosophy, and politics available and attractive to those who believe they have no interest in them.

Legions of readers have learned all that already, of course, while delighting in *The Phoenix Guards* and *Five Hundred Years After*. Now, with *The Viscount of Adrilankha*, they will rediscover that delight. And, far from quailing at the threatened lawsuits prompted by the publication of this wonderful volume, we at Glorious Mountain look forward to a long and mutually rewarding relationship with Paarfi of Roundwood and his creations.

—Luchia of North Leatherleaf, publisher

Preface

Concerning the Fall of the Empire, Lord Adron e'Kieron, and the "Dragon-Jhereg War"

This preface is addressed specifically to those who have read our earlier histories of *The Phoenix Guards* and *Five Hundred Years After*; readers to whom this volume is their first introduction to those characters with whom we have concerned ourselves are invited to pass over it with full confidence in having missed nothing of any significance. Indeed, it is our firm hope that such readers will need no introduction other than this volume, and we will confess to having failed in our duty should any reader feel himself bewildered because of unfamiliarity with history in general, or with our history in particular.

That said, we wish to indulge our right as the author to address certain issues that have arisen from the publication of the works mentioned above.

Some students of history who have done us the kindness to follow us through our previous volumes have raised questions concerning a supposed unpleasantness within the House of the Dragon, and of a "war" between the Dragon and the Jhereg, and of the influence of these events on the fall of the Empire—questions, no doubt, encouraged by information disseminated by our brother historians. We have been accused of neglecting to pay sufficient attention to these affairs when we treated with the matter of Lord Adron e'Kieron and what is popularly called "Adron's Disaster."

For those who have not made the assiduous study of history that might lead to these questions, allow us to mention a few facts which might, hereafter, permit us to both clarify the events of this vital yet confusing stage of history, and explain the reasoning which led us to make those choices we made.

A certain Dragonlord, the Count of Kee-Laiyer Meadows, who was the Dragon Heir for a short time early in Tortaalik's reign, was killed in battle with an army commanded by Sethra Lavode. There were accusations that Lord Adron e'Kieron, who had been the

Dragon Heir before and after, had had Kee-Laiyer assassinated in the middle of the battle, and had then protected the assassin. There was bloodshed over the dispute, but the issue was never resolved because the Interregnum intervened. Moreover, several powerful Dragonlords were struck down by Jhereg assassins owing to some complications that many believe stemmed from the affair mentioned above.

It is perhaps true that the author has been culpable if, as some say, these facts conceal issues important to an understanding of Adron's Disaster, which matter was lightly treated with in our previous history. It is, however, the opinion of the author that neither the squabble within the House of the Dragon nor the dispute between the Dragon and the Jhereg had much bearing on Adron's decision to use elder sorcery against the Orb; and, as the reader is by now aware, the author has diligently avoided any digressions of any sort in unfolding the history of Sir Khaavren and his friends.

The reader may recall that when we were first introduced to Lord Adron, in our history of *The Phoenix Guards*, he was then the Dragon Heir. When he appeared in our later history of *Five Hundred Years After* he was the Dragon Heir. If there was, in between, a period of time, more or less prolonged, in which he was not the Heir, we can hardly be held responsible for failing to describe events that fall outside of the realm of our investigations.

But we feel it our duty, in any case, to separate fact from myth; truth from legend; possible from impossible. We will acknowledge, then, that there are stories—and these from reliable sources—that have linked Mario Greymist, who slew the Phoenix Emperor, with Lord Adron. While these stories, perhaps, have their origin in someone who knew Adron well, we should also add that these stories have come from one who also knew Mario, and who had reason to wish history to hold a higher opinion of the assassin than, perhaps, he deserves. We nevertheless maintain that under no circumstances would Lord Adron have used an assassin, nor given sanctuary to one. We defy anyone, however well informed, to point to anything even Adron's detractors of the period have said, that would lead us to believe the Duke of Eastmanswatch would countenance such methods under any circumstances whatsoever.

We should add that the vilification of Lord Adron that has occurred since the Disaster is as natural as it is predictable; nevertheless, this author will not indulge in such conduct himself. Whatever else he was, Adron was above all a human being, with all of the strengths and weaknesses that implies: there is no more reason to treat him as an inhuman monster than there is to present him as a military genius. As we have attempted to do with all those who pass through our pages, we endeavored to present him as he was, leaving judgment to the reader. Those who have censured us for "apologizing" for the Duke in our previous work no more deserve our attention than do those who have accused us of "bending the fabric of history to sustain a dubious maxim," as one supposed historian has suggested.

There nevertheless remain two valid questions: Did the quarrels within the House of the Dragon, and between the Dragon and the Jhereg, contribute to the fall of the Empire? And, if so, is the historian negligent in having failed to discuss them?

In the opinion of this historian, the rôle played by these two quarrels in the fall of the Empire is negligible at best — the disagreement over who was to be Heir, which occurred early in Tortaalik's reign, was resolved well before the end of it; and if a certain bitterness lingered among the supporters of Kee-Laiyer, it was an impotent bitterness. More importantly, those few wizards who were assassinated by the Jhereg could have no effect on the power unleashed by Lord Adron's spell, and to claim that, had they been present, he would not have required the spell, is to engage in the most base and unhistorical sort of speculation.

The figure at the center of this controversy is, of course, Adron's daughter, Aliera, who appears to have made certain comments to the Enchantress of Dzur Mountain. If Aliera did make these comments, then we should point out that they were made to Sethra Lavode, who then somehow relayed them to another party, from whose mouth or pen they fell into the hands of a supposed historian. The reader is encouraged to consider: Aliera makes an interpretation; Sethra summarizes this interpretation; some third party records this summary; a historian writes based on this record. How far removed we are from truth! To call this "hearsay" is to accord it far more weight, even, than it deserves.

This historian, we may add, has, over the years, had the honor to carry on a limited but fascinating correspondence with Sethra Lavode, in the course of preparing for the work (as yet unpublished) from which, accidentally, sprang our two previous histories; and the Enchantress has never mentioned any such conversation to this historian.

In short, we would like to say that, while historical speculation is, perhaps, an amusing pastime, it has no place in serious works of history; and this author has avoided, and will continue to avoid, such speculation in the course of laying before the reader the interesting lives of those few persons with whom these narratives have concerned themselves.

There are other remarks that could, perhaps be made; but we long ago made the choice, regarding these works, to avoid insulting our readers by explaining matters with which anyone is likely to be familiar. We would no more offer an explanation, then, of conditions obtaining during the Interregnum, where we begin our narrative, than we would describe the location of Adrilankha itself.

With this firmly established, we hope the reader will, without further delay or digression, allow us to embark once more on a narrative journey through a stormy and enchanting time in our recent past.

—Paarfi
2/2/10/11 (Norath. II: 181)

The Viscount of Adrilankha

BOOK ONE

The Paths of the Dead

In Which We Introduce the Principal
Actors in Our Drama, and Most of Them
Set Out on Diverse Missions

Chapter the First

How a Traveler Wishing for a Name
Met a Coachman Wishing for a Drink
And a Bargain Was Reached

It was on a Homeday in the early summer of the 156th year of the Interregnum that a traveler entered a small village in the East. This village was, we should say, far to the East—farther than any except the most intrepid of explorers have ventured, for it involves crossing the range of mountains that lie beyond the Laughing River, and descending, from there, into a land of myth, legend, and, if we are to be permitted, history. Knowing, as we do, that few of our readers will ever venture into these lands, we hope we may be permitted a moment to sketch the peculiar landscape that might greet the traveler who emerges from the narrow Grinding Pass between Mount Horsehead, also called Hookjaw Mountain, and the Broken Mountain, which may also have other names, although these have not come down to us.

In this place the traveler in his coach or the reader on his couch would find a gradually widening gorge or valley descending from the mountain in the place where a furious river had once run. The valley is as green and lush as one might expect from what had once been the bottom of a river, while above it stand ranks and rows of greyish rock, cut or molded into the strangest of formations, some standing two or even three hundred feet high, and many of them appearing almost manlike in their aspect. These are called by those who dwell in the valley the Guardians, and these Easterners, a peaceful agricultural tribe called Nemites, believe, in fact, that these rocks contain a sentience that watches over them. What is more significant, however, is that all of the neighbors of the Nemites, including the warlike Letites to the north and the fierce Straves to the south, also believe it, for which reason the Nemites have dwelt in this valley for years upon years without the least disturbance.

While phenomena such as strange and oddly beautiful rock formations—caused by we know not what fluke of wind, water, and earth—might well serve to protect these Easterners from others of their own kind, one could hardly expect them to do any good against the less superstitious human; especially those of the House of the Dragon who, after all, had dwellings not twenty leagues away, on the other side of the Broken Mountain. What, then, has protected the Nemites from the Dragonlords? Could it be that, in fact, they are correct in their beliefs concerning the formations of stone that seem to watch over them day and night? Perhaps. Yet it seems to us that the answer lies more in geography than in magical philosophy. The very existence of the Broken Mountain has served, for thousands of years, to shunt large groups to one side or another of the Nemite Valley, and both of its sides, or "flanks" to put it in the military terms of the House of the Dragon, are guarded by the very tribes who are filled with superstitious dread of the Guardians. In this way, one might say that the Guardians have, indeed, done exactly what the Nemites believe them to do.

The astute reader will have observed that we have explained why the valley is safe from the west, from the north, and from the south, and is, no doubt, furiously wondering what lies to the east. The author would like to assure the reader that we have not forgotten this cardinal direction, but intend to take him there directly; indeed, it is for the purpose of this easterly journey that we have introduced the Nemites who, though certainly of interest in and of themselves, form no part of our history.

To the east, then, is one of the more peculiar features of landscape to be found anywhere in the world. It is as if the gods who made the world had decreed that no one should be permitted to pass eastward from the land of the Nemites. To begin, the valley is sealed off by a sheer cliff of granite—to all appearances, a slab of rock nearly four thousand feet high, three miles wide, and running almost straight up. From its peak, it runs down to the east in a slope only slightly less sheer. How such an object could occur in the course of nature is a curiosity rivaled only by the Rising Waterfall of Cordania or the Steam Caves of Northern Suntra. But however imposing Man might consider this object, Nature, evidently, did not deem it sufficient, for beyond "the Rise," as the Nemites call it, is a land of bogs and mires, where what few dry patches exist are liable to turn into quicksands whenever the sudden and unpredictable rains visit the district. This useless, boggy area continues for several miles—all the way, in fact, to Thundering Lake, or Lake Nivaper as some call it: that wide, blue, scenic, but terrifying lake, surrounded by harsh rocks and subject to the sort of weather that one might anticipate finding at sea, but should hardly expect to encounter in a freshwater lake, whatever its size.

The Thundering Lake dominates the region both physically and economically, and should the author indulge in a description of the various small kingdoms and independent villages that thrive or struggle along its shore the reader might well grow impatient, to the chagrin of the author, who prides himself on laconicity. Therefore, bowing to the reader's understandable desire to learn what there is in this region that bears upon our story, we focus our attention upon a village directly opposite the Lake from the the Rise. This is the village of Blackchapel.

Alas, little is known of the strange gods and demons who were once worshiped here by the heathen Easterners, but at some point, most likely around the middle of the Third Cycle, an enclosed altar was built to one or more of them, which became a center of prayer and commerce. In the opinion of this historian, the first chapel (there have been at least six) was probably erected to a fish god, because the district has thrived on fishing for as long as anyone can recall, and because certain markings in and around the altar could be interpreted as crude representations of primitive fishing gear.

Blackchapel, for most of its history, was a quiet little village. Indeed, the noted traveler Ustav of Leramont, one of the first human beings to visit, noted that a day spent in the village was, as he put it, "as exciting as watching two pieces of granite involved in a staring contest," and added, "I eagerly looked forward to my night's rest as a means of relieving my ennui."

We go back, then, to the 156th year of the Interregnum—which is, we should add, nearly a hundred years before the rest of our tale begins—when a young warlock came to this village, traveling from the south. He was remarkably tall for an Easterner, towering well over everyone he chanced to meet, and he was, moreover, thin of figure. He had dark hair and eyes, and was dressed simply in a black shirt, black trousers, and short brown cloak, and was equipped with a sword, a knife, and a small satchel which contained a heavier shirt, a longer cloak, and a change of underclothing. We should take a moment, before continuing to follow this young man, to say two words about the term "warlock." It is, as a translation from the Eastern *boszorkány*, simply the masculine form of the word for "skilled one" or "witch." But throughout various Eastern cultures, this word has acquired other meanings, as a young nobleman who grows in power gradually acquires additional lands, dwellings, and retainers.

In some cultures, the word has come to mean "enemy." In others, "servant of dark powers." Yet in other places of the East it means stranger things, such as "man who dresses as a woman," or "traitor to one's lord," or even "man who knows the secrets of women," this latter indicating that among some Eastern cultures the practice of witchcraft is considered a woman's skill, although no other evidence has been found to support this belief.

In this case, however, when we call this traveler a warlock, we mean simply a man who has studied the heathen arts of Eastern witchcraft. In fact, though initiated into these arts, this young man had not progressed in them to any great degree, but, rather, had only recently come to the point where, according to the "school" of witchcraft practiced by this young man and his teachers, he had to undertake a journey and attempt to find a guide or a path into what the Easterners called the "spirit world." Upon the actual meaning of this term, if any, the author will not speculate, this being, after all, a work of history, not a treatise on magical philosophy or a study of primitive superstitions.

The young man had not, in fact, traveled far, his home was in the manor house of a minor noble not twenty miles away, so upon his arrival at Blackchapel, which he conceived as only the first leg of his journey, he was well rested and eager for whatever adventures might await him. We need hardly add that he did not anticipate these adventures, or, in fact, any other that might await him in Blackchapel; and yet, as the reader has no doubt surmised by the fact that we have taken it upon ourselves to make reference to this place, it chanced that he was incorrect.

The day having nearly reached evening when his feet brought him to Blackchapel, his first order of business was to procure lodgings for the night, which he set about doing in the simplest and most natural way: he made a polite greeting to the first Easterner he met, and inquired as to any inn that let rooms by the evenings, or of any persons who might take in strangers for a pecuniary consideration. As it turned out, however, the first Easterner he met was a certain man named Erik, who was unable to be of much help to him. This Easterner could be described, by any standards, as ignorant. In fact, he could be described as ignorant not only by any standards, but upon any subject. While everyone is, of course, ignorant upon some subject or another, Erik maintained his ignorance in any and every matter he came across, and even improved upon it when he could.

The traveler, then, spoke to this fellow, saying, "My good man, I wish you a pleasant day, and hope indeed you are finding it so."

Erik considered this for a moment, then said, "Well?"

"Well, there is a question I would wish to ask you, if it is no trouble: Do you know a place where a traveler such as myself might secure lodgings in this charming village?"

"How, lodgings?"

"Yes. That is, a place where I might spend the night, enjoying more or less of comfort."

"Ah, yes, I see. Well, I must consider this question."

"Yes, I understand that. You, then, consider the question, and I will wait while you do so."

"And you are right to wait," said Erik promptly, "for I have even now begun considering."

"And I," said the young warlock, "have begun waiting."

In the event, it seemed that the traveler had far more success in waiting than Erik had in considering; for his waiting was accomplished with considerable skill—that is, not a shift of feet nor a quiver of an eyebrow betrayed impatience, whereas, after the span of some ten or fifteen minutes had elapsed, the considering had yet to bear fruit. At the end of this time, Erik, still with a countenance that spoke of deep consideration, turned and wandered off. The traveler, initially startled by this action, at length concluded that the other had discovered an answer, and the traveler determined to follow Erik, who wandered through Blackchapel on some errand of his own, and at just about the time the traveler realized that Erik would not lead him to what he sought, he noticed, in a two-story stone bungalow* set back from the road, a small sign saying, "Let Rooms." Now, our friend the traveler could imagine no reason for anyone to put up a sign suggesting that others let rooms; but, to the left, he found it easy to imagine that someone who found calligraphy a chore might save himself the trouble of scripting out, "We have rooms to let," and might, indeed, shorten it to, "Let Rooms." The possibility that this was the case was so strong, in fact,—that he immediately resolved to test it by entering the bungalow and inquiring. We need hardly add that this resolution was no sooner made than acted upon.

---

*I know that "bungalow" implies a single-story dwelling, but it is also the only possible translation for the Northwestern "tyuk-kö," which is what the original mss uses. Take it up with Paarfi.—SB

Entering, then, he found himself in a narrow, dingy room, lit only by a single candle, this candle being the sole occupant of a tiny, square table, the table being accompanied by a plain wooden chair, and the chair being occupied by a skinny, balding old Easterner, who looked up from under bushy eyebrows that were astonishingly black compared to the grey of what remained of his hair. Without saying a word, the Easterner waited for the traveler to speak. This the traveler did, and almost instantly, by pronouncing the words, "Have you, in fact, rooms to let?"

The old man stared up at the warlock for some few moments, as if startled by his exceptional height. The traveler was used to this, however, and merely waited for the inspection to be completed. Eventually it was, and the old man said, "You wish for a room for tonight?"

"You have said it exactly. So well, in fact, that I cannot improve upon it. I wish for a room for tonight."

"It chances that we do have one. Fourteen fennick for the night, which includes one meal and a bath."

"That does not sound too expensive, only—"

"Yes?"

"What is a fennick?"

"Ah. What currency have you?"

"I? I have the coinage of Esania."

"Well, that is perfectly good coinage, and in those coins, we would we ask nine pennies, and we will add a breakfast to make up the difference."

"I see. Yes, that is most fair, and I should be glad to take the room on those terms."

"Well then, young man, it is yours, for as long as you wish. Climb the stairs, and it is the doorway on the right."

The traveler carefully counted out nine pennies, then made his way up the stairs and, finding the room with no more trouble than one might suppose after hearing the simple directions, let himself into it. He looked around and noted with pleasure that the bedding appeared to have no holes through which straw could emerge, and that, moreover, the room possessed both a chair and a window. He set his satchel on the floor, and studied the view from the window. As there was little of interest to him, and less of interest to the reader, we will forebear to describe the scene upon which he looked, and merely follow him as he left his room in order to have, as he thought, a brief walk through the town before retiring for the evening and continuing his journey in the morning.

He came down the stairs, then, and turned up the narrow street to see if he might find a public house where he could take a glass of wine and meet a few of the local denizens. It took him some time to locate it, because it was a small house unadorned with any sign or indication of its nature, but at length he happened to notice that it was uncommonly busy for a simple home and asked a passerby, who confirmed his deduction.

Upon entering, the young warlock observed a single room, well lit by hanging lamps. There were a few hard wooden chairs scattered about, but most of the patrons were standing in groups of four or five drinking beer or wine. Discovering that he felt suddenly uncomfortable, the traveler made his way to a corner that appeared to be more-or-less deserted, and which, moreover, contained an unoccupied chair. This chair, we should say, was next to a small round table, which table contained a head full of dark, curly hair, which head was attached to a body that occupied the table's other chair. Presuming that this other individual was in no condition to object to company, the traveler at once seated himself, and set about considering how to acquire for himself something to drink.

Several moments passed, during which our friend became acclimated to the warmth of the room, and the atmosphere, in which humanity commingled with stale wine and the sweet harshness of burning tobacco leaves, inhaled for their mild euphoric effect by many of the patrons. Eventually, a portly woman carrying a tray full of glasses came by, and, before the young man could speak, set down before him a mug of wine that was so dark as to be almost black. He accepted it in the spirit of inquiry, and paid for it with a coin that the hostess looked at carefully before accepting. She hurried on, and he tasted the wine, finding it to be very dry and acidic. Though hardly a connoisseur, he did have something of a palate, and winced slightly at the taste.

"You should," said someone, "have asked for the reserve. It costs only a little more, and is not nearly so harsh, with a not unpleasant peppery aftertaste. Or, better yet, the *brandy*, which, while falling short of excellent, has the virtue of quickly causing the drinker to stop caring about such niceties as taste." We should explain that *brandy* is what the Easterners call that class of wine which is distilled after being fermented; that they have a special name for this drink may, indeed, give us several significant clues about the Eastern culture, but now would not be the time for this discussion, interesting though it might be.

It took the traveler a moment to identify the speaker, but eventually he realized that it was none other than his companion at the table, whom he had taken to be asleep. Though this individual had not moved, his eyes were open, and he gave no appearance of intoxication; nor did he slur his speech, though he spoke Olakiska, the language of the district, with an odd rhythm, rather like a horse about to jump an obstacle, then suddenly stopping and reconsidering the affair, and continuing in this manner throughout the length of the sentence.

Notwithstanding the odd speech, which meant only that the speaker was, like so many others, not native to the region, the traveler replied politely, saying, "I thank you for your advice, and will avail myself of it the next time our good hostess passes by."

"You are most welcome," said the other, still not moving. "Might I inquire as to your name?"

"You may, indeed, inquire, but, alas, I cannot tell you."

"How, you cannot tell me?"

"I'm afraid that I cannot."

"You will pardon me if I find that singular."

"Well," said the traveler, "there is an explanation."

"Ah, well, that is less astonishing. And will you give me this explanation?"

"Certainly, and this is it, then: I cannot tell you my name, because I am traveling to find it."

We should note that, during this entire conversation, our friend's companion had not stirred from his position of resting his head upon his arm, and his arm upon the table. Upon hearing this, however, he lifted his head, showing a trim mustache, a few strands of hair upon a strong chin, a thin, narrow face with deep-set eyes, and a small mouth, all of which were framed, as it were, by masses of curly black hair tumbling down to his shoulders. He then said, "Ah. I comprehend."

"How, you comprehend?"

"Yes. You are training in the arts of the warlock."

"You have understood me exactly."

"That is hardly surprising; I have been acquainted with warlocks before. My name is Miska."

"How do you do, Miska?"

"I am, to my deep regret, entirely sober. This is because I do not have sufficient coinage to remedy the condition. If you would be good enough to buy me a drink, I will repay you by giving you a name."

"As to giving me a name, well, that may not be as simple as you pretend. Yet I will gladly buy you a drink nevertheless."

"Splendid. You are an amiable fellow, and I believe I like you." Miska then turned his head and called, in voice that carried throughout the room, "Two *brandies*, my good woman!"

The traveler, who, in fact, would have preferred the reserve wine, decided not to say anything, and soon enough two small glasses of *brandy* appeared before them, for which the warlock-in-training cheerfully paid. He then sipped his, winced again, and set his glass down; Miska, for his part, drained his glass in one long swallow, his head thrown back, then set the glass down on the table with a hard *crack*. He wiped his lips with the back of his hand and said, "Your name is Dark Star."

"Dark Star?"

Miska nodded.

"Why?"

"Why?"

"Yes, why is that my name?"

Miska looked at him, and it seemed to the young warlock that the other's black, black eyes were seeing deeply into him, and he said, "Because in the land of Faerie all the stars are dark, but you will be the darkest. You will give light, but few will know it. Your rod will be black, your home will be darkness, but you will shine. You will be the Dark Star of Faerie."

"I will go to the land of Faerie?"

"You will."

"Dark Star."

"Yes. Or, in my own language, Sötétcsilleg."

"I do not believe I could pronounce that."

"Do you speak the language of the Silatan? In that language, it would be Morrolan."

"That is not one I speak."

"Then, in the language of Faerie —"

"But I am able to pronounce it."

"Let us hear you."

"Morrolan."

"Well, there you have it. Your quest is complete. What will you do now, Dark Star?"

"What will I do now?"

"Yes, my friend Sötétcsilleg. Your quest is complete. Will you now return to your home?"

"Oh, but I had more to do than merely acquire a name."

"Ah, more?"

"Oh, yes, indeed. In fact, that was to happen near the end."

"Well, what else have you do, Morrolan? Perhaps we will dispatch those tasks as easily."

"What else have I to do?"

"Yes, yes. Come Dark Star. Tell me your tasks and we will consider them together. After all, you have bought me a drink."

"And you have given me a name."

"Then it may be that we have the beginning of a fine partnership. Or, perhaps, a legendary friendship. At all events, come. Let us hear what you have to do."

"Well, in addition to a name, I am to find a holy artifact, and a place of power, and a kindred soul. Ah!"

"Excuse me, you say, 'ah.'"

"Well, and, if I do?"

"It would seem that, to say 'ah' in that tone of voice, my dear Sötétcsilleg, would indicate that something has occurred to you."

"Well, in fact, something *has* occurred to me."

"And that is?"

"Well, it is this: Perhaps you, my good Miska, are my kindred soul."

"Alas, good Morrolan, it seems unlikely."

"How, unlikely?"

"Yes."

"But why?"

"Because I am only a coachman."

"Well, and if you are?"

"The kindred soul for whom you search is someone with whom you can make many journeys, and, in each one, you will grow closer together. As for me, well, once you have completed this journey, my work will be done."

Morrolan considered this in silence, at something of a loss for how to respond. At last he said, "Would you care for another *brandy*?"

"If we are not kindred spirits, Dark Star," said Miska, "at least, it seems to me, we understand one another, and that is not so little."

Morrolan acquired more *brandy* for Miska, and a glass of the reserve for himself; we should add that, as Miska had promised, this wine was a noticeable improvement over either of the other drinks. Miska, for his part, seemed content to sip his *brandy* on this occasion, rather than quaffing it as he had the first glass.

Morrolan watched the other for a moment, wondering at the whims of fate and fortune that bring people together, and said, "How is it you come to be in Blackchapel, Miska? For it is clear that you are not from here; and are, in fact, Fenarian, if I do not mistake your accent."

"I am of all places and all times," said Miska. "At least, when I am drunk. When I am sober, yes, I am Fenarian, and was most recently employed by a nobleman of that land, who took an excursion to visit the Lake Nivaper in order to fish and to swim. He failed to catch any fish and so for reasons best known to himself he chose to get drowned, leaving me in a foreign country without employment." Miska then belched prodigiously and swallowed about half of his drink. "I decided, then, to come here because I have been here before and fancy their *brandy*."

"So you are, then, waiting for something to come along?"

"Something always does, my dear Sötétcsilleg, in a day or a year or a hundred years."

"A hundred years is too long for me, good Miska; I doubt I shall live that long."

Miska gave him a quick glance, but made no other reply.

Morrolan said, "You have, then, his coach?"

Miska shook his head. "I gave it into the care of the servants who came to look for his body."

"And so, you must use your feet to return?"

"Yes, my good Morrolan, if I return."

"Ah, then you may not return?"

"It is possible that I won't return, or that my return will be delayed. There is nothing waiting for me there."

"And so?"

"And so, I drink. I drink, and I wait to see what is in the cup fate sets before me. It is not a bad life, Dark Star. You do the same, only—"

"Yes? Only?"

"Only you are unaware of it."

"Perhaps you are right. Then, you believe that some fate or destiny has caused us to meet?"

Miska shrugged. "Who can say?" He drained his glass, then, and stood up suddenly, appearing perhaps a bit unstable on his feet, but he said, "Come. Let us continue your quest."

"What, this very instant?"

"Why not?" said the coachman.

Chapter the Second

How Morrolan Met Someone
Who Was Not, in Fact, a Goddess

Morrolan nodded and stood, leaving his wine unfinished, taken by a sudden desire to move forward in his mission. "Yes, let us do so, then," he said, and followed the coachman out of the house and into the street. The air was clear and bracing after the closeness of the public house, and very dark, as this Eastern village had not yet found a way to light its streets, so the only light came from that which spilled, as it were, out of a few windows behind which lamps or tapers were burning.

As they stepped out, they were greeted by someone who said, "A very pleasant day to you, sir. I see that you found a room."

"Why, yes," said Morrolan. "And I thank you, sir, for your assistance earlier." We need hardly add that the irony of Morrolan's statement was lost on Erik, for, of course, it was he who had spoken.

"Good evening to you, Erik," said Miska. "I hope the night finds you well."

"Why, as it chances, it does," said Erik. "And I hope the very same to you, uh . . ."

"Miska," prompted the coachman.

"Yes, Miska," said Erik. "That is right," as if Miska required reassurance. "Are you two off to visit the goddess?"

"Goddess?" said Morrolan. "I was unaware that a goddess had taken up residence here."

"How, you were unaware of this fact?"

"Entirely, I assure you."

Miska said, "Tell me, my dear Erik, when this goddess arrived."

"Oh, as to that, I have not the least idea in the world. But I know she is here, for I saw her not five minutes ago near the chapel."

"That," said Miska, "is a good place to find a goddess."

"Why, do you know, that thought had not occurred to me."

"Well."

At this, Erik smiled and continued on his way.

"A goddess?" said Morrolan.

"I hardly think so," said Miska. "Were it, in fact, a goddess, the good Erik would have identified her as something else entirely."

"Ah," said Morrolan.

"Nevertheless," said Miska, "I see no reason not to walk over to the chapel and make our observations."

"Yes, let us do so."

This decided, they set off, Miska leading through one or two turns of the little streets of Blackchapel, until they came to the place for which the village was named. The original Blackchapel, was, in fact, no more than a large black rock of the type the wizards call sparkstone, which, coming to the height of an Easterner's chest, was peculiarly flat on the top, giving the appearance of a high table, or altar, and stretching out some five feet in length, and perhaps three or four in depth. Upon its discovery, somewhere far back in prehistory, it became, quite naturally, a place where the Easterners would gather to practice their primitive rites. At times the altar was open to the sky, at other times it was covered by some structure or another.

The most recent form of the temple had come to be several hundred years before, when a priest of the Three Sisters, who were much worshiped in the East, caused to be built a small temple around it, made of sparkstone, obsidian, pumice, and other black stones that could be found in the district, from which the village soon gained its name. There were two large stone doors to the chapel, also black, which would have been difficult to open were they, in fact, ever closed; but by custom they remained open at all times, and it was at these doors that our friends at length arrived.

Upon entering the chapel, which was lit by half a dozen torches evenly spaced upon the wall to the left and the right, and which emitted thick, oily smoke that blended into the dark walls and ceiling, they at once saw a figure standing at the altar, facing them.

"Well," remarked Miska quietly. "Erik was closer to the truth than I'd have thought."

This comment was drawn from Miska by the sight of the individual who stood at the altar, and was, perhaps, more of a comment on Miska's taste in female beauty than in any attribute of this person. On the other hand, we cannot but admit that "beauty" as the concept might apply to an Easterner is not something of which this historian could claim to have any knowledge or appreciation—indeed, it is obvious that such an abstraction as "beauty" is hardly meaningful except within a species. This said, however, it does not mean that the historian can abnegate his duty of sketching, however briefly, every new person who brings himself to the reader's attention, and with whom the reader will be expected to spend some time. This description may appear before the individual appears, as the individual appears, or even, in some cases, after the reader has come to know the individual more or less well; but appear it must, and so, the time being so convenient, we will pause now to say two words about the woman who faced our friends from across the altar of Blackchapel.

She was, then, small, even by Eastern standards, slight, with dark hair around a narrow face dominated by large, bright eyes, and she wore a plain black garment, rather like a robe, save that it was belted at the waist and fit rather snugly, and, as that was all our friends could see as they entered, it will have to do for our initial sketch.

While her frame was slight, her voice was strong as she said, "Greetings, my friends. I have been expecting you."

"How," said Morrolan. "Expecting us?"

"For some reason," murmured Miska, "that does not astonish me."

"Yes, indeed," she said. "I knew the time, and the place, although I did not know you would be a, that is, I did not know who precisely. And I knew you would be accompanied by a guide, although I did not know the nature of the guide. I take you to be a coachman, sir?"

Miska bowed at this.

"There are many stories of coachmen."

"Indeed, madam. And coachmen, on their part, take revenge by telling stories of everyone else."

"Yes, I have heard of this. And your name, my good coachman?"

"Miska."

The woman nodded. "Very well, Miska. You have done well. Here is your fee." So saying, she threw him a small purse, which he caught out of the air.

"How," he said. "That is all for me?"

"You wish more?"

"Indeed."

"What more would you wish?"

"How much is available?"

"Nothing," said the woman.

Miska sighed. "Well, I should at least like to know how this all comes out in the end. You perceive, it might give me another story."

"I have no doubt," she said, "that you will come to learn about it, sooner or later. But for now . . ."

Her voice trailed off, her sentence punctuated by an eloquent look. Miska interpreted the look, bowed to each of them, and, addressing Morrolan, said, "Well, at least some of your tasks are now completed." With this he backed out of the chapel, leaving Morrolan alone with the strange woman.

"I am called Arra," she said after Miska had left.

"I am Morrolan."

"Morrolan?" she said. "'Black Star.' An auspicious name."

"I hope so. And who—"

"I am a priestess."

"Ah! Yes, of course. I should have realized. A priestess of—?"

"The Demon Goddess. I serve her. You will serve her as well."

"You think so?" said Morrolan.

Arra nodded. "Yes," she said. "In fact, I am entirely convinced of it."

"Well then," said Morrolan. "Perhaps you are right. But will you do me the honor to explain why I will do this?"

"Because you wish for knowledge, and for power."

"And I can gain these things by serving the goddess?"

The priestess indicated by a sign that, in fact, he could.

"Well," said Morrolan, "I do not wish to say that I doubt you—"

"That is good. You should not doubt me."

"—but how am I to know that serving her will lead me to knowledge and power?"

"Oh, you wish to know that?"

"Yes. In fact, I so strongly wish to know, that I cannot conceive of committing myself to the goddess before this question has been answered."

"But then, what do you know of the goddess?"

"Very little. I know that her feast day falls in the winter, and that she is one of the Daughters of Night, and that she is said to take an interest in certain of the smaller kingdoms."

"Have you heard that she takes an especial interest in those who study the arts of the witch?"

"I had not heard this. In fact, I had thought that was one of her sisters."

"They are sometimes hard to tell apart."

"Very well."

"Nevertheless, it is true."

"Then I accept that she interests herself in the study of the Art. What next?"

"Next? She is very powerful."

"That is but natural in a goddess."

"That is true, but, moreover, she is loyal."

"Ah! She is loyal, you say."

"I not only say it, but I insist upon it."

"Well, I admit that makes a difference."

"And then?"

Morrolan suddenly found himself in one of those moments where the direction of one's whole life can change in an instant. Another might have hesitated, but Morrolan was not of a character for hesitation, and, moreover, he had set out from home with the idea in mind of putting himself into the path of just this sort of event.

"Very well, I accept," he said. "Is there a ritual or a ceremony?"

"Yes, exactly."

"Well, when shall we perform this ritual?"

"Unless you can think of a reason to delay, well, we can do so at once."

"I can think of no reason," he said.

"Then let us begin," said Arra.

Morrolan went forward to the altar and, towering over Arra, he said, "What, then, must we do?"

"Will you agree to serve the goddess?"

"I will."

"Very well, then."

"How, that is it?"

"No, but it is a good beginning."

"I see. Well then, what next?"

"Next is the consecration."

"Ah, the consecration!"

"Exactly."

"Well, but—"

"Yes?"

"What is being consecrated?"

"Your soul, to the goddess."

"Ah."

"Then you have no objection?"

"None at all. One's soul must do something, after all."

"That is true, though I had not thought of it in precisely those terms."

"And from this, I will get power?"

"You will."

"And will there be a cost for this power?"

"Of course."

"And that is? For it is always good to inquire as to the cost."

"Yes, I understand that. Well, the cost will be that you must serve the goddess."

"Oh, I have no qualms about serving her."

"It is good that you do not. Next, when you die—"

"Yes?"

"She will then have disposition of your soul."

"What happens when I die does not concern me excessively."

"That is good. Then can we begin?"

"I nearly think so."

"Very well, then."

As to the exact nature of the ritual through which Arra led Morrolan, we must confess that it has not come down to us; indeed, even if it had, we would no more reveal its details than would a Discreet reveal the intimacies which had been confided to him. Yet we can say that the matter consumed several hours, and involved various rare herbs, long incantations, body paints of certain colors, some amount of blood from both participants; and was, as far as Morrolan was concerned, physically and emotionally exhausting. When it had at last been concluded, at very nearly the exact hour of midnight, Morrolan fell into a deep sleep, stretched out behind the stone altar.

While he slept, Arra cleaned up the devices and material which had been used in the consecration, and, while she did so, Morrolan had a dream, which he later reported this way: "I was standing knee deep in a large, calm lake, that seemed to be Lake Vidro, only there were no trees along the shore, only large boulders. And as I stood there, I thought that I was looking for something, but I could not remember what it was. Then the water was disturbed, and a whistle-fish broke through the surface and looked up at me, and it seemed that its eyes were two jewels, one green and the other red. After it had looked at me for a moment, it dived into the lake, and I knew I was to follow it. I did so, holding my breath, and under the water, which in my dream was very clear, I swam easily to the bottom, and there I saw, sticking in the sand at the bottom of the lake, surrounded by glittering light, a short black staff or wand. I took it in my hand, and it came away easily. I swam back toward the surface, which now seemed an impossible distance away, and I thought I should never make it, but at last, just as my lungs seemed ready to burst, I broke out onto the surface, and at that moment, I woke up, gasping for air."

This is how Morrolan tells the story of his dream of the black wand. We confess that Morrolan is capable of exaggeration, prevarication, disingenuousness, and making something up out of whole cloth, wherefore we cannot insist upon the truth of the matter.

In any case, it was dawn when he emerged from the chapel, the Easterner called Arra behind him, Morrolan appearing pale and exhausted.

Morrolan said, "What now?"

"Well, how do you feel?"

"How do I feel?"

"Yes. Do you feel at all different than you did last night?"

Morrolan considered this question carefully, and at length he said, "Yes. I do. It is difficult to describe —"

"You feel as if there is a presence, just past the corner of your eye. You feel almost as if you were being watched, but by a benign presence. You feel as if you had a way of touching something that you didn't have before, only there is nothing there to touch. Does that come close?"

Morrolan considered for a moment, then said, "No, I cannot say that it does."

"Well, you are right; it is difficult to describe."

"Yes."

"At all events, your soul is now consecrated to the goddess, so that anything you do, you do for her. And anyone who attempts to thwart you, will be thwarting her."

"It is an honor," reflected Morrolan.

"It is that," agreed Arra.

"Well, what now?"

"Now we begin to gather witches."

"Gather witches?"

"Exactly."

"You must explain why we would wish to do this."

"I shall do so at once."

"Then I am listening."

"Are you aware that when two witches work together, they can create a spell more powerful than either acting alone?"

"I have heard that, yes."

"Can you imagine a hundred witches working together?"

Morrolan thought for a moment, then said, "No."

"It can be done, as long as there is a focus."

"Ah. And what is the focus?"

"I am," said Arra.

"We will gather a hundred witches?"

"With the blessing of the goddess, we will gather a thousand."

"A thousand! Well, I think that will be enough. But where will we find them?"

"They will come to us."

"How, they will come to us?"

"Yes. They will hear of Blackchapel, and they will come."

"How do you know?"

"The goddess has told me."

"Then I shall not dispute with her."

"You are right not to."

Morrolan looked out into the morning of Blackchapel and considered the future.

Chapter the Third

How a Dragonlord with an
Ambitious Cousin Considered
The Possibility of
Becoming an Emperor

We will now, with the reader's indulgence, turn our attention from a place so far east that it is beyond the old border of the Empire at the time of its greatest expanse, to a place that is very nearly at the western edge—that is, to the far northwestern region of the continent, on a peak called Kâna, in the Kanefthali Mountains. It behooves us, before going on, to say two words about the district in general and this mountain in particular.

In the earliest days of the Empire, when the seventeen tribes (or sixteen, or twenty-one, depending on whether the number is submitted by a culturalist, a biologist, or a rationalist) united under the Dragonlord Kieron the Conqueror and the Phoenix Zerika the First and began moving east, among the first discoveries was a mountain range filled with, in the first place, large veins of iron ore, and, in the second, the race of the Serioli, who were mining this ore and turning it into such objects as were useful to themselves, many of which were also useful to the seventeen tribes. Here arose one of the first disagreements between Kieron and Zerika, a disagreement eventually won by the Phoenix, who, after using the newly created object that would come to be called the Imperial Orb to solve the language problem, negotiated with the Serioli for much of this ore, for the secrets of bladesteel, and for the rights to a portion of the mountain range itself. This portion centered around four of the mountains: Koopyr, famous for its large twin peaks where so much mountain buckwheat was grown and for its fertile valleys where oats grew and flatfoot sheep grazed; Needle-at-the-top and Redground, with their rich iron veins; and Kâna, which looked back north upon the others, with vineyards and orchards along her lower slopes.

With the agreement made, the district was populated, for the most part, by the tribe of the Vallista, except for portions of Kâna in which several Dragonlords took up their abode to provide a defensive fastness in case of a retreat by the armies of Kieron. Over the long centuries after Kieron and the rest of the tribes had marched away, the region became nearly its own country, developing a language in which the tongue of the Dragon combined with the Northwestern language and included elements of the speech of the Serioli, until the eastward expansion ended and, toward the end of the Third Cycle, the unity of trade, military matters, and communication began to form what came to be the Empire (or, to be more precise, what many finally realized had been an Empire all along).

The fall of the Empire was felt in the Kanefthali Mountains (now, for a long time, nearly devoid of Serioli, and those few confined to the far north, on such peaks as Lostway and Brownhead) as a strong tremor, and many of the old fortresses of the area collapsed and were ruined, along with many of the working mines; but in a lower valley of Kâna called Whiteside, near a village of the same name, there was a Count named Skinter, of the e'Terics line of the House of the Dragon, whose keep, constructed low and strong and in conformity with the landscape, survived the shaking and rending of the ground. Shortly before the disaster he had been involved in gathering certain forces around him, in preparation for a dispute with a neighbor over an insult Skinter planned to deliver as soon as he calculated he had amassed a sufficient army. Skinter's intended enemy was a second cousin who had, over the previous century, acquired fishing rights to a certain lake, control of a particular vineyard renowned for its fortified wine made from late-apples, and the affections of the daughter of a local baron, all of which Skinter wanted, and none of which survived Adron's Disaster. In fact, the second cousin himself succumbed to the first tremors by drowning while attempting to enjoy all three of these acquisitions at once.

This left Skinter, also called Whiteside, relatively safe, without enemies, with a large standing army, without anyone to whom he was responsible (the Duchess of Kâna and most of her family having been in Adrilankha at the time of the Disaster, and the remainder having unfortunately been at home during the aftershocks) and with a great store of ambition. To round out this list, however, we ought to add that he had no means to feed over an extended period of time such an army as he had gathered. When we consider these conditions, and remind ourselves that he was, after all, a Dragonlord, it should come as no surprise that he began to widen his circle of dominance.

When he did so, he made the same discovery that thousands of other warlords of the era, going through the same process, discovered: For the most part, the aristocrats, the tradesmen, and even the peasants welcomed the firm hand of a leader; they had been "free," that is, without the Empire, for too short a time to become habituated to anarchy (this was, we should point out, within the first few years after the Disaster), and they were nearly all lost, confused, and frightened, and any semblance of order was greeted with a sense of relief; Skinter's army had rarely to draw sword, lower spear, or set catapult to secure the first victories.

These victories gave the Duke of Kâna, which title he assumed after completing the subjugation of that duchy, a broader area from which to secure food for his army, but it also required of him that he station portions of this army in each of his newly conquered territories, to insure that no other potential warlord, envying him his success, would be able to raise an army to replace or overthrow him and that no leader should rise among the subdued peasantry; he thus required a larger army, he thus required even more territory to support this army, and he was thus forced to continue his expansion, albeit necessarily at a slower pace as the area to be conquered grew geometrically.

This pattern—the lone aristocrat acquiring, building, or already possessing an army needing more land to feed the army, and then a larger army to protect the land—was repeated thousands of times during the period of history we call the Interregnum, but what made Kâna, as he now styled himself, unique was the presence of his cousin, a certain Marchioness of Habil, herself of the e'Terics line of the House of the Dragon; a lady with no ambition herself, but with a good knowledge of history, a head for strategy, a skill with arithmetic, and a fierce loyalty to her cousin. On a certain day, scarcely twenty years after the Disaster, she spoke to Kâna as he broke his fast and contemplated his position. Before letting the reader in on this interesting conversation, it is only necessary to say, by way of sketches, that Kâna and Habil, although cousins, looked like brother and sister, were often mistaken for brother and sister by casual observers, and have even been identified as such by careless historians. They were quite typical Dragonlords, rather short than tall, and marked by hollow cheeks, deep-set eyes, and curly brown hair that each wore to the shoulder. Kâna wore the black and silver of the Dragon warrior; Habil, though not actually a warrior, did the same.

This being established, let us endeavor to discover what they said to each other on that morning some score of years after the Disaster, as they took their ease in Kâna's dining room.

"Let us consider," said Habil.

"Very well," replied Kâna. "I am willing to consider. Only—"

"Well?"

"What do you wish to consider?"

"Acreage of farmland," she said.

"Ah. Well, what of it?"

"In this district, it requires some thirty or thirty-five acres to produce sufficient grain for the usual Teckla family that works it to feed itself for a year."

"Very well. And then?"

"And then, for each ten additional acres the family produces, we are able to feed—that is, pay—an additional soldier for our army."

"But then, there are the vineyards, which produce wine that we sell, and the orchards, which produce fruit, not to mention livestock and—"

She made a dismissing motion with her hand. "You complicate the issue needlessly. The figures work out to be very nearly the same."

"You are certain of these figures? That is, you have made a study?"

"No, I read them in a book."

"Do you trust this book?"

"Oh, certainly. It was published by the University Press before the Disaster."

"Very well, then, I accept the figures. What of them?"

"Suppose I have thirty renters, each renter, on average, has—"

"What does 'on average' mean?"

"It is unimportant. Each renter, let us say, farms fifty acres."

"Very well, let us say that."

"When we subtract from this the amount the renter is entitled to for his own use, either to eat or to sell, which is, by chance, very close to what he needs to keep himself and his family alive, we find we have the amount needed to support one soldier, along with the portion that goes into your bin, and eventually, your treasury."

"Yes, yes, or larder, or wine-cellar. I am familiar with this process. What you are saying, then, is that we are able to support one soldier for each peasant family."

"That is correct."

"This also came from a book?"

"The same book."

"Perhaps I should read it."

"I will lend it to you."

"Well, I accept these figures. And then?"

"After reading the books, I did my own calculations."

"I am not surprised that you did. But —"

"Yes?"

"What did these calculations tell you?"

"That in order to effectively defend the land in these times, with brigands and armies everywhere, we require one of two things: either one and a half soldiers for each peasant —"

"Half of a soldier is hard to imagine."

"— or we must arm the peasants."

"A risky proposition."

"Exactly."

"And then? What is your conclusion, my dear cousin?"

"There is yet a third method."

"I am anxious to hear it."

"Each time we gain an area equal to fifty acres, and, in doing so, use fewer than one soldier for each fifty acres conquered, we stay afloat, as the Orca say, for a little longer."

"Ah. I understand."

"Yes. That is why we are driven to keep expanding."

"Well, and so we expand."

"But there is a limit, you know. The expansion must necessarily slow down, because there is time required to secure each new area, and as the circle widens —"

"Circle?"

"Say, rather, as your holdings grow, it will soon take so much time to see to the arrangements that, well, the entire structure will collapse."

"Having seen the Disaster," remarked Kâna, looking around nervously, "I mislike the thought of structures collapsing."

"As do I."

"But permit me to put a question."

"Very well," said Habil, "ask your question."

"If this is how it works —"

"Oh it does, I assure you."

"How was the Empire able to function?"

"Because it was an Empire, and everywhere was order, and there was little bickering, and so only a small army, and that managed by the Empire itself, could keep order over a large area. In fact, rather than requiring one and half soldiers for each peasant, it required scarcely one soldier for each thousand peasants. You perceive there is a great deal of difference."

"Yes, yes, I see that. But is there a solution?"

"I believe there is."

"And what is that?"

"A new Empire."

"How, a new Empire?"

"Exactly."

"But that requires a new Emperor."

"Yes, exactly."

"And where might we find such an Emperor?"

"I believe I am looking at one."

"How, me?"

"Are you not a Dragonlord?"

"Well, yes."

"And have you not proved your ability to win battles?"

"Battles, yes. But to govern such an area, and that without the Orb—"

"The lack of the Orb is a problem."

"I nearly think it must be!"

"But I have a solution."

"Have you then?" said Kâna admiringly. "I recognize you so well in that!"

"I think so," said Habil, blushing.

"Well, I should be glad to hear it, Marchioness."

"A system of counselors, of observers, and governors of territories."

"I see. Advisers, then, to suggest actions, and spies to be sure I am informed of what is going on in all parts of the Empire, and rulers of sections to carry out my orders in their territories."

"You have understood exactly."

"But how am I to conquer such a large area, when you have already said that expansion such as we have been engaged in is doomed?"

"I have thought of this, too."

"I am not startled that you have."

"Shall I tell you what I have thought of?"

"I should like nothing better."

"This is it, then: You need counselors, observers, and governors."

"Ah, ah!"

"You understand, then?"

"I think so."

"Well, let us see."

"Advisers to help plan the campaigns, spies to make certain I am aware of what is going on around me and throughout the Empire at all times, and rulers to secure each area as it is conquered."

"Precisely."

"And," said Kâna, his eyes beginning to sparkle, "as we fully secure each area, there will be fewer soldiers required to maintain control, and thus these warriors can move out, while food for them, and fodder for the horses, which we cannot forget, will move out in regular paths to feed the army that is advancing."

"You have grasped my plan exactly. What do you think of it?"

"My dear cousin —"

"Well?"

"I think I will be Emperor."

"I nearly agree."

"Have you anyone to suggest for those rôles of which we have spoken?"

"Some. We will discover more as we begin our campaign. Come now, have you any maps?"

"Why yes, many."

"Good. I perceive that you have finished your omelet and your bacon, and are now drinking your third cup of klava, whereas I have finished my biscuit and my sausage, and am just pouring my second cup of tea, so let us retire to the library, and consult these famous maps, and begin to plan this campaign of which we have been speaking."

"An excellent suggestion, and one that I subscribe to with all my heart."

Thus began Kâna's campaign, which at its start was one of the countless efforts of minor aristocrats to preserve the few holdings they had, and which by its end was so much more.

Chapter the Fourth

How a Band of Road Agents
Met a Sorceress Who Was Not,
In Fact, Picking Flowers

On a spring day in the 229th year of the Interregnum, a woman could be seen to be picking flowers in a meadow near the banks of the river that the Easterners call the Naplemente, which name, we believe, translates to "the last of the light." The name was given it by an Eastern explorer who, having traveled as far from his homeland as he was willing to go, saw it as the farthest western point he could discern; he therefore called it by his country's name for the end of the day, or, perhaps, the place where the last of the daylight is seen. It still goes by this name among some, especially Easterners living within the Empire, but it is more often known as the Adrilankha River, for the simple reason that it passes through this city before finding its way to the ocean.

The meadow to which we direct our attention, however, was nearly three hundred miles north of this city, and there were no cities nearby, though, to be sure, there were no small number of inns and tiny villages, as more than a few roads ran in diverse directions through the region.

As to the woman picking flowers, we should say that she was eight or nine hundred years of age, with narrow eyes, a clear noble's point beneath dark hair that curled around her ears, a small mouth, and a face that showed that she had lived no easy life. While she was unencumbered, she traveled with a mule, which held a heavy pack, and one item of especial note: that being a staff of white wood, polished until it nearly gleamed, and featuring a small reddish marking on one end. Other than this staff, she appeared to have nothing more than what anyone might take for extended travel in the woodlands.

Watching her as she made her slow, painstaking way through the meadow, one might suspect her of being a midwife or herbmaster, until the observer realized that she was not, in fact, picking the flowers, so much as searching through them—indeed, her concentration was so fixed upon the ground that she did not, at first, realize that she was not alone.

When she at last became aware of it, she looked up with a sharply indrawn breath to find eight or nine horsemen watching her from a distance of only a few yards.

"A good day to you, madam," said one of them. "You appear to have lost something."

"And a good day to you, sir. I am called Orlaan, and, as you have deduced, I have, indeed, lost something."

The horseman looked at his companions and, with something like a smile, said, "Tell us what you are looking for, then, and, as we are all gentlemen here, we will help you find it."

"Will you, indeed? Why, I should be most glad for the assistance, and I will tell you at once."

"Well?"

"I am searching for a soul."

The horseman stared, then, frowning, said, "I beg your pardon, madam, but I fail to understand what it is you do me the honor to tell me."

"But, what could be simpler? There is a soul somewhere hereabouts."

"I . . . that is to say, a soul?"

"Exactly."

"Well, how did you come to lose it?"

"Oh, I never had it."

"But . . . then, it is not your soul?"

"No, it belongs to another."

"But, how is that possible?"

"For another to have a soul?"

"No, no. For there to be a disembodied soul. I have never heard of such a thing."

"It was a strange effect of Adron's Disaster."

"But that was two hundreds of years ago!"

"Oh, yes."

"Then you have been searching for it all this time?"

"Oh, certainly not. It was scarcely a hundred years ago that I realized it was missing. It took me that long, you perceive, to train my skills to the point where had an awareness of such things, and to perform the divination that revealed that it existed."

"But now you know it exists?"

"I have Seen it, yes."

"And it is here?"

"As to that, I cannot say. I traced a line from Dragaera City—"

"Dragaera City! That is a sea of amorphia, from all I have heard."

"Well, so be it, then. From the sea of amorphia to Dzur Mountain, and I began my search at the edge of the sea, as that is where I happened to be when I made the discovery, and my search has, so far, brought me here."

"But, well, what will you do if you find it?"

"Oh, I will find it."

"Very well, what will you do *when* you find it?"

"I will put it into that staff which you observe on my mule."

"Well, and then?"

"I have not the least idea in the world. But I am convinced it will be useful. Such an object—"

"Madam, I believe you are doing yourself the honor of mocking me."

"Not in the least," said Orlaan coolly.

"You should be aware, madam, that we—that is, my friends and I—had only intended to rob you of your mule and your possessions, and perhaps to sport with you a little. But, as you have chosen to mock us—"

"Oh, I have been aware of your intentions all along."

"Have you? Well, you do not appear worried."

"I have no reason to be worried."

"And, would you care to tell me why? Quickly, if you please; you perceive my associates are becoming impatient."

"I will be as fast as the Great Flood of Thuvin."

"Very well, I am listening."

"I have mentioned that I was near the Sea of Amorphia."

"That is, the Lesser Sea."

"Yes, yes. The Lesser Sea. Well, can you imagine what I was doing there?"

"Why, I have not the least idea in the world."

"I was coming to an agreement with it."

"With the amorphia? The Gods! You consider me too credible by half!"

"Not, perhaps, a conscious bargain on its part, but I was learning how to speak with it, to convince it to do what I wish. In a word—"

"Elder sorcery!"

"Exactly."

"Pah! I do not believe you."

"Well," said Orlaan, shrugging. "It then remains only for me to convince you."

Some hours later, a certain Teckla, who had been kept by the brigands to cook for them and help with tasks around their encampment, observed that his band had not returned. After consulting with himself (there being no one else around with whom to consult), he went off searching for them in the direction in which they had departed. Soon enough, he found what remained of them, and could only speculate on what sort of catastrophe could have left these blackened and burned remains. He did, we should say, feel a slight twinge of sorrow—the brigands had not been as unkind to him as they might have been, but then he realized that, with the booty they had left, he would be able to live comfortably for many years, if he managed it well. And, when his means began to run low, he could, no doubt, hire a boat to bring him down the river to seek his fortune in the city.

As for Orlaan, there was no sign. It had happened that, on that day, she had found what she had been seeking.

Chapter the Fifth

How Arra Prevented Aging
And Morrolan Discovered
His Growing Notoriety

I t so happened that on a spring day Morrolan entered the chapel
at Blackchapel, looking for his Priestess, Arra, who was, naturally enough, often to be found there, as it was not only where
she consulted with penitents, and not only where she conducted her
services, and not only where she worked with and trained what had
come to be called "the Circle," but was also where she lived.

Having introduced the subject of living quarters, and, moreover,
observing that the reader last had occasion to look in on Blackchapel
several scores of years earlier, we consider it out duty, before continuing, to say two words about Blackchapel as it was at this time—that
is to say, in the 243rd year of the Interregnum (although, the reader
must not forget, an Interregnum that had no direct effect and little
indirect effect on matters this far to the East of the old bounds of the
Empire).

Since we have last visited, then, there have been considerable
changes. In the first place, what had been a sort of low, swampy field
north of the chapel had been drained by clever engineering on the
part of a certain Cecilia, and a series of low cottages had been built
there to the house those who had been steadily arriving in the
village—or, more properly, the town—ever since Arra had begun her
work.

Blackchapel had absorbed these new citizens in the simplest possible way: When they were not engaged in their training in the magical practices, or working with Arra to send out the strange psychic
calls to attract more of their number, they put their talents at the disposal of the local citizens. The most annoying of the pests who disturbed the local agriculture were now almost unheard of. Lost
livestock no longer remained lost. There had not been a bad year for
fish as long as the current generation could remember.

All of these services for the townspeople were performed at the absolute insistence of Arra, who pretended that the instant the Circle became a burden on Blackchapel, the slow, steady, peaceful growth of the Circle would be, at best, interrupted. Morrolan, for his part, paid little attention: he had the single-mindedness (and, to be sure, the accompanying tendency to be oblivious to everything outside of his immediate focus) that seems to be as much the birthright of the young Dragonlord as the fierce temper and callous disregard for life.

To be sure, Morrolan was of a naturally cheerful disposition, and had had no occasion for any display of temper. The townspeople considered him something like their pet demon (though, of course, they would never think of using such terms to his face) and as such, considered him something like a living token of good fortune, and he made friends easily both among the townspeople and the witches. These friendships were hampered only by Morrolan's observation that the people who surrounded him—indeed, everyone except himself and Arra, who were marked by the special favor of the goddess—tended to grow old and die at an alarming speed.

Over the decades, the distinctions tended to diminish between the two groups: local peasant girls could not help but find the witches fascinating, and no one is as attractive to a peasant boy as a woman with the mysterious powers of a witch. The populations therefore tended to mix, with only those newly arrived remaining separate, for a time, from the life of Blackchapel.

And so, as we have said, there was nothing but harmony in Blackchapel between those whose families had dwelt there for generations uncounted, and those who drifted in to become part of the Circle, a harmony that, so far as Morrolan knew, was entirely natural and normal, he being unaware of Arra's diligent work to maintain this state.

Arra, for her part, could not help but be aware of the aspects of Morrolan's character to which we have referred, and so, without complaint, simply added to her duties all of those matters that can be called "politics"; that is, the requirements of maintaining harmony between her witches and the locals of Blackchapel.

On the occasion of which we now write, she heard Morrolan call her name, and so emerged from a back room into the chapel itself, dressed only in a long towel of a particularly absorbent material, and with water streaming from her hair and collecting in small pools on the hard stone floor.

"I beg your pardon," said Morrolan. "I was not aware—"

"It is nothing, milord," said Arra. "I was merely immersing myself in sanctified water to which certain salts and herbs have been added, as part of the process of maintaining my youth. The favor of the goddess does a great deal, but, you perceive, even she can use aid in her endeavors from time to time."

"Oh, as to that, you seem to have maintained all of your youth with no change, so far as my eyes can see."

"You are most kind."

"Not at all. And, come to that, when I look in the glass, I do not seem to have particularly aged myself, which speaks strongly for the powers of our goddess, and the rejuvenating effects of the Circle, does it not?"

"Oh, in your case I believe there are other reasons," said Arra, smiling. "But tell me, what is it that you wish? For I am convinced that you did not enter, calling my name in that strong voice, without having had in mind some particular issue."

"Oh, as far as that goes, you are entirely correct. But, before discussing it, I should rather wait until you, that is, until—"

"Until I should have dressed myself, my lord?"

"You have said it precisely."

Arra, we must confess, took a certain pleasure in embarrassing Morrolan, but she merely said, "Very well, I shall return in a moment, properly attired."

Morrolan bowed, and Arra left, although not without permitting the towel to drop just as she vanished through the doorway. Soon she was back, properly covered in her priestly robes. "I hope," she said, "this causes you less discomfort, my lord."

Morrolan bowed.

"Well then," she said when they were seated, "what is it that you wish to discuss with me?"

"A peculiar thing happened."

"Well, I am listening."

"I was on my way from my apartments to the dry goods store, when I happened to pass a stranger—that is, someone I had not met before."

"Yes, I understand. A stranger. They pass through Blackchapel from time to time. Indeed, many of them end up joining the Circle, at which time they cease to be strangers."

"Well but this stranger—a clean-shaven gentleman of middle

years with a large belly and very little hair—seemed to be looking at me in a very peculiar fashion."

"Yes?"

"That is, he was staring at me."

"I understand."

"And then—"

"There is more?"

"Yes. He stopped Claude, who happened to be passing the other way, and spoke to him, pointing at me in a way I considered impertinent at best, and probably rude."

"Yes?"

"And, after that, he stopped, dropped to his knee, and bowed to me!"

"Well?"

"But, my dear Arra, why would he, a stranger, have done such a thing?"

"No doubt he has heard of you."

"Heard of me?"

"Why, yes. You cannot imagine that what we have done has not been noticed, and that you are not seen as the mover behind it."

"What we have done? You mean, our Circle?"

"Precisely."

"But why?"

"Why, milord? You wonder why?"

"Yes, exactly. And, if you know, I should consider it a great favor were you to tell me."

"Then I will do so."

"I am listening."

"You must consider that we have gathered together three hundred and eighty-three witches. We have been working together, learning more of the Art, and sending out messages to all with the sensitivity to hear them—messages that reach farther and farther as we add more to the Circle."

"Well, I know all of this."

"But, nothing like this has ever been done before!"

"I had not known that. But still—"

"And we have done more. Do you recall last year, the Seeing?"

"You mean, when you saw the raid that was to be conducted on Carrick?"

"Exactly. And we warned them, and the raiders were driven off."

"Oh yes, certainly, I can never forget it any more than I can forget the ten barrels of *oushka* that we were sent as a mark of gratitude. But—"

"My lord, you seem not to understand."

"Understand? I do not understand? Goddess! I have been telling you for an hour that I do not understand!"

"My lord, for a hundred miles around, everyone knows of the Circle, and, to them, the Circle is you."

"Me?"

"You."

"Arra, what do you mean, the Circle is me?"

"I mean that everyone has heard of you, and of the Circle, and sees them together."

"For a hundred miles around?"

"Maybe two hundred."

"They know the Circle, and know me?"

"Your description travels by word of mouth—they perceive you are a very distinctive man."

"Well, but—it is strange."

"Oh, I do not doubt that it is. But it is true."

Morrolan frowned and considered the matter. Arra waited patiently while he did so. At length he said, "Arra, a thought has occurred to me."

"Well, and it is?"

"That band of raiders, would they have heard of us, too?"

"It is possible, yes."

"Are there very many of them?"

"Oh, yes, certainly. They come from considerably less than a hundred miles away. They are from a region called Sylavya, around thirty-five or forty miles around the lake, and, whenever they have a bad harvest—which happens often, as the god they worship does little to give them good harvests—they plunder those around them."

"Yes, I see. Well—"

"My lord?"

"It has come to my thoughts that if we should continue warning their victims of impending raids, they may take it ill."

"That is possible, my lord. As I consider it, I think it is very possible."

"So I had thought."

"Do you think, well—do you think we ought to stop giving these warnings?"

"Oh, no!" said Morrolan. "I certainly would suggest nothing so drastic as that!"

"That is well. For a moment, I was afraid—"

"Yes?"

"I was afraid that you were beginning to show your age."

We will advance in time by something like a year from the time of our previous chapter, though remaining in the same geographical position—that is, in the village of Blackchapel. As we look upon the village (or, perhaps we should say, the town), now in full summer of the 244th year of the Interregnum, the astute observer might notice a few changes since we were last there: The public house where Morrolan met Miska is entirely gone, except for its brick chimney, which stands as a monument. Of the place where he spent his first night, not even a chimney stands, although there are a few scattered stones about to show where it once stood. The cottages that had been built to house those of the Circle are vanished, save for smoking ruins. Indeed, there is scarcely a house or building remaining at all on what was once the main street of the village. Nor, in fact, are there people in evidence; the street would appear to be entirely deserted, save for a small number of rats scurrying about looking for anything edible, and a smaller number of dogs sniffing about after the rats.

After a close inspection, the observer might conclude that some sort of disaster had occurred in and around Blackchapel, and, in this, the observer would be entirely correct.

To find the cause of this catastrophe, let us journey to the chapel itself, which, although showing signs of damage—a few stones have been pried out, and there are some indications that an attempt was made to burn it—is still standing, and is, moreover, occupied: Morrolan and Arra stand at the altar, conversing with one another, which conversation we will take the liberty to intrude upon, at very nearly the point where matters of interest to us are being discussed. At the moment we have chosen, Arra is just saying, "Everyone is in hiding now."

"That is best," said Morrolan.

Arra nodded. "They will reappear soon."

"It happened quickly?"

"While you were in your trance."

Morrolan said, "It seems that I only spent two or three hours in my attempt at astral traveling."

"How was the effort?"

"There was a point when I felt that I was very close to achieving something."

"Well, that is good."

"But they came and went during that time?"

"Yes," said Arra. "They were very fast. Indeed, they were gone in less than an hour. I came to get you, but it was over already."

"They killed many people, didn't they?"

"Nine were killed, twenty or thirty more hurt, and, as I have said, the entire village has been razed."

"And did they steal as well?"

"No. They burned and killed, that is all."

"Indiscriminately?"

"So it seemed."

"Were any of the Circle hurt?"

"Ricardo sustained a cut on his left arm that went to the bone; he is being attended to. And Marya hurt her ankle in avoiding them. That is all."

"We were lucky."

"Yes, milord."

"What were they after?"

"I believe, my lord, that they were looking for you."

"For me?"

"They took Tamas, and beat him to make him tell them where you were."

"He didn't tell them?"

"He didn't know."

"Is he all right?"

"Bruised, no more."

"I must see for myself what they have done."

"I understand, milord."

We trust the reader will understand if we do not follow Morrolan too closely. We confess that the sight of burned-out structures, and, even more, the twisted and bleeding remains of what once were people, will no doubt appeal to some of our readers. Indeed, we are not unaware that there are entire schools of literature which devote themselves to enthusiastic depictions of exactly such events, dwelling

in loving detail on each drop of blood, each broken limb, each ago-
nized scream, each countenance made grotesque by an expression of
pain. Of course, it is the nature of the *history* as it is written that any
tendency within literature will find a reflection within it; and naturally the reverse is true, because those who create literature read history as much as those who write history read literature.

We understand why some of our brothers find themselves drawn
to such depictions: whereas history becomes stronger when the emotions of the reader are engaged, literature absolutely requires it; and
dwelling on agony in its most graphic form is an easy way to engage
the emotions of the reader. Yes, we understand this, but will not ourselves indulge in such appeals to the most base and unsophisticated
instincts of our intended audience, because we hope and believe that
those who have done us the honor to follow us through these histories will best respond to a higher order of stimulation.

However, while we are not choosing to show the reader what
Morrolan saw on the streets of Blackchapel, we must, nevertheless,
insist that *Morrolan* saw all of it. He spent hours on the streets, speaking with the injured, consoling the bereaved, and shaking his head
over the damage to the village. It should not be necessary to make the
observation that Morrolan, after living there for a hundred years,
knew well all of those who had been killed or hurt; indeed, had
known all of their families for many generations, and the tears and
groans could not leave him unmoved.

When he returned at length to the chapel, Arra, upon seeing his
countenance, involuntarily stepped back from him, for she had never
seen him in this mood, nor had she realized that he was capable of
such wrath as he now displayed, though still tightly contained. His
eyes were lit with such a hate that, while it had been seen on a thousand thousand battlefields in the Empire, had, perhaps, never been
seen before on this side of the Eastern Mountains. His hand had
gripped the hilt of his sword. His teeth were clenched, and his words,
when he spoke, were delivered in a low, even tone through lips that
barely moved.

"Let us see, then. They killed and burned without stealing, and
they were looking for me."

"Yes."

"Whence came they?"

"The northeast."

Morrolan nodded. "Then that is where I will go and look for
them."

"How, look for them?"

"Yes."

"Milord—"

"Well?"

"There were seventy or eighty of them. And, while our Circle now numbers considerably more, well, they are witches, not warriors."

"I said nothing of taking the Circle."

"How, you will attack seventy or eighty of them?"

"Why not?"

"With that number, they will probably kill you."

"Perhaps."

"And, if that is what they came here to do, and failed, why gift them with exactly what they wanted?"

Morrolan frowned as Arra's reasoning penetrated the rage that consumed him. "Well, there is something in what you say," he admitted.

"I think so, too."

"Only—"

"Yes?"

"They have burned and destroyed my village, and killed nine of my people."

"Well, and?"

"I wish to kill them."

"That is but natural. Perhaps—"

"Yes?"

"Perhaps the goddess will help."

"You think so?"

"It is possible."

"Has she spoken to you?"

"Not in a hundred years."

"Well?"

"It can do no harm to ask."

"That is true. Let us ask, then. What is required?"

"Very little."

"Then let us attempt it."

"Place your hands upon the altar."

"Very well, I have done so."

"Now close your eyes."

"They are closed; what next?"

"Now you must think about the goddess."

"How, think about her?"

"Yes."

"But, what shall I think about her?"

"What you know about her."

"But in truth, I know very little."

"You have feelings for her."

"Well, yes."

"Concentrate on those."

"It is difficult, Arra. I feel little now except anger."

"You must do your best."

"Very well."

"Now you must visualize her."

"Ah. Visualize her."

"Yes. That means to picture her in your mind."

"Oh, I know what it means well enough, only—"

"Yes?"

"What does she look like?"

"I assure you, I have not the least idea in the world."

"Well, that will make it more difficult."

"That is true, but you must do the best you can."

"Very well."

"Are you visualizing her?"

"As best I can."

"That is good. Continue doing so."

"What then?"

Arra did not respond; or, rather, her response was not to him. She began speaking in some language that Morrolan was unfamiliar with—indeed, a language he had never before heard pronounced. At the same time, he noticed that the altar seemed to be growing warm beneath his hands; he considered remarking to Arra upon this strange phenomenon, but then thought better of it.

He did his best to do as Arra had bid him, difficult as it was to concentrate when in his heart he wished for nothing except to confront his enemy and rend them. Nevertheless, he tried.

He created a picture of the goddess in his mind, thinking of her with flowing yellow hair, and bright eyes, dressed in a gown of shimmering white; at the same time he held to his feelings about her, those being composed of a measure of fear, a touch of awe, and even perhaps an element of love. In his mind—already trained, as it were, by his studies of the heathen Eastern arts, which teach discipline if nothing else—the droning of Arra's voice gradually faded from his awareness. As sometimes happens in that state when one is no longer fully awake, and yet is not entirely asleep, his thoughts began to slip out of his control, and take almost the form of a dream. On this occasion, Morrolan did not afterward remember any details or events from the dream; only that it seemed to him that he left his body, and for a while he was aware of a presence all around him. He was also aware of time passing, though he could not tell how much; it could have been minutes, hours, or days. Arra continued her chant, or, if the reader prefer, her incantation, but Morrolan had ceased to be aware of it in the way that the noise of the chickering, however irritating when it begins, soon vanishes from one's awareness so thoroughly that one is startled and even a little puzzled when it abruptly ceases.

We shall not, however, carry the analogy any further. The sound did not abruptly cease; rather, Morrolan gradually became aware that some time had passed. He then realized that Arra was no longer standing next to him, but, rather, had collapsed onto the floor next to him. Once fully aware of this occurrence, he lost no time in kneeling next to her. Or, to be more precise, he began to kneel next to her, but, for reasons he did not at once understand, he continued down until he was next to her indeed, on his back, staring up at the dark ceiling of the chapel. After some thought, he came to the conclusion that whatever he and Arra had done had been more exhausting that he had at first realized. He considered further and decided he would take some time before attempting to rise.

After a moment, he said, "Arra? Are you well?"

"Sword," she said, which seemed to be a not entirely responsive answer.

"I beg your pardon," he said after a moment, "but I fail to comprehend what you have done me the honor to tell me."

"Sword," she repeated.

"Well, I do have a sword," he said. "Shall I draw it? I am not quite able to do so at this moment."

Arra shook her head, tried to struggle to her feet, and failed. "Sword," she said.

Morrolan would have shrugged, but he lacked the strength to do so, wherefore he decided to wait until either he was able to move, or matters became clearer.

Presently Arra stirred, and said, "My lord Morrolan, are you well?"

"Well enough. Did you speak with her?"

"Yes. She said you must have a sword."

"Well, yes. If I am to attack these people, I must indeed. But, as it happens, I have a tolerably good one."

"No, she means a particular sword."

"Ah. That is different."

"Entirely."

Arra struggled to her feet, leaning upon the altar. Morrolan, not to be outdone, did the same, and soon they were, more or less, standing next to each other.

"Did she say what it was about this sword that makes it special?"

"No."

"Did she say anything about where to find it?"

"In fact, she did not."

"Hmmm. That makes it more difficult, then."

"Yes, I can see that it might."

"Did she say anything that might help me to find it?"

"She said that, when the time came, it would find you."

Morrolan thought about this for some few moments, then said, "This would require me to wait before acting against those who raided Blackchapel."

"And?"

"You know, I think, that I am not of a disposition to enjoy waiting."

"Yes, I know that."

"I am at this moment less inclined to wait than I have ever before been in my life."

"I know that, too, milord."

"And, moreover—"

"Well?"

"If we do nothing, what is to stop them from returning?"

"Oh, as to that—"

"Well?"

"There is more the goddess told me."

"I am listening."

"We must leave Blackchapel."

"How, leave?"

"Yes, exactly."

"That is hard."

"It is. But consider: we are not strong enough to fight them, and they know where we are."

"Both of those statements are true," admitted Morrolan.

"And moreover—"

"Yes?"

"The goddess has said so."

"Well, that is a strong argument."

"That is my opinion; I am gratified that it coincides with yours."

"And our Circle?"

"What of them?"

"Will they be willing to leave Blackchapel?"

"If you lead, they will follow."

"You think so?"

"I am convinced of it. Consider: You are their leader, who has brought them together, and they have all learned more of the Art from this, and share in the power we are gathering."

"That is true."

"And consider as well that, if they stay here, they will be subject to more depredations from jealous or frightened neighbors."

"The Goddess! You are right about that, too!"

"Then, are you convinced?"

"Nearly."

"Well?"

"There is something I wonder about."

"And that is?"

"When we leave Blackchapel—"

"Yes, when we leave?"

"Where do we go?"

"Oh, as to that . . ."

"Yes?"

"I have not the least idea in the world, I assure you."

"But then, we cannot set out without setting out in some direction; that is a natural law."

"Oh, I do not quarrel with natural laws."

"Then we must determine, if not a destination, then at least a direction."

"Perhaps we will receive a sign."

"You think we might?"

"It is possible."

"Is the goddess known for giving signs?"

"She does sometimes, when it suits her purposes."

"Well then, perhaps it will—what is that?"

"What is what?"

"I heard something."

"What did you hear?"

"Something clattering, outside of the chapel."

"Clattering?"

"And the sounds of horses' hoofs."

"Perhaps it is a coach."

"Well, if there is a coach, perhaps there is a passenger."

"That is not impossible."

"Let us look."

"Very well, let us do so; I believe that I am able to walk now."

"As am I."

"Then let us go outside."

"Very well."

Chapter the Seventh

How Morrolan Is Astonished
To Learn Something that the
Reader Has Known All Along

Having made the decision to determine the exact nature and cause of the sound outside of the temple, Morrolan and Arra stepped around the altar, and took what seemed to them to be a long walk to the doors. They stepped out and blinked their eyes in the sudden brightness.

"It is a coach," said Arra.

"And a coachman," said Morrolan. "Miska, is it not?"

"The same," said Miska, as he climbed down.

"I am pleased to see you still among the living. I would have thought—"

"No, my good Dark Star. Priestesses of the Demon Goddess are immortal, elfs are long-lived, and coachmen—"

"Yes, what of coachmen?"

"We are eternal."

"Very well, I accept that you are eternal. In any case, I am pleased to see you. I would offer you *brandy*, only it chances that I have none."

Miska shrugged. "It chances that I have a flask of it, so I require no more at the moment."

"That is well," said Morrolan. "Tell me, what brings you here?"

"I am delivering a passenger."

"A passenger?"

"Yes, indeed."

"How did you acquire this passenger?"

"She was kind enough to buy me a flask of *brandy*, so I offered to bring her to where she should be."

"Ah, and this is where she should be?"

Miska shrugged. "So it would seem, for I am here."

"Is that how you know?"

"Assuredly. You must understand, my dear Sötétcsilleg, that when I set out upon a journey, I do not always know where I am going. But I always know when I have arrived, and, as I have said, I am here."

"Well, that is true," put in Arra, who had been following this conversation closely.

"Then," said Morrolan, "let us meet this famous passenger."

"You are about to," said Miska.

"Then we await you," said Morrolan.

Miska, having by now climbed down from his box, stepped up to the door, with its two windows, both of which were shuttered, and struck the door twice with the knuckles of his right hand, evidently as a signal or warning; after which he grasped the door handle and, with a practiced maneuver, turned it, which not only permitted him to open the door, but, at the same time as the door opened, caused a small stairway to descend from the coach to the ground. The coachman held out his hand, and another hand, this one covered in a green glove, took it delicately, after which appeared the arm connected to the glove, then a face, then neck and shoulders, until at length all of the mysterious passenger had appeared, set foot upon the stairway, and descended to the ground.

In addition to her gloves, which, as we have already said, were green, she wore a gown of the same color (with the addition of white trim) that fit very close, left bare her right shoulder, and, save for a few small ruffles, was without decoration. In addition to this, she had a white wrap of some sort of fur, and for jewelry she wore a pair of small, plain, gold ear-rings and a ring upon the fourth finger of her right hand in which three tiny rubies were set in silver. Her hair was rather dark than otherwise, and her face narrow and angular. Her figure, as could be clearly discerned from the tight fit of the gown, was quite slim; but what caught everyone's attention at once was her height, which was nearly the equal of Morrolan's, which height, as we said earlier, was such as to tower well over all the Easterners with whom he surrounded himself.

"My good Dark Star, and my dear Arra, I present to you the Lady Teldra."

"It is a great pleasure to meet you all," said the one called Teldra, "but, I must say that I am especially pleased to meet you, Lord Morrolan, as I had no idea I was to have the honor of meeting, here so far to the East, another such as I."

Arra and Morrolan bowed, and Morrolan said, "Another such as you? You must refer, then, to the fact that we are both exceptionally tall? Well, but permit me to say that your surpassing beauty commands my attention far more than the mere distance between your forehead and the ground upon which you do the honor to tread."

This speech, as it happened, was remarkable in two ways: for one, it was the first time anyone had heard Morrolan assume such tones and manner; and, for another, it seemed to everyone present that Morrolan had overlooked something that, to them, seemed obvious—more than obvious, in fact, it seemed conspicuous.

Miska was the first to point it out, saying, "How, you think she made reference to her height, when she observed that you two have something in common?"

"Well, I had thought so. Do you refer to something else?"

"Entirely. Or, rather, we refer to a cause of which her height, and your own, is merely an effect."

"Well, I am most anxious to hear about this cause."

"How, you do not know it?"

"Know it? Why, I cannot so much as hazard a guess about it."

"How, you cannot even guess?"

"I have said so."

"And yet, I have trouble believing it."

"Oh, you should believe it, and for two reasons: in the first place because I have said so, and in second place because it is true."

"Well," said Miska, "you begin to convince me that you really are unaware of what we are suggesting."

"That is good. But there would be something better."

"Oh, and what would be better?"

"If you would enlighten me. For I confess that I am entirely perplexed—so much so, that you might as well call me Erik."

At this, Teldra in turn looked puzzled, but Miska gave a gesture indicating that it was not worth explaining. Arra, in the meantime, was staring at Morrolan with undisguised astonishment. The latter, observing her countenance, said, "What, you too?"

"My lord," said Arra, "would you permit me to ask you a question?"

"If it will help me to comprehend, you may ask three."

"This, then, is the question: Have you never wondered why it is you are so much taller than everyone around you?"

"Why, I had thought it rather a fluke, in much the same way that Kevin is so much fatter than everyone else, or that Lara has hair that is so much redder than everyone else's."

"But you cannot fail to notice that you have lived for more than a hundred years, whereas those around you rarely achieve half that age."

"But, my dear Arra, you have lived as long as I."

"But you know that this is a gift from the goddess, for I have explained it to you."

"Well, and could she not grant me a similar gift?"

Arra could only respond to this with an eloquent shrug, as if to say, "I am at a loss for how to go on."

At this point, Miska could no longer contain himself, and began to laugh—and his laugh, the reader should understand, consisted of no small chuckles, but rather big, booming guffaws, and were accompanied by a rocking of his whole body, and tears streaming down his face. Morrolan frowned. "Do you know, I am becoming annoyed," he remarked.

Miska, for his part, did not notice, being too occupied with laughing, but Teldra said, "Please, my lord; forgive him. He means no offense, and does not laugh at you, but, rather, at the absurdity of the situation, which, I assure you, is as unlikely as any I have ever encountered, or am likely to."

"Well," said Morrolan, a bit mollified, "if you would be good enough to explain it, perhaps I will see the absurdity as well."

"That is not unlikely," said Teldra.

"Well then?"

"Permit me to try," said Arra.

"Do so, by all means," said Morrolan and Teldra. (Miska said nothing, as he was still endeavoring to stifle his laughter.)

"You have," said Arra, "heard of elfs?"

"Elfs? But of a certainty. They live in the West, over the mountains."

"That is true," said Arra, "although some of them, from time to time, come east to our side of the mountains."

"Well, and if they do?"

"Well, then, sometimes they settle down and live here."

"Why should they not? There is good country on this side of the mountains."

"Well, of what does living consist?"

"Living? Well, it consists of walking, of sleeping, of eating—"

"And having children?"

"Well, yes."

"And dying?"

"Well, yes, dying can be seen as part of living, if you wish."

"I more than wish, I insist upon it."

"Very well, if you insist, I accept it."

"Good then. Let us see what we have."

"Yes, let us do so."

"We have elfs who have crossed the mountains, and had children, and died."

"Yes, as well as walking and eating and sleeping."

"Oh, I do not say they didn't do those things as well."

"That is good, for if you did, I should have to dispute with you."

"But for now, let us consider only having children and dying."

"Very well. It is sad when those things happen together—that is, when two people die soon after having a child, for that leaves the child an orphan."

"Exactly."

"I know of this, because it is what happened to me."

"Exactly," said Arra. "Now do you comprehend?"

Morrolan frowned. "But we were speaking of elfs."

"Well, and what do we know of elfs?"

"They live on the western side of the mountains."

"And what else?"

"They have magical powers."

"What sort of magical powers?"

"Oh, as to that, I have no idea, I assure you."

"Well, they live a very long time, do they not?"

"Yes, so I have heard."

"And they are very tall, and thin, and, in addition, they have no beard."

"Yes, I believe I have heard that too."

"Have you ever shaved, my dear lord?"

"I? Well, I have never had the need."

"And then?"

Morrolan stared at her, comprehension at last coming to him. Miska was at last able to stop laughing, and just watched Morrolan with an amused twinkle in his eye.

At last Morrolan said, "Do you pretend that I—"

"Exactly," said Arra.

"Impossible!"

"Not at all."

"But why would no one have mentioned it to me?"

"I, for one, assumed you knew."

"As did I," added Miska.

"But those who raised me—"

"Almost certainly wished to conceal your nature to protect you."

"I cannot believe it," said Morrolan.

"You cannot doubt it," said Arra.

"And yet—"

"Well?"

Morrolan fell silent, considering what he had been told. At last he said, "I am an elf?"

"As much as I am, myself, my lord," said Teldra. "Although I am an Issola, and you are, to judge from your countenance, a Dragonlord."

"You perceive, I do not comprehend what these terms mean."

"Then, if you wish, I will explain."

"I think I am not yet ready for more explanations."

"I understand," said Teldra, "and will wait until you are ready."

"That will be best."

Miska wiped tears of laughter from his face and said, "Well, it was worth a drive of three hundred kilometers just to be here for this moment."

Morrolan, in the meantime, stared at his hands as if he had never seen them before. "I am an elf?" he murmured.

"We call ourselves human," said Teldra gently.

"Who does not?" said Arra.

"Or Dragaeran, if you prefer," said the Issola.

"Dragaeran," said Morrolan, as if trying out the word to see how well it fit into his mouth.

"I wonder . . ." said Teldra.

"As do I," said Morrolan. "I wonder many things."

"I do not doubt it in the least," said Teldra. "But there is a thing I wonder in particular."

"Well, and what is that?"

"I wonder about your family name, and who your ancestors were, and so on."

"Oh," said Morrolan. "I know that."

"How, you know?"

"Of a certainty. While I know little of those who bore me, I at least know my family name. Is it important?"

"Important?" said Teldra. "I nearly think it is!"

"Well, and why is it important?"

"Because from it, we can, with some work, learn many things that would be of interest to you."

"What sorts of things?"

"Your lineage, any ancestral holdings you might have, your family history."

"How, you pretend we can learn these things merely from my name?"

"It is likely, although it may take some few years, and much traveling."

"Well," said Arra suddenly, "it seems to me that we were just discussing the idea of travel, were we not?"

"That is true!" said Morrolan.

"Travel?" said Miska. "And to where were you considering travel?"

"We had not yet made that decision," said Morrolan. "We were waiting to see if the goddess wished to give us a sign."

"And," said Arra, "I nearly think she has. Indeed, were the sign any more prominent, it would block our view of the sky."

"Lady Arra," said Morrolan, "I agree with you entirely."

"Well," said Teldra. "Let us see. First of all, if you will tell me your family name, then perhaps even from that I can make a guess as to a destination for which to start."

"You wish me to tell you now?"

"If you would be so good."

"Very well. My father's name was Rollondar, and—"

"Rollondar?"

"Yes, that was it, and my—"

"Rollondar e'Drien?"

Morrolan looked at Lady Teldra, who had, quite against custom of the Issola, interrupted him, and had even done so twice, and who was now staring at him with an expression of astonishment on her countenance.

"Yes, my family name, I learned, was e'Drien. But tell me, for I am curious, why this seems so remarkable to you, for I perceive that you are startled."

"I am, indeed, and I will tell you at once why it is so."

"I am listening, then."

"Here it is: I know exactly who your father was, and, moreover—"

"Yes? Moreover?"

"I know where to find your ancestral lands."

"Ah! I have ancestral lands."

"Indeed you do."

"Are they far from here?"

"Rather, yes. Across the mountains, down a long river, and within a hundred leagues of the great city of Adrilankha, which lies along the Southern Coast of what was once the Empire."

"That does sound like a long way," said Morrolan.

"It is no quick journey."

Morrolan turned his face to the west, and used his hand to shield his eyes from the Furnace which, in the East, was blazing brightly enough to be annoying to anyone who looked at it.

"Yes," said Teldra, as if reading his thoughts. "It is to the West that our destiny lies."

Morrolan nodded, and continued staring. After a moment he turned to Lady Teldra and said, "What else do you know of my family?"

"I know one thing that will amuse you, I think."

"Well, I do not mind being amused."

"If you do not, then I will tell you."

"Do so."

"It is this: Your name, Morrolan, means Dark Star in the language of the Silites, who lived in this region many, many years ago, and whose language is still spoken by some."

"Well, and if it does?"

"Your father also took his name from the same tongue, and it means, 'Star that never fails.'"

"Ah. That is remarkable. A coincidence, do you think?"

"It is," said Arra, "unlikely to be a coincidence when the goddess is at work."

"Well, that name was given me by the good Miska here."

They looked at Miska, who merely shrugged.

"'Star that never fails,'" repeated Morrolan. "Well, did he fail?"

Teldra said, "I would think, looking at you, my lord, that he did not."

Morrolan nodded.

"And then?" said Arra.

Morrolan shrugged. "Do you, Arra, speak to our Circle. Tell them whither we are bound, and have them meet us there as best they can in their own time, and, moreover, have them spread the word to every witch that we will gather there."

"I will do so."

"Someday we will return, though; there is a debt here that I have not paid." With this he sent a dark glance to the northeast.

"Then we are leaving?" said Arra.

"Yes. And if you wish to accompany us, Lady Teldra, we should like nothing better."

Teldra bowed and said, "I should be honored, my lord."

"And you, good Miska?"

"Me? No, my dear Dark Star. I believe I must return to my own land, now that I have delivered the Lady to you."

"As you wish. But you must not fail to call on me, should you require me."

Miska shrugged, as if to say that, save for his preferred drink, there was little he was likely to need.

Morrolan nodded and looked to the west once more. "We leave at daybreak," he said.

Chapter the Eighth

How the Society of the Porker Poker Came to Exist, and How It Had Its Final Meeting

It was on a Farmday in the middle of winter in the 246th year of the Interregnum that the Society of the Porker Poker met for the last time. The Society had already had its number diminished in several ways: first when the Tsalmoth, Stagwood, had taken to the road to pursue his desire to be a bard; next when Flute, of the House of the Hawk, had become disgusted with the bickering of certain of the other members and ended her association with the Society; and most recently by the exodus of Mialand, of the House of the Lyorn, who had married and gone to live with her husband in the iron center of Lottstown, far to the East. With all of these desertions, more or less justified, the Society now numbered only four. All the members of the Society were between one hundred and three hundred years old—in other words, at the age where adulthood looms over one and demands an end to childish things, but the enthusiasm of youth has not yet been lost. Were the Empire still in place, no doubt they would have long before scattered and been pursing whatever lives their inclinations had led them toward, or at least living each in his own household; but the Interregnum had the effect, in addition to all of its other effects, of keeping families more firmly bound together, as if to provide a better defense against the untamed world outside the doors of the family manor.

The names of these four will, no doubt, mean little to the reader, yet our duty as historian requires that we introduce them at this time, in hopes that, hereafter, they will mean more, and will stir in the reader's heart and mind whatever feelings of affection or disdain the unfolding of this history will engender. They are, then: Lewchin, Shant, Piro, and Zivra.

Lewchin, the only daughter of a Marchioness of the House of the Issola, was a hundred and ninety or two hundred years old, tall, dark, and rather frail in appearance; she was distinguished by that grace of speech and manner which always marks those of her House. She lived with Shant, who was nearly the same age as she.

Shant was the oldest son of a Dzurlord; and although he and Lewchin could not marry, owing to the difference in their Houses, they nevertheless lived together as husband and wife, as many did during that period of spiritual as well as material decay called the Interregnum. Shant was short and stocky for a Dzurlord and distinguished by green eyes and wavy fair hair that he wore in perpetual disarray, covering his noble's point.

The third member was Zivra, who was something of an enigma. She appeared, at first glance, to be the Dragonlord she dressed as, and as, indeed, were her guardians. Yet she had blond hair, rare among that House, and fair skin; and above all she displayed a coolness and evenness of temper and a calm attitude that made one think more of a Lyorn noble. From the shape of her ears and her noble's point one could easily believe her ancestors were Dragons, yet again, she lacked the sharpness of feature that one would have expected; instead her face was rather heart-shaped, her lips thin, her nose small, and her eyes widely spaced and vibrant. A casual observer might suspect her of being of mixed Houses, yet there was some indefinable quality about her that denied this. She was soft-spoken, yet there was no hesitation in her judgments of people or events, and she seemed, moreover, to be looking always ahead, as if there were something in the distance, or the future, that was calling to her. She was the oldest member, being two hundred and forty or two hundred and fifty years old, and if she still lived with her guardians, rather than having struck out on her own, it was because her guardians, having no offspring of their own, had made her their heir, and, being old themselves, desired her assistance in managing the family estate.

The remaining member of the Society was Piro, who was the Viscount of Adrilankha and, moreover, he for whom this history is named. His mother was Daro, the Countess of Whitecrest, and his father was Khaavren, who had been the Captain of the Phoenix Guard at the time when the last Emperor was assassinated and the city of Dragaera dissolved into a sea of amorphia; and who is someone of whom we entertain hopes the reader will not have forgotten from those earlier histories in which he played no small rôle. Piro was, therefore, of the House of the Tiassa, as could be seen by the white and blue he affected; his quick smile; his bright, intelligent eyes; his lean form; and his long, nervous hands. He was, at this time, just about one hundred years old, and was the youngest member of the Society.

These characters being sketched, we will now, with the reader's permission, give a brief history of the Society itself before moving on to the events of its last meeting. It had been formed, then, some forty or forty-five years previously, when some of its founders were barely more than children. The present members, along with a few others, had long been friends; indeed, had already formed bonds of common sympathy natural to a group of children of the same social class living near each other. They would often form parties of pleasure in which they would walk or ride into pasture or jungle areas near the outskirts of Adrilankha, where they would hunt or fish or simply sit and talk in the manner of children, and, later, in the manner of young adults.

On one such occasion, walking through the Generous Wood near the ruins of Barlen's Pavilion on the west side of the city, they happened to disturb a wild boar, who panicked and charged them, snorting and bristling. Shant happened to be carrying a sword he had recently acquired—a poorly wrought sword, to be sure, but one that had a point nevertheless, and before he knew it, he had drawn it and held it out between his friends and the boar. The boar, with surprising intelligence, had stopped short of this formidable obstacle, and stood its ground, snarling and snorting, at which time Shant gave a halfhearted lunge, which punctured the skin of the boar, and which puncture, in turn, sent the beast scampering back into the woods.

The friends, the danger now averted, relieved their tension through the sort of laughter that often follows fright—especially fright that, in the event, proves unfounded. Shant was declared a hero, to which he responded, between giggles, by holding his sword aloft and saying, "I dub thee Porker Poker." The friends then immediately swore eternal allegiance to the Society of the Porker Poker, a name which stood them in good stead in the years that followed. We do not, by the way, know which members of the Society were actually present at the time, because the story was so often spoken of among them that those who were not there could soon tell it as well as those who were, and even see it in their minds, and so everyone eventually forgot who had truly been present—the incident had become the common property of the Society.

One by the one, members drifted away because of other interests, marriage, or relocation. Shant acquired a better sword, but kept

Porker Poker suspended by wires on the wall of the parlor of his home in Adrilankha, which home he later shared with Lewchin. It was here, then, that the Society met in the small but tidy parlor of Shant's family home in Adrilankha, with Porker Poker—to which, by custom, they solemnly offered the first toast—still on the wall above them.

The toast being done, they set about, as they had so often before, engaging in conversation. "Well," said Shant, "has anyone anything to report that concerns the Society? That is, has anything of interest to any of the members happened since we last gathered? I can say, for my part, that it has been a pleasant enough week, but nothing has happened that is worth reporting." In fact, it was rare indeed for anything to have "happened," yet this usually served as an effective gambit for opening the conversation that was the meat and bread of the Society's meetings.

On this occasion, Zivra shifted in her chair, as if she would speak, but didn't. This was noticed by Lewchin, but she decided that, if Zivra preferred to wait before giving her news, then Lewchin would respect this preference. Piro, on the other hand, said, "I do not know the significance of it, but I can report that a messenger has arrived and put the manor into something of an uproar."

"How, an uproar?" said Lewchin.

"Well, that is, a subdued uproar."

"What precisely," Shant inquired, "is a subdued uproar? For you perceive I desire precision of all things."

"I will describe it as best I can," said Piro.

"I await your description with all eagerness," said Shant.

"Here it is, then: A messenger arrived some four days ago, that is, the day after we last met."

"Well?" said Lewchin. "Whence came this messenger?"

"That I cannot tell you, only—"

"Yes?"

"He was a Teckla, and he wore the livery of the House of the Dragon."

"There is nothing remarkable in that," said Shant. "Dragonlords often hire peasants to run errands, and it is only proper that they wear the Dragon livery under such circumstances."

"Oh, I agree, there is nothing remarkable in that. Only—"

"Well?"

"His message."

"What was it?"

"I assure you, I haven't the least idea in the world."

"How," said Zivra. "You have no idea?"

"None at all, on my word of honor."

"And then?" said Shant.

"All I know is this: The messenger spoke to the Count my father and Countess my mother for some time, and then departed, and after he left—"

"Well?" said Shant. "After he left?"

"There were unmistakable signs of agitation in the behavior of the countess and the count."

"And yet," said Lewchin, "they gave no indication of the cause of this agitation?"

"Exactly. Indeed, far from giving a reason for it, they made every effort to hide it."

"The Horse!" said Shant. "It is a regular mystery."

"So it seems to me, my dear friend," said Piro.

"But," said Zivra, "what could the explanation be?"

"I could not guess," said Piro. "Only—"

"Well?" said Lewchin.

"I intend to attempt to discover it."

"You have not yet done so?" inquired Zivra.

"I have tried, but I have not yet succeeded."

"Well," said Zivra under her breath, "there are mysteries abounding these days."

"I will," said Piro, "certainly inform the Society when I have learned something."

"And you will be right to do so," said Shant.

"Perhaps it is an impending invasion by the Islanders, or news that roving bands of Easterners have made it this far. Or, yet, it may be news of bandits nearby, or even of another onset of the Plague."

"Speaking of the Plague," remarked Shant.

"I would rather not," said Zivra, with a grimace.

"Refusing to speak of it," said Shant sternly, "will not cause it to vanish, any more than refusing to speak of the marauders from the sea or the reavers from the East will prevent them from appearing."

"And, therefore?" said Zivra.

"Therefore, I propose to speak of the plague."

"Well," said Piro. "Let us speak of it, then."

"I have heard of a marvelous preventive."

"Ah, have you then?" said Piro, sitting back with the attitude of one prepared to listen to something either interesting or amusing, and not yet certain which it was to be. Lewchin glanced quickly at Shant, something like a smile apparent from the crinkling around the corners of her eyes. Zivra raised her graceful eyebrows slightly and gave no other sign.

"Indeed," said Shant. "And I will share it, if you like."

"Well, do so then," said Piro.

"This is it: The first symptom of the Plague is that one begins to feel tired, is it not so? First, the victim finds himself sleeping a great deal. This is followed by a reddening of the features, a dryness of the mouth, a shortness of the breath, a fever, delirium and then either the fever will break, or death will follow soon after."

"Well, this is all true," said Piro. "And then?"

"You will agree, I think, that these symptoms follow in a regular order."

"Yes, indeed."

"Well then, if one was able to stop the disease in its early stages, it would never reach the latter stages."

"That is but logical."

"Well then, I have learned of an herb that, when chewed, will prevent sleep."

"And so you believe—"

"Well, if, as we have agreed, the first symptom is prevented—"

"Then the poor fellow will simply remain awake until lack of sleep sends him out of his senses."

"Well, what of it?"

"For my part," said Piro. "I should rather have a clean death than lose my mind."

"Pah! Brain fever can be cured. Death cannot."

"You cannot mean you would prefer madness to death."

"You cannot mean you would prefer death to madness."

"Absurd!"

"Impossible!"

"They are," quietly observed Zivra to Lewchin, "beginning once more."

"I nearly think they are," agreed Lewchin. "And quickly, too."

"Ought we to do something?"

"Yes, perhaps we should."

"And have you an idea?"

"I have."

"Well?"

"I believe," said Lewchin, "that we should have another glass of wine, for yours is quite empty, and mine is no better."

"An admirable plan," said Zivra, and poured. Shant and Piro, meanwhile, had raised their voices and begun pounding on the furniture in order to emphasize certain points in their dispute. After some few minutes, however, Zivra and Lewchin, through an exchange of looks, decided that the conversation could be stopped without risk of an inordinate amount of knowledge or understanding being forever lost to the world.

"Gentlemen," said Zivra, in a sweet voice with which she somehow contrived to penetrate the sounds of controversy. "I beg you to leave off for a moment."

They stopped, glanced at Lewchin and Zivra, then at each other, after which they adopted abashed expressions. "Well?" said Piro.

"I have something to say," said Zivra. She pronounced these words with no particular expression; in fact, she used the same tone of voice in which she might have announced that the coffee was roasted and seasoned and ground and ready to be brewed (for she was, in fact, adept at this craft, though such mastery had grown rare after the Disaster), yet in some indefinable way, everyone understood that Zivra was about to say something of importance; consequently, no one spoke, but rather everyone waited for her to continue, which she did at once and in this fashion: "My guardians have informed me that I am to be leaving for some destination for some length of time."

"How, leaving?" said Piro.

"Precisely," said Zivra.

"Do you mean, leaving Adrilankha?" said Shant.

"Yes, that is it."

"For some destination?" said Piro.

"For an *unknown* destination."

"Then, you do not know where you are going?" said Lewchin.

"You have understood me exactly."

"But," said Piro. "Your guardians must have at least given you a reason."

"Not the least in the world, I assure you," said Zivra.

"But, when will you be leaving?" asked Shant.

"To-morrow," said Zivra.

"To-morrow!"

"Early in the morning."

"The Horse!" said Piro. "So soon?"

"Nearly," said Zivra.

"But, then, has something happened?" said Shant. "For to be told that one must pack up and leave, with only a day to prepare, well, there must be a cause for it."

"That may be," said Zivra. "Yet, if so, I assure you I know nothing about it."

"And will you be returning?" said Lewchin.

"Ah."

"Well?"

"I know nothing about that, either."

"But," said Piro, "did you not interrogate them?"

"How, interrogate my guardians?"

"Yes."

"Not the least in the world. They made the announcement, and I—"

"Yes, and you?"

"Well, I submitted. It seemed to be a matter of grave urgency, and a matter, moreover, about which strict secrecy must be observed, for otherwise they would have answered those questions they knew I had before I should ask them."

"And therefore," said Shant, "you didn't ask them?"

"Exactly."

"You must write to us," said Piro.

"And often," added Shant.

"I will," said Zivra.

"It is a shame," said Piro, "that the Orb is lost, for with sorcery we could communicate directly, mind to mind, as they did in the old days."

"Sorcery is not required," said Shant. "There are those who can so communicate without it."

"Oh, indeed?" said Piro. "Well then, do so now."

"That I have not learned this art," said Shant, "is no proof—"

"Gentlemen," said Lewchin. "If you please, let us not start this again."

"I must confess," said Zivra, "that I shall miss even the arguments on natural and magical philosophy."

"Well," said Lewchin. "I will take notes, and then send them to you with my letters."

"Ah! I anticipate much pleasure in their perusal."

Lewchin frowned and pursed her lips, studying her friend, and then said, "There is more, isn't there?"

"How, more?"

"You know or suspect something you have not yet told us."

"Ah," said Zivra, and smiled. "Well, I ought to have known I could not fool you."

"What is it?"

"Well, I only suspect—"

"That is," put in Shant, "you fear."

"Well, yes, I fear. I have been told that I am to meet someone."

"How, meet someone?" said Piro.

"Exactly."

"Then you fear—"

"That I am to be married."

"But your guardians wouldn't do that!" cried Lewchin.

"Alas," said Zivra. "I don't know. They will tell me nothing, only that I am to go, and that I will meet someone, and all will be explained."

"I confess," said Piro, "that it sounds, well, I do not like how it sounds."

"Nor I," said Shant.

"Nor I," said Lewchin.

"But it is a mystery," added Piro. "That much is clear."

"If it is a mystery," said Shant, "then it is *not* clear."

"I meant—"

"Well, but what can be done?" said Zivra quickly.

"We will carry you off ourselves!" said Piro.

"How, carry me off?"

"Exactly," said Shant.

"To where?"

"Well," said Piro, "to, that is—"

"Anywhere," said Shant. "The jungle."

"Neither of you," said Lewchin, "is being sensible. Consider—"

"Well?" said Shant and Piro.

"We do not know that marriage is contemplated, we only suspect."

"That may be," said Shant. "Yet it is bound to be unpleasant, or they'd have told her what it was. Come, Piro, what do you think?"

"I am entirely in agreement with Shant."

"And I," said Zivra, who seemed caught between laughter and tears, "am very much afraid I must subscribe to Lewchin's opinion. We cannot run off merely on a suspicion. Besides, if it is a marriage, perhaps I will like him."

"You think so?" said Piro, doubtfully.

"Well—"

"It doesn't matter," said Lewchin. "We will not, in fact, be carrying her off."

"And yet—" began Shant.

"But," continued Lewchin, "our friend will write to us, and soon we will know, and then—"

"Well?" said Piro. "And then?"

"And then we will do what we must."

She said this coolly, and with no expression in her voice. The others looked at each other and nodded solemnly.

The rest of the day's events continued under a certain pall, and with the not-unaccountable feeling of something ending. No one said that the Society was now, in effect, dissolved; yet everyone, in his own way, seemed to feel it. They drank but sparingly, as if none wished to have his memory clouded by wine, and they spoke, even Piro and Shant, in low tones, recalling past adventures and sharing plans, hopes, and dreams for the future, until well into the night.

At one point, Piro said, almost as if speaking to himself although his words were addressed to Zivra, "Do you think that you might at last learn something of your origins?" Then, realizing he'd spoken his thoughts aloud, he held himself very still, an apology on his lips, for this was a subject that had never been spoken of.

Yet Zivra only nodded, as if the question were the most natural one in the world, and said, "I have had that thought. Perhaps I will, but then, perhaps not."

For years this had never been broached, and now that it was, no one quite knew what to say, until Lewchin said, "Has it troubled you not to know?"

Zivra frowned and said, "You wish to know if it has troubled me?"

"Yes," said Lewchin, "if you would care to tell me."

"Well, I will answer your question."

"And?"

"No, for some reason it has not. It has always seemed to me as if—"

"Yes?" said Shant. "As if?"

"As if there was a reason why the names of my parents and the circumstances—and even the House—of my birth has been hidden from me. I have always known, or seemed to know, that I would find out at the right time."

Said Piro, "And this, perhaps, is the right time?"

"Perhaps."

"And," added Lewchin, "you have never questioned your guardians?"

"Never," she said.

"But," put in Shant, "you will tell us if you find out? For you perceive we are curious about everything that affects any member of our Society."

"Yes, I understand that, and by my faith I will tell you everything I can."

"That is all we can ask," said Lewchin, with a look to Shant to make sure he understood to whom these words were, in fact, addressed.

After that, the conversation drifted to other subjects, and continued until at last Zivra announced that she must retire, for the following day would see her busy in completing her preparations for departure in the earliest hours, and in setting out while it was still quite morning.

The reader, who has only just been introduced to these four persons, will not be interested in hearing of the words and tears which poured fourth as Zivra and Piro took their departure from Lewchin and Shant, so let us pass quickly by with only the statement that there was no shortage of protestations of mutual affection and promises of letters to be exchanged often and visits to be made when possible.

The routes taken by Piro and Zivra ran together for some distance, and so, after mounting their respective horses, they continued together for some time.

"Do you think," said Piro, "that we will all ever meet again?"

"As to that," said Zivra, "I cannot say. But at least you will be able to see Lewchin and Shant when you wish."

"That is true. Do you know, I envy them."

"Because they have found each other?"

"Yes, that is it exactly."

"They are fortunate," said Zivra. "Before the Disaster, they should never have dared to display such an arrangement, one being a Dzur, the other an Issola."

"Well," said Piro, shrugging, "at least one good thing, then, has come from the Disaster."

"You think so?"

"How, you disapprove?"

"Of Lewchin and Shant? Of course not, they are my friends. I shall miss them. And you, as well."

"It is a new stage of our lives, Zivra. Yours, and mine as well."

"You are right. And I accept it, only—"

"Well?"

"If it is to be without the friends I love, it will be hard."

"Yes. But here is the bridge, and this is where we part."

"I believe—"

"Yes?"

"I believe we will see each other again, Piro."

"It is my dearest wish, Zivra."

We ought to say that, upon leaving Piro, Zivra went to a place the reader might not expect, met with a most remarkable person, and had a conversation of considerable interest. The reader may rest assured that we will reveal place, person, and conversation when it is proper to do so. Nevertheless, we believe that we should waste no time in following the principal actor in our history: the Viscount of Adrilankha. He directed his horse through the streets, oblivious, as he always was, of the danger of riding alone through the city at night, until, without incident, he returned to the high cliffs above the sea, and thus to Whitecrest, which was the name of his home, as well as the district in which the city of Adrilankha was situated. There he gave his mare into the care of the night-groom and was about to enter the home, when he observed, in the dim light that came from the windows of the manor, the form of a man, who stood like a statue near the servants' entrance of the keep.

Chapter the Ninth

How the Viscount Met His New Lackey, With Necessary Digressions During Which Something Is Learned of the Countess and Count of Whitecrest

Piro touched his sword, which, having been removed from the saddle, was hung from the sheath-belt over his shoulder. On consideration, however, he did not draw it, but approached the figure before him, whereupon this person turned and presented a respectful bow, as to a superior, which the Viscount found unusual, as they were as yet unable to see each other clearly. Piro continued forward, and finally stopped a few feet away, at which time he acknowledged the salute and said, "I give you good evening, visitor."

The visitor repeated his bow, as deeply as the first time, and said, "I am not yet even a visitor, noble lord, yet I aspire to be more."

"You aspire to be more than a visitor?"

"I do, my lord."

"Well, let us see, then." Piro was close enough so that, squinting in the small amount of light that filtered down from an open window above, he was able to see that the stranger, who was holding his hat in his hand, had no noble's point. "Come, what are you doing here?" asked the viscount.

"My lord, I am waiting."

"How, waiting?"

The Teckla bowed once more. "Yes, lord: waiting."

"But, then, for what are you waiting?"

"I am waiting for the door to open."

Piro was momentarily confused, uncertain whether he was being mocked. He said, "You are waiting for a servant to answer the door?"

The visitor respectfully bowed his agreement with this assessment.

"You perceive," said Piro, "that there is no one to come to the door, as we have no doorman. It is unlikely that the Countess or Count would have heard you, and the other servants have, no doubt, retired for the evening."

"Then that," said the one who was not yet a visitor, "more than adequately explains why I have not been acknowledged or admitted."

"Well," said Piro, "but how long have you been waiting?"

"Four hours and a quarter," said the Teckla.

"Four hours and a quarter?"

The visitor nodded solemnly.

"But then, how are you able to know the time to such a precise degree?"

"Ah, does Your Lordship wish me to explain?"

"Yes, that is it exactly: I wish you to explain."

"I will then."

"I am listening."

"As I became aware that I might be standing here for a good length of time, it came to me that the time would pass better were I able to keep my mind occupied."

"Well, I understand that, for standing in one place often leads to ennui. What, then, did you do?"

"Your Lordship may perceive that, it being dark, there was nothing to look at."

"Yes, I understand that. And therefore, being unable to see?"

"Being unable to see, well, I listened."

"Ah! And what did you hear?"

"I heard many things, my lord: the waves crashing upon the cliffs, the hollow clop of a shod horse along the stone streets, the rattle of carriage wheels. But among them was the peculiar chitter that I recognized as the hunting call of the ratbird."

"Yes, I know that chitter."

"And I, too, for I have spent a great deal of time in forest, wood, and jungle; and I know that the male ratbird, who always hunts with his mate, makes this call at regular intervals, each time receiving a response from his mate, who is also hunting, until one or the other has made a kill. Your Lordship may perceive that the important thing is the regularity of the call, which is astonishingly consistent for each pair on each night."

"I am not unaware of this phenomenon," said Piro. "And then?"

"I had a thought."

"As you listened to the ratbird?"

"Yes, exactly. In fact, it was listening to the ratbird that inspired the thought."

"Well, but what was this famous thought?"

"My lord, it is was this: If the ratbird demonstrates this behavior in forest, wood, and jungle, why, then, should it not demonstrate the same behavior when entering the city?"

"Why, that was more than a thought, it was very nearly an idea."

"Was it not? And then, my lord, having nothing else to do, I counted the interval between calls, and discovered that, with this pair—ah, there it is again!—eight minutes and twenty-one seconds elapsed between calls. Now, as I am something of an arithmatist—"

"The Trey! Are you then?"

The Teckla bowed. "I was thus able, merely by keeping track of the number of times the ratbird made its call, to discover two things."

"And what are these two things you have discovered? For you perceive you interest me enormously."

"In the first place, that I have been waiting at this door for the amount of time that I have had the honor to inform Your Lordship."

"That being four hours and a quarter."

"Now, in fact, four hours and twenty-five minutes, or close to it."

"I understand. And, the second thing you have discovered?"

"There are very few rats in the environs of Your Lordship's keep."

"Ah. I understand."

"I am gratified that I have been able to answer Your Lordship's question."

"And I am gratified to learn that there are so few rats, although it does make me wonder why the ratbird should venture this far into the city."

"Ah, my lord, with Easterners to the east, and Islanders to the West and South, and plagues and brigands all around us—"

"Well?"

"Well, the city and the jungle become closer each year."

"That is true, I think. Yet there remains the issue of what I am to do, for I am loath to leave you standing here for another four hours and a half, or more."

"That is as Your Lordship wishes."

"Well, since there is no one else to speak to you, I shall do so myself."

"That is very kind of Your Lordship," said the Teckla, and he put himself into an attitude of waiting.

"Why have you come to the door?"

"I have come for a position, my lord."

"How, a position? What sort of position?"

"Doorman and lackey."

"Ah, ah! You heard, then, that such a position was open?"

"Exactly. I heard that such a position was open, and I have not only heard it, but —"

"Well?"

"I think I have very nearly proved it."

"Indeed, I think you have. How did you come to hear about this position?"

"Gossip, my lord, from local gossips, which is often the best if not the only way to learn anything."

"And what exactly did you hear? For, you perceive, I was raised to believe in precision in all things."

"If I may say so, my lord, that is only just, and so I will tell you what I heard."

"That is what I wish to know."

"It was just this: The Countess and Count of Whitecrest require a doorman and lackey. This doorman and lackey, so I was told, must be of good character and have letters of reference."

"And you have such letters?"

"Indeed, my lord." The prospective servant touched his breast to indicate that he carried them within his blouse.

"Well, follow me, then."

Piro led the way into the house, through the buttery, larder, and kitchen, and so into the gentle confines, where he lit a few more tapers, then sat and held out his hand. The Teckla removed a neatly tied scroll of papers from his bosom, slipped it from an oilskin envelope, and presented the scroll to the Viscount, who untied it, unrolled it, and glanced through the various letters and documents contained therein. After a moment he said, "Your name is Lar?"

"Yes, my lord. My name is Lar, and Lar means me."

Piro rolled up the documents and tied them once more. "Well, Goodman Lar, it is late, and I am not the one to whom you must speak. I have looked at these recommendations, and they appear to be entirely regular, so that I will permit you to spend the night within these walls. You may find a corner of the kitchen, and then in the morning you may speak with the Count."

"Thank you for your kindness, my lord," said the Teckla, accepting his scroll. Meanwhile Piro, whose eyes had quite adjusted to the light, took a good look at the Teckla. He was rather shorter than the Viscount, but sturdy-looking, as if he had spent some time in physical labor, he had the round face of his House, and, moreover, a face with no expression on it, yet Piro, who even at his tender age had some skill as a physiognomist, thought he detected a certain intelligence in the set of Lar's eyebrows and the lines of his forehead.

Piro cleared his throat and said, "Two words."

Lar stopped in mid-bow and looked up, presenting a slightly comical aspect. "My lord?"

"When you speak to the Count—"

"Yes? When I speak to the Count?"

"You may wish to be, well, laconic."

Lar straightened up slowly, frowning a frown of bewilderment.

"There is something about you," continued Piro, "that inspires my sympathy, and I wish to help you."

"I am grateful," said the Teckla. "And yet—"

"Your comportment," explained Piro. "My father the Count is, well, he is not a cheerful man, and I am afraid that he will not wish to be attended by a cheerful servant. And my mother, well, as she manages the affairs of County Whitecrest, she leaves the estate and the domestic matters to my father."

"How, not cheerful?"

"Exactly."

"And yet, he is a Tiassa."

"Well, I know it is strange."

"My lord, it is—unusual."

"You perceive, there are reasons."

"Oh, as to that."

"Yes?"

"Well, my lord, is it not the case that there are reasons for everything?"

"You think so?"

"So I have been told, my lord."

"Then you are educated."

"I know my symbols, and I know my numbers, and I know that there is a cause for every effect."

"Then you wish to know the cause for this?"

"If Your Lordship would care to tell me, well, I would listen."

"This is it then. You know about Adron's Disaster."

"Trout! I nearly think so! I was a young man when it happened, and a thousand miles away, and yet I remember feeling the ground shake beneath my feet, and I was nearly brained by a large pitcher falling from a shelf."

"Well, then, my father was a friend of Adron."

"How, Adron himself?"

"Exactly."

"Ah! I had not known of this circumstance."

"There is more."

"How, more?"

"He was a servant to His Majesty, the Emperor."

"A servant?"

"And more than servant."

"More than a servant?"

"He was—"

"Yes?"

"Captain of the Phoenix Guards."

"He!"

"Exactly."

"And yet, His Majesty was assassinated."

"Precisely."

"Well, much is explained then. And yet—"

"Well?"

"Has he been brooding on this subject for two and a half hundred years?"

Piro made a gesture with his hands. "It has grown worse, so I am told, these last hundred years or so. But nevertheless . . ."

"Well, that clarifies matter, my lord. Only—"

"Yes?"

"The position, as I have been informed, is not that of servant for the Count."

"How, it is not?"

"Not the least in the world."

"Well, but then, what is it, my good Lar?"

"It is lackey to his son."

"His son?"

"Exactly."

"But I am his son."

"So it would seem, my lord."

Piro looked at him again. "You are, then, to be my lackey?"

"That, at any rate, is the post for which I have the honor to apply."

"And yet, good Lar, I give you my word that I had no idea any such position was requested."

"It is only very recent, my lord. That is, within the last few days. And then again—"

"Yes? Then again?"

"It is also possible that I have been misinformed."

"What use have I for a lackey?"

"Oh, as to that, my lord—"

"Well?"

"I assure you, I have not the least idea in the world, although I am convinced, my lord, that the Count your father must have a reason."

"Oh, I am certain that he does, and, moreover, I am equally certain that, in time, I will learn what it is. But, in the meanwhile, as it concerns me—"

"Yes?"

"I will look again at your letters of recommendation."

Lar bowed and passed them over. Piro this time studied them more carefully than he had at first. "You have traveled extensively," he remarked after some few minutes.

"Well, that is true."

"What has taken you on these journeys?"

"Is Your Lordship aware of the expression 'to follow one's nose,' meaning to travel according to mood, and to instinct, thither and yon, with no plan, hoping to find one's fortune?"

"I have heard this, yes. And?"

"My lord, I have followed my stomach."

"Ah. I understand. Well, at any rate, you have no fear of travel."

"None. You expect to be traveling?"

"I have no expectations. But the fact that my father the Count wishes for me to have a lackey may indicate something of his plans for my future. Then, again, it may not. I see you cooked for a band of mercenaries."

"Highwaymen might be a more accurate term, my lord, or road agents as they are sometimes called."

"I see. Well, then you have no fear of a skirmish or two."

"Oh, as to that, there have been times when the very air was thick with the sounds of battle, and steel flashed, and bodies fell, and blood flowed freely, and yet I stayed at my post cooking venison with way-berries as if it were nothing at all; I assure Your Lordship that, with regard to my duties, I am utterly without fear."

"Well, that is good," said Piro.

"Then there is to be an expedition of some sort, my lord?"

Piro shrugged. "I have no such plans, but, whatever the Count's plans for me may be, I have no intention of staying here for-ever."

"Ah! My lord is ambitious?"

"Nearly."

"So much the better."

"Oh?"

"A young man without ambition is an old man waiting to be."

"Ah. I perceive you are a philosopher."

"My lord? Not the least in the world."

"You say you are not?"

"My lord, I must nearly insist on it."

"Very well, if you will have it so. But tell me, how did you come to the line of work you occupied—that is, cooking for a band of highwaymen?"

"I will tell you, my lord, if you wish it."

"Wish it? I nearly think I have asked."

"This is the answer, then: In my youth, I was granted use of a small parcel of land from the estate of Baron Halfwing, which estate, my lord, was situated in the lowlands some eighty leagues west of the city and along the coast."

"Well?"

"That is, my lord, it was *quite* along the coast, so that I could dip my feet in the ocean without leaving the land I had been allocated."

"Ah! Yes, it is clear to me now. With the fall of the Empire . . ."

"Exactly. It soon came to pass that I had no land, but, rather, a small parcel of ocean. And being thus tied to no place—the Baron, you perceive, having no inclination to insist that I remain in the water, nor being in a position to insist on anything—I found myself free. I have neither the patience nor the inclination to fish, my lord, and so I took the opportunity to set out onto the road to make my fortune."

"Well, and have you made your fortune?"

"I have my life, which, as Your Lordship may agree, is a fortune to a man such as I."

"And have you family to support, as well?"

"A younger brother, but he is getting along well enough on his own."

"Ah. And what is he doing?"

"He? Oh, he is doing as I did—that is, cooking for a band of highwaymen."

"I see. It is as well you know some of these, for it may prove helpful should some of them set on us if we travel."

"Indeed, it may save Your Lordship's life."

"Or the lives of the highwaymen."

"Trout! That is true! But then, a life is a life, and if some are of more importance to us than others, it does not make these others worthless."

"It is, no doubt, living near the sea that has made you a philosopher."

Lar spread his hands, as if to say that if Piro wished to insist that the prospective servant was a philosopher, said servant would not dispute the issue, but instead, although disagreeing, would remain, if we may, philosophical about the difference of opinion.

The reader may, perhaps, be confused about the apparent liberty in conversation between Teckla and nobleman; if so, we can only give our assurance that, by all accounts, this was one result of the fall of the Empire—the courtesy and respect due one's social superior seemed to fall apart even as did the ties of land, fortune, and honor that they supported, so that, in some places, one might listen to an hour's conversation between two persons unaware that one was a nobleman and the other a servant. To be sure, this did not happen at all times and in all places, and one can also find occasions, especially in the duchies far from any large city, where such distinctions increased, as if the desire for tokens and symbols of respect could replace the actuality. We will not waste the reader's valuable time by attempting to account for this peculiar alteration in social custom, but will instead leave it up to the reader to decide how much consideration the phenomenon merits; having both represented and pointed it out, we consider our duty fulfilled and our goal achieved.

Piro's goal was, at least for the moment, also achieved: He had learned enough about the Teckla to convince himself that by letting the fellow into his house he was not, as they said at the time, "letting the brigand onto the coach," and he had, moreover, given himself a certain amount of information to think over during the night; this much done, he showed the Teckla to a spot where he might rest and be warm until the morning, after which the Viscount took himself off to his bedchamber to consider the events of a day rather more full of significance than he had expected it to be. To a Tiassa who had not yet passed the mark of his first century, events full of significance cannot fail to bring cheerful ruminations, wherefore it was a contented young man who fell asleep that evening in Whitecrest Manor.

Chapter the Tenth

How the Arrival of an Envoy
Caused Turmoil in Whitecrest Manor

By contrast with the sentiment with which we closed the previous chapter of our history, it was a discontented and ill-humored older man who, in the form of our friend Khaavren, woke up early the next morning and, after dressing himself, made his way down the stairs. We trust that we have dropped sufficient hints to prevent the astute reader from being unduly startled by the changes that have taken place in our old friend since we last saw him two and a half hundred years before; and we do not, moreover, wish to give needless pain to those readers who have done us the honor to concern themselves with the brave Tiassa whose activities have formed the center of these histories; all of which is to say that we propose merely to glance briefly at the Count of Whitecrest, and give only the barest outline of what he has become, thus saving ourselves from the vicarious unhappiness the poor soldier has suffered in the time that has elapsed since the assassination of the Emperor and the fall of the Empire.

As the reader will, no doubt, have deduced, Khaavren's failure—or, rather, what Khaavren *perceived* as his failure—to protect the Emperor had preyed upon his mind and spirit, leaving him, to some degree, a sad and bitter man, inclined to keeping his own counsel, and to torment himself mercilessly for every failure in his long and active life. To be sure, this bitterness had occurred only gradually during the last two hundred and fifty years, yet the alteration of his character, like the rot in a fruit, had come with ever-increasing speed once first begun, so that the last thirty or forty years had seen more change than the previous two hundred.

These changes were reflected in the set of his jaw, which gave the appearance of hiding teeth perpetually clenched; and in his hair, which had become quite grey; and in the unnatural rigidity of his posture, which gave the impression, when he walked, of an utterly inflexible spine, as if he had suffered some disabling injury, and above all in his eye, which lacked the gleam of joy and ambition that had marked his countenance even when he had been, for all anyone could see, content to be merely a soldier, carrying out the humble yet exacting duties of his office. Moreover, though he retained, perhaps, some skill in swordplay, for such skill is based in part on knowledge of the art and science of defense that is not subject to the whims of the body, he had lost nearly all of the strength, quickness, and stamina which had made him, at one time, such a formidable opponent and one of the most feared and respected swordsmen in the Empire. His condition could be observed from the sagging of his muscles and the shortness of breath that accompanied even such a mundane task as climbing the stairs up to his bedchamber. To all of this, for the sake of completeness, we should add that his left hand, wounded on that long-ago day in the last, desperate battle to stop Adron, had never entirely healed, so that it remained somewhat stiff, and unable to close, and caused him a certain amount of discomfort, especially on cold, wet nights.

And yet no one, least of all a Tiassa, is made up only of one characteristic; no one, that is to say, can be entirely lacking in complexity and contradiction. In the case of our old friend, the reader ought to remember that, at nearly the same time as the events which had marked what he saw as the great failure of his life, he had met a woman—to be precise, Daro, the Countess of Whitecrest—who had brought him a kind of happiness and contentment he had long despaired of achieving. His life with her, which resulted in a son in whom he had no small degree of pride, had worked, in some measure, to offset the sense of defeat that beset his spirit, so that at times, most often in the evening, as he sat in the drawing room before the grand hearth and played at sparrows with his son, or drew rounds with the Countess, or dealt dog-in-the-wood with both of them at once, a certain aspect of peace and happiness would settle over him; too often, however, it would be dispelled by some stray thought which would bring to mind those last days and hours of the Empire, and he would fall silent, and Daro (and, later, Piro) would know that he was asking himself once more what he could have done differently to have saved the life of that well-intentioned but ineffectual man whom the gods and the Cycle had made the last Emperor. At such times, wife and son would fall silent, as if in respect for his thoughts, and provide what little comfort they could by their presence.

To be sure, in case it is insufficiently clear to the reader, it was the influence of his wife and son that had, as it were, held off for so long what might be called the disease of his spirit. These spells of bitterness or despair seemed to grow worse and more frequent as Piro grew older; almost as if the son in which the Count took such pride were a reminder to him of his own ambition, and the devastating blow it had suffered. Yet both mother and child knew him to be of a kindhearted disposition, and loved him all the more for the pain—physical and spiritual—that he carried with him.

This was Khaavren, then, as, dressed in dark, baggy pants tucked into his tall boots and a thin blue blouse, he made his way down the wide central stairway of Whitecrest Manor, and so into the kitchen, where he found the cook deep in conversation with a Teckla he did not recognize, although the reader, jumping ahead to the correct conclusion that it is none other than Lar, will have knowledge ahead of the good Tiassa.

Khaavren, whose ears had remained as sharp as they had been on that long-ago day when the Emperor had done them the honor to make an observation respecting their obedience to their owner's desires, was able to ascertain that the conversation between the unknown and the cook concerned the identity of the unknown, wherefore from the force of old habits he took a moment to wait and listen. A moment was all it took for the Tiassa to learn something concerning the identity of the unknown, at which time he stepped forward and said, "I bid you good day. I am the Count of Whitecrest."

Lar bowed very low and stated his own name, adding, "I was informed—"

"Exactly," said Khaavren. "You have letters of recommendation?"

Lar, remembering Piro's advice of the night before, contented himself with nodding, bowing, and respectfully offering the documents in question. Khaavren accepted them and led the way back into the drawing room, where, after sitting and inviting Lar to do the same, he asked many of the same questions Piro had asked earlier, albeit in briefer form and receiving more laconic answers. At one point in the interview, the side-door clapper made its sonorous report, and Khaavren suggested Lar find out who was there; upon returning the latter announced coolly and without expression that a certain Teckla was at the door inquiring about a position as doorman and lackey.

"You may tell him," said Khaavren evenly, "that the position is filled."

Lar bowed without comment and turned to carry out his duty. Upon his return, Khaavren suggested that he see if he could find

something with which to break his fast, after which he might introduce himself to the cook, the maid, and the stable-boy (who was also
the night-groom), these being the only three other servants currently
employed at Whitecrest Manor. "You will," remarked Khaavren, "be
informed of your duties at a later time, save that, as you know, you
are to answer the door and—" He was interrupted again by the door
clapper. He smiled and said, "To-day you will, no doubt, be spending
a certain amount of your time informing those who arrive of your
new position."

"Yes, lord," said Lar, and once more went off to answer the door,
this time returning to say, "My lord, a messenger."

"How, a messenger?" said Khaavren, frowning. "And from
whom?"

"He would not say, my lord. But he is dressed in the livery of the
House of the Phoenix."

These words had such a profound affect on Khaavren that even
Lar, who scarcely knew him, could see that he was experiencing
strong emotion. The Tiassa nevertheless mastered himself sufficiently
to say, "Pray find the Countess and inform her, after which you may
show the messenger into—well—into whatever room the Countess
may wish."

"Your pardon, my lord, but—"

"Well?"

"Where might I find the Countess?"

"Ah. At the top of the stairs, turn there to the right. At the far end
of that corridor, on the right, will be a small anteroom where you will
find her maid. Speak to the maid."

Lar bowed and went off to fulfill his orders, which he did with
careful precision. Khaavren sat where he was, thinking and remembering, but not speculating. That is, it is not so much the case that he
knew, or thought he knew, what the message was; or even that he
didn't care; it was that he had long ago simply stopped wondering
about things. He knew that he would either find out or not, and it
would have an effect on him or it would not, and it would be good or
it would be bad, and he saw no reason to permit his thoughts to run
ahead of the facts, especially when his thoughts were so entirely
occupied with all of those recollections engendered by the phrase
"House of the Phoenix," which recollections we will, in respecting
Khaavren's privacy, refrain from making explicit to the reader,
although the reader can, no doubt, form whatever conclusions he
wishes, especially recalling that the Viscount had already spoken of a

certain turmoil engendered by a letter. Should the reader conclude that the earlier letter and the present messenger are related, we will at once endorse this opinion; but should the reader choose, instead of speculating, to merely await the unfolding of events, a choice by which we are flattered in that it indicates trust in the narrator, we will give our word that the source and purpose of the messenger will be revealed before too many pages have passed.

After some few minutes, Lar returned and stood before Khaavren.

"Well?" said the Tiassa.

"Madam's compliments, and would the Count be kind enough to attend her on the terrace?"

"Very well. Do you, then, bring us coffee."

"I will do so at once," said Lar. "Unless—"

"Well? Unless?"

"If Your Lordship should wish it, and you have the filter, I know how to brew klava."

Khaavren's visage brightened slightly, and something like a smile came to his lips as he said quietly, "Do you, then? I have not tasted klava in three hundred years. Yes, by all means, bring us a pot."

"Honey and cream?"

"Exactly."

"Are there biscuits and bacon?"

"Perhaps. Bring us what there is."

Lar bowed and went off to attend to his duties, while Khaavren made his way onto the terrace, which stood in the rear of the house and offered a view out over the ocean-sea—a view which had, in fact, improved with the Interregnum, now that Kieron's Watch no longer stood in the way off to the southwest. The morning breeze came in from the sea, which required use of the appropriately named "morning-coats," which were left on pegs near the terrace door. Khaavren donned his, which was colored a pale blue with white embroidery, then sat in his chair facing the wide expanse of reddish-orange ocean far below him. An instant later the Countess emerged, in a morning-coat of lyorn red against which elaborate stitching in brown could barely be seen (the Countess, we should add, though a Tiassa, always affected the colors of the House of the Lyorn, because they suited her and because she cared very little about the dictates of fashion). Khaavren rose and took both of her hands in his, smiled, and escorted her to a seat next to his, where they sat together for a few minutes, until Lar appeared and announced, "An envoy from the

Enchantress of Dzur Mountain," causing Khaavren and Daro to frown in sudden consternation, because Lar, in his inexperience, had first announced the visitor as a *messenger* rather than an *envoy*, the latter of which required the hosts to rise to greet him out of courtesy for his principal.

They managed this, however, without any clumsiness. Daro bowed her head and said, "I am Whitecrest, and this is Lord Khaavren." The envoy bowed very low and did not, of course, give his name, but did accept the chair that was offered, out of respect for his office, and he also gratefully accepted the klava that Lar brought, and which was so good that the Count and Countess immediately forgave Lar his error.

The envoy, we should add, was not a Teckla, but appeared from his features, at first, to be verily of the House of the Phoenix itself, so that for just an instant the Countess and Count found themselves startled, until they recognized, by the shape of his cheekbones and nose, that the visitor was, in fact, a Dragonlord—those of the House of the Dragon tending to often resemble superficially those of the Phoenix.

"Your Lordships perceive," began the envoy, "that I wear the Phoenix livery."

"We had even remarked upon it," said Daro.

"It is for this mission only. I have taken service for this task at the request of she whom I serve. You might say that I have been loaned from one master to another. Yet I daresay my visit is not unexpected."

"That depends," said Daro, "on whose behalf you come."

"I serve one called Sethra Lavode, whose name is, I expect, not unknown to you."

"That is true," said Daro. "I have heard that name pronounced before."

"Sethra, on her part, serves one called Zerika."

"Zerika?" said Khaavren. "I do not believe I know her, but—"

"But the name," said Daro, "is significant."

"She is," said the envoy, "the last being born of the House of the Phoenix."

Khaavren and Daro looked at each other.

"Her mother," continued the Dragonlord, "was the Princess Loudin, the Phoenix Heir at the time of the disaster. Her father was—"

"Vernoi," said Khaavren, suddenly remembering a conversation he had had with that worthy gentleman, a scant few days before the fall of the Empire.

"Exactly," said the other. "Vernoi died in Adron's Disaster, but he had—"

"Sent his wife out of the city some days before."

The envoy frowned. "Ah. You knew of this circumstance?"

"At one time," said Khaavren. "And yet, until you brought it to mind, I had not given it a thought in more than two hundred years."

"Well, yes. It seems the Lord Vernoi had a premonition of catastrophe, and sent his wife, the Princess Loudin, to a safe place some days before the Disaster, where she was delivered of a child."

"Zerika."

"Exactly. Now the Princess herself scarcely survived the birth of her child by a year, falling to the first wave of Plagues that accompanied the Disaster, but the child survived, and has been raised by foster parents, and it is now at last time . . ." His voice trailed off and he looked expectantly at Khaavren.

"Yes? It is now time?"

"Well, Sethra Lavode deems the time is ripe."

"The time is ripe for what, my dear sir?"

"As to that, I cannot say."

To hide his confusion, Khaavren busied himself in pouring more klava, adding cream and honey, and drinking. At this moment Lar, who had slipped away unseen, returned with a plate full of warm biscuits, a tub of butter, and a jar of apple marmalade, all of which conspired to put the conversation in abeyance for some few minutes. During this time, Daro, who had spoken little, studied her husband, wondering at his thoughts but unwilling to intrude upon them.

After a biscuit or two had been consumed by each of the three, the Countess said, "We were not expecting you until next week."

The envoy nodded. "In the event, the passage was not as difficult as we anticipated, yet it is a long passage, and through treacherous regions."

"I understand. Well, you are welcome here."

The envoy bowed his head solemnly and said, "Here is my signet and a letter." He rose and gave these items into the hand of the Countess, who looked at them and passed them on to Khaavren, who, after making certain of the handwriting and the description contained in the letter, and the authenticity of the signet, gave them back to the envoy. Reading Sethra Lavode's description, however, caused Khaavren to pay closer attention to the individual before them than perhaps he had hitherto, whereupon he frowned suddenly, and staring hard at the Dragonlord, suddenly pronounced the word "Uttrik."

The envoy nodded. "I have the honor to be his son."

"Well," said Khaavren, smiling for the second time that morning, "You resemble him." Then, no longer smiling, he said, "And how is my old friend?"

"Alas, sir, he was in Dragaera at the time of the Disaster."

Khaavren bowed his head. "I'm sorry," he said in a voice so low it was nearly a whisper. "I had not known that he was so close by in those last days. I wish . . ." His voice trailed off from a whisper to less than a whisper—in fact, to silence.

"I scarcely knew him, sir," said the envoy.

Khaavren nodded and said in a stronger voice, "I had the honor and pleasure of knowing him well. Your name, young man, is Kytraan?"

"Yes, my lord."

"Well, Kytraan, you are always welcome in my home, whether you have an errand or not, in memory of a good man, a good fighter, and a good companion." He glanced at Daro for confirmation, and she nodded solemnly.

"Thank you, Lord and Lady," said the envoy.

As if to emphasize this greeting, Lar appeared once more, this time with a plate full of bacon and onions, which he set on the table before drawing discreetly back, which bacon and onion dish was at once sampled by those present.

We trust the reader will allow us, during this lull in the conversation, to briefly sketch Kytraan, the son of that Uttrik whom some of our readers may recall from our history of *The Phoenix Guards*. He was, then, a well-proportioned young man of about three hundred or three hundred and twenty, perhaps slightly short for a Dragonlord, yet with long arms and legs that gave the opposite impression when he sat. His hair was of a light brown shade, as were his eyes, and he bore a Dragonshead pendant with the jewels that marked the line of Lanya. His movements were slow and graceful, almost like a Lyorn's, and from his countenance one would think that he smiled but rarely.

After a few minutes of silence, during which the three of them ate bacon and onions, drank klava, and stared out over the sea, Daro said, "We received a message from Dzur Mountain, that is, from the Enchantress of Dzur Mountain, that we should prepare to receive an envoy, and that we should prepare our son for a journey, but there was no reason given."

Kytraan smiled. "And yet, you began to do so at once, didn't you, even though you had no notion of what would be asked?"

Khaavren shrugged. "I know Sethra Lavode."

The envoy started to speak, but Khaavren cut him off with a gesture. "Lar," he said, "have the Viscount dress, and bring him here."

The servant, who had been standing by some distance away, bowed and left to carry out his orders, and some half an hour later Piro, dressed and alert thanks, in spite of his abbreviated rest, to the recuperative powers of youth, appeared before them, with a cheerful word to his father, a kiss of the hand to his mother, and a respectful bow to the stranger, who was introduced at once as an envoy from the House of the Phoenix.

"The House of the Phoenix?" said Piro, frowning in bewilderment.

The envoy bowed his agreement, after which they all sat down, having, we should have mentioned, stood upon the Viscount's entrance. Piro was then given some time to eat and drink, during which he manfully attempted, with only limited success, to conceal his curiosity and impatience and to give the impression of eating and drinking with the relaxed ease that became his rank. Both the effort and its failure were noted, we should say, with both pleasure and amusement by the Count and the Countess.

"My son," began Khaavren without preamble when at length Piro had set aside his plate, "you are called upon to serve — I will not say the Empire, for the Empire no longer exists, but the memory of what was, and the hope of what may be again." He stopped and spoke to Kytraan. "Will you say I am wrong?"

"I will not," said Kytraan.

Daro said, "What exactly does the Enchantress wish of our son?"

"That I do not know. Only that he is to come with me to Dzur Mountain, a distance of some sixty-five or seventy leagues. I have arrived sooner than I had expected, and so if you wish to delay the departure, there is no reason why you should not, but I can give you no more information than I possess."

"That is only natural," said Daro, who glanced quickly at Piro, and then looked away. We trust the reader is able to understand what might be passing through the mind of a mother at such a moment — a moment, that is, when she is preparing to see her only child leave home for the first time, and, moreover, to leave home on a quest of uncertain results and unknown dangers. As for Khaavren, he was not immune to these feelings, yet there were other emotions as well flitting through his nerves—emotions having to do with recollections of when he had first set out from home, and of what he considered his failures since that time, and of a certain hope that his child might in some measure redeem him, and of sorrow that he would not have the chance to redeem himself, and of many other delicate shades and nuances of feeling that accompanied these.

As for Piro—for we will not hesitate to take advantage of our position as narrator to flit hither and yon into the mind and heart of whomever we wish—it may be that buried somewhere within him was a certain regret for leaving his family, perhaps for-ever, and there may have even been the smallest hint of apprehension with regard to setting out toward unknown dangers, and it is even possible that he felt some strains of loyalty toward the cause his father had served for so long; but all of these emotions were drowned and submerged by one: the sudden longing to set out and to make his way in the world, for better or worse, for good or ill, for fortune or catastrophe.

Each of the Great Houses has, as is well known, its own characteristics: the heroism of the Dzur, the ferocity of the Dragon, the cleverness of the Yendi, the nobility of the Lyorn, and, of course, the enthusiasm of the Tiassa. But some of these Houses, as is also well known, have also their similarities; and it is worth noting one point of similarity that the Tiassa share with the Dragon and the Dzur: their inability to keep their thoughts from being fully and immediately reflected on their countenances. Daro and Khaavren, then, saw at once what was passing in the mind of their son, and responded in the same manner: They gave a smile that was at once fond and a little sad, and reached out and took each other's hands. Kytraan, upon witnessing this conjugal meeting of minds, coughed in confusion and looked away.

"Well," said Daro after a moment, letting go of Khaavren's hand with a gentle squeeze and recovering herself, "we must confer as to details, but, at any rate, you, good Kytraan, will spend the night beneath our roof, to which end you must be shown to a room. The servant—" She paused, realizing she didn't know the servant's name and the servant could not yet have knowledge of the manor. "The servant," she continued, "will have the maid show you to a room, and we will meet again at dinner."

Kytraan rose and bowed, and allowed himself to be escorted from the room, leaving Daro, Khaavren, and Piro alone. When they had seated themselves again, Khaavren said, "You understand there may be danger."

"I understand that."

"I trust you will acquit yourself bravely, because you are, after all, a Tiassa."

"Yes, Father, and more-so because I am your son."

"Well, it is true I have never lacked for courage, although there have been times—"

"None of that," said the Countess gently. "Be brave, my son, but not foolish."

"I give you my word," said the Viscount, "that I will be inspired and guided by your examples, and I will always hold to those principles by which I have been raised."

"Well," said Daro, "let us hear those principles."

"You wish, then, for me to recite them?"

"Exactly. We will see what you have learned."

"Very well. I think you will not be disappointed. I will recite them now."

"I am listening. What are your principles?"

"To seek understanding before taking action, yet to trust my instincts when action is called for. Never to avoid danger from fear, never to seek out danger for its own sake. Never to conform to fashion from fear of eccentricity, never to be eccentric from fear of conformity. To preserve the honor of my name and House, and to cherish the memory of the Empire. To always care for my horse, my lackey, and my equipage as if they were part of my own body. To hold myself to higher standards of conduct than I hold another. To never strike without cause, and, when there is cause, to strike for the heart. To respect, love, and obey those whom the gods have made my masters, for their sake when deserved, for my sake should my masters be unworthy, and for the sake of duty at all times. To be loyal to my House, my family, my name, and the principles of the Empire."

"That is it," said Daro. "Now see to your horse, lackey, and equipment, for you will leave in the morning."

Khaavren responded to this with a sharp intake of breath. Daro looked at him quickly, but he nodded. "A delay," he said, "would only . . ."

"Yes," said Daro.

Piro stood, respect battling excitement in his address, yet he bowed and walked from the terrace without unseemly haste before breaking into a run that took him through the manor and out to the stables, to give his favorite horse an extra measure of grain, and to begin the other preparations necessary for his journey.

The Count and Countess of Whitecrest took klava on the terrace overlooking the Southern Coast of Dragaera; the sight, smell, and sound of the sea filled their senses. Khaavren never took his eyes from the reddish waves.

"My lord," said the Countess. "For what do you look?"

"Ships, my lady, from distant ports."

"Someday you will see them," she said.

After this they spoke no more for the better part of an hour. At length, Khaavren said very softly, "It seems that I did some good after all."

"You speak of the Princess Loudin?"

"Exactly."

"Well, but speak more clearly."

"It is nothing," said Khaavren. "Only that, in this one matter, it seems that I was a tool of the gods."

"And does this give you joy?"

"I feel that, in some measure, the burden is eased."

"Then I am glad."

Khaavren looked at her quickly. "It cannot have been easy, my dear, to—"

"Come, do not speak of it. Rather, let us watch the ocean-sea and wonder at its farther shores."

"Yes, let us do that."

And that is what they did, until at last Daro took her leave to be about the business of Whitecrest. Khaavren sat where he was until, well after noon, he was joined by the Viscount, who saluted him respectfully and, at Khaavren's sign, sat next to him.

"You are ready to leave in the morning?" said Khaavren.

"Yes, sir, I am."

"How will you travel?"

"Sir, I will take my horse, and, with your permission, we will load the supplies on the seveck gelding, who is large and strong and will also carry the lackey; unless you, my father, believe we should take a mule. Yet I thought to bring as little as possible, and thus travel the more quickly."

"No, no, my son. I subscribe to your plan exactly."

"Then that is what I will do."

"And you will leave early, will you not?"

"Before it is light."

"In fact, before the Countess and I have risen."

"That is our intention, sir, for I know that you have said that an early start on the first day is of utmost importance in a long journey, and so I have taken your words to heart."

"That is good, Viscount. And you have come to see if I have any other words, that is, any last words of advice to you before you leave?"

"Exactly."

"I am gratified that this thought came to you. Well, I do not, for I have taught you what I could, in words where I could not do so by example, and whatever you have learned must serve you as best it can. What of your friends?"

"I shall write to them this evening."

"That is well. It is important that we not neglect our friends, for they are our anchors, and good friends can hold in any storm, provided we do not cut them loose." He laughed. "You perceive what living near the sea has done to my habits of speech."

"You have had good friends, sir, have you not?"

"I have indeed. But distances have grown longer since the Disaster, and we no longer have the posts, so that one must remain ignorant of what is passing with old friends, unless one is Sethra Lavode."

"Apropos, sir."

"Well?"

"Do you think I will meet her?"

"It seems you may. And if you do, you must not fail to present my respectful greetings."

"I will do so, sir."

Neither spoke then, for a moment, until the Viscount said, "My lord?"

"Yes, Viscount?"

"You wish you were going, don't you, instead of I?"

Khaavren sighed. "I am in no condition to go, Viscount. I could perhaps still lift my old sword, but I could neither cut nor parry. And my old bones do not allow me to sit astride a horse for more than a few hours. And if this mission is what I suspect it is, it requires someone who . . ."

"Yes, sir? It requires someone who . . . ?"

Khaavren shook his head. "No, you will go forth, and do what must be done. That is all of it."

"Yes, sir. I will not disgrace you."

"No, Viscount, I am certain that you will not. And you will bid a fond farewell to the Countess before you go?"

"I will visit her in her chambers as soon as I have left you, sir."

"Good." They sat once more without speaking; then Khaavren said, "What do you think of your lackey?"

"He pleases me, sir, for he seems to have some courage, and his conversation amuses me."

"That is best. A lackey can sometimes be almost a friend, you know, and I will tell you that, to this day, I wonder what has become of my old servant, Srahi, and I hope that she is happy with her companion, whose name was Mica, and who serves my friend Tazendra of whom I have told you so much."

"I will not fail to attend to Lar, sir."

Khaavren nodded, and then, with an effort, he rose. Piro did the same. "Come, Viscount, embrace me, and then take your leave of your mother."

"Gladly, sir," said the young man, and embraced his father with enthusiasm and affection, after which, with a last tender salute, he re-entered the manor. Khaavren, for his part, sat down once more and continued looking out over the ocean, where none could see the glistening in his eyes.

Chapter the Eleventh

How the Duke of Galstan,
Whom the Reader May Remember as Pel,
Has Acquired New Responsibilities;
And a Brief Discussion of What
These Responsibilities May Entail

Early the next morning, if one were able to look out over the broad expanse of terrain that had once been the Empire, one would have found, in fact, that almost nothing worth our notice was occurring. To be sure, the western half was still covered in darkest night, but even in that portion upon which we have turned our attention, that is, on Whitecrest Manor in Adrilankha, all the observer might have observed was this: Three figures, those being Piro, Kytraan, and Lar, walked to the stables, secured their provisions and supplies on a pack animal, mounted horses, and began riding slowly east.

In some sense, this may be considered a momentous occasion, because of all the later events set in motion by this simple departure; yet it is a startling truth that simply because an event has historical importance, that does not necessarily make it interesting; and as the reader has the right to demand that everything in a romance be both significant to the unfolding of events and absorbing in its own right, the author has no choice but to leave these three individuals to find their own way onward, while the reader is guided toward matters by which his imagination and sympathy may be evoked.

At the moment, then, when our three friends are setting out, we must look hard for any activity of both interest and significance to our story; much of the land is asleep, and, of those who are awake, nearly all are involved merely in the day-to-day life that takes up most of the time and energy of the aristocrat, the tradesman, the peasant, and, if truth be known, even the historian. The exception could be found, if one looked, in the far northwestern portion of the continent, on a peak called Kâna, in the Kanefthali Mountains, where a certain Dragonlord with the same name as the peak to which we have just alluded and his cousin have, since we last saw them, achieved an expansion that is certainly worthy of note.

Much (indeed, in the opinion of this historian, most) of Kâna's success can be attributed to his ability and determination to find the most talented individuals in different areas of expertise and recruit them into his project. By the time a half century had elapsed from the Disaster, he had fought, subdued, and killed or recruited all of the smaller warlords in the area around the mountains; by the end of the first century he had established communication, intelligence, and transport lines to the Ocean-sea in the south and west, and nearly to the desert in the East. Over the next century, he bargained and traded with those larger holdings near the mountains, and then, one by one, swallowed them, until, by the time of which we have the honor to write, that is, near the middle of the third century of Interregnum, he controlled almost a third of the land that had once been the Empire, and his influence was felt over another third.

We should mention in passing, by the way, that, some fifty years previously, his agents had learned of Khaavren, and had considered recruiting him, but had decided against it upon learning of his general demoralization and weakness of body and spirit. Should they have attempted to add him to their number, it is impossible to say if they would have succeeded, or how history might have unfolded differently.

But if Kâna (or, more precisely, Habil acting through Kâna) missed Khaavren, there is another of our acquaintances who was not missed, that being Pel, who gravitated toward the gathering of power as naturally and inevitably as an orca will swim toward a place in the water where blood has been spilled. Pel had, a hundred years before, been a minor and almost accidental pawn in Kâna's vast information network; but in the manner of the Yendi that he was, he had learned more on his end of the "wire," as it was called, than Kâna had learned from his assistance, and Pel had soon grown more and more important in this organization, showing a talent for not only the gathering of facts, but for making almost uncannily correct deductions from the fewest threads of information until, for the half century leading up to the time of which we have the honor to write, he had, in fact, been in charge of the operation of what Kâna still called spies and Habil called observers and Pel only referred to as his "friends."

On the occasion of which we now write—that is, some time before dawn on the day Piro set out from Adrilankha—Pel, who is actually the Duke of Galstan, had arrived at the same library in which, two centuries before, the plans for the campaign were first laid. At this time Pel, if time had added more than two centuries to those which had already passed beneath his feet, showed them no more than he had when last we saw him, still being dark of hair and eye, fine of skin, and graceful of gesture. In the library already were Kâna and Habil, who were leaning over a detailed and skillfully drawn map of the desert of Suntra. Pel, upon entering, made a respectful bow.

"Good day to you, Galstan," said Kâna. "You have something to report?"

"I do," said Pel, "if you wish to hear it."

"I wish to of all things," said Kâna. "My cousin and I were engaged in debating the virtues of attempting to take the western portion of the desert of Suntra, compared to the advantages of working around it to the south. We are, as yet, undecided, and if you have any information that will make our decision easier, well, we should like nothing better than to hear it."

"On that subject," said Pel, "I do have certain things to say."

"Well?" said Habil.

"I have heard from my friends that a certain warlord, named Fwynn, has been gathering strength for the past score of years, anticipating an effort on your part to take the western portion of Suntra. His base of strength seems to be to the north of the desert, where he can call on some six thousands of trained and organized warriors, while he has a garrison of some four thousands at this point, all of whom are mounted and ready to move at a moment's notice."

"Then perhaps," said Kâna, "if we go north, rather than south, we can cut the forces off from each other."

"Rather," said Habil, "we are likely to be caught between them; we have only eleven thousands available to us, and it will take some little time to move more into position."

"Can our eleven thousands take the garrison, do you think?" asked Kâna of Pel.

"If they can arrive without being seen," said Pel, "then it could be managed. For that, however, an attack from the far north is indicated, because they are not watching from that direction. If Your Venerance wishes, a detailed report of the roads and watering spots can be ready by morning."

Habil and Kâna consulted each other by look, then both nodded. "Is there anything else?" said Habil.

"There is, Marchioness."

"Well?"

"You know where our chief danger lies in the future, do you not?"

"You have told us," said Kâna, "that Dzur Mountain must be taken into account."

"Exactly," said Pel.

"Well?"

"I have, therefore, kept a constant watch on Dzur Mountain, and even had followed all of those who have left it on errands of one sort or another."

"And that is well done, I think," remarked Habil.

Pel bowed.

"But then," said Kâna, "has something happened?"

"Exactly," said Pel. "And, if you wish, I will tell you what it is."

"Do so," said Habil. "You perceive we are both listening avidly to your every word."

"Yes," said Kâna, "what has the Enchantress been doing?"

"She has," said Pel, "been sending out messengers. And moreover—"

"Yes?"

"She has been summoning people to her."

"Troops?" said Kâna.

"Not troops," said Pel, "but individuals."

"What individuals?" said Habil.

"I don't yet know all of them, but one, at least, I know, and that is the Viscount of Adrilankha, who I have learned, thanks to the sorcerous communications methods you have given me access to, just a few hours ago set out in the company of the messenger from Sethra."

"Exactly who is this Viscount?" said Kâna.

"The son of an old acquaintance of mine," said Pel; "that is, the son of Lord Khaavren, who commanded the Phoenix Guards until the Disaster."

"Ah, I have heard of him," said Kâna. "He was not to be trifled with when he was in his prime."

"Exactly," said Pel. "Nor is his son, if the blood flows true."

"And, is there something you recommend we do?"

"No, only be aware of it. Sethra Lavode is preparing a stroke, whether against us or in some other direction I cannot yet say, but I would caution Your Venerance to remain aware of her. And for my part, I intend to redouble our vigilance on Dzur Mountain and environs."

"Very well," said Kâna. "What else?"

Pel sighed. "I fear Sethra Lavode," he said. "We cannot storm Dzur Mountain, we cannot counteract her sorcery, we cannot undermine her diplomacies, all because, in the first place, she is skilled and powerful, and, in the second place, we know so little about her. What is the source of her power? What is her nature? What is her age? We know none of these things, but have only speculations."

"Perhaps," said Kâna, "she is powerless since the fall of the Empire. Is it not true that she has not left Dzur Mountain in all that time?"

"It may be true," said Pel. "To be sure, we do not know that she left. But how can we tell? She hasn't been tested."

"How then," said Habil, "can we test her without committing ourselves?"

"There may be a way," said Pel. "There are young Dzurlords, and even Dragonlords, who may be convinced to stand against her, which would give us some indication of how much we need fear her."

"You can arrange this?" said Kâna.

Pel bowed. "But there is still another consideration."

"And that is?" said Habil.

"It may be that we need not fear her, but, rather, we can enlist her."

"How, enlist her?" said Kâna.

"Exactly. If she believes that we are the best hope for the Empire, why, then it may be that she will aid us, rather than thwarting us."

"How, then, are we to determine this?" said Habil.

"That is the question," said Pel. "That is what we must consider."

"Would it be safe," said Kâna, "for us to send an envoy?"

"How, ask her directly?" said Pel. "I had not considered that."

Habil chuckled. "I am not astonished by that, my good Yendi. Yet what do you think of it?"

"It may be the best solution," admitted Pel.

"We must carefully consider who to send," said Kâna.

"I have an idea," said Habil.

"I should be glad to hear it," said Kâna.

"I believe I can think of someone who is polite, subtle, observant, discreet, courageous, and intelligent. Someone who is able to follow orders, yet able to exceed these orders, or change them, if circumstances require it. Someone who, in short, has all of the virtues needed for this mission."

"I agree with your list of needed virtues," said Pel. "It remains only for you to give us the name that goes with the list."

Habil, instead of answering, merely smiled, and continued looking at Pel. His eyes widened slightly when he realized what was being said, but then, after an instant's consideration, he bowed.

Chapter the Twelfth

How the Author, Forced Against His Will
To Write of the Viscount's Travels,
Attempts, for the Sake of the Reader,
To Make Travel Interesting

It has long been known by those who take up the pen and write for a populace greedy for distraction, that among the most difficult tasks of the writer are those caused by circumstances in which the characters whom the reader has been following must go from one place to another. The author must somehow account for the journey, and to merely say, "They traveled; they arrived," often leaves the reader with the feeling that something important has been missed; yet to actually describe the passage of one day after another, each filled with nothing more than the routine of the traveler, is, more often than not, to invite ennui; that is, in a word, to bore the reader.

To be sure, those who write pure history are sometimes able to escape this dilemma under the guise of pretending that, as nothing of significance happened, nothing need be said. Alternatively, the historian may be so fortunate as to have history provide a good supply of incidents with which to keep the reader amused; some historians, notably the witty and erudite Cropperwell, seem to specialize in historical events that feature exactly this sort of circumstance.

As for the writer of the popular romance, each has sought after methods of treating this difficulty, with more or less success. The fabulist will invent adventures of the most absurd variety; the minutist will describe the scenery through which characters and readers are passing to the tiniest detail; the summarist will omit the journey, contenting himself with the assertion that it has occurred; while to the metaphorist the journey becomes the reason for the story itself; and then there are those, such as the delightful Madam Payor with her "Greentide Romances," who invent characters who are, for one reason or another, incapable of traveling; or the clever Tremmel of Brock, who uses as a device actions that center on a certain specific location and brings all the events to the characters who dwell there; thus escaping the problem entirely. Any of these choices, and of others we have not troubled to mention, are reasonable and proper if carried out with sufficient skill and dexterity, yet it seems to us that what is most significant to the reader ought to be that which is most significant to the characters who occupy the reader's attention, and this is doubly true in the case of the historical romance, where we are not at liberty to invent incidents, but must rather be content with those events with which history has provided us, and then fulfill our task of casting them in an entertaining as well as an informative light.

For this reason, then, it has been our approach, which has met with a certain success, to direct the attention of the reader toward events which have caused significant changes in the personality, or, at any rate, the disposition of those whose actions have attracted our interest; that is, if the struggles of the journey itself, or the conversation among the travelers, or certain incidents have had a profound and lasting effect, that is where we will ask the reader to lend us his attention, so that we, in turn, may repay him by providing him with a deeper understanding of those characters, and with whatever degree of entertainment is naturally afforded by the incidents we are called upon to reveal.

All of which brings us to a time exactly a week into the journey, to a small fire where Piro, Kytraan, and Lar sat in order to feel simultaneously warm and protected. The jungle around them was alive with night noises, the loudest being the nickering of their own horses, who were themselves rather close to the fire, as if entirely uncertain about what sorts of animals might live nearby and what these various species might think about horse as a delicacy. With these noises the crackle of the fire competed, as if to assert the continuing drama of man's invasion of wilderness; yet together these sounds—the jungle noises of nature, and the sound of the burning of nature's artifacts by man—produced a certain music, or at least a backdrop of sound, against which the soft conversation of Piro and Kytraan harmonized in its own way, while providing, should the reader choose, another, deeper metaphor concerning man and nature, but one of which the author will eschew the explicit drawing.

As we make our study, we will find Piro saying, "But, my dear Kytraan, you must have had your share of adventures."

To this, the worthy Dragon said, "Perhaps, but not as many, nor as adventurous, as you might suppose. To have one's sword blooded for the first time in order to prevent one's skin from being punctured is an adventure, or feels like an adventure at the time, even if one's attacker is an innocent beast and hardly a threat."

"Well, I understand that," said Piro, thinking suddenly of Porker

Poker and feeling unaccountably homesick, albeit just for an instant. "And then?"

"Well, the second or third time it happens, unless the threat is more severe, or the goal to be accomplished is greater, it is no longer an adventure, but merely an annoyance. Now, it is true that I have, once or twice, encountered bandits or highwaymen —"

"How, you have?"

"As I said, once or twice, and yet —"

"Well?"

"Well, never during these encounters was there an occasion to draw steel, for such as these will rarely attack a man who may choose to fight back."

"Ah, I see."

"Upon first leaving Dzur Mountain, I fancy I saw a dragon, but it was far away and asleep, and may indeed have been nothing more than a peculiar formation of rock, such as occur there to provide grist for the stories about the Enchantress."

"Then you don't believe the stories of the Enchantress changing people into stone and into animals?"

"I don't know," said Kytraan reflectively. "I could, perhaps, believe either one by itself, but I cannot imagine why she should wish to turn someone first into one and then into the other. Moreover, I cannot see why, if she had the power to do such a thing, she would fail to simply kill the intruder."

"There is some justice in what you say," admitted Piro.

"Do you think so?"

"I am sure of it."

"Well, then I am satisfied."

"But, continue. You were discussing adventure."

"Ah, yes, so I was. Well, to conclude, I expected adventure on my way to visit you, good Piro, but I am forced to say that nothing happened beyond my being woken in the night by some unknown man or animal, which promptly retreated upon the introduction of another stick to the fire that has always been the best friend of the woodsman."

"You say you had been expecting adventure, but had you been hoping for it as well?"

"Ah, as to that —"

"Well?"

"I don't say I wasn't."

"If your journey hither, alone, was uneventful," said Piro regretfully, "then, with two of us, it is unlikely we shall encounter much to cause excitement."

"That is my opinion," said Kytraan. "Yet consider whither we are bound: is it not adventure enough to visit Dzur Mountain? And consider that you go there in pursuit of some sort of mission. My friend, I fully expect, if adventure is your desire, adventure is what you will have, and that before too much time has passed."

"Well, that is true," said Piro. Then he laughed and said, "Though I have heard that those who have had the most desire the least when all is over."

"And I have heard the same. And yet —"

"Well?"

"You know of your father's friend, Tazendra?"

"I have heard of her, yes. But then, she is a Dzur."

"That is true; such feelings do not apply to Dzurlords."

Piro sighed. "I should love to meet her, and those others of whom my father speaks with such fondness, and of whom my mother tells such stories."

"Your father does not tell stories?"

"Of himself? Rarely. The memories are, I believe, too painful."

"It is a shame, though," said Kytraan. "In those days, there were heroes. And, as you know —"

"Well?"

"Girls like heroes."

"That is but natural," agreed Piro. "Indeed, that would be sufficient reason for adventure, even if there were no others."

"You have expressed my thoughts so well that I can do nothing except agree."

Piro nodded. "That, then, is the plan: we will have adventures, and then we'll meet girls."

"I am in complete agreement with your plan, my friend."

"Ah, you call me your friend."

"Well, and if I do?"

"I am gratified, and I hope you will do me the honor of allowing me the same privilege."

"Of a certainty, my dear fellow. Here is my hand."

"And here is mine."

"There, we are friends."

"Good. Now, who has the first watch?"

"Our worthy servant, Lar."

"Lar, are you on watch?"

"Entirely, my lord, and I give you my word that nothing larger than a rollbug will escape my eyes, and nothing louder than a damp leaf will escape my ears. And this will be easier, as I am now in a region I know well."

"You have been here before?" asked Piro.

"With those brigands of whom I told you, my lord."

"Then there may be brigands about?"

"Oh, yes, indeed. They like this region, because of the large number of roads that pass and intersect, many of which are still in use."

"Well, then, you will wake me in three hours?"

"As nearly three hours as I can manage, my lord. You perceive there are at present no ratbirds in the vicinity."

"How, ratbirds?" said Kytraan.

"I will explain on another occasion," said Piro. "Very well, then, to bed, and perhaps sleep can relieve these muscles of some of the stiffness they acquired from being on horseback for so long!"

"That is not likely," remarked Kytraan. "You perceive that sleeping on the ground is not conducive to easing sore muscles. Nevertheless, it will pass. Very soon, you will not even notice."

"I hope you are right," said Piro, and, almost on the word, he had drifted off to sleep.

In the days that followed, they continued along trails and paths that had been cut through the jungle, stopping at streams to fill their water-bottles, and looking at the desolation of what had once been villages along the various larger waterways, until at last, with a surprising abruptness, the jungle turned into grassland: long, seemingly endless, and with no explanation of why it should make such a drastic change with so little warning; nevertheless what had once been a road still ran through it, so their rate of travel was unchanged. As the hours and days passed, they visited one or two villages that were not quite deserted, but found little to say to the dispirited inhabitants, and so, finding nothing that appeared to be an inn, they proceeded on, keeping their horses to a gentle walk, and speaking little even among themselves.

Late one evening, after they had been on the road nearly two weeks, and Piro was scarcely noticing his muscles, as they were about to make camp, they saw the flickering of another light, a few hundred meters away; and by mutual consent they turned their horses toward this light. They stopped just inside the ring of illumination given off by what proved to be a campfire, so that whoever it was whose camp they were visiting could see their number and their faces. For an instant, there was a stillness; Piro could hear nothing save his own breathing, Kytraan's, and the jingle of the harness of Piro's horse, which horse, we should add, gave Piro a quick look as if it wondered why they had stopped, before abruptly shaking its head, stamping its right forefoot, and snorting.

This silence, or near-silence, was broken at last by Kytraan, who said, "I give you good evening, stranger. We are travelers, and wonder if you would do us the honor of sharing your fire for the evening. We have wine, bread, cheese, and certain salted meats which we have but lately tested and found good, and we are more than willing to share them."

The reply came after only an instant. "Come, then," said the stranger, a woman from the sound of her voice. "I have boiled coffee, dried fruits, salt, and biscuits, and I am, like yourselves, entirely willing to share."

They dismounted, hobbled their horses, and approached the fire, where sat a woman who, though it was difficult to see in the flickering of the fire, seemed to be about eight or nine hundred years old. It was impossible to guess her House, but she had, at any rate, a noble's point, which seemed sufficient for the moment.

"I am Kytraan e'Lanya of the North Pinewood Hold. This is my companion, Piro, the Viscount of Adrilankha."

"I give you good evening. I am called Orlaan, and I am not a traveler at all, but, rather, I live here."

"How, you live here?"

"Exactly. I am attempting the study of sorcery, and the control of certain forces, and, you perceive, such matters are best performed where there is no one around, in case of a miscalculation."

"Well, I understand," said Piro. "And permit me to wish you well in your studies."

"You are courteous," said Orlaan, "and I wish you a safe and pleasant journey. But come, your servant appears to have nearly finished laying out the food; let us then eat together, after which you will no doubt wish to rest."

"An excellent plan," said Kytraan.

This being agreed upon, they carried it out at once, and for some time there was little speech, mouths being occupied with exploring such concepts as goat cheese on bread with slices of dried apple, and how this might compare to the same cheese with salted kethna on a savory biscuit. During this time, Piro took the opportunity to study their host; yet he could learn little. Her clothing was the darr skin and leather of a traveler, and her face, seen only through the flickering light of the fire, revealed little save narrow but bright eyes, rather fair hair and skin, and a few small scars such as one might expect on someone who lived in the wilderness. As they ate, Piro began to grow uncomfortable, because it seemed to him that Orlaan kept sneaking glances at him. This naturally made him curious, but he refrained from asking any questions. Orlaan, however, did not refrain, but rather proved that Piro had not been imagining her interest, because she said, "You are the Viscount, you say, of Adrilankha?"

"I have that honor," said Piro.

"Adrilankha is a large city along the coast, is it not? It used to be a port, if I am not mistaken."

"You are correct. It is in the county of Whitecrest."

"Ah. And your father, then, is Whitecrest?"

"My mother, the Lady Daro."

"Daro," she repeated, as if she had heard the name pronounced before, and was trying to collect it. "And is your father still living?"

"He is," said Piro. "I am, you perceive, one of the fortunate ones."

"Indeed," said Orlaan. "My own father was in Dragaera at the time of the Disaster."

"I am sorry."

"The Cycle turns," said Orlaan. "Or, at any rate, it did," she amended. "And might again."

"The gods may know," agreed Piro. "But come, what of your studies? I have heard that some are trying to learn once more the art of sorcery as it was practiced before the dawn of history, when there was no Orb. Is this not dangerous?"

"Dangerous? Yes, it is dangerous. And yet, we have an advantage that the sorcerers of those bygone days did not."

"And that is? For you perceive I am curious."

"What young man is not curious? To answer your question, our advantage is this: We know it can be done."

"Ah. That is true. We know, for example, that a device can be built to control the power of amorphia."

"Exactly. And it is toward this end that we direct our efforts."

"In hopes of restoring the Empire?"

"Perhaps, someday. Or of creating a new one. Or, often, merely of learning."

"And yet, to enter the amorphia without the intercession of the Orb, well, the thought frightens me."

"And well it should, young man, for it is nothing to be entered upon lightly. And, you perceive, I have put several thousands of miles of distance between me and the sea of amorphia, as a precaution, so I am not entirely foolhardy, as some are."

"As some are?"

"Why, yes. There are those who venture to the very shores to work, and even, I am told, some who have entered the sea bodily, there to work with the stuff of chaos itself."

"How, entered the sea?"

"Yes, entered the sea itself, although—"

"Yes?"

"Well, I have heard of none who have emerged after doing so."

"I wish you well in your studies; for it seems to me that these studies may be of great benefit to us all."

"So I hope, young man," said Orlaan. For an instant, Piro thought he saw a peculiar gleam in her eye, but then he decided it had been a trick of the firelight.

There was no more speech that night, as everyone felt the need for sleep, and when they awoke the next morning, they found that their companion of the night before had left.

"For my part," opined Lar, "I am just as glad. Did you mark the peculiar look in her eye? I wish I had been able to see her more clearly."

Piro merely shrugged, and permitted Lar to assist him, and then Kytraan, onto their horses. This being done, they turned the head of these horses and, without another word, resumed their journey toward Dzur Mountain.

Chapter the Thirteenth

How Khaavren Received an
Unexpected Visitor

At very nearly the same hour that Piro and Kytraan were mounting their horses, Piro's father, that is to say, Khaavren, was standing in his study at Whitecrest Manor, where, careless of the cold, he had thrown open the window in the eastern end of the room and was looking out over, or rather past, the city of Adrilankha, as if his eyes could span the leagues and pick out the form of his son now lost in the distance and the terrain. He had been standing in this way for some few hours, and might well have been standing so even longer had not Daro, guessing his mind, come to the study and found him, whereupon she stood next to him for perhaps a quarter of an hour, not speaking, after which he stirred and said, "Do you suppose we would feel it if something were to happen to him?"

"I think we would," said Daro.

Khaavren nodded, and at that moment came a faint booming, as the great door clapper was pulled down below. "Hmmm," said Khaavren. "We hire a servant, and he is gone almost at once."

"That was the intention, was it not?"

"Yes," said Khaavren, "that is true."

"Perhaps Cook will answer it."

"Or perhaps not," said Khaavren. "And it is the front door, from which we may deduce that our visitor has pretensions to nobility, and ought not to be kept waiting. I will, therefore, personally endeavor to see who has come to visit us, and, in thus bestirring myself, I will engage in more activity than I have in longer than I care to consider." He accompanied these words with a smile, from which Daro was to understand that his self-mockery was meant in jest; she, however, knew him well, and understood the meaning behind words and countenance. Khaavren walked down the stairs, trudging, yet with a hint of his old martial step still remaining in his gait.

He was on the stairs between the first floor and the main when he met Cook, who had, in fact, answered the door, and after doing so was now on her way up. Upon seeing Khaavren, she stopped and made a bow. "My lord—" she said.

"Well?"

"There is a gentleman to see you."

"A gentleman?"

"Yes, lord."

"Well, has he a name?"

"Indeed he has, my lord. In point of fact, he has two of them."

"How, two names?"

"Exactly. In case, he said, one should be insufficient to identify him."

"Well, and what are these famous names?

"My lord, he said that he is called Galstan, and adds that, should this identification be insufficient, he is also called—"

"Pel!" cried Khaavren, nearly bowling over the poor cook in his haste to arrive at the bottom of the stairs and behold his friend once more.

"—Pel," concluded the cook as she nimbly stepped to the side of the stairway, which was, fortunately, rather wide.

"Pel!" cried Khaavren again, before he had even reached the entry-way. "Come in, come in and be welcome."

Pel, evidently hearing him, came forward, and they met in the corridor outside of the parlor, where they embraced fervently and said nothing, except for Khaavren, who murmured, "Ah, Pel, Pel."

At length, Galstan pulled back slightly and said, "Yes, my friend, it is I. But come, what state have I found you in?"

"Not good, my old comrade, not good. Come in, though, come in. My wine-cellar, thanks to the gods of the vine, is not entirely depleted, and you shall have the best there is. This way. You remember the Countess, do you not?" This last, we should add, was said of Daro, who had come down from the study and was now waiting in the parlor.

"Of course," said Pel, bowing and kissing her hand. "Madam, I am, as always, enchanted."

"The pleasure is entirely mine," said the Countess, "and I hope you do not begrudge it, for in no way am I so selfish as in my desire to have good friends around, wherefore I hope you will do us the honor of staying with us for a long time; I know that I speak for my husband the Count as well as for myself in saying that the longer you will be here, the more we will be pleased."

"Bah," said Pel with a smile. "What have you married, my dear Khaavren? A Tiassa who looks like a Lyorn and speaks like an Issola."

Pel handed his coat to the cook, who was, as the reader may have noticed, taking the rôle of butler; the cook then proceeded to open, decant, and pour the wine. "Ah Pel," remarked Khaavren, "it is good to see you! Have you had a long journey?"

"Tolerably long," said Pel. "Six days ago I was in the Kanefthali Mountains."

"Six days!" cried Khaavren. "Impossible! How could you have arrived so quickly? It is a fifteen hundred miles and more!"

"The post," said Pel.

"The post? Cha! There has been no post for two hundred and fifty years."

"And yet," said Pel, "there is again, and the proof is that I am sitting here before you, when a week and a day ago I was, in fact, more than five hundred leagues away, as we measured leagues in the city in the old days."

"But, then, who has put together a post that covers that distance?"

"Oh, you wish to know that, do you?" said Pel, smiling.

"I more than wish to know," said Khaavren. "I think I even ask."

Pel smiled and waved his hand in a dismissive gesture. "Then we will speak of it, in due time. But first, I will claim my right as a guest to question you."

"You wish to question me? My dear friend, I recognize you so well in that! Always questioning, always wanting to know, always with some plan or another. But this time, star me if I can imagine what I might know that could interest you."

"How, you cannot guess?"

"Not for the life of me."

"Then I will tell you."

"I ask for nothing better."

"This is it then: I wish to question you, my good friend, about your health, and about your doings, and about your happiness, and about all that concerns you; in short, about everything a friend might wish to know about another friend, when they have not seen each other for two hundred and fifty years."

"Ah, Pel. There is nothing to say. I exist, my friend, nothing more. I exist, and am content with my family, my estate, my books, and my memories."

"Your family, good Khaavren?"

"Why yes. The Countess you know, and I have a son, as well."

"Ah! A son!"

"Very much so. He is near his first century, and as fine a boy as I could wish for."

"And do you tell him so?" said Pel with a smile.

Khaavren sighed. "I'm afraid I do, Pel. I have become the doting father, and I cannot conceal from him how I feel, yet it seems to have done him little harm."

"Well, well. And when will I have the honor of meeting him?"

Daro said, "Oh, as to that—"

"Yes?"

"I'm afraid he is not here."

"Not here?" said Pel, looking from one of his hosts to the other. "Well, when will he return?"

"I cannot say," said Khaavren. "He is on a mission, you see."

"How, a mission?"

"Exactly. Just as, in the old days, you and I would set off on missions for His Majesty, whom the Lords of Judgment receive"—Pel bowed his head briefly and touched his breast as Khaavren spoke these words—"and as, I daresay, you still do from time to time."

"Who, I? You think I still go on missions?"

Khaavren gave a brief laugh. "Hang me if I don't think you are on a mission now, my old friend."

"Oh, but what of you, Khaavren? Surely you have not given up missions?"

"I? Entirely. I am a broken-down mill, or an old suit of clothing, and no one would offer me a mission, nor would I accept one if offered."

As he spoke, a certain shade passed over Daro's countenance, but she did not comment. Pel, for his part, did comment, and in the following terms: "Bah!"

"I tell you the truth, Pel," said Khaavren. "Two hundred years ago the Islanders attempted to invade, and I ran back and forth all along the lines of defense, it was very nearly with my own hand that the invaders were pushed back; and I think I accounted for six or seven of them myself."

"Nine," put in the Countess.

Khaavren smiled, and resumed his argument. "Well," he said, "if the Islanders were to attack again to-day—"

"Yes? If they were to attack?"

"Then I should make my contribution by turning command over

to someone who might be able to lead, for I could not. Oh, I might consult on tactics, if I were asked to, but nothing more."

"I cannot believe it."

"Cha! If you saw what an effort it was for me to so much as lift my sword, well, you would be convinced. And so, when missions come, they go to my son."

"Well, but what is this famous mission?"

"Ah, as to that, I cannot say, except—"

"Yes?"

"It was our old friend, Sethra, who sent for him."

"Ah! But you don't know what the Enchantress wanted with him?"

"Not the least in the world, on my honor."

"Hmmm," said Pel.

"But tell me," said Khaavren, "what is this about a post working once more?"

"Oh, you wish to know that?"

"Yes, yes. In one thing I am not changed: I still have some curiosity. And you perceive that to have the post working once more, when for two hundred and fifty years there was none, well, it is like the sudden rising of the waves here on the coastline, in that it implies a great deal more activity than is at once visible."

"Well, that is true."

"So, then, will you explain?"

"I should be glad to do so, and this instant, if you wish."

"I wish for nothing else in the world."

"This is it, then: Someone has, on his own initiative, put together a post."

"Well, and for what reason?"

"For what reason?"

"Yes."

"Why, to aid in communication and travel."

"Well, that much is clear, only—"

"Yes?"

Khaavren frowned and considered. "What aren't you telling me, Pel?"

Pel laughed. "Ah, it is good to see you once more, my friend. Yes, yes. His name is Kâna, his domain is large, and his ambition is boundless."

"Kâna," said Daro, as if, taken by the feeling the this name might become important, she wished to commit it to memory.

"Kâna," said Khaavren. "Yes, that name has come to my ears."

"Well?"

"Well," said Khaavren, "I have heard little enough. What more can you tell me?"

"Nothing, my friend. I have told you what I may."

"There must be more than that, if his posts extend all the way from Kâna to the Coast, and you are able to use them."

"Well, that is true, but, you perceive, I am not allowed to tell all I know, even to you."

"But there must be one thing you can tell me."

"And what is that?"

"Why you have come to visit me."

"Oh, as to that—"

"Well?"

"You are right, there is no reason not to tell you."

"Then you will do so?"

"This very instant."

"Then I await you."

"It was just this: I wanted the chance to see for myself how you were getting along."

"How I was getting along?"

"Exactly."

"Well, and how am I getting along?"

"In my judgment, admirably."

"Ah, I see."

"You see?"

"Yes. Whatever ravages neglect may have perpetrated upon my body, my mind has not yet wasted away entirely, and I begin to understand a little more."

Daro glanced at Khaavren with an expression of both fondness and amusement. Pel, for his part, permitted an ingenious expression of surprise to cross his countenance, and said, "You pretend there is something to understand?"

"I am nearly certain of it. But come, will you have no more wine?"

"A little, perhaps."

"And some for you, Countess?"

"Thank you, yes."

"Well, here you are, and you. You see, my friend Pel, I am still capable of standing up when I wish, and the wine-bottle does not tax my strength exceedingly."

"My dear Khaavren—"

"But enough of this, old friend. Shall we show you to your room?"

"Ah, I am sorry to say it, but I am on an errand, and this is only the briefest stop."

"Shards! Do you mean to say that you will arrive on my doorstep after three hundreds of years and then leave without spending even a single night beneath my roof? Impossible!"

"You are no stranger to duty, my old friend, and that is what calls me now."

"Impossible," repeated Khaavren.

"At least," said Daro, "you will stay and eat with us, will you not?"

"After which," said Pel smiling, "it will be too late to travel? Well, so be it. I will stay and eat, and will remain with you tonight, and we will drink wine and reminisce until it becomes so late that my departure tomorrow will be delayed, and I will lose nearly an entire day. Come, will that satisfy you?"

"Ah, my old friend, I will not be satisfied until the four of us are living once again under a single roof, but that can never be, I think, and so I will take my pleasures where I can find them, and be content."

"The beginning of wisdom," said Pel.

"Or dotage," murmured Khaavren.

Cook, upon being informed of a guest for dinner, was, after an initial and short-lived panic, positively delighted; guests for dinner, and thus the requirement for creative efforts, had now occurred twice within a month; this would not only be reflected in the budget for the month, and was not only entertaining in itself, but it meant that there was a chance that the Count would begin, once more, to show an interest in food for its own sake—an interest he had not shown in a hundred years. This would not make up for the departure of the Viscount, whom she missed, we should add, for himself as well as for the way the young man appreciated a good meal; but it would help a little.

She therefore spared no effort, requiring the maid to run down to the market for the freshest squabs, the choicest cuts of kethna, a supply of goose fat, cresent-onions, striped mushrooms, marrows, basil, peppers, and saltpea pods; all of this while she, the cook, rummaged in the cellar for the best wines, the purest flour, the freshest garlic, and the most active yeasts. She had been trained, the reader ought to understand, at the same Valabar's Restaurant that still exists in Adrilankha today, and from which those most concerned with victualing still hire, or attempt to hire, the cooking staff; it being said that a man who has cleaned tables at Valabar's will absorb more of the art of cooking than the head chef for any other inn or tavern in the Empire; an exaggeration which, if not entirely true today, was much closer to the truth during the Interregnum.

We should add as an aside that, should the reader believe that Cook was giving herself all of the exciting work while forcing the maid to engage in the drudgery, nothing could be further from the truth. While the maid had the pleasure of a pleasant walk into town (with, as always, a few extra pennies in hand to spend as she pleased) the cook, with full confidence in the maid's abilities to garner only the best of the supplies for which she had been dispatched, was engaged in carefully washing and seasoning all of the pots, pans, and utensils required by her exacting profession; at the same time, she cheerfully arranged her mind for the frenzy of preparation and execution that would begin upon the maid's return.

None of this, of course, was apparent to Khaavren, Daro, or Pel, who gave the order for the meal to be prepared and then continued chatting, entirely oblivious to the flurry of activity in the back rooms of Whitecrest—or almost oblivious, the exception being that Khaavren had to show Pel to his room himself, the maid being otherwise occupied.

Pel did not, in fact, require any rest, and so, after a cursory inspection of the room, carried out for the sake of custom, he returned at once to the parlor, where the conversation continued without interruption until Cook herself, dressed in her finest outfit of pale blue and white, with the Tiassa insignia apparent, announced that dinner was ready, whereupon they proceeded into the dining room and engaged in a meal where, if there was perhaps more ceremony than might have been strictly called for, the diners were inclined to forgive it because of both the rarity of the occasion and the quality of the food. When the sweet (a puff pastry filled with thin slices of cheese and covered with strawberries) had been digested along with a good quantity of fortified wine, the diners made their way back into the parlor.

Should the reader feel annoyed at the brevity with which we have described the meal, we can only say that, under these circumstances, what was most important was not the meal, but that which occurred before it and after it, and so that is where we insist the reader's attention be turned, and we are thus refusing to indulge in a misplaced desire for sensuous gratification at a time when our duty demands we concentrate on other areas: to wit, the conversation that took place, especially between Khaavren and Pel—a conversation destined to have far-reaching effects on the history of both individuals, and, thus, on the history we have taken it upon ourselves to relate.

Once the participants were seated in a relaxed posture, the conversation, to which we have just had the honor to refer, turned toward the conditions prevailing in what had once been the Empire. It came as no surprise to Khaavren, and should come as no surprise to the reader, that Pel was exceptionally well informed of the major movement throughout the territory that had until Adron's Disaster been ruled from Imperial Palace in the city of Dragaera, and for some time kept up a stream of gossip concerning lords of small areas attempting to expand, or of marauders terrorizing unprotected districts, or of the difficulty, in many cases, of telling one from the other. He spiced the anecdotes with observation of a more general character, touching on the failure of certain long-established customs and the emerging of new, sometimes inexplicable ones; as well as making shrewd observations and daring predictions.

"Do you know," he remarked during one lull in the conversation, "I believe our old friend Aerich, Lyorn that he is, must be truly scandalized by what has become of rank. A man born before the Disaster as a baron often simply decides that he is now a count, or even a duke, and so he is called unless someone nearby decides to take issue."

"Indeed?" said Khaavren. "And what of you, who were, I believe, actually a duke?"

"I? Oh, I claim no title anymore. It seems pointless, when I am not engaged in the general scrabbling for land or power."

"How, you are not?"

"No more than you are, my dear Khaavren. Less, in fact, as you have some responsibility to a certain amount of territory, whereas I am responsible for nothing and to no one."

"For nothing and to no one," Khaavren echoed. "Well, yes, I understand that. Perhaps you are right, then, and titles mean nothing. I should dearly love to learn what Aerich thought of the matter."

Pel nodded, watching Khaavren closely. "What," he said, "is it that you're not telling me?"

"I?" said Khaavren. "Not telling you? Now, that is a peculiar question for you to ask, don't you think?"

Pel sighed and looked away. "I cannot help but be worried for you, my old friend, whatever other concerns may be occupying my thoughts."

"Concerned for me?" said Khaavren. "Well, it is good of you to be concerned, but there is no need. The sculpture of Kieron the Conqueror stood for a score of centuries outside the Dragon Wing in the Palace, and the elements played such havoc with it that twice each century artisans were called in to repair it, yet I am certain it didn't care. In the same way the forces of nature work on old men like me, but that is only part of life, and there is no need to be concerned about it."

"You! Old!"

"Beyond my years, Pel, for reasons you know as well as I. Yet there is no cause to be sad on my account. I have a good home, a family, and all is as it should be, and I even have my footnote in history to console myself with when the dream-winds blow. I am as contented a man as you are likely to find, and, I tell you frankly, that when I see you scheming as of old I feel nothing but fondness, and I would no more expect you to tell me everything you are thinking than I expect you to worry about this old statue that is content to stand before the gate of its keep and provide a nesting place for the birds who flock about it with such careless abandon."

During this uncharacteristically lengthy speech, Pel's frown grew deeper, and at its end he glanced covertly at Daro, to see if her countenance expressed worry, pity, impatience, annoyance, or if she were carefully keeping all expression from showing; what he noticed was a frown of puzzlement that was, had he known it, nearly the twin to his own. It seemed clear that there was something about what Khaavren had said that, in some measure, bewildered her, yet she said nothing. Pel, after some thought, realized that he could do no more.

"Very well," he said. "You have told me not to worry, so I shall not."

"That is best, believe me," said Khaavren.

"I do," said Pel.

The conversation turned, then, to other topics, and, pleasant as it was for Khaavren, and, indeed, for Pel to be reminded of the good times of the past, such reminiscences, we know, would hold but little interest for the reader, and moreover the details of this conversation would do nothing to bring forward the story we have taken it upon ourselves to tell, wherefore we shall content ourselves with the remark that the conversation continued well into the night, and was ended only by the drooping lids of both Khaavren and Pel, Daro having retired some time earlier. Khaavren then showed the guest to his room, after which he took himself to his own and fell into a sleep which, though deep, was not without dreams, the dreams being full of images from the adventures of the past, and especially of Aerich, whom Khaavren still missed bitterly.

The next morning, Khaavren and Daro were up early to greet their departing guest, who, after breaking his fast with them, left amid embraces all around. As he rode out of the gate and down the streets of Adrilankha, Khaavren continued staring after him for some time, until, at last, Daro said, "There is something on your mind, I think."

"Yes," said Khaavren.

"Well?"

"I am thinking about what he told me."

"Did he tell you so much?"

"That he did, Countess. I know him, and I know how to interpret his words, and read his lies, and fill in what he doesn't say, so that he has told me a great deal."

"But what did he tell you?"

"That there a great power brewing in the Kanefthali Mountains, and that he has allied himself with it in some capacity, and this may bring about a conflict with none other than Sethra Lavode herself."

"He said all that?"

"He did."

"It must have been after I had retired for the evening."

Khaavren smiled briefly, then said, "The fact is, I am troubled."

"How, troubled?"

Khaavren nodded. "Great events are afoot."

Daro looked steadily at Khaavren, who, in turn, was staring off into the distance, as if he could see the future, and what he saw troubled him.

Chapter the Fourteenth

How Kâna Met with Representatives
Of the Great Houses

It should come as no surprise to the reader that, as Pel prepared to take his leave of Khaavren, there were other activities occurring in other parts of what had once been the Empire. This is because of that phenomenon of history called "simultaneity," which avers that events do not always happen in a neat orderly manner, one after the other; but rather that many things can happen at the same time. Thus, for example, during the Eleventh Issola Reign, while in Dragaera City the Baron of Karris was preparing an expedition to venture into the eastern jungles in search of exotic birds, at that same moment, in the desert of Suntra a caravan of traders was forming that, on their way to the port city of Adrilankha, would be passing through the jungle; and it was in this way that there came the fateful meeting between Ricci of Longgarden and Nessa of Kobi that resulted, some few years later, in the Battle Beneath the Hills and the subsequent rise to power of the Chreotha who became the Empress Synna the Fourth. This is just one example out of thousands of the phenomenon of simultaneity, and serves to point out one of the difficulties in writing—and, consequently, reading—history: that is, while historical events of significance are inclined to happen at the same time, it is nevertheless obvious that they can be treated by the historian only one at a time, as if they had happened sequentially. Hence, the writing of history is bound to introduce certain inaccuracies, and the reading of history is bound to produce certain misconceptions. It is the hope of the author that these inaccuracies and misconceptions can be held to a minimum by the expedient of making the reader aware of this circumstance, which we have just endeavored to do by our discussion of simultaneity, which, now that it has been made, can be set aside as we turn our attention to an example of this phenomenon of more direct moment to our particular history than the events, thousands of years in the past, when the bird-watcher met the game hunter.

We therefore turn our attention and the reader's to a place very nearly upon the opposite side of the continent from Adrilankha, that being the Kanefthali Mountains, in particular, to the mountain called Kâna and the duke of the same name, whom we hope the reader will not have forgotten in the brief time since we last encountered him. We observe, then, the Great Hall of the manor, where the Duke has gathered together, in addition to his cousin, a collection of notables brought in not only from the surrounding region, but from great distances away as well. In addition to certain advisers to the Duke, and to the servants who kept the guests supplied with wine, there were, in total, some fourteen guests; a number that has a significance that, the reader may be assured, we will reveal in due course.

Both the Duke and his cousin spent some little time among their guests, greeting each by name and welcoming them, until the moment seemed to be right, at which point Kâna took himself to a place before the hearth and said, "I am Skinter e'Terics, Lord of Whiteside, Duke of Kâna; also by right of conquest, Duke of Harwall, Tenmoors, and so on and so on. My friends, for so I hope I may call you all, if you would do me the honor to give me your attention for some few moments, well, I will endeavor to explain why I have asked you to attend me at this time and in this manner."

This speech, short though it was, produced the desired effect; that is, the guests, instead of speaking among themselves, at once gave their attention to Kâna.

"You cannot fail to have observed," he began, "that, including myself and my cousin, and excepting only the House of the Teckla—for reasons that, I am convinced, need no explanations, and the House of the Phoenix because there is none left—each House in the Cycle is represented in this room."

Most of those present had, indeed, observed this curious fact; the few exceptions, such as the ancient and stooped Iorich Lord Newell, quickly looked around and gave out more or less quiet exclamations as the realization struck home.

"Some of you," continued Kâna, giving a bow to Her Highness the Jhegaala Princess Eaner and Her Highness the Dzur Princess Sennya, "are, in fact the Heirs for your House. Others," here he indicated the Tiassa Lord Röaanac, the Chreotha Countess Deppian, and the Jhereg Lord Beck, "are or have been Imperial representatives of your House. The rest of you have, to say the least, great influence within your House."

Kâna paused, then announced, "The Cycle is irretrievably broken. There is no Empire. There is no Orb. There is no communication. There is no trade." He cleared his throat, then, and said, "Here, from these mountains, we have been attempting nothing less than restoration of the Empire."

These were greeted by looks of frank astonishment, followed by murmurings of surprise in some cases, outright disbelief in others, and comments of the form, "I knew it all along," from a few, such as the Yendi Lady Casement, who was seated next to Lord Deppian. The latter replied with a shrug, and turned his attention back to Kâna.

"No doubt," continued the Dragonlord after he deemed that sufficient time had passed, "you now understand why I have asked you here. You—that is, you who are in this room—will be the foundation of the new Empire. Some of you are aware of how much progress we have made, to the rest of you, if you will do me the honor to direct your attention to the map behind me, permit me to say that all of the area colored red is now entirely under our control, whereas the area in pink is under a control which is less than absolute, in that it still requires a military presence, but is, nevertheless, mostly secure. You perceive that very nearly a sixth of the area that was the old Empire can be considered already part of the new Empire—which Empire we have not even yet declared. In terms of our forces, we have—but the numbers are unimportant. Let us say we have enough.

"My friends, we have made great progress, and our future seems, if not assured, then at least extremely favorable. We have our armies, and more than this, caravans now regularly travel to two coasts. And we have reintroduced the posts. But then, you may ask, what is your rôle? For what reason have I caused to be assembled representatives of the Great Houses? Well, this is an astute question, and, moreover, one that deserves an answer. If you will do me the honor to continue giving me your attention, as you have so graciously done till now, well, I will explain."

Various reactions from those to whom he spoke indicated that such an explanation would be welcome, wherefore he continued, saying, "It is time to prepare for the transition. That is, hitherto we have been a conquering army; soon we will be an Empire. In order to go from one to the other certain things are needed. That is, in the first place, there must be an Imperial Palace; for this, of course, we turn to Lord Cenaaft of the House of the Vallista. Next, we require something to take the place of the Imperial Orb—that is, a means of communication, and, if possible, a way to give the Empire control of the

Sea of Amorphia. This, naturally, will be the province of the Marquis of Mistyvale of the House of the Athyra. There will be the matter of creating laws, for which we will turn to the House of the Iorich, represented here by Lord Newell. And so on. In other words, my friends, I say to you that it is time we got down to business.

"That concludes what I have to say. Should any of you have any questions, well, I would consider it an honor to attempt to answer them, which answers I will give to best of my ability."

For a moment no one spoke; rather as if, they having consumed a large meal, a veritable feast of information, some amount of time was required in order to permit the mechanisms of digestion to work sufficiently to permit the resources to become available for use. Then the Marquis of Mistyvale rose. Mistyvale was an old wizard of imposing stature, if somewhat stooped now from age. He still carried his now-useless wizard's staff, a length of hickory that, when resting upon the floor, stood taller than the Marquis. His hair had gone entirely grey, and his face was more full of wrinkles than an almshouse is full of beggars, and his voice, when he spoke, was barely over a whisper. He said, "There are matters, Lord Kâna, of which you should perhaps be aware."

"Well then, Marquis, I hope you will condescend to inform me of them."

"If you wish, Duke, I will tell you."

"I wish for nothing else in the world, and, moreover, I should not be surprised if everyone else in the room was anxious to hear anything you should do us the honor to tell us."

"In that case," whispered Mistyvale, "I will tell you at once."

"We ask for nothing better."

"It is simply this: It is impossible to create the Orb, or anything like it."

"How," said Kâna. "Impossible?"

"Yes," whispered the Marquis.

"And yet, it was done once."

"That is true."

"Well, then?"

"In the first place, we know of no deposit of trellenstone sufficient for the purpose, and nothing else will do. And, in the second, of all of the secrets that the Orb contained, it never held the secret of its own making, and as Zerika the First never told anyone, that secret is now lost to us."

"Well," said Kâna, "these are certainly problems. Yet—"

"My lord," said the Lyorn, the Count of Flowerpot Hill and Environs.

Kâna broke off, and said, "Yes, Count?"

The Count, whose name was Ritsak, was a thin, frail man of around fifteen hundred years, with an unhealthy-looking pale complexion and a strong, booming voice, which voice he used to good effect, saying, "I have a question."

"Ask it, Count. And I promise that, if it is within my power, I will answer it."

"I will ask, then."

"I await you."

"You speak of an Empire, my lord."

"Well, and if I do?"

"An Empire necessarily requires an Emperor."

"Yes, that is but natural."

"Well then, who is to be this Emperor?"

Kâna shrugged. "The last reign was that of the Phoenix."

"Well, and?"

"That of the Dragon must necessarily follow."

"Ah. It will be, then, a Dragonlord?"

"Yes. No doubt one who has proven his fitness to be Heir."

"In that case, my lord—"

"Yes? In that case?"

"My House cannot condone such a thing."

"How, your House cannot condone rebuilding the Empire?"

"Not in this way."

"But then, Count, have you a reason?"

"I nearly think I do."

"And what reason is that?"

"It is because we have no reason to believe the Cycle has turned; and if it has not, it is still the Reign of the Phoenix."

"Bah! The Cycle has been broken."

"Well, and if it has, then there is no reason for the natural successor to the Phoenix, that is, the Dragon, to claim the throne."

"In that case, Count, we will claim the Throne not according to the Cycle, but according to the arguments more usual with the House of the Dragon, those being the arguments of blood and conquest."

Ritsak, with no hesitation, replied, "An Empire formed upon that basis is an Empire where steel and terror take the place of wisdom and law, and it will be an Empire without the House of the Lyorn."

Kâna cast a quick glance at his cousin, who returned a look that said, as clearly as if she had spoken aloud, "We need this man."

We hope we have delineated Kâna's character well enough to show that he had certain virtues; yet it is undeniable that the ability to make quick decisions, to respond to sudden change in circumstances with an improvised idea, was not one of his particular skills. Faced, then, with a situation requiring such action, all he could think of to do was, to put it in terms military, mount a delaying action. He said, therefore, "I believe, my dear Count, that I can convince you to see matters in a different light."

The Lyorn looked doubtful, and said, "You think so?"

"I am certain of it. But it will take a certain amount of conversation, and so, if you will permit me, I will continue with other matters, and you and I together will find a time for our discussion."

"Very well," said Ritsak. "To this, I agree."

Kâna bowed his thanks and said, "Let us, then, return to the subject of conversation my lord Mistyvale did us the honor to speak upon, that being the creation of an Orb."

The Count bowed his agreement.

"Then," said Kâna, "let me ask this. Is it not possible, with all the knowledge of the House of the Athyra, to find a way to permit the Emperor communication with his subjects?"

Mistyvale frowned, and was silent for a long moment, then at last he said, "If that is all you wish, it may be possible."

"All we wish?" said Kâna. "The Gods! We wish for a great deal more than that! Yet, it is a beginning."

"Oh," remarked the agèd Princess Sennya. "And yet, for my part, I wonder at what goes beyond the beginning."

"How, you wonder?"

"Yes, exactly, I wonder."

"Come, Your Highness, for so I will call you, even though the Cycle has been broken. Tell us what you mean. Speak plainly."

"Well, you perceive that I am a Dzur, therefore I am unable to speak other than plainly."

"And that is good."

"I will tell you then."

"You perceive that we are all listening."

"Then this is what I wish to say: What will you do, Kâna, if some of the Houses refuse your Empire?"

"What will I do?"

"Yes, exactly."

"That is a frank question, and I will be equally frank in my answer."

"I ask for nothing less."

This was, in fact, a question that Kâna had anticipated—in fact, more than anticipating it, he had expected it—and so he and his cousin had spent some time in discussion concerning how to answer it. Should the reader be curious as to results of this discussion, be assured we will explain at once, and, in the simplest possible way: that is, we will permit the reader to hear how he answered the question the Princess Sennya did him the honor to ask, and thus the reader will be able to deduce the results of the discussion without the historian taking the time to make an explanation that, with the results of the conversation clearly laid before the reader, is easily seen to be not only useless, but unnecessary.

Kâna, then, answered the Dzurlord by saying, "Your Highness, we are building an Empire, and hope to rebuild the Cycle. Should we be opposed by any force, we must of necessity give battle, hoping that the caprices of chance and the intervention of the gods, as well as our own skill and force of arms, will be sufficient to the task. Yet, with this clearly understood, we do not propose to force anyone to join us. Indeed, it is our belief that, soon enough, it will be clear to everyone that there is no reason to oppose us, but, on the contrary, every reason to join with us as soon as possible."

Sennya frowned, as if she needed to work this out to be certain she was not being threatened. At last she decided that she was not, and gave Kâna a brusque nod.

The Dragonlord then said, "We do not, in fact, expect anyone to answer our question now; on the contrary, it is our intention to present the information, and then permit you to take as much time as you require to consider the matter, and to perhaps formulate questions, which we promise to answer to the best of our ability. Therefore, permit me to suggest that we together enjoy a repast my cooks have prepared, after which those of you who live nearby may wish to return to your homes, and the rest of you those rooms to which we showed you when you did us the honor to agree to be our guests, and we will resume our conversation in a week. Has anyone any reason to put forth why this plan should not be adopted?"

In the event, no one had the least objection, and, in fact, many considered it admirable. So agreeable was this idea, in fact, that it was put into action at once, and everyone adjourned to the dining hall, where they were seated at a large circular table that Kâna had had built for the occasion and that permitted everyone to sit according to his House's position in the Cycle. Here they were given a feast of a whole roasted kethna along with a selection of vegetables and wines calculated to please the wide variety of palates that had been gathered. It was generally conceded by everyone except Kâna that the feast was, indeed, the most successful part of the evening.

Certainly this was the opinion of Princess Sennya, Dzur Heir. She had not been unduly impressed with anything she had heard on this day, and she reflected, as she lay upon the bed in the room Kâna had allocated for her use, that had it not been for the meal, the journey would have been useless.

"I wonder," she said to herself, "if I wish to remain for the meeting next week, or simply return now to Blackbirddriver and to my daughter."

Her thoughts, having arrived at her daughter, came to rest there, and a warm smile spread across her features. "I have made many errors in my life," she admitted to herself. "I have been foolish, and self-indulgent, and irresponsible, and even, on one occasion, weak. Yet I still have Ibronka, and, through her, there is a future, for me, and for my land where the Blackbird River rushes through canyon and gorge, white-capped, proud, lovely, and dangerous. Not unlike my daughter herself, come to that. That one could break some hearts if she chose, and I mean that in ways beyond the metaphorical, for her wrist is strong and supple, her eye keen, and she knows nothing of fear, and her mind is as sharp as her blade. Black hair, black eyes, small, yet as fierce as a dzur—as fierce as I was when I was young. Perhaps the gods have forgiven me my lapse, for they have graced me with a daughter to make up for—well, for the one who is lost.

"It must have been a gift of the gods," she reflected, "for not only had I thought myself too old to have a child, but, when the Plague took my lord Ibron before he could see his daughter, it somehow spared me. I must never fail to give thanks each day to Barlen for this gift, and I must remind myself to permit no more lapses.

"Apropos," she continued, "what of this Kâna? Can he, truly, bring back the Empire? It would be a grand thing indeed for my daughter to be raised with all the benefits of civilization that I enjoyed. And yet—do I trust him? Is he anything more than another power-hungry Dragon warlord? I wish I knew."

She stared up the ceiling for some few moments, as if there were writing upon it that would tell her what to do. She considered that her duchy was located directly in the path of Kâna's expansion, and observed, "If I do not support him, I must prepare to oppose him. And, come to that, if I oppose him, I must see to it that my daughter is safe, because she is old enough to wish to give battle, but not yet old enough to fulfill her wish. I should send her away. But then, to where could I send her?"

She sighed, and continued her reflections until, at last, she slept.

Chapter the Fifteenth

How Röaanac Returned Home
And Had to Make Difficult Decisions

As the Princess reflects and sleeps, we hope the reader will permit us to follow Lord Röaanac of the House of the Tiassa, who had said nothing during the gathering, but rather contented himself with thinking his own thoughts, which pursuit he found so satisfying that he continued it during the sixteen-hour journey to his home in the lush Valley of Three Seasons at the feet of Mount Lostway in the Kanefthali Mountains. When he reached the manor, also called Three Seasons, his servant, a Teckla of perhaps a thousand years whose name was Haro, had seen him soon enough not only to alert his family, but also to be waiting outside to hold his stirrup and tend to his horse, all of which earned him a smile and a nod.

"Welcome home, my lord," said Haro.

"It is good to be back, Haro," said Röaanac.

He took himself into the manor itself and embraced his wife, after which he offered her his arm.

"It is good to see you home again, my lord," she said.

"It is good to be home, my lady."

These statements, though required by the formality husband and wife are always owed to each other, were said with sufficient emotion that their truth could not be doubted on either side. They made their way into the manor, which was small, as manors go, having in all fewer than twenty rooms, yet spacious and comfortable, as is typical for the home of a Tiassa. In the hallway, Röaanac was greeted by his only child, a girl of some ninety or ninety-five years called Röaana.

"Ah Röaana, come and embrace your father."

"Gladly," said the girl, and did so.

After embracing him, the girl said, "My lord father, I hope all is well, and that your journey proved satisfactory."

"It went as I thought it would," said Röaanac with a shrug. "That is, a Dragon warlord behaving like a thousand other Dragon warlords, only this one has been rather more successful, and thinking to call his domain an Empire, as he has already been doing for some time, now wishes to enlist the other Houses, so that he may become recognized as more than a Dragon warlord."

"And," said his wife, who was called Malypon, "will anything come of it?"

"Nothing good, at any rate," said Röaanac. "The fool even believes he will convince the House of the Lyorn to join in his madness. Still—"

"Yes?" said Malypon. "Still?"

"It occurs to me that some trouble could result."

"Trouble? How? Do you mean for us?"

"Not for us, my dear, because I long ago agreed to his terms and conditions, and became his vassal."

"Oh, I am well enough aware of this fact. But then, if not for us, what do you mean?"

"In fact, my lady, I am not certain; it is just a notion that has made its way into my head that this Dragonling could be dangerous."

"My lord husband, I have known you too long to ignore those notions that work their way into your head. What ought we to do?"

Röaanac frowned. "I am, as yet, uncertain. Let us consider the matter."

"Very well, let us do so."

"But not, perhaps, at this instant."

"Of course, my lord. You've just returned from a journey, and, I am certain, stand in need of, first, sustenance, and after that, rest."

"My lady, you understand me exactly, so that no husband has ever been better pleased."

"Well, that is only just, because no wife has ever had a better husband. But now, let us see what we can find in the kitchens."

"Sir and Madam," said Röaana, "if you will give me leave, I will retire for the evening. I have eaten, and it was only for the pleasure of embracing you, my father, that I have remained awake until now."

"Of course, child," said her father. "Come, embrace me once more, and your mother, and then you may retire."

Röaana made her way up the stairs to her room, where, after starting a fire in her hearth and changing into her night clothes, she took a moment as she often did to step out onto her porch, where, during the day, she had a view of the Coldwater Lake and much of the valley, and, at night, she could see twinkling lights from the vil-

lage of the same name as the lake. The breeze was chilly on this evening, so she did not remain out-of-doors long, but the time was, nevertheless, sufficient for us to quickly sketch her.

As Tiassa go, she was perhaps slightly short, yet so well propor-
tioned that the sternest critic could have found no fault. As to her
face, here, too, she had been gifted by nature with all that a connoisseur of beauty could request. Her eyes were narrow and, if we are
permitted, feline beneath brows that, being the same color as her
hair, was of such a light brown it was nearly blond; and these eyes,
which were her most striking feature, seemed to glitter and sparkle
with mischief or delight in the most endearing way. She had the ears
of her house—that is, more pointed than those of an Athyra, but less
so than those of Dzur. Her nose was straight, her lips full, her chin
strong, and she had, moreover, a way of flipping her long hair impa-
tiently behind her back that made her doting father shake his head
in pity for those who would likely fall under her spell, should she
decide to play the coquette.

As we look upon her, then, we find that she has not yet come
back into the room, and so we will take it upon ourselves to listen as
she holds conversation with herself, as many Tiassa are wont to do.

"It is clear," she began, "that Pepé is upset, and is hiding something from me. I suppose I should be angry at him for treating me
as if I were a child, but I know that to him I will still be a child
when I have seen my two thousandth year, and so there is no sense
in becoming angry. I only wish there were something I could do to
help him. Of course, Mamé will do all that is required, as she
always does.

"I wonder," she continued, staring out at the valley, "what I will
do when I no longer have them near at hand for counsel? For it is
certain that someday I will go forth into the world on my own. Even
now I feel that urge, to go, to explore, to find—or, rather, to *create*—
my own place.

"Perhaps it will be soon. It is true, there is much I have to learn;
yet I know that, somehow, I will leave my mark upon this world. Ah,
if only I had been born in the days of the Empire; then I should be
able to travel the world, to find my place. Well, but it is useless to
complain about what cannot be helped."

She stared out at the night, shivering, and suddenly became
aware that she was cold, after which she went back indoors and to
her warm bed.

After their daughter had retired, Röaanac and Malypon sat in the kitchen and ate soft rolls with good butter and the crumbly, pungent cheese of the region, along with dried figs, followed by hardtack, which Röaanac always ate because he pretended it would keep his teeth strong. All of this was washed down by fermented apple cider, made from apples out of their own orchard, strengthened by the extreme cold temperatures that could be found in the winter by a short trek up the mountain—the same mountain that the two of them could, at least during the daylight hours, see vanishing into the orange-red Enclouding through the open window of the kitchen. Even now, at night, they knew that the view was out there, and so, in their mind's eye, they could see it as if it were daylight.

"My lord," said Malypon.

"Well, my lady?"

"I have an opinion."

"I recognize you so well in that!"

"It is true, I often have opinions."

"And, my dear one, they are more often right than they are wrong."

"It may be that this one is also right."

"That would not startle me. Perhaps, if you will tell me this opinion, I will agree with it."

"We will soon see, for I am about to tell you my opinion."

"This very instant? Well, then I am listening."

"Here it is: In my opinion, my lord, you are more worried than you were willing to let on in front of Röaana."

"Ah! Is that what you believe?"

"It is, my beloved."

"Well, you are not far from the truth, dear heart."

"Ah!"

"You perceive, I believe there are some who would oppose this Kâna, and, moreover, would oppose him with fire and sword."

"And you worry because you have agreed to be his vassal?"

Röaanac shook his head. "Not so much for that reason. Our agreement is very limited, and includes a certain token tribute and the pledge not to revolt against him, but it does not require me to fight on his behalf."

"Well then?"

Röaanac sighed. "Even though I am not required to fight with him nor to defend him, well, we are, you perceive, located in the very heart of his domain."

"But my lord husband, it would seem to me that, in that case,

should conflict arise, we are located as far as can be from what Dragons refer to as 'the front.'"

"What you say is true, my dear wife, and yet —"

"Well? And yet?"

"That is only true if the conflict should take the form of tradi-
tional military action."

"Yes, I see that. And you think it will not?"

"I worry that someone might strike for the heart. It is, after all,
what I would do."

"I concede the possibility, my lord. But what then?"

"What then? Well, I worry about our daughter."

"Yes, that is true. I should mislike seeing her in the middle of
such an affair; I fear being unable to protect her."

"That is it exactly."

Malypon nodded and said, "I understand. And yet —"

"Well?"

"What can we do?"

"Oh, as to that, well, I confess that I have no idea. But come, I
believe I have done my share by announcing the problem; it is now
your turn to find the solution."

Malypon smiled and said, "How, you pretend I can solve this
problem?"

"It would not astonish me if you could."

"I can think of nothing else than to send her away."

Röaanac sighed. "Yes, in truth, it is all I can think of. And yet,
where we can send her? You perceive, our family are all gathered in
this district, and thus she would be no safer with, for example, my sister, the Baroness of Shalebrook, than she would be here."

Malypon considered for a moment, then said, "You know, do you
not, that my brother, Shalicar, is married to a woman named
Norissa."

"Well, and if he is? For, you perceive, Shalicar and Norissa live
not forty miles from our doorstep; it is for this reason that we are so
often victims of your brother's experiments in combining fruits to
produce wine."

"Yes, that is true, only —"

"Well?"

"Norissa has a sister."

"Ah! I had not known this circumstance."

"I am aware of it, because she often speaks of her; and, indeed,
my brother and his wife, from time to time, speak of visiting this sis-

ter, although they never do so because of the dangers of the roads in this day."

"Well then, who is this famous sister?"

"In truth, my lord, I do not remember her name, yet she is Countess of Whitecrest, which is the county that contains the seacoast city of Adrilankha."

"And you think this Countess might be willing to take our daughter until the danger is past?"

"I will prevail upon my brother to ask, and my brother cannot refuse me—no more, then, can his wife refuse him, nor her sister refuse Norissa."

Röaanac nodded. "It will be hard for our daughter."

"And harder for us, my lord. She is so young!"

"Yes, she is. And yet, I tell you that I think it is the best thing to do."

"Well, I do not dispute that. Except—"

"Yes?"

"The roads are hardly safe."

Röaanac chuckled. "You forget that I am vassal to Kâna. Shards! It must be good for something! I will claim my right as vassal to arrange an escort for her."

Malypon nodded. "Yes, that would ease my mind."

"And so?"

"And so I will write to my brother, and that to-morrow, and, well, we will see."

"Yes, we will do that. And shall we speak to Röaana concerning this matter?"

"I believe, my lord, that we should waste no time in doing so. It is true that she is young, yet she is no child, and should know what we intend, and why."

"With this plan I agree," said Röaanac.

"Very well, then, to-morrow we will speak with her, and, moreover, we will write to your brother."

"We are in complete agreement."

"Yes. And we will be more than in agreement if—"

"Yes, if?"

"If we agree that it is time we retired for the evening."

"Ah, I am so much agreement with this plan, that I will go ahead of you and kindle the fire that has already been laid in the hearth of our sleeping chamber."

"That will be best, believe me, because I am so weary that my eyelids are prepared to close upon their own without so much as consulting with me."

"Then, my lady let us be certain that these famous eyelids are facing upward before they close."

And so, this agreed upon, the two Tiassa retired for the night, and, after a long and sound sleep, arose the next morning prepared to put their plan into operation.

Chapter the Sixteenth

How Piro Met the Bandits
He Had Almost Been Expecting

It was red dawn and there was a cold wind from the south when Piro, Kytraan, and Lar began the next stage of their journey toward Dzur Mountain. For some time, they traveled in silence; Lar because he was attempting to accustom himself to being laconic, the others because they were deep in their own thoughts, especially of their destination. This particularly occupied the attention of Piro, for reasons that will require no explanation if the reader will but for a moment put himself into our young Tiassa's position: To be journeying toward Dzur Mountain, toward the Enchantress of whom so much was said and so little known, accompanied as it were by all of the vague fears and oft-told stories concerning her power, temperament, and capabilities, would have been enough to have kept busy the imagination of a thousand Piros.

The path required but little thought: the direction was well known and Lar had, at one time, dwelt in the area and knew many of the landmarks. "And," said Kytraan, who had made the journey not long before, "soon enough we will see Dzur Mountain in the distance, and then it will be all too easy to continue." Lar could not repress a shudder as Kytraan said this; a shudder the Dragon and the Tiassa pretended not to see.

In a day or two the the terrain assumed a character of grasslands occasionally dotted with woods, yet there were still roads, or at least paths, that took them, according to Lar, close enough to the direction they wished to go. As night fell they would find one of the wooded areas, and sleep there in a clearing around a fire they would keep burning all night. After several days, the woods became denser and more frequent, until soon they were traveling through what could only be described as deep forest.

Around this time the Tiassa began to notice that Lar was displaying certain peculiar signs, until, at last, Piro felt called upon to remark on it. "Come, good Lar," he said, "it seems to me that you have been behaving oddly, this last day or two."

"How, Lord, oddly?" said the Teckla.

"So it seems. Have you noticed it, Kytraan?"

"Do you know," said Kytraan, considering, "it nearly seems that I do, although I had not remarked on it until just now."

"Well then," said Piro, "the case seems to be proven."

"And yet, my lord," said Lar, "I confess I am entirely unable to understand in what manner I have been behaving that is unusual."

"Well then, I will explain."

"I am listening."

"This is it, then. In the first place —"

"Well, in the first place?"

"It seems to me that for the last day or two you have been disturbed and agitated."

"How, I?"

"Indeed, yes."

"I admit it may be possible."

"And, in the second place —"

"There is more?"

"Yes. In the second place, you have been frequently looking over your shoulder."

"Have I been doing this?"

"Yes. So much so that I have noticed."

"Well. It may be true."

"Come then, have a you a reason for this behavior?"

"Nearly."

"Well?"

"In the first place, Your Lordship may have noticed that I have a nervous disposition."

"I will not deny that. And then?"

"In addition, I have a certain keenness of hearing and sharpness of sight that comes from having lived for so long in the wild."

"Very well."

"And not only that, but I have been cursed with a certain vividness of imagination, which inconveniences me from time to time."

"Lar, you must admit that, as an explanation, these reasons you give are not entirely satisfactory."

"Then I will explain further."

"I will be glad if you will do so."

"Here it is, then: The idea has been growing on me for the last few days that—"

"Yes?"

"Well, that we are being watched."

"How, watched?"

"And even followed."

"Impossible!" said Kytraan.

"How impossible?" said Piro.

"Well, then, unfortunate," amended the Dragon.

"I will permit unfortunate," said Piro. "But, Lar, are you certain?"

"Not the least in the world, my lord. Had I been certain, I would certainly have said something."

"Ah, I see. Well, can you imagine who might be watching or following us?"

"I am sorry to say that I can. I have, as I have had the honor to mention, a very active imagination."

"Well, and who do you imagine it might be?"

"Well, we are now traveling in the very district where I once lived as a bandit."

"How," said Kytraan. "You, a bandit?"

"Or, rather, a cook for bandits."

"So it might be your very band?"

"Another like it, my lord. It is unlikely to be mine, as they all met with an incident."

"Do you mean an accident?"

"I beg Your Lordship's pardon, but there was nothing accidental about it."

Kytraan looked at Lar with open astonishment. Piro, for his part, said, "Well, what then is to be done? It seems we must at least remain alert. And yet, if we are being followed by brigands, why have they not attacked us?"

Lar said, "That, my lord, is exactly what I have been wondering."

"Perhaps," said Kytraan, "they have some deep plan."

"Or perhaps," said Piro, "it is not bandits, but someone else."

"Or perhaps I have merely imagined that we are being followed. You perceive, my lords, that I haven't seen or heard anything, precisely, it is more that I have had a sense of it, and think I hear things, and almost see things. And yet—"

"Well?" said Piro. "And yet?"

"I am very nearly convinced."

Piro and Kytraan looked at each other, each asking without words if the other gave credence to the Teckla's impressions. Piro finally shrugged and said, "We should be fools if we did not exercise caution, yet, until we know for certain if we are being followed, and if so by whom, it is difficult to know what precise action is called for."

"In that case," said Kytraan, "we ought to attempt to discover the answers."

"That is well taken," said Piro. "How ought we to go about it?"

"In the simplest possible way."

"And that is?"

"We will go forward a little more, and then step off the trail, hide, and see who comes along."

"I agree with this plan," said Piro.

"Then let us act on it at once. I see a grove of cedars ahead which, by the formation of their growth, should suit our purpose admirably."

The decision was no sooner made than acted upon; the trio rode in among the trees and waited, watching the path, speaking, when they spoke, only in whispers.

And, indeed, they did not have to wait long before there appeared exactly what they had feared: a band of seven men and four women, well mounted, well armed, poorly dressed, with no clear indication as to House. Piro, for his part, felt his breath catch in his throat and his hand involuntarily strayed to the hilt of his sword. He looked over at Kytraan, who was at that moment looking at him, and it seemed to Piro that the same thought was going through both of their minds at once, this thought being something in the nature of, *We forgot to decide what to do if we discovered our pursuers.* They could hardly ignore the fact that they were outnumbered eleven to two, and yet how could they let the brigands pass without a challenge? Piro knew well the stories of those contests in which his own father along with Kytraan's father and their friends had happily accepted battle against greater odds than this; could he, therefore, do any less? He hesitated, uncertain, while the eleven riders passed before them, unconcerned, not even looking to the side.

While Piro was considering the matter, Kytraan had been making his own calculations, the results of which were communicated to Piro by the sound of a sword coming free of its scabbard. We must say to the young Tiassa's credit that, upon hearing this sound, he did not hesitate, but at once drew his own weapon, so it was almost as one that the two horsemen urged their mounts out of concealment, coming out behind the brigands.

The bandits, of course, reacted predictably: they wheeled their horses quickly, drew swords, and held themselves ready, relaxing a little when they saw only two enemies. One who was in the rear (which, the reader ought to understand, meant he had been leading before they turned around), called out, "Look around, there may be more of them." As he spoke, he rode forward, so that soon it was he who was confronting Piro and Kytraan; a few others, following his orders, studied the surrounding woods. At this point Lar emerged, weaponless, and placed himself behind the Dragon and the Tiassa.

Piro, meanwhile, studied the bandit who stood before him. On horseback, at least, he gave the impression of being rather small, with a narrow face, a noble's point, and features that suggested the House of the Chreotha, though he wore only brown and grey traveling garb. He held his sword with that relaxed tension that speaks of one who knows its length.

"Well now," he said. "What is this?"

Piro was saved from the necessity of finding something to say by Kytraan, who managed to have some words ready to hand. They took this form: "We thought perhaps you were looking for us, and so we came to you."

The brigand frowned, however, and said, "Looking for you? I don't think so."

"You don't think so?" said Kytraan. "That is to say, you were not looking for us?"

"Not to my memory. But I may be deceived on this point. Who are you?"

"My name is Kytraan, of the North Pinewood Hold, and my companion is the Viscount of Adrilankha."

"Well, I must say I have never before heard those names pronounced, so that I cannot claim to be looking for you. Unless —" and here comprehension appeared to grow in his eyes. "Unless this is your way of saying you wish to join my band, in which case I'm forced to disappoint you by —"

"Join your band?" cried Kytraan. "I hardly think so."

"That is well, then."

"But sir," said Piro, who at last managed to find his voice, "is it not the case that you have been following us?"

"Following you? Well, if so, it is only because it so happened that you have been preceding us."

Kytraan looked at the brigand, then glanced at Piro, and back. He cleared his throat. "Well, I must confess this conversation is hardly going in the direction I had expected."

"Things rarely go the way we plan," said the other, shrugging. "But what would you have? It is clear you intended to fight all of us. If that is still your wish, we can oblige you, although it seems point-less. My name, incidentally, is Wadre."

Kytraan shook his head, "No, we are not Dzurlords, to fight to no purpose except the fighting."

Wadre smiled. "Nor are we."

"I must say," said Kytraan, with a small bow executed from horseback, "that you seem remarkably amiable for a brigand."

Wadre shrugged, appearing to take no offense at the label. "If I am amiable to those I intend to rob, why should I not be amiable to someone toward whom I have no such intention?"

Kytraan could find no answer to this question; Piro, for his part, could not help but burst out, "But why do you rob people?"

Wadre shrugged. "Robbing animals would seem unproductive."

"There is some justice in your observation," said Kytraan.

"No," said Piro. "I mean—"

"I know what you mean," said Wadre. "But, come, what would you have us do instead?"

This question required some thought, and Piro began forthwith to think. Kytraan, meanwhile, said, "But then, if you are robbers, why do you *not* rob us?"

"Have you anything worth stealing?" said Wadre.

"Well, in fact, no," said Kytraan, after reflecting.

"Well."

Piro nodded to indicate that he was satisfied with the answer.

"In that case," said Wadre, "it only remains for us to wish you a pleasant journey."

"And to yourselves, well, I hope your ventures are prosperous."

"You are very kind," said Wadre, and bowing, he led his band away.

As they were leaving, Kytraan said, "Come, my dear Piro, do you think you may have gone too far?"

"In what way?"

"Well, you wished them prosperous ventures."

"And if I did?"

"Well, consider that they are road agents. For them to have prosperous ventures—"

"Well, your argument is valid. And yet—"

"Well?"

"Consider: Whom would you rather see prosper? Noble highwaymen, or fat merchants?"

"You think they are noble?"

"Perhaps not. I must consider this. They *seemed* noble."

"Yes, you consider that, while I consider the entire issue of fat merchants."

"Excellent. We will both be considering, and that will help the hours and days of the journey pass more pleasantly."

"With this plan, I am in complete agreement."

In this way, then, they continued. Yet before we either continue this journey, or turn our attention to those other persons with whom the reader is familiar, we believe it may be instructive to look, for the briefest of moments, to Wadre and his band of road agents, who are now riding off in another direction, looking for plunder should it appear, or a pleasant day's ride should it not. As Wadre had expressed it once, "We prey on the helpless, but not too hard, and not too often."

As they rode, Wadre's lieutenant rode up to join her chief. She was a woman named Mora, with narrow eyes, short hair with curls concealing a noble's point, and a small mouth with thin lips. The two of them rode knee to knee for some few moments, until at last Wadre said, "Well?"

"Well, they were a strange band."

"Yes, Mora?" said Wadre, who knew his lieutenant never spoke merely to make conversation.

"I think they are marked."

"You saw this?"

"Yes, or felt it."

"I am not startled by this news. Yet are they marked by destiny, or by fate? That is, do they ride to glory or to doom?"

"As to that, I cannot say, only—"

"Yes?"

"We have crossed their path."

"And so?"

"In some way, we are now bound up with them."

Wadre nodded. "I feared it may be so. You are certain?"

She shrugged. "One can never be certain, but I think it likely."

"Well, in that case, Mora, let us wish them the best of fortune."

"Yes," said Mora. "Let us do so."

Wadre gave a glance over his shoulder, but the strangers had long since vanished from sight.

We return to Piro and his friends the next day when, in the light of the morning, they were able to see Dzur Mountain standing up against the northern sky. As Piro looked up at it, Kytraan said, "We must bear to the left here, and travel until I am able to recognize, by certain signs, where to turn again in order to strike the path that will lead us up the mountain."

Piro nodded and said, "Well, let us then turn. It still seems to be a long way off; will we arrive today?"

"Before the afternoon has turned to evening, if we make good time."

"Then let us endeavor to make good time."

"Very well," said Kytraan. "I agree to this plan."

Lar made no remark, nor did he give any indication about whether the making of good time was to his liking, or if he should have preferred to delay as much as possible. For the sake of completeness, we should add that the morning, as well as being hazy, was chilly, so that our friends saw their breath before them, as a reminder of how cold they were. They sat close to the small fire upon which Lar had made the "camp-coffee" they gratefully consumed as they studied the mountain before them.

Piro said, "Is it true what they say about her?"

This was not the first time he had asked this question, in one form or another; nor was it the first time Kytraan had replied with a shrug of his shoulders. Lar packed up the gear in the various saddle-bags, prepared the horses with saddle and bridle, and said, "My lords, we can leave whenever you are ready."

Kytraan and Piro arose at once, indicating that they were, in fact ready that very instant.

"Soon I will be able to judge for myself," said Piro, and climbed into the saddle. Piro's horse, a reddish-brown mare called Brush, gave him a quick look, as if to say that she would be delighted, if only because it would be the end of her work for a while.

Kytraan set off, and Piro rode beside him, Lar bringing up the rear. They at once turned in such a way that the wind was blowing into their faces, so by common consent they pulled their cloaks up to cover themselves.

"The Horse," murmured Piro. "We nearly appear to be brigands ourselves!"

"What did you say?" asked Kytraan, who was unable to distinguish Piro's words through the muffling of the cloak.

Piro shook his head and huddled more fully into his cloak, shivering. Kytraan, notwithstanding the need to stop several times to look for landmarks, led them well, finding paths that brought them ever higher up into the rocky heights of Dzur Mountain. By noon, they were well into the mountain, so that it had long ago lost its form; indeed, by the peculiar trick of mountainous terrain, while they knew they were climbing, they could no longer see their ultimate destination, but rather the next rise ahead of them always appeared to be the last, although Kytraan assured them they had yet some distance to travel. They stopped and ate without starting a fire, in part because they all wished to arrive quickly, in part because, although they had climbed well into the mountain, the day had nevertheless become warmer, and in part because there was nothing at hand to burn. Having finished their meal of bread, cheese, and dried fruit, they mounted once more and continued.

"We are rather high up now, aren't we?" asked Piro some time later.

"I don't know our elevation, but yes, I believe so."

Piro happened to glance back at about this time, and noticed that Lar had a peculiar expression on his face, as he looked up. Piro slowed down until he was knee to knee with the Teckla, then said, "Come, my good Lar, something seems to be troubling you."

"I do not deny it, my lord," said the servant.

"Well, tell me what it is."

"You wish me to do so?"

"Yes, and this very instant."

"I will tell you, then."

"I am listening."

"We are climbing."

"Yes, that is true."

"Moreover, we are gaining height."

"Yes, that is natural when we climb."

"So I had thought!" exclaimed Lar.

"And then?"

"Well, it seems to me if we go much higher, we shall reach the Enclouding."

"Well, it is possible we shall reach it."

"But then, I have understood that to reach above the Enclouding is to, well . . ."

"Yes? Is to what?"

"To have one's soul ripped from one's body."

"Oh, indeed, have you heard that?"

"All my life, my lord. Indeed, I have been told the Enclouding is nothing more than the disembodied souls of those who have entered it."

"How is that possible, Lar? Consider that a thing cannot be what it absorbs, otherwise, well, there would be nothing to do the absorbing before the first thing was absorbed."

Lar tried to work this out. At length he said, "But consider that every living thing absorbs substances into itself and makes them part of it, only we call it 'eating.' Indeed, I believe that is what it means to be alive."

"I have said that you are a philosopher, Lar. Now I insist upon it."

"I would never venture so far above my position to dispute with you, my lord. Yet —"

"Well?"

"You perceive, this has not allayed my fear."

"Very well, then. Consider that the Enchantress lives above the overcast."

"But it is well known that the Enchantress has no soul."

"Ah! I had not known this circumstance."

"Well, but then?"

"You should also consider our friend Kytraan, who has been to Dzur Mountain, and returned."

"So he claims," said Lar doubtfully.

Piro considered, then he said, "Very well, my good Lar, here is what I will do. I shall be riding ahead of you."

"Yes, my lord?"

"Well, as we are on the same trail, and as the trail is climbing, it follows that I will reach the Enclouding before you do."

"Your reasoning seems good to me."

"Well, I will enter it, and I will let you know if my soul is ripped from my body, and if it is, well, you will have leave to ride back down."

"That is very kind of you, my lord."

"Cha! It is nothing."

This difficulty being settled, Piro spurred his horse back up to where Kytraan continued to lead. Piro noticed that, in fact, the Enclouding did seem very low. He wondered for a moment if the Teckla's superstition could be correct, but then, he decided, he was hardly going to turn back now, and he would know soon enough.

And, in fact, it was perhaps an hour later that Piro noticed an odd smell: a mixture, as it were, of certain harsh odors, with a kind of tangy sweetness, none of which he could identify. At the same moment, he realized that the ground had acquired a bit of a reddish tinge, and, moreover he could no longer see more than ten feet in any direction; it occurred to him that he was, in fact, passing through the Enclouding. He turned back to the Teckla and said, "Well, I seem well enough so far."

Lar shrugged, as if to say he was resigned to his fate. We should add, lest the reader feel later that he was held needlessly in suspense, that there were no ill effects from passing through the Enclouding; in fact, even Lar instantly forgot the danger as he suddenly got his first clear sight of Sethra Lavode's home, or her "lair" as some have styled it, at the top of Dzur Mountain. As if by common consent, they all drew rein to look at it. Although not apparent from a distance, even on those occasions when the Enclouding was of sufficient altitude for Sethra's residence to be visible, this portion of Dzur Mountain was formed of smooth, dark blocks of stone, rising up at a sharp angle and, from below, appearing majestic and awe-inspiring. From the angle at which our friends studied it, it seemed to form a pyramid, its walls sheer and with no evident means of entry; not even a window was apparent.

After some few moments, Lar remarked, "My neck hurts."

"That is natural," said Kytraan. "For, you perceive, you have been staring at a tall object for some time, and thus your neck has been asked to hold a position it was never intended to."

"That is true!" exclaimed Lar. "All is explained, then!"

"I am glad of it," said Kytraan.

Piro said, "You have truly been there, Kytraan?"

"I have truly been there."

Piro continued staring upward for a moment longer, then said, "Let us go on."

Kytraan shrugged.

They turned their horses up the slope, where the path seemed to be carved out of the middle of a corpulence of grey slate that towered well over their heads. It was as they were passing through this that a voice called to them, saying, "Permit me to suggest, my friends, that you come no further, unless you wish your heads to be sent down the hill without your bodies, which I give you my word will make further journeys on your part inconvenient."

Chapter the Seventeenth

How Piro and His Friends, Upon at Last Reaching Dzur Mountain, Met Someone Whom We Hope the Reader Will Consider an Old Friend

The three of them stopped upon hearing this remarkable speech, and looked toward the voice, which came from well above them. Even looking up, however, they could not see who had spoken, because the Enclouding was so low on that day that they had by now quite passed through it. The reader may, indeed, wonder why it is that being above the level of the Enclouding made it difficult to see who had spoken to them; rest assured we will explain at once. Once past the Enclouding, there was, in fact, nothing between them and the Furnace, which was visible, as it is in the East and upon the top of certain mountains. As is well known to those who travel to such regions, the Furnace is not only hot, but, just as a fire that gives off heat also emits light, so the Furnace, which emits enough heat to warm the entire world, also gives off so much light that one cannot stare into it without feeling more or less pain; indeed, there are cases of travelers being blinded by nothing more than looking into the heart of the Furnace in all its incandescent glory. In this case, it chanced that the speaker stood more or less between our friends and the Furnace, and so it was quite impossible for any of them to get a good look at her.

Recognizing at once that the speaker was a woman, however, Kytraan, while attempting to shield his eyes from the glare and still look at it—a futile effort, we might add—said, "Is that you, Sethra? It is I, Kytraan, and I have returned from the errand upon which you did me the honor to send me."

"Well," said the other, "I do not doubt that you are Kytraan, but if you are correct about that name, you are still wrong about the other, for I am not Sethra."

"So much the worse," said Kytraan.

"Well," said the other.

"If you wish to fight," said Piro, "we will happily oblige you, because it is our duty to continue to the home of the Enchantress, and duty is a stern master."

"How," said their interrogator. "Your duty?"

"Nearly," said Kytraan. "The Enchantress sent me to bring this gentleman to her, and he has agreed. It is, therefore, both of our duties."

"You perceive," said the other, "that if she wishes to see you, that is entirely another matter. I am only here to keep away visitors she does *not* wish to see—which class of visitor, you perceive, have been appearing in no small numbers of late."

"In truth?" said Piro.

"It is as I have had the honor to tell you."

"Well," said Kytraan, "but then, you perceive, we have no quarrel."

"No," said the other, in tones of deep regret. "It appears we have none."

"Cha!" said Piro. "It nearly sounds as if you are sorry that we cannot slaughter each other."

"Well," said the stranger. "I do not deny it. But, alas, it seems I must be denied the pleasure."

"You perceive," said Piro, "that being slaughtered would not be nearly so great a pleasure for us."

"Oh, I understand that. But I was so looking forward to fighting you both at once, as I have had not such an opportunity for some years."

"Cha!" said Piro. "She is not lacking in confidence."

"A moment, please," said the stranger.

"Well?"

"If I am not mistaken, that is the second time you have used the expression 'Cha.' "

"Well, and is it not a good expression?"

"Oh, I have nothing against it, I assure you. Only—"

"Yes?"

"Star me if I don't think I've heard it before."

Piro shrugged. "I am certain there are others who have used it. As for me, I learned it of my father, who would say it at times when an oath seemed called for."

"Well, there is nothing wrong with that."

"I am glad you think so."

"Only—"

"Well?"

"Bide a moment, while I contrive a way to come down from this rock without breaking my neck."

"So much the better," said Piro, "as looking up at you is causing my neck to become quite stiff, and my eyes to water at the same time, and I have nevertheless been quite unable to make out any of your features, so that, in truth, I cannot even tell of what House you are."

"Oh, as to that," said the other, looking around for a means of descent, "can you not guess?"

"Well, I might take you for a Dzurlord."

"And you would be right," she said, eventually finding a ledge where, with two jumps, neither of them from too great a height, she could make her way to the path. She gave them a deep bow. "I am, indeed, of the House of the Dzur, and my name is Tazendra Lavode."

"Tazendra!" cried Piro.

"Lavode!" cried Kytraan.

"Exactly," said Tazendra, who, as no doubt the reader realized some time ago, was none other than our old friend.

"Then you," said Piro, coming to the same conclusion as the reader, "must be that very Tazendra of whom my father has so often spoken."

"Well, but that would depend upon who your father is."

"Why, he is Khaavren of Castle Rock."

"Cracks and Shards!" cried Tazendra. "You are Khaavren's son?"

"I have that honor."

"But this is delightful! Come, my boy, let me embrace you!"

"Gladly," said Piro, filled with emotion at meeting one of his father's old comrades. They embraced warmly, after which Tazendra held Piro at arm's length and looked him over carefully. For his part, Piro studied the Dzur of whom he had heard such stories. By any standards, she was still a beautiful woman, her hair was still long and quite black, her eyes still piercing, and her skin still as smooth as any courtesan's. Moreover, she had that quality about her that comes with a body that is in supreme good health, well conditioned and athletic. These observations left Piro with a certain confusion, for the lady before him was without question an attractive woman, and Piro could hardly be insensitive to this; yet he was also acutely aware that she was a friend of his father, and looking at her the way a man looks at a desirable woman made him uncomfortable. It is only fair to add that Tazendra, for her part, had no trace whatsoever of this confusion.

Kytraan, who had no part in any of this, waited a moment, then coughed discreetly, commanding the attention of Tiassa and Dzur.

"Your pardon," said Piro, flushing slightly. "Tazendra Lavode, this is my good friend Kytraan e'Lanya of the North Pinewood Hold, the son of Uttrik, whom you may recall."

"An honor," said Kytraan.

"A pleasure and an honor," said Tazendra happily. "Uttrik's son? Shards!" Tazendra appeared about to speak more, no doubt to ask questions about Uttrik, but Kytraan spoke first, saying, "I observe that you have added the appendage 'Lavode' to your name."

"How, you noticed that?" said Tazendra, looking pleased.

"Very much so."

"Well, it is true."

"And I am glad it is, only—"

"Yes?"

"Well, what does it mean?"

"What does it mean?"

"Yes. I know of Sethra Lavode, but—"

"You do not know of the Lavodes, the magical arm of the Emperor from time immemorial?"

"Well, I have heard certain stories, it is true."

"Oh, on my honor, they are all true."

"And yet, were the Lavodes not all destroyed in Adron's Disaster?"

"Pah! You know very well that Sethra still lives. Or, that is to say, she exists."

"Well, that is true of Sethra."

"And if Sethra exists, why can she not cause there to be more Lavodes?"

"If you put it in those terms, my good Tazendra—"

"Oh, I do, I assure you."

"Well, then I can make no answer."

"And there you are."

"But I still congratulate you upon it."

"As do I," put in Piro.

"Thank you," said Tazendra modestly.

"You are, then, a wizard?" continued Kytraan.

"Well, not yet, but I hope to become one once there is an Empire again."

"I wish you well of it."

Tazendra bowed and appeared about to say more, but Piro interrupted, saying, "Your pardon, my good Dzur, but is it not time to continue, and to meet Sethra?"

"Yes," said Kytraan. "And we must introduce you to Zerika."

"How," said Tazendra. "You know Zerika?"

"No, but I am told that she would be here by the time I returned, and that Piro was to meet her."

"Well, let us go, then."

Piro at once dismounted and prepared to lead his horse. Kytraan frowned; then it occurred to him that Tazendra had no horse, and none of them, of course, could be expected to ride the lackey's mount, so Kytraan dismounted as well, and Lar did the same.

"This way," said Tazendra, and guided them up the path.

It soon became evident that, even had they chosen to remain mounted, they would have quickly had to dismount, for the path rose sharply until at last they were helping the horses to negotiate the incline, rather than the reverse.

"This is not as easy as some things I have done," gasped Piro as they struggled.

"The more difficult the climb, the more satisfying the view," said Kytraan.

"Then," said Piro, "I think this view will be breathtaking, for, by the Horse, the climb is nothing less."

Tazendra, of them all, appeared to have no difficulty making her way up, and even helped to pull the animals as she did so; whereas Lar was huffing and puffing as if to take in all the unused air that might be found for the surrounding miles.

At last they came to a place where the ground leveled off, a sort of wide ledge, with sheer grey rock before them and the path forking to either side. They took a moment to recover from the exertion of the climb; then Piro, looking from one path to the other, said, "Which way?"

"Forward," said Tazendra.

Piro looked at the unyielding grey rock before him, then turned back to Tazendra, a look of inquiry upon his countenance.

By way of answer, Tazendra turned to Kytraan and said, "Would you care to do the honors, my dear Dragon?"

Kytraan bowed and said, "With pleasure, my good Dzur."

This said, Kytraan walked forward as if he would go through the rock itself, but then stopped directly before it, placed his hand upon the grey slate, and appeared to push lightly, whereupon a door swung open in the edifice, as if to mock Piro for not having seen it before. They all became aware at once of the odor of fresh straw wafting out from it, as well as other, less pleasant, but equally familiar odors.

"Cracks and shards," said Piro.

Kytraan stepped aside. "Welcome to Dzur Mountain," he said. "Or, at any rate," he amended, "to its stables."

Piro shrugged. "As we have horses, it is good to find the stables."

"That was my thought as well," said Tazendra, and led them into the stables, where they found all that was necessary to see to the comfort of their animals. Lar, without a word, set to work.

"When you have finished," Kytraan told him, "go through that door, climb the stairs to the very top, and follow your nose until you find the kitchens."

"Yes, my lord," said Lar, and continued his ministrations to the horses. This matter attended to, Tazendra led them through the very door Kytraan had just indicated. Here they were at the bottom of a narrow stairway that curved to the left and, as Piro looked up, seemed to go on forever.

Kytraan said, "Had you thought you were done climbing?"

Piro shrugged, and followed the Dragon and the Dzur up the stairway.

While it is undeniable that Piro and Kytraan, if not Tazendra, were wearied by the long climb up from the stables, yet we do not believe it necessary to weary the reader by bringing him along that same climb, the more-so as the exhaustion of our friends precluded any conversation, and, in addition, it cannot be denied that there is little to say of a long stairway, in which each stair is much like another, and the wall, save for the occasional torch, is without features. To be sure, they did pass three or four landings, each with a doorway, but, as they did not trouble to open these doors, there is little reason to speculate upon what lay upon the other side. Let it be said, then, that, after a long time, they reached the end of the stairway, at which time Tazendra pulled open the door, and they stepped into the residence of Sethra Lavode.

Piro was so filled with awe that he was unable to move, until Kytraan said, "Come, my friend, it is only a corridor. You may as well wait until you meet the Enchantress before being struck dumb."

Piro swallowed and nodded. "Lead on, then; I am with you."

We shall no more describe the twists and turns of the passages and stairways they now took than we earlier described the stairway; suffice it to say that presently the three of them found themselves in a room of bare, grey walls, appointed with large chairs that were themselves, to all appearances, carved out of stone, although these chairs were covered with padding to provide comfort. One wall held a massive hearth, which was burning with a bright fire, although Piro could not see what was actually burning in it: there was no sign of wood, but only what appeared to be several rocks. We wish we could solve this mystery for the reader, but, alas, we know no more than Piro, from whose report we know of it, what strange magic was causing this fire.

Tazendra at once sat down in a chair as if there were nothing remarkable in being in Sethra Lavode's lair.

Piro said, "Should we not inform her that we are here?"

"Pah," said Tazendra. "She knows."

Piro started to ask how she knew, but then, on reflection, merely nodded. At this point, someone entered who was clearly not Sethra. In the first place, the individual gave no appearance of being undead, and, in the second place, was a man. He was of middle years, and rather short than tall. He wore black and bore the insignia of the House of the Dzur upon his shoulders, yet his features were those of the House of the Teckla, distinguished by thick, black eyebrows that seemed always to be in motion: rising, falling, or attempting to compress themselves together. Piro found the effect distracting.

The Teckla bowed to them, and said, "I am Tukko. May I bring any of you refreshment?" His voice was high, and reminded Piro of the door to his father's study, which was always so much in need of oil that the entire manor was alerted each time it was opened or closed.

They each asked for wine, and Tukko bowed and walked out, returning shortly thereafter with a sparkling sweet Truil for Tazendra, a white Furnia for Kytraan, and a full, red Khaav'n for Piro. Piro sipped it, identified it at once by the dry, spicy flavor with a hint of nuttiness, and the mild tingling upon the tongue, a combination produced only by wines from that district, whereupon he graced Tukko with a glance of inquiry.

"In honor of your family," said Tukko in explanation.

"Ah, then you know who I am."

Tukko bowed, which gesture he managed to make at once stiff and undignified. This confused Piro, until it occurred to him that Sethra would have little use for a servant skilled in the ways of court, especially in the ways of a court that no longer existed. After bowing, Tukko said, "You will observe a small rope near the Lady Tazendra's left hand; should you require anything else, pull upon it; I will hear, and will return." With these words and another clumsy bow, he left the way he had come.

Piro said, "Will the Enchantress be here soon?"

Tazendra shrugged. "Soon? Late? Who can say?"

Kytraan smiled. "Are you anxious to meet her?"

"The word *anxious* is well chosen, my friend," said Piro, smiling. "I must confess to you, the stories one hears about her give rise to a feeling not unlike trepidation. Yet while you have not told me that these stories are true, neither have you said that they are false. You perceive, therefore, I don't know what to believe, and I therefore don't know what to expect, and, therefore I am, as you have said, anxious."

"Well, but I have not told you for the best of all possible reasons: I don't know."

Tazendra said, "For my part, I believe them."

"All of them?" said Piro.

"Why not? That is no more foolish than if I believed none of them."

"Cha! I nearly think I agree with you."

"Do you?" said Tazendra, smiling. "Well, that is good, then. It is pleasant to find that Khaavren's son agrees with me. In the old days, you know, he often agreed with me."

"Did he?" said Piro. "Well, that does not astonish me."

Tazendra nodded. "The truth is, when I would suggest an idea, why, it was most often Khaavren who was the first to agree with me. 'Tazendra, my friend,' he would say, 'I think that is an excellent plan you have suggested, and I, for one, vote that we adopt it at once!' That is how he would speak to me."

"I am certain that is just how it was," said Piro, who was certain it was nothing like that at all.

"Oh, those were grand days! Adventure at every turn! To save this Dragonlord, to foil this Jhereg, to protect this Emperor—"

She stopped suddenly as if fearful that Piro might take her words amiss. The Tiassa shrugged, however, and said, "And adventures are gone now?"

"Oh, I don't say that! I had thought they might be, but then Zerika appeared last week—"

"Ah! You mention Zerika!"

"Well, and why should I not?"

"It is only that I am curious about her."

"Well, and it is right you should be, because she will save us all."

"How, she will save us?"

"Yes, but first we must save her."

"You perceive," said Piro, "that I am now bewildered."

"You are? But, what has bewildered you?"

"Why, you have said she will save us, and we must save her, and she has changed everything, and yet, I have no idea of who she is."

"Ah! And you wish to know why I said all of those things about her?"

"That is exactly what I wish."

"Well, I said them for the simplest possible reason: because that is what Sethra said, and I am convinced that if Sethra Lavode said it, it must be the truth."

"So then," said Piro, "is that why I am here? To save Zerika?"

"Oh, as to that—"

"Well?"

"I have not the least idea in the world, I assure you."

Kytraan looked up suddenly. "Well, but here is someone you can ask, if you wish."

Piro stood up, startled, and turned to see a tall dark figure standing in the doorway.

"Piro," said Kytraan, also rising to his feet. "I am honored to introduce you to Sethra Lavode, the Enchantress of Dzur Mountain."

BOOK TWO

In Which Sethra Lavode's Plans
Are Not Only Revealed, but Attempted
To Be Put into Action

Chapter the Eighteenth

How the Gods Concerned
Themselves with the Momentous
Events That Were Taking Place

According to the Athyra scholar Ekrasan of Sibletown, writing in the Eleventh Cycle during the Reign of the Issola or the Tsalmoth, we forget which, there are four classes of literature: The ironic, which concerns the actions of men to whom the reader is invited to feel superior; the realistic, which concerns the actions of men with whom the reader is invited to identify; the romantic, which concerns the actions of men the reader is invited to admire; and the mythic, which concerns the actions of the gods.

We must confess that we have nothing but admiration for the worthy Athyra: it was he, after all, who first identified the Five Parts of Literature, and who, moreover, took the first Chair in the great debate before His Imperial Majesty Fecila the Third over the ban on works of fiction proposed during the Eleventh Vallista Reign, with the result that a destruction of literary works that we shudder to contemplate was, in the end, avoided.

Nevertheless, upon this point, we must dispute him. It seems to us that, in any serious work, all of these classes are contained, and all the issues within them addressed; and if more or less emphasis is placed on one or the other in a certain work, this does not mean that the others are not present, by implication if not explicitly, in every work of literature that merits the name.

If we were to use our own humble effort as an example, we might say that our treatment of Tazendra could be considered ironic; whereas when we address ourselves to certain of the Teckla, such as Lar, we strive for the strictest realism; many of those persons who make their way through our history are, at least in the opinion of the author, admirable: Sethra Lavode, Aerich, and, we hope, many others.

Yet we have not, hitherto, dared to directly address the gods in this work. Indeed, we would not do so now, except that at this point our history absolutely requires it.

Therefore, we must ask our reader to permit us to take him to the very Halls of Judgment, where those beings who control, as best they can, the fate of our entire world sit and pass judgment, not only on all of those who come before them, but on all of the events that take place over which they exert, or attempt to exert, some measure of control.

While it is beneath our dignity as historian to plead excuses to the reader, we must, nevertheless, explain that to describe the Halls of Judgment is no easy task. In the first place, this is because there are few witnesses who have returned with such a description. In the second place, it is because the descriptions that do exist seldom agree. And in the last place, it is because the realm comes from the dreams of the gods themselves. The reader may consider the problem for himself: if the reader could dream and then make that dream real, and share that dream with a score of others who were making their own dreams real, and if some observer were to enter this place which was an intersection of all of these dreams, and if, moreover, the dream was constantly changing as new presences were added and removed, well, we beg liberty to doubt the reader's ability to precisely—or even meaningfully—describe the place he had visited.

This noted, however, we will say that, by all accounts, the Halls of Judgment were spacious. Let us say, then, that we observe a large open space, such as the Terraces of Finance behind the Silver Exchange in the old city of Dragaera. And like the Terraces of Finance, there is no ceiling, but neither is there the Enclouding of the Empire, nor the sparkling holes in the sky that are visible in the East; rather, there is simply naked, empty blue-black sky. There is no light of lamp or torch, nor is there the natural light of the Furnace; rather the Halls of judgment are perpetually in that state that comes just after twilight; one can see clearly enough, but one always wishes for just a little more light.

As for the gods, they sit upon "thrones" that are as diverse as their characters, to say nothing of their forms. They sit in a great circle—so great, indeed, that were the reader to stand directly before one and by turning his head look around, he could only barely see the one directly behind him. Yet, by the deep wizardry that is a part of the Halls of Judgment, three or four steps are all that is needed to be before the other, and he whom one had been addressing before would now appear to be an incalculable distance behind. The conclusion is inescapable: in this dream of place, distance has no meaning.

We have put this chapter here, interrupting Piro's arrival at Dzur Mountain, for two reasons: the first is that, insofar as we can judge, it was at just about this point in history that what follows actually occurred. But secondarily, it was to emphasize that *time*, as it applies to the Halls of Judgment, cannot be understood as the normal, orderly progression of moments where it is elsewhere experienced. From everything we know, at least this much is clear from those few who have entered the Halls of Judgment and returned to the normal world: a day spent in the Halls might be an hour outside of it; or it might be a year, or ten years. The conclusion is inescapable: in this dream of sequence, time has no meaning.

We have used the terms *sorcery*, and *necromancy*, and *witchcraft*, and *wizardry*, to refer to the different techniques of holding in abeyance natural law—or, to be more precise, temporarily substituting one set of natural laws for another. These different forms of magic are understood to different degrees, and, after the manner of all branches of science, the efforts to understand them more deeply never cease. To use is to learn, and to learn is to use better, and to use better is to learn more deeply. This is a continuing process, and one that gives meaning to the term *progress* (however much certain desert-born mystics might sneer at the word). Yet, in the timeless, placeless place that we call the Halls of Judgment, the realm of the gods, there are no natural laws, because all is a dream of the gods. And where there are no natural laws, there can be no abeyance of these laws. Where everything is possible, nothing is possible. Where all laws of magic and reality operate, no laws of magic and reality apply. The conclusion is inescapable: in this dream of truth, magic has no meaning.

Of course, this confusion of distance, time, and magic will make no difference to the residents of the Halls of Judgment, by which, be it clearly understood, we mean the gods; we are not at this time concerned with those poor souls who wear the purple robes and are the servants of all who pass beyond Deathgate Falls; nor with those who await judgment or rebirth; nor those who, like Kieron the Conqueror, have simply chosen to remain within the Paths for a time more or less protracted. As we look upon this scene, he who is, some believe, the most powerful of all the gods, that being Barlen, sits in a chair that appears to be a stone that has been chiseled to conform to his reptilian shape. Always near him are the Three Daughters of Darkness, who appear very nearly human, and whom we know as Verra, Moranthë, and Kéurana. Some say Verra, who is either the eldest or the youngest, is Barlen's lover; upon this subject the historian will not speculate. Others might be here as well: Ordwynac, the embodiment of fire; Nyssa, who most often appeared as a dim shape floating in the air; Tri'nagore, similar to Barlen, although larger and darker; Kelchor, the cat-centaur; Trout, supposed to be the wisest of gods.

All of these, and, perhaps, others, sit in a great circle, and communicate with each other by pure thought, thus eliminating, the reader should understand, the need for them to speak each other's languages, because many of them do speak different languages, and some, such as Ordwynac, are believed to have no means to speak at all (a proposition which, frankly, this historian finds dubious, if not impossible).

As we listen in on this conversation, there are questions that, no doubt, will at once occur to the reader: First, the reader will be curious as to how we will reproduce thoughts from the minds of the gods. To this question, we will say the way thoughts are always reproduced—that is, we will turn them into language. If there are perhaps certain turns of phrase that are introduced in this way, the reader may be assured, at least, that the most important aspect of the thought, that is, the *substance*, will be faithfully rendered.

But then, the reader might wonder, how can the historian pretend to know conversations that occurred where distance, time, and magic have no meaning, far from anywhere, and only within the minds of beings who are not subject to the understanding of a mere human. This is a more difficult question, and deserves an answer that is as honest in its substance as it is brief in its exposition.

The answer, then, is this: While we cannot, for the reasons outlined above, know precisely what was expressed, nevertheless, we can know from testimony of those monks who commune with the gods, and those priests who intercede with them, and those sorcerers who have made pacts with them, some of what they did during this fascinating era of our history. And, as the thought is to the deed as the road is to the destination, so, by examining the results, we can arrive at certain conclusions concerning their thoughts. Moreover, we have, from writings that go back far into the depths of history, certain clues concerning the personalities of these deities. Last, we know that the Orb was present, and the Orb cannot forget, and hints that Her Majesty the Empress has been gracious enough to drop are also useful in providing us with material with which to make informed guesses.

It is true, the ability to make an informed guess is often over-used and mis-used by historians and pretended historians: It is well known, for example, that the military historian is at his best when giving the names of field officers who fell in battle, and at his worst when attempting to explain the reason for the general officer to have made a certain decision at a certain time. Nevertheless, we believe that, just as there are times when conclusions are so obvious that the cold recitation of fact and nothing but fact best serves the ultimate goal of history, which is the discovery of *truth*, still, there are other times when a judicious application of careful, responsible guesswork is not only permitted, but very nearly required. We further contend that this is just such a circumstance, and we hope the reader will be willing to give us his trust as we explore these difficult yet vital matters.

To begin, then, Kelchor spoke, saying, "Great matters are stirring in what was once the Empire of Men."

"That may be," said Ordwynac. "But need we concern ourselves? That is, does it involve the Cycle? Or is it only more playing by those who have already wasted the opportunity we gave them."

"It was not wasted," said Moranthë.

"It was not their fault," said Kéurana.

"Opportunity *who* gave them?" said Verra.

"Nevertheless," said Ordwynac. "The question is, do these 'great matters,' as you call them, involve the Cycle, or do they not?"

Nyssa said, "They involve the Enchantress of Dzur Mountain, at any rate, for I have seen her stirring."

"Well," said Kelchor, "that is something. I have known her as long as any of you, and you will all agree, I think, that she rarely involves herself in trivialities."

"So then," said Barlen, "it may involve the Cycle. In fact, I begin to become convinced that it does."

Ordwynac said, "Very well, it involves the Cycle. And yet, the Cycle is broken—"

"The Cycle is never broken," said Barlen. "Only the Empire is shattered, but the Cycle which was its foundation cannot be broken, for it is part of the fundamental nature of the universe. As long as there is one living being—"

"There is no remaining Phoenix!" said Ordwynac. "How can the Cycle survive with no Phoenix?"

"There is one," said Moranthë.

"Actually two," said Verra, "though they are both female."

"How, there are two?" said Barlen.

"Yes," said Verra.

"You are certain?"

"The House of the Phoenix is my watch," she said. "I am certain. There are two."

"I am astonished," said Barlen. "This may change everything."

"And yet," said Verra, "as I have said, they are both female."

"Then," said Ordwynac, "that is the same as if there were none."

"How so?" said Kéurana. "You perceive, if two is the same as none, then all of the sciences must be redefined, beginning with arithmetic."

"Because," said Ordwynac, ignoring the irony the goddess did him the honor to share, "these are beings who require a male and a female to reproduce."

"And so?" said Verra.

"And so, even if there is a Phoenix now, there can never be another, and so, by the time the Cycle returns to the Phoenix, it will be broken."

"You know little of the Phoenix," said Verra.

"And less of the Cycle," added Barlen.

"Then explain it to me," said Ordwynac.

"And to me as well," said Kelchor, "for, you perceive, I do not understand how the Cycle is to survive either, and, if there is to be no Cycle, well, then why are we here?"

"You explain it," said Verra to Kéurana. "The breeding of humans is your domain; I cannot explain why two that are hidden can produce one that is seen."

"Let Moranthë explain, because she understands the phoenix and its significance, and how it lives when it dies, and creates when it destroys, and prophesies while making its prophecies come to pass."

"No, let Verra explain," said Moranthë, "because she comprehends the Cycle better than I, and moreover knows how, to preserve itself, it can summon the phoenix, and even cause people to fall in love who otherwise might not have met."

"Well," said Verra. "That is true, but it needs help from time to time."

"Yes," said Barlen. "And I believe that now may be that time."

"You think so?" said Kelchor.

"Very possibly," said Barlen. "At least, the fact that the Enchantress is stirring is, as Verra has said, not insignificant."

"But," said Ordwynac, "is that all? Are there other signs?"

Moranthë turned her gaze away for a moment, then said, "The Cycle has not turned."

"Well," said Ordwynac. "What does that mean?"

"Nothing," said Moranthë, "except that, if you have been paying attention, you will observe that Time is slowing down. And if Time is slowing down, and the Cycle has not turned, then, well, then it means something else."

"That is true," said Ordwynac.

"And," added Kelchor, "I can tell you that one of the warlords, a certain Kâna, is growing in power at an alarming rate."

"He wishes to found an Empire?" said Nyssa.

"It seems so," said Kelchor.

"Perhaps," said Tri'nagore, "he is deserving of the Orb himself."

"Hardly," said Verra coldly. "He is a Dragon, and the Cycle still points to the Phoenix."

"Very well," said Ordwynac. "What other signs are there?"

"How," said Kéurana. "Isn't that enough?"

"Not for Ordwynac," said Moranthë. "He is lazy, and looking for an excuse not to have to do anything."

Ordwynac glared, but did not otherwise speak.

"Two young girls will meet," continued Moranthë. "A Dzur and a Tiassa. I do not know why I have been drawn to this meeting, but drawn to it I was. It is caused by the machinations of Kâna, and may be significant. The Dzur is likely to be the Dzur Heir when the present Heir comes to us. As for the Tiassa, I do not know."

"What else?" said Ordwynac.

"There is," said Verra, "a joining of East and West."

"How, a joining?" said Barlen, who seemed startled by this news.

"At least, there is the potential."

"Explain."

"Very well. A Dragonlord, raised in the East, is gathering power and moving west."

"Well, and if he is?"

"He is of the e'Drien line."

"Forgive me, Verra, but I am not as familiar with the lines of the Dragon as you are. What is the significance of this?"

"Surly you remember Drien, do you not? You were there when he was judged."

"Yes, I know him."

"He had the ability to bring disparate forces together, and to forge powerful combinations. He did this in battle, and in politics, and in the subtle social weavings where small things can have great effects."

"Well, I understand. And this descendant of his is moving west?"

"Yes. With a force of witches and an Issola, and—"

"Yes?"

"A pact with me."

Barlen frowned. "You made this pact without consulting any of the rest of us?"

"Yes," said Verra.

"Knowing the sort of effect it could have?"

"Yes."

"Why?"

"Because I wished to."

"And you believed that was sufficient reason?"

"I not only did then, but, what is more, I still do."

"And yet, now we are all involved with this man."

"Not in the least."

"How, we are not?"

"Only I have made a pact with him."

"And yet, through this pact, he has a hand in the Halls of Judgment. And a foot in the Empire. And his head in the magic of the East."

"Well, he is flexible."

"There is no question of joking, Verra."

"Very well, then let us not joke, but rather be as serious as an Iorich."

"That is what I wish."

"Well?"

"This Dragonlord may come into conflict with Kâna, or with Sethra. The results are unpredictable."

"I favor results that are unpredictable."

"You favor—!"

Moranthë broke in, then, saying, "There is more. This Kâna has allied himself with a certain Yendi, who has plans that I cannot read, but that stretch out still more."

Barlen shook his head. "I do not like this. There is too much happening too quickly, and we are not fully aware of it, nor of what it means."

"We can never be fully aware, nor can we always know the meaning," said Trout, speaking for the first time.

"And then?" said Barlen.

Nyssa said, "Perhaps now is the time to watch, and to wait."

"That has never been my particular skill," said Verra.

"I know," said Barlen.

"Where is the phoenix now?" asked Nyssa.

"If you do not know," said Ordwynac, "how are the rest of us to?"

"If she has any sense," said Moranthë, "she is hiding."

"Hiding," said Kéurana, "and waiting until her moment."

"Which moment," added Verra, "may not occur for nearly an entire Cycle."

"We have an opportunity," said Barlen, "as well as a danger."

"An opportunity?" said Kelchor. "What sort of opportunity?"

"To inflict a blow upon Those We Do Not Name."

"Why," said Verra, "do we not name the Jenoine?"

"Hush," said Barlen.

"What sort of opportunity?" said Ordwynac.

"We have the Orb in our possession," said Barlen. "We have the chance to have Nyssa engage with it, and remove some of the, if I may use the term, rough edges."

"But think of the power that would give these mortals," said Kelchor. "Consider, even without that, they very nearly destroyed the entire world."

"They did not use the Orb to do that," said Verra.

"That is true," said Kelchor. "Nevertheless—"

"If they have the power," said Moranthë, "they can be of even more help to us."

"And more danger to themselves," said Kelchor.

"Can we trust them?" said Nyssa.

"Never," said Ordwynac.

"Sometimes," said Kelchor.

"I trust the line of Kieron," said Verra.

"And I," said Barlen, "trust the House of the Phoenix."

"That is right," said Ordwynac. "One of you trusts the line that nearly destroyed the Orb, and the other trusts the House that could not protect it."

"For my part," said Nyssa, "I trust Sethra Lavode."

"That we know," said Ordwynac, "else we'd never have permitted her to leave the Paths."

"Well, and do you regret the decision?"

"It is too soon to know. Ask me again when next the Cycle brings the Phoenix to the top, and I will tell you then."

"Very well, I will ask."

"And I will answer."

"What we should do," said Barlen, "is send forth an emissary."

"An emissary?" said Kelchor. "Come, that is not a bad thought. Someone who can push them in the right direction."

"No," said Barlen. "We do not know the right direction any more than does Sethra; to push them could be to destroy them. That is not what I meant."

"What then?" said Kelchor. "If not to give counsel?"

"I meant help of a more practical kind. Those We Do Not Name may become active the instant this Phoenix emerges with the Orb, if, indeed, she does so."

"If we permit her to," said Ordwynac.

"For my part," said Nyssa, "I believe she should not be permitted to, because of what her race did with the Orb the last time, if for no other reason."

"Her race," said Verra, "created the Orb."

"And yet—"

"Now is not the time for that discussion," said Barlen. "For now, the question is this: What have they to defend against Those We Do Not Name? Sethra Lavode and Dzur Mountain, it is true, as well as Sethra's apprentice. But these may not be enough. That is why I believe that we should send them an emissary. If we decide not to give them the Orb, well, the emissary can be recalled."

Verra said, "We could send them Kieron the Conqueror. His shade has been here longer than any other, and I know he would like nothing better than to go forth and engage in battle once more."

"No, it is not battle and war that worries me."

"It worries me," said Kelchor. "The stirring of this warlord from Kâna could ruin everything."

"Nevertheless," said Barlen, "Kieron is too unpredictable, as are all of his race. The last time, he came within a hairsbreadth of attempting to take the Orb himself and undoing all our plans. Do you pretend he could be controlled now?"

"He would abide by an oath," said Kéurana.

"He would not take such an oath, sister," said Verra.

"Well," said Moranthë, "but what then?"

"One of us?" said Kelchor.

"Never!" said Nyssa. "Those We Do Not Name would know at once. Our hope is that, however strong they are, they are slow to act, and so we may have prepared for them before they are aware of the opportunity. If one of us emerges, they will look, and they will see, and they will know, and we will be lost."

"That is true," said Barlen.

"What then?" said Kelchor.

"A demon," said Trout.

All of those assembled looked at him. After a moment, Barlen said, "How, a demon?"

"Yes," said Trout. "One sensitive enough to know when the Others may attempt to gain entry, skilled enough to aid Sethra in preventing that entry, and, moreover, a demon whose presence will not alert them."

There were nods from around the circle. After a moment, Nyssa said, "I know one."

"That doesn't astonish me," said Verra.

"Who?" said Barlen.

"She comes from the World of Seven Doors," said Nyssa, "and she knows six of them."

"How, six?" said Verra, appearing astonished for the first time.

"And she is not entirely unacquainted with the seventh."

"But, how is it we have never heard of her?"

"She is without ambition."

Moranthë said, "How could one without ambition have learned six of the doors?"

"She is well supplied with curiosity."

"And no little skill, it seems," added Kéurana.

"That is true," said Nyssa.

"And yet—" said Kelchor.

"Well?" said Barlen.

"To set a demon loose upon the world, uncontrolled."

"That is true," said Barlen. "It is not something to be done lightly."

"As for the demon," said Nyssa, "I vouch for her behavior."

"In that case, I like this plan," said Kelchor.

"I have no objections," said Ordwynac.

"If Ordwynac has no objections," said Verra, "than I believe there must be a flaw. Nevertheless, I am in favor."

"And I," said Kéurana.

"And I," said Moranthë.

"And I," said Trinagore.

"And I," said Barlen.

"And Trout, proposed it," said Verra.

"Has anyone any objections to make?" asked Barlen, now speaking to all of the gods and demigods present in the Halls of Judgment. No one responded, and so Barlen said, "Very well, Nyssa. Summon the demon, so that we can instruct her."

"I will do so," said Nyssa.

Chapter the Nineteenth

How Sethra Lavode At Last, Much to the Relief of Piro And, No Doubt, of the Reader, Reveals Her Ideas; And a Difficult But Necessary Distinction Is Made Between Intentions and Plans

Piro stared at the Enchantress for some few moments; indeed, he stared at her until, eventually, he realized that he was doing so, at which point he dropped his eyes and attempted to apologize, only to find that he could not manage to bring up the required words, which had evidently lodged themselves in the back of his throat, creating an obstruction that threatened to make breathing problematical. Sethra Lavode, who was perfectly aware of what was transpiring within the young Tiassa's mind and heart—not to mention his throat—chose to ignore it, and merely said, "Welcome to Dzur Mountain, Viscount, and thank you for agreeing to visit me."

To this, at least, Piro knew how to respond: he bowed very low. Sethra continued, "And welcome back, Kytraan. You succeeded admirably, and in good time."

"It was nothing," said the Dragonlord, bowing in his turn.

It must be said that there was little about the Enchantress, at least upon first glimpse, to match Piro's expectations. She appeared to be a slim woman, not exceptionally tall, rather gaunt of face, with long, black hair that set off the pale skin which was her only remarkable feature. To look at her, one might at first think of her as a Dzurlord from the slant to her eyes and the point to her ears; yet a closer inspection would reveal the bridged nose and high cheekbones characteristic of the House of the Dragon. Further, she had the strong chin that denotes determination, and the close eyebrows which would indicate that she spent a great deal of time in her own company. Her countenance indicated a reserved warmth, if the reader will permit such a formulation.

"Please, sit down," she said. "I trust the journey was without incident?"

"Entirely," said Kytraan. "We met only harmless beasts, friendly sorcerers, tame brigands, and a Dzurlord who was willing to listen to reason. As the journey to Adrilankha went quickly, we took our time returning and made a holiday of it. Moreover, the weather did nothing untoward, beyond a sprinkle of rain as I was on the way to Adrilankha, and a bit of misty chill this morning. Therefore, you perceive, the journey was entirely pleasant and free from any occurrences which might give rise to complaints."

"That is well, then. I have sent word that you are here; certain individuals will be arriving in order to meet you, after which we will have conversation."

"And then," said Piro, whose throat had now become sufficiently free of obstructions that he was able to force words past it, "will I learn why it is my presence here was requested?"

"How, you have some curiosity about that?"

"I do not deny it," said Piro.

"Well, I think your curiosity will be satisfied."

"That is well, then," said Piro. "And will Zerika be there as well?"

"Oh, as to that, I am not certain. She is reading, and studying, and attempting in only a few weeks to learn what should take years, and so she is, you perceive, busy, and, when not busy, she is resting."

"Well, I understand that," said Kytraan. "And yet, I am anxious to meet her."

"For my part," said Piro, "I admit to some interest as well to have the honor of meeting this lady who, it seems, has asked for me, although I have never, so far as I know, laid eyes upon her."

"You will meet soon enough," said Sethra. "In the meantime, I beg you to be patient, and to recover from your journey, and to enjoy what hospitality I can manage to show you."

"I shall do as you say, madam," said Piro.

"And you will do right to do so," said the Enchantress. At this moment, Tukko walked in the door behind Sethra. Piro just had time to notice that he was carrying the satchel that had lately been hanging from Piro's saddle when the Enchantress, without turning her head, said, "Tukko, be good enough to show Piro to his room, where he can rest until food is prepared."

The servant stood before Piro and waited. The Tiassa rose and bowed to his hostess, whereupon Tukko led him out of the room by the door in the far side. Piro realized that, in fact, he *was* rather weary, and looked forward to resting quietly for a while: young though he was, he had already discovered the joys of ease that many only discover at an advanced age.

Tukko set Piro's bag down and left the Viscount to his rest. The room, though not large, was well appointed, and the bed not uncomfortable; and, moreover, the sheets were clean and cool. These observations, be it understood, were the last Piro made for some few hours, when a clap outside of the door made him aware that he had been sleeping. Upon rising, Piro opened the door, where a Teckla he did not recognize bowed to him and said, "My lord, I am informed that a bath has been drawn for you in the bath-room, and, moreover, dinner will be ready in half an hour."

"Very well," said the Tiassa.

The Teckla bowed once more, making a marked contrast with Tukko, and went off down the hall, limping slightly. Piro found the bath to be rather warmer than he was used to, yet very pleasant, and so, rested, bathed, and dressed, he found himself to be very hungry indeed, and took himself back the way he had come with no little eagerness.

When Piro reached the sitting room where he had first met Sethra Lavode, he found it empty except for Tukko, who said laconically, "This way," and walked out of the other door. Piro followed him for some few minutes, through doors, hallways, and up a set of stairs, until they arrived at a small dining room, where were seated the Enchantress, Kytraan, and Tazendra, as well as two women Piro had never seen before, all of whom stood as Piro entered.

The Enchantress spoke, saying, "Sorceress, Sethra, I should like you to meet Piro, the Viscount of Adrilankha. Viscount, this is the Sorceress in Green, and this is Sethra the Younger."

"A pleasure, Viscount," said the two women.

"An honor," said Piro, bowing to each, and, moreover, adding a smile to his bow for reasons which we will hasten to explain.

We trust that, as Piro takes his place between Sethra Lavode and Kytraan, and the others sit down once more, the reader will permit us to say two words about the mysterious and intriguing Sorceress in Green, a person about whom history speaks much, yet knows little. She was exceptionally tall, and from her general aspect and complexion, one might take her for an Athyra, although, in fact, no one has established her House for a certainty. This historian will not indulge in speculation upon matters for which no proof is available, unlike some of those who have suggested, on the basis of no evidence whatsoever, that she was one of those unfortunates born of a mother from one House and a father from another. That she was of noble blood is certain; a cursory glance at her long, delicate hands and the haughty arch of her eyebrows were sufficient to establish this even if one ignored her noble's point. She had thin lips, a sure sign that she did not often let her emotions escape her heart, yet she had also the narrowness of the eyes that indicate a fierce temper. Her hair was a light brown, and would have been rather wavy than otherwise, save that it had been severely bound up at the nape of her neck. And, as the reader no doubt has already deduced, she invariably affected green garments, for reasons which we cannot state with certainty, although we can speculate that it was because she found the color more pleasing than other colors, especially favoring a dark green, such as that found in the needles of certain evergreen trees.

Her real name, like her lineage and House, are unknown, and a few historians, as well as several scores of popular writers masquerading as historians, have advanced theories more or less preposterous and explanations more or less prosaic to answer these questions. But whatever her origins, her subtlety as a sorcerer is indisputable, her fame stretching as far back as the Fifteenth Tsalmoth Reign, when she created the Wall of the Circling Winds to hold back a tidal wave that threatened large portions of the southwestern coast. Later, during the Fifteenth Chreotha Reign, she was brought in by Sethra Lavode during the Littleshell War, where by herself she held at bay the entire sorcerers' corps of Baron Niefivre for three full days, permitting Sethra to make the flanking maneuver that won the war for the Empire. From there, her fame, at least among those who studied the magical sciences, grew quickly; indeed, she was one of only three sorcerers from outside the House of the Athyra who were offered command positions in the Guard during the Seventeenth Athyra Reign; a position, we should add, which she declined, pretending she had finished with Court life.

As to her age, there is no one who can say; except that it is generally accepted that she is one of oldest living human beings, although her skill at her art combined with her vanity insured that her appearance was that of a girl of not more than two or three hundred. Piro, not in the least indifferent to these charms, and, perhaps, less aware of her fame than would be someone more familiar with magical history, added a warm smile to his bow.

For her part, Sethra the Younger was a slightly shorter, heavier, and darker version of her namesake, although those features of Sethra Lavode that made one think of the House of the Dragon, such as the sharpness of the chin, the hook of the nose, and the depth of the eyes, were accentuated in her apprentice. For that, of course, is what Sethra the Younger was: the latest in a long line of apprentices to whom the Enchantress had wished to teach her art, hoping that, someday, one of them would assume the power of Dzur Mountain, whatever that might be, and permit the Enchantress to retire peacefully. In character, Sethra the Younger was, one might say, Sethra Lavode carried to an extreme: more ambitious, more jealous of her prerogatives, more arrogant, and fiercer. Yet, for the sake of completeness, we must say that, from certain words that Sethra Lavode has let fall over the years, apprentice was not unlike what master had been years and years ago, when Enchantress and Empire were young together. Sethra the Younger's greatest moment had occurred during the Third Battle of Hartstongue Wash. On this occasion, she was serving as a brigadier under Sethra Lavode, who had entrusted to her the Flooding Pass, vital as the supply line to the army, with the instructions "If they wish for this real estate, you must bargain with them for it, and be certain you get a good price." Now Sethra the Younger, intrigued by this formulation, decided to take it more literally than it had been intended, and so, when the Duke of Softrock threatened her position, she came forward under a flag of truce, and said to him, "My dear Softrock, I believe you wish to control this pass."

"Well, and if I do?"

"Then you may have it."

"How, you surrender it?"

"Exactly. But I must receive for it one-third of your command, to be sent back to the prison camps behind our lines."

"What? A third of my command?"

"Yes, my dear Duke. That is the price. And, if you are wise, you will take it!"

"Bah! The price is too high."

"You think so? Well then, come and see if you can gain it for any less," upon which she returned to her lines, and, in the event, defended the ground with such skill and ferocity that the Duke lost some ten percent of his force in killed, wounded, and captured, and at no time came close to taking the position. We hope this story will serve to tell something of the character of Sethra the Younger, for it is all we wish to say of her at this time, and therefore the reader is obliged to be satisfied.

Once everyone was seated, Tukko came forward and poured wine, while the Teckla Piro had seen earlier went around with a platter of finely chopped kethna, mountain mushrooms, scallions, rednuts ground into a powder, and sweet peppers, all wrapped in an unraised bread of the type eaten in the northern reaches of Suntra; the combination resulted in a very small package with, if the reader will excuse the expression, a very large flavor.

"Blood of the Horse," said Piro when he had tasted one. "May I ask who prepared this?"

Sethra gestured toward Tukko, who gave a nod that could, perhaps, be interpreted as a bow if one were sufficiently liberal in one's interpretation.

"Much is explained, then," said Piro. "It is splendid."

"I am glad you are pleased," said the Enchantress, who was, in fact, only nibbling at her own. The others, we should add, made no secret of their pleasure at the food. Sometime later, the next course was served, which consisted of various vegetables served with a sort of cream sauce flavored with the same wine they were drinking; we can say that this was as successful as the first.

As they ate, Piro said, "I had thought that, perhaps, the mysterious Zerika would do us the honor of joining us for this magnificent repast."

"I had hoped so," said Sethra. "But she was too exhausted from her labors, and has decided that rest is a more urgent requirement than food."

"Well, I understand that," said Piro, who could remember being that tired, and who, indeed, had been in very nearly the same state a few short hours before.

Several more courses followed, courses which, with the reader's permission, we will not detail, save to say that they included fish caught that very day in the fast-flowing streams of Dzur Mountain, and roasted game-bird in a sauce of wine and fruit, and other delicacies of the region. It was while the bird was being served that Tazendra happened to remark to the unknown Teckla, "I seem to have dropped my fork, Mica, and should be glad to have a new one."

"Mica!" cried Piro.

The worthy Teckla said, "Yes, my lord, that is my name."

"But then, are you the Mica of whom my father, that being Khaavren, the Count of Whitecrest, has spoken of so often?"

The Teckla, who was, indeed, our old friend and Tazendra's lackey, turned bright red, and veritably beamed with pride, and could only stammer and bow, so great was his joy at the thought that Khaavren not only remembered him, but had spoken of him to his son. Indeed, so overcome was the good Mica that he had to be reminded again to bring his mistress the fork she had requested.

We can only add that from this moment on Mica would as gladly have allowed himself to be cut to pieces for Piro as he would for Tazendra herself.

By the time they reached that portion of the dinner reserved for the sweet, which, in this instance, took the form of an assortment of local berries in a cream sauce with vanilla sugar, everyone was relaxed and ready for conversation. Nor were they disappointed in this, for the Enchantress, though she enjoyed pleasing guests with a delectable repast as much as anyone, had, in point of fact, brought everyone together with the idea in mind of having a certain amount of discussion; a discussion to which the repast had been only intended as a prelude.

She began, then, in this fashion: "My friends," she said, "for so I hope I may call you, I have brought you here with a purpose in mind."

"Well," said the Sorceress in Green with a bow of her head, "that is all right, but I hope that you will do us the honor to tell us this purpose."

This sentiment was echoed by nods and murmurs of agreement from around the table. The Enchantress herself said, "In fact, I am about to do exactly that."

"How, this very instant?" said Kytraan.

"Yes. In fact, I am about to begin."

"Well," put in Piro, "for my part, after a journey of nearly two hundred miles, I think I should like nothing better than to know the reason behind the journey."

"Listen, then, and you will understand."

"We are listening," said everyone at the table, giving Sethra Lavode their full attention.

"This is it, then: My friends, I propose to restore the Empire."

"Blood of the Horse," said Piro.

"Ambitious," said the Sorceress in Green.

"A worthy goal," cried Kytraan.

"If anyone can do it, it would be you," said Sethra the Younger.

"For my part," said Tazendra, "I nearly think I am in favor of it."

"Well then," said the Enchantress. "If we're all in favor of it, I see no reason not to do it."

Tazendra said, "But—"

"Yes?"

"Oh, I agree it would be a good thing, but, well, it seems that doing so might present difficulties."

"Oh," said the Enchantress. "I do not dispute that."

"You do not? Well, that is good then. Because, you perceive, what you have expressed is a desire—"

"Oh no, my dear Tazendra. More than a desire: an intention."

"Very well, I accept that it is an intention. And yet—"

"Well? And yet?"

"And yet it seems to me that we need a plan."

"Ah, a plan."

"Exactly."

"Well, Tazendra, and do you have one?"

"Who, I?"

"Yes, you."

"Not the least in the world. Why, so far am I from having a plan, I don't even have the intention. You perceive, you had that."

"Well, that is true, but you agree that it is a good intention, do you not?"

"Oh, certainly. And that is all the more reason why we need a plan."

"And yet, Tazendra, you say you do not have a plan."

"Say it? My dear Sethra, I insist upon it."

"Well then, I am convinced: You have no plan."

"I am glad we agree," said Tazendra.

"Yes. All is well, now."

"Oh yes, all is well, except—"

"Yes, except?"

"The difficulties."

"Oh, yes; the difficulties."

"Yes. What will do about them?"

"We will overcome them," replied the Enchantress laconically.

"For my part," put in Kytraan, "I am all in favor of overcoming difficulties. Indeed, I should feel my life wasted were I never to have the opportunity to overcome difficulties."

"I very nearly agree with you," said Tazendra.

"Do you, indeed?" said Kytraan. "Well, that pleases me greatly."

"I am glad that it does. But, as to these difficulties, I wonder—"

"Oh, you wonder?" said Sethra Lavode.

"Well, yes. Many years ago, my friend Pel pretended that wondering was a sign of intelligence, and I have therefore taken the opportunity to wonder whenever I at all could."

"For my part," said the Enchantress, "I am not far from agreeing with him. But tell me, what do you wonder?"

"Just this. I wonder *how* we are to overcome these difficulties."

"Oh, as to that . . ."

"Yes?"

"To overcome them, we need a plan."

"Exactly what I was thinking!" cried Tazendra, slapping her hand on the table with such force that the pottery rattled. "Shall we formulate one?"

"Why not?" said Sethra, who, if truth must be told, found the conversation not unamusing. She continued, "Well, in the first place, let us see: what are these difficulties?"

"What are they? Well, to begin with, there is no Orb."

"That is true," remarked Piro, who had been listening quietly, but was suddenly struck by the extreme justice of this remark.

"Yes," said the Enchantress. "That is true. But come, let us investigate. Why is there no Orb?"

"Why?" cried Tazendra. "Because Lord Adron destroyed it, that is why!"

"You think so?" said the Enchantress, smiling a little.

"Why, I am very nearly certain of it. I was there, you know, when the city was destroyed, and was the Orb not in the city?"

"Oh, it was in the city."

"And could the Orb survive an explosion large enough to create a Sea of Amorphia?"

"No, it could not."

"Well then," said Tazendra, "there you have it. If the Orb was in the city, and everything in the city was destroyed, then the Orb was destroyed."

"Well, my dear Dzurlord, you reason like Clybur himself, only—"

"Yes?"

"You are wrong."

"But, in what way am I wrong?"

"In this way: The Orb was not destroyed."

These words produced an effect in the room similar to that a harlot might make walking into the Citadel of the Deniers; everyone sprang to his feet and began speaking at once, and for a moment, confusion reigned. But then the Enchantress cleared her throat, and such was her power that everyone stopped speaking, sat down once more, and awaited her words.

"I repeat," she said at last. "The Orb was not destroyed."

"But," said Sethra the Younger, "how is that possible? If it was in the city at the time of Adron's Disaster—"

"Well, it was."

"But then, as Tazendra said—"

"Oh, she was right, as far as she went."

"Then how could it have escaped destruction?"

"Shall I explain?"

"Explain? I think we have been asking for nothing else for an hour!"

"The explanation, then, is this: The explosion itself may have seemed instantaneous, but it was not. That is, the entire affair lasted some few seconds, perhaps three or four."

"Well," said the Sorceress in Green, "so it lasted three or four seconds. And then?"

"In the first second, the Orb was able to detect it. In the second, to know what it meant. And in the third, to act."

"To act?" said Tazendra. "But, in what way did it act? For, you perceive, it did not act to stop the Disaster, or, by the Horse, I think we should know it."

"Stopping the Disaster was beyond it, that is true. But the Orb had still the power to transport itself away."

"Transport itself!" cried the Sorceress in Green.

"By itself?" said Sethra the Younger, narrowing her eyes. "Or did it have help?"

"Oh, as to that," said the Enchantress, "who can say? What is important is that before the catastrophic waves of amorphia reached the Imperial Palace, the Orb had removed itself."

"But," said the Sorceress in Green, "where did it remove itself to?"

"Ah!" said the Enchantress. "That, in fact, is what I asked myself."

"Well?" said Tazendra. "And did you answer yourself as well? For it is one thing to ask one's self a question; I have done so many times. But to—"

"Yes, I answered it. That is, I had a theory."

"Oh, a theory!" said the Sorceress in Green. "It is good to have a theory."

"Yes," said Sethra the Younger. "But theories must be tested."

"My theory has been tested, and it has been proven correct."

"Then," said Kytraan, "where is the Orb?"

"You wish me to tell you?"

"I should like nothing better, I assure you."

"Then I will. The Orb lies, at this moment, in the Paths of the Dead."

"Blood of the Horse," said Tazendra.

The Enchantress nodded. "It is in the keeping of the Lords of Judgment."

The Sorceress in Green shrugged. "Well, it is in good hands, in all events."

"Yes, that is true," said Sethra Lavode.

"And yet, I do not see that it is much better than it would be had it been destroyed. Consider: No one who is living can enter the Paths of the Dead, and no one who is dead can leave it. Unless—"

The Enchantress seemed to read her thoughts, because she said, "No, the Lords of Judgment would not surrender it to me, nor could I leave if I were to return there."

"Well, then—"

"But there is a way."

"Indeed?" said Sethra the Younger. "Well, I, for one, wish to hear of it."

"As do I," said Tazendra.

"And I," added the others.

"I will explain," said the Enchantress. "The one thing that would allow someone to return out of the Paths is the Orb itself."

The Sorceress in Green chuckled. "Now there's a pretty riddle," she said. "I shall be curious to learn how you solve it. We cannot enter the Paths unless we have the Orb, and we cannot get the Orb unless we enter the Paths."

"Pah, there is nothing to prevent a living man from entering the Paths of the Dead."

"There is not?"

"No, provided he is able to survive the descent of the Falls, and the hazards of the Paths themselves, and avoid becoming lost."

"As I said," said the Sorceress.

"Well, but most of the hazards of the Paths will have no effect on a living man. And the descent can be managed in many ways. Indeed, some believe that the Falls will refuse to take a life, so that one cannot drown in the Blood River even if one wishes to."

"And do you believe this?"

The Enchantress shrugged.

"But then," said Sethra the Younger, "will the Lords of Judgment release the Imperial Orb into our hands?"

"They will release the Orb to only one person," said the Enchantress.

"Well?" said Tazendra. "And that is?"

"To the Empress."

"But you perceive," said the Dzurlord, "that there is no Empress."

"No, but there is an Heir," said Sethra Lavode.

"How, an Heir?"

"Exactly," said the Enchantress.

"Ah," said Sethra the Younger.

"You say, 'ah,'" said Sethra Lavode.

"Well, and if I do?"

"You have, then, guessed the name of the Heir?"

"Say rather," said Sethra the Younger with a bow as to a master, "I now understand who your guest is."

"Zerika," said the Sorceress in Green.

"Exactly," said the Enchantress. "Zerika, of the House of the Phoenix, will be the next Empress."

"That is all very well," said Sethra the Younger, "but—"

"Yes?"

"Who will be Warlord?"

"Oh, as to that, the Empress will decide."

"Will she? Then I, for one, am more ready than ever to aid her in any way I can."

"And your help will be appreciated, I assure you," said Sethra Lavode.

"And mine?" said Tazendra.

"Certainly."

"And I hope I can be useful," said Kytraan.

"I have not the least doubt that you will be."

"And I?" said Piro.

"Ah, you," said the Enchantress. "Yes, indeed, I think you will be very helpful indeed."

"Well, that is good then."

"Blood of the Horse!" cried Tazendra suddenly.

"What is it?" said the others.

"Well, I have just realized something."

"And what have you realized?" asked the Enchantress.

"I have just realized that we now have not only an intention, but we very nearly have a plan."

"That's lucky," said Sethra Lavode.

How Wadre's Band Met the
Mysterious Orlaan, and the Results
Of Their Conversation

At around the same time as Piro was getting his first look at Sethra Lavode, Wadre and his band of brigands were getting their first look at someone with whom we have already a passing acquaintance, for it was none other than the woman, Orlaan, whom Piro, Kytraan, and Lar had met in the woods, and with whom they had had a brief conversation.

It was not, in fact, far from that place, that is, within sight of Dzur Mountain, that Wadre and his band observed the sorceress seated before a small fire. Wadre, on his part, studied her for a moment, then, satisfied, signaled his band forward. Very quickly they had surrounded her, while she sat upon the ground and looked around at them with no trace of fear upon her countenance, but, rather, only what appeared to be mild curiosity.

"I gave you good day, madam," said the bandit. "I am called Wadre."

The woman rose then, and said, "I am Orlaan, and I welcome you to my home."

"Your home?" said Wadre.

"Exactly."

"You live here?"

"I live here."

"Here? In this clearing, where there is no roof, nor even walls?"

"Exactly."

"But, if I may say so, this is hardly a safe place to live, madam."

"Well, but where is a safe place to live in such times as these?"

"What you point out is valid."

"It is kind of you to acknowledge it."

"It is nothing. But still—"

"Yes?"

"It would be good to have shelter, and maybe even concealment."

"Concealment? But, from what might I need concealment?"

"From what? You don't know that there are brigands in these woods?"

"The Trey! Are there?"

"I give you my word on it."

"And have you met some?"

"I have."

"And are they frightening?"

Wadre considered. "Well, I shouldn't like to meet a whole band of them when I was alone."

"Pah. What could they do to me?"

"What could they do? Well, they could rob you!"

"Of what?"

"Of what?"

"Yes, of what could they rob me?"

"Well, of money, for example."

"I have none."

"You have no money?"

"Not so much as a silver orb."

"Then, perhaps, you could be robbed of food?"

"I have none of that, either."

"What do you say? You have no food?"

"None."

"But, if you will permit a question—"

"Oh, ask, by all means."

"Well, how do you live, if you have neither food nor money."

"I use my art to attract game, much as the athyra does in the wild."

"The deuce!"

"It is as I have said. And so—"

"Yes, and so?"

"Well, I have nothing in which a brigand could be interested."

"Oh, as to that, well, I do not deny it. But I must say you interest me."

"I interest you?"

"That is to say, you intrigue me."

"Well, what is intriguing?"

"When you speak of your art, what do you mean?"

"Ah, that. Well, I speak of sorcery."

"Sorcery!"

"Yes, sorcery."

"But there has been no sorcery since the fall of the Empire!"

"Well, that has been true until now."

"Until now?"

"Yes, exactly."

"Now, today, this very hour?"

"No, to be more precise, some hundred and fifty years ago."

"But what happened a hundred and fifty years ago?"

"I lit a fire."

"Well, but, you perceive, I light fires every day."

"Oh, I do not doubt that. But do you light fires using the magical arts? That is, using sorcery?"

"Why, no I do not. And you did?"

"Oh, you perceive, it was only a small fire."

"And then you began to bring animals to you?"

"Yes, exactly."

"And it has been working?"

Orlaan gestured toward the fire, where a norska was slow-cooking over a spit.

"Ah," said Wadre. "You do, in fact, have food."

"Enough for a meal, yes."

Wadre considered all that he had heard, and finally said, "But one thing still puzzles me."

"Well, tell me what it is, and perhaps I will be able to give you such an answer that you will understand."

"Before you succeeded in gaining those magical power of which you speak —"

"Yes, before that?"

"How did you live?"

"Oh, I have a small cache of gold."

"Gold? But you said you had none!"

"I was not, perhaps, entirely truthful."

"I see that you were not."

"Well, but what would you expect me to say when surrounded by brigands about to rob me?"

"I do not deny the extreme justice in what you say, only —"

"Yes?"

"Are you not afraid that we will now rob you?"

Orlaan walked over and carefully removed the norska from over the fire. Holding the spit with her left hand, she made a careless gesture with her right, and, in an instant, the flames leapt up thirty or thirty-five feet. Wadre and the others in his band recoiled. The very top of the flame seemed at first to dance and sway and even lean over, as if to touch first one of the brigands, and then another, all in response to the pointing of the forefinger of Orlaan's right hand, although in fact none of them were actually touched. After a moment, she pointed down, and the flames receded. After giving the norska a slow, careful inspection, Orlaan then put the spit back on the fire, and turned to Wadre.

"No, I am not afraid," she said.

"Just so," said the road agent.

He turned to his lieutenant, Mora, and said, "I am sufficiently convinced. Are you?"

"Entirely," said Mora.

"And the others?"

"I believe I speak for all of them, Captain."

Wadre turned back to Orlaan. "On reflection, we have determined that, in point of fact, we have no business to transact with you. We therefore wish you a good—"

"But," said Orlaan, "it may be that I have business to transact with you."

Wadre shifted uncomfortably in his saddle. "Well, if you have something to say, I give you my word of honor I would never be so lacking in courtesy as to leave without giving you a chance to say it."

"That is good. Then you will listen?"

"I assure you, I will do nothing else while you do me the honor to speak to me."

"That is best. But perhaps you could listen better were my mouth at the same height as your ears."

"There is something in what you tell me. Would you like the use of a horse?"

"Perhaps it would be easier for you to dismount than for me to mount."

"Just as you say," said Wadre, and, endeavoring not to appear nervous, climbed down from the saddle. He turned to the other brigands and said, "Stand easy, my friends. I will have conversation with this lady, and then, well, then we will be on our way. In the meantime, keep a lookout, so that our conversation will not be disturbed."

"That was well done," said Orlaan.

"Do you think so?"

"I am certain of it."

"Then I am satisfied."

"Come, sit next to me."

"Very well, you see that I am sitting."

"And are you listening?"

"With all of my attention."

"Then I will tell you a story."

"I like stories, if they are good ones."

"I think mine is a good one."

"I will listen, and judge."

"I can ask for no more."

"Begin, then."

"Years and years ago, I was in Dragaera City."

"I presume this was before Adron's Disaster?"

"That is natural, as there was no Dragaera City after it."

"That is true."

"As it happens, however, it was only just before it; that is, within minutes of the Disaster itself."

"Then you had a narrow escape?"

"The narrowest."

"Very well. I enjoy hearing about narrow escapes."

"Oh, it was narrow, and not only because of my proximity to the city, but also because I was attacked."

"How, attacked?"

"Viciously."

"By whom?"

"By a set of scoundrels whom I was only barely able to escape, and who, in fact, murdered my father before my eyes."

"The trey! Did you kill them?"

"There were four of them, and only one of me. I was barely able to escape."

"The cowards!"

"Yes, they were certainly cowards."

"Did they die in the city?"

"Not in the least. They are still alive."

"What, to this day?"

"To this day."

"But, do you know where they are?"

"Some of them. I hope to learn about the rest."

"Yes, I understand that."

"And moreover, one of them has a son, and I do know where he is."

"The son?"

"Yes. And from him, I can certainly learn where his father is. And to kill the scoundrel's son seems fitting revenge for the murder of my father."

"Well, I don't say that it isn't."

"So I shall kill the son, and then I shall hunt down and kill the other four."

"I understand."

"Do you like my story?"

"It is full of pathos."

"Well, but there is a reason I told you of it."

"I had suspected this might be the case, madam."

"Your suspicions are well founded."

"Are they? It pleases me to hear you say so, madam, for I take a certain pride in my suspicions."

"Have you, then, any more suspicions?"

"Oh, many. For example, I suspect—"

"Yes, you suspect?"

"I suspect that you wish our aid in hunting down and killing these people."

"There! You see? Once again you have proven yourself clever in the matter of suspicions."

"Then I am right?"

"Entirely. And the proof is, I am about to make you an offer for your help."

"I am always glad to listen to an offer, madam."

"This is it, then. If you give me your loyalty, and aid me in my endeavors, I will see to it that you become both wealthy and powerful."

"Well, I have no objections to wealth and power."

"Do you not? That falls out well, then."

"Yes, that is my opinion."

"Then you accept?"

"I do not say that I decline, and yet—"

"You hesitate?"

"I must consider."

"Oh, I have nothing against considering."

"That is good."

"But tell me what you consider. It is possible I can help in your considerations."

"Well, I am considering how *much* wealth and power we might expect, in comparison to the amount of danger involved."

"You think there will be danger?"

"I would suspect, madam—"

"Ah! You are suspecting again!"

"—that were there no danger, you would need no help."

"I don't deny what you say."

"And then?"

"Should I succeed, I can promise you more wealth than you have dreamed of, and, I think, sufficient power."

"You say, should you succeed."

"Yes."

"And if you fail?"

She shrugged. "Should I fail, I do not think you will be concerned with wealth."

"I understand."

"Have you any more questions?"

"You say that you can find these people?"

"I will find them."

"I do not doubt you."

"Have you any other questions, my good brigand?"

"Only one."

"And that is?"

"Are any of those you seek by any chance the Enchantress of Dzur Mountain?"

"Sethra Lavode? Not the least in the world."

"In that case—"

"Yes? In that case?"

"I agree to your proposal."

"And the rest of your band?"

"They follow me."

"Very well, then. We have an arrangement."

"A mutually beneficial arrangement, I hope."

"Yes, let us hope so."

Chapter the Twenty-First

How Aerich Required a Plan
And Was Confident That Pel
Could Supply One

With these negotiations concluded, we hope the reader will permit us to turn our attention elsewhere; for if the reader has lost track of our old friend Pel, rest assured that the author has not. Indeed, we should long ago have caught up with him had he, in fact, done anything worthy of note; yet, as he had not, we chose not to waste the reader's time by describing his travels until he reached a destination worthy of our observation. That he has now done so will be obvious to the astute reader, wherefore we will endeavor at once to give him the attention he merits.

As we look, then, he is riding through a stone archway which our readers may remember as the entrance to Brachington's Moor, the home of our old friend Aerich. He came, that is, past the tall hedge which surrounded the estate and so onto the grounds, following the curves of the road past the pond and the garden toward the door. On this occasion, Fawnd was informed by one of the staff of the approach of a visitor, and looking out of an upper-story window, recognized him at once, whereupon he lost no time in informing his master. The reader may be good enough to remember that Fawnd was a servant of Aerich who had, one one occasion at least, taken the role of lackey and acquitted himself well enough, and even had the honor to play an important part in helping certain of Khaavren's household to escape Dragaera just before the city erupted into violence and destruction. Since then, age had come upon him, giving him a slight bend in the middle, adding lines to his face, and slowing his movements; yet he remained Aerich's servant, and in this capacity, all unknowing, he had acquired a grace quite rare among Teckla.

Thanks to this most efficient servant, before Pel had so much as dismounted from his horse, there were already stable-boys rushing to hold his stirrup and tend to his mount, and the door to the manor had already opened, and Aerich was standing in the doorway to greet his guest. Unlike Fawnd, Aerich was not in the least bent or weathered by the years; he stood straight and graceful, his dark curls falling over a dressing gown of red silk embroidered with gold thread, and his face, though certainly showing lines of age and care, shone with nobility; to those who saw him for the first time, it was as if one of the ancient warriors from the youth of the Empire and returned and now stood before them: a figure clothed in dignity, calm as Watcher's Lake and wise as a Discreet.

In many ways, we should note, Aerich had been lucky: there were no large cities near him, and so the plagues had all but missed his district, and the duchy of Arylle was not in the path of any invaders, nor was there a great deal of wealth to be gained from it. To be sure, he had been forced to take steps against the growing numbers of brigands, but even in this regard his domain had escaped the worst of the infestations; Arylle was, then, almost an island of civilization in a sea of barbarity, and at the center of that island sat Aerich: vigilant, careful, learned, and dignified; a representative, as it were, of a world long passed away.

Pel smiled warmly upon seeing his old friend—an expression, we should add, to which his countenance was not accustomed. For his part, Aerich came forward to embrace him.

"My dear Galstan!" he said. "What a joy this is!"

"Galstan!" he cried. "Bah, what is this? To you, I am always Pel, I hope."

"Pel it is, then. Come, come inside, my friend. However urgent the business that brought you here, you will have a glass of wine and give me some of your company."

Pel took Aerich's arm and said, "How, you pretend I am here on business?"

Aerich chuckled. "I do not expect the dragon to form an alliance with the dzur, I do not expect the jhereg to pass up untended carrion, and I do not expect my friend Pel to be without plots and conspiracies."

"Oh, my friend—"

"No, no. If you do not wish to tell me, well, I have no need to know. But do not try to convince me that you are paying this visit with nothing in mind but to pass a few pleasant hours or days in the company of an old friend."

Pel chuckled as they crossed the threshold into the manner. "No, you are right, as always, my friend. I am here for a purpose."

"Good. You tell the truth, then. But wine first, and a toast to our absent friends."

"I agree to this plan."

They entered the sitting room, where Fawnd had already pre-pared glasses and a decanter. When they each had a glass, they lifted them, and Aerich said, "To Khaavren and Tazendra."

"To Tazendra and Khaavren," said Pel. "Ah. I perceive you have not lost your taste for the Ailor wine."

Aerich smiled. "For once, you are wrong, my friend."

"Bah! Wrong?"

"This is my own wine we are drinking."

"What? Your own?"

"Yes. Of course, the Master Winemaker I hired is a certain Corniff, who is from —"

"Ailor, of course. Well, I should expect nothing less of you."

Aerich bowed to acknowledge the compliment, and said, "Have you met Khaavren's son?"

"No, I have not had that honor."

"Nor I. Yet I hear that he is a fine boy."

"And I have heard the same."

"Well?"

"Well, the next generation is gathering. You and I seem not to have done our part, my friend."

Aerich chuckled. "That is true; I am unmarried, nor have I any prospects. But what of you?"

Pel shook his head. "I, my friend, am not the problem today."

Aerich gave a small smile and said, "There is, then, a problem?"

"Yes, I'm afraid there is, and it is not a question of joking."

"Well, then let us speak of it. What is this problem?"

"Our friend Khaavren."

"Ah!"

"You say, 'ah.'"

"Well?"

"I know what it means when you say that."

"And so?"

"And so, you knew there was a problem with him?"

"I have suspected it from what our friend omits from his letters."

Pel nodded. "I have just been to visit him."

"And?"

"He is a broken man, Aerich."

The Lyorn shook his head. "It is as I feared."

"We must do something."

Aerich glanced up sharply. "Is that what brings you here?"

"Yes and no, my friend. I have business in this region, it is true, but only the business of passing through it on my way to another place where I am engaged in certain works of charity. It was the thought of Khaavren that led me to stop here."

Aerich nodded. "I believe you, my friend."

"And then? Can you go to him?"

Aerich shook his head. "I had thought about it, and several times I very nearly went, but—"

"Yes? But?"

"I do not believe it would help him."

"How so?"

"To see me, my friend, would remind him of the best times of his life, and how they are gone now. It would drive him deeper, no matter what I said."

Pel sighed. "I am afraid you are right. And yet, we must do something. We cannot leave him in that condition."

"That is true, but what?"

Aerich shook his head. "If I knew, believe me I should have done it already. We need an idea, and our friend with the ideas is no longer with us."

"Perhaps," said Pel, "we should find another Tiassa to inspire us."

"Yes," said Aerich, suddenly struck by an idea. "Perhaps we should."

"Bah. I was jesting, my friend."

"I was not," said the Lyorn.

"What, you think we should find another Tiassa?"

"Yes, of a particular sort."

"I'm afraid that I don't understand."

"Well, then I will explain."

"Do so, I am listening."

Aerich explained while Pel listened carefully. When the Lyorn had finished, he said, "Come, what do you think of my plan?"

"I believe, my friend, that there is some merit in it."

"You think so?"

"Yes, only—"

"Well?"

"How will you convince this Tiassa to do what you wish?"

"In fact, my dear Pel, I have a plan for that, too."

"I should be most happy to hear this plan."

"This is it: I will have you do it."

"How, me?"

"Exactly."

"You pretend that I can convince him?"

"I do not know if you can convince him, Pel, but I am certain you can arrange for him to do as we wish, one way or another. He lives within a day's easy ride, and you always have means of communication at your disposal. I do not know how you will arrange it, but I am certain you can do so."

Pel considered this for some few moments, then said, "My friend, I believe that I have thought of a way."

"That does not astonish me."

"Would you like to hear it?"

"No, I think I would rather not. I have no need, for I have implicit faith in you."

Pel chuckled. "Very well. I will proceed to make the arrangements, and then —"

"Yes?"

"Then I must be about the charity work that brought me to this district."

"I recognize you so well in that, my friend!"

"Well, we are what we are."

"Your argument, my dear Galstan, is irrefutable."

"Bah. How often must I remind you that to you, I am always Pel?"

"I have not forgotten; I merely remind you that I know well that there are more sides to you than one."

"My friend," said Pel, "do I perceive a hint of criticism?"

Aerich shook his head. "Not the least in the world. You cannot be other than what you are, and I love you for all our shared pain and glories and would not change you if I could. But you must forgive me, as well, if I cannot help but let you know I am not deceived."

The Yendi smiled. "You can no more help being you than I can help being me."

"Then let us drink, this time, to ourselves."

"I agree."

This plan was no sooner agreed to than acted upon. Pel, after draining his glass, said, "Farewell, then, for this time, my friend. I must go see about a fire."

"And may it burn well and brightly," said Aerich.

Pel left the next morning, after a warm embrace from Aerich which he returned in full measure, after which he was helped onto his horse, bowed once more, and turned his horse's head away from

Brachington's Moor. As he passed through the archway, he murmured under his breath the words "It is good, and rare, to have friends." He traveled for several hours, letting his horse, which was a brown and white mare of the Cramerie breed, which Aerich had always favored for its endurance and its noble appearance, proceed at a walk. After several hours had elapsed, he murmured under his breath the words "I hope it won't be necessary to kill too many innocent people."

The reader may be interested to learn that these two statements, separated by hours and miles, were, in fact, the product of one continuous chain of thought. On the chance that the reader might be curious about how such apparently disparate thoughts could lead one to the other, we will take it upon ourselves to intrude on the thoughts of the Yendi in order to satisfy this curiosity.

To begin, then, Pel was reflecting not only on all the memories he had shared with Aerich, but also with Khaavren, whom they intended to help if they could manage to do so, which led to his first remark. From there, he considered Tazendra, whom he had always especially loved, perhaps because her simplicity formed such a compliment to his own complexity. As the miles passed, he recalled many of the incidents that formed the association of which he was a part, and, moreover, he considered the ways of friendship, formed in furnaces of shared trials, and, though this thought made him happy, he knew with a certain sorrow, that, while the friendship remained, the youth that surrounded and enriched it was gone forever.

"But then," he reflected, "so many things are gone. 'Cha,' as my old friend Khaavren would say. I have seen what an innkeeper must do in order to procure ice for patrons who wish their drinks cold. And I have passed rivers, once the domain of those giant man-made fish called 'barges,' now almost empty, as transportation is broken down in every phase. Speaking of rivers, half of the bridges have collapsed, and the others are no longer safe. The landlords cannot trade, one with the other, and, in the same way, the merchants cannot safely acquire those things the peasants need. And, while I am not of a disposition to be ordinarily moved by the suffering of people I don't know—indeed, I have always found it easy to maintain equilibrium in the face of others' misfortunes—still, I have seen too much, too many since the collapse of the Empire, to say nothing of the Plague, which seems to re-emerge each time we think we have forgotten about it. And, how can it not? Such a mundane matter as the disposal of refuse, which was solved tens of millennia ago, is now a problem that each village must solve anew, and without sorcery, and without the means to easily communicate its solution to others. And then, the arts of the physicker relied so heavily upon sorcery that what was once the most easily cured illness is now fatal as often as not.

"But then," he continued, "that is why we were engaged in rebuilding the Empire. Or, at least, that is a good reason to do so, even if it is not my own reason, which has far more to do with my desire to hold an important post within it. And why should I not? Before Adron's spell got out of control, I was well on my way to becoming a Discreet, from which position I would have access to sufficient secret knowledge to achieve whatever goals I might set myself. Since that was denied to me, well, then I must find access to this power another way, and what better way than to be instrumental in the forming of the Empire that is to be? Perhaps I shall even be mentioned in history, which would be amusing. It may be that this Empire will be built upon the bodies of many of those it is to serve. But, one way or another, if I am to achieve my ambitions, and, incidentally, to help those unfortunates who now suffer from want of what the Empire provided, it must be done. I hope it won't be necessary to kill too many innocent people."

It was at just this point that he recognized the village he was looking for, a small village, like thousands of others in the region, yet in this village, he had been informed by his spies, there was a small enclave of Easterners who, like the Valabars of Adrilankha, had been permitted to dwell there from time immemorial.

He rode his horse slowly through the muddy main street of the village, until he came to a small brick house at the end where, after tethering his horse, he clapped. The door opened, and a tiny, frail-looking woman opened the door. Pel had no way of guessing her age, yet her hair was still mostly dark, and her features not exceptionally wrinkled. She looked up at him fearfully. He said, "You are a friend of the man who knits rocks?"

Her eyes widened, and she seemed confused, but after a moment she said, "He does not knit, he crochets."

"Well, that is good enough."

"Please come in," she said.

Pel did so, not bothering to remove his hat. Without preamble he said, "I require an enchantment."

"Would you like to sit down?"

"No."

"Would you care for refreshment?"

"No."

"Well then, what sort of enchantment do you require?"

"The subtlest kind."

"Oh?"

"A man must have an idea planted in his head."

"That is easily done, especially if the idea is not too far out of the ordinary."

"Oh, this idea is very ordinary for him; indeed, he is always looking for it."

"Very well. It can be done."

Pel removed a gold coin and placed it carefully on the table. The Easterner, who had neither given her name nor asked for Pel's, looked at it and shrugged. "You must," she explained, "give me the name of the man who is to have this idea, and you must also tell me this idea he is to have, in as much detail as possible."

"I will do so. I have the name here, and I will explain it to you fully, with exact detail."

"And you will do right to do so."

"It is most important," said Pel, "that he not only have this idea, but that he not have any idea it was given to him from the outside."

"Of course," said the Easterner. "He will believe the idea comes from himself."

Pel nodded. "That is good," he said. "I depend on you."

"You may," said the Easterner.

Chapter the Twenty-Second

How Ibronka, Only Daughter of
Her Highness Sennya,
Came to Begin an Adventure

Some three hundred and ten or or three hundred and twenty leagues southwest of Mount Kâna there is a region called Harata, which name comes from "Hvaer-itha," which, in the ancient language still preserved by the House of the Dragon, means "several hills," or something very like it. It should not, we should add, be confused with the name of the town of Hartre, to the south, which derives from "Hara-itha," meaning "several winds."

Harata is, indeed, a place of rolling hills, in addition to a large number of small ponds, gentle meadows, and, here and there, small wooded areas, the whole of which is populated mostly by Dzur and Lyorn, as well as the occasional Tiassa and, of course, the Teckla; but more than all of this, it is populated by sheep.

It is well known that most of the Empire's wool came from this district. In the days of the Empire, the wool had, most often, been transported to the Elbow River, from which point it could be loaded on ships, which might journey to Hartre, or to Elde Island, or to barges that would make their way along the Grand Canal from Candletown to Dragaera City. From this, the reader might deduce that the Elbow River was vital to the entire district; we can only say that such a deduction would be entirely correct.

The Elbow River was named by a certain Tiassa who, seeing it from atop Blackbird Mountain, fancied that it resembled a bent arm as its westerly course made an abrupt southward turn as it was joined by streams running from the mountain to which we have just had the honor to refer. As for Blackbird Mountain itself, there is little to say about it, except that it does not, in fact, contain an abundance of blackbirds; rather it was named for Lord Blackbird, of the House of the Hawk, who first discovered it, and then named it after himself. He also named the stream that flows down from it, the river that the stream becomes and which flows into the Elbow River just at the elbow, and the surrounding district.

The region was first settled in the Chreotha Reign of the Eighth Cycle, and, when it was raised to a duchy in the Issola Reign of the Ninth Cycle, the first Duke, who happened to be a Dzurlord, naturally took for his title Duke of Blackbird. It is equally natural that Lady Blackbird of the House of the Hawk protested, and what followed was a battle in the justice chambers of the Iorich. It happened that Lady Blackbird retained as an advocate the famous Sir Neevya, whereas the Duke of Blackbird enlisted the aid of the brilliant Lady Jutatil, with the result that the struggle before the Justicers lasted some seven hundred years, and set several precedents which are still referred to often in disputes of this kind. In the end a compromise was reached: Lady Blackbird was given sole possession of her title, and the name of the duchy was changed from Blackbird to Blackbirdriver, which is why the single largest political division within the geographical region of Harata takes its name from what is, in fact, little more than a stream, and one that passes through the duchy for only a score or so of miles.

The reader should understand that for this entire region the Interregnum, with its breakdown of trade, was nothing short of catastrophic; yet it should be said that within the county of Larkspur, where the Duchess of Blackbirdriver had her seat, matters were not as bad as they were in many other counties, this because of certain lowlands at the base of the mountain which, combined with the extreme heat of the summer and the moderation of the winter, permitted the growing of fieldrice, which, along with mutton, at least kept starvation at bay, this being more than could be said for much of what had been the Empire.

The manor of Larkspur was a long, low structure, and had been built after the old one had failed to survive the tremors that accompanied Adron's Disaster. The new house, in addition to being low, was built solidly of stones that had been brought up the Elbow River at great expense and difficulty because of the breakdown of transportation to which we have already alluded. It was, in general, a comfortable manor, though less imposing, as it were, than might be expected of a Dzurlord, and an Heir at that. But after her experiences during the last years before the Interregnum—experiences which, we hope, the reader will permit us to skip over for now—Sennya had determined that, instead of the ostentation usual for a princess of her House, she would instead cause to be built a home in which she could raise her daughter—the daughter who was now, to her, the only reason for living.

This daughter, to whom we have now made mention on more than one occasion, had not yet reached her ninetieth year. She was distinguished by the narrow eyes and pointed ears of her House; but nature had also graced her with thick, dark hair that she permitted to grow so long that it fell to her waist. Other than this, she was small, but, rather than being frail, gave the impression of strength and sinew contained in a package from which it might explode at any moment; and, although she was too young for those marks of character to be revealed upon her features, one would, upon seeing her, nevertheless gain the impression of a latent ferocity, overlaid with a ready smile and a mind that was sharper than, perhaps, one might usually expect in a Dzurlord. Her aspect was of one who smiled often and laughed much; and, in the opinion, at any rate, of her mother, she required only opportunity to make a name for herself that would bring honor to her clan and her House; indeed, her cradle song had been Beed'n's "Dance of the Six Battle Flags," which did little to put her to sleep, but, at least in Sennya's opinion, instilled in her a good martial spirit and a disposition toward victory and triumph.

As we look upon her, that is, at the very instant when our history requires we devote a certain amount of attention to her actions, we see her seated by the window of her room. We must add that this is a place she often sat, staring out that window. Of the many beautiful and scenic wonders of this world upon which the gods have been pleased to set us, it must be admitted that the view from Ibronka's window was not the most spectacular. Indeed, other than very plain, unadorned fields of grass upon which sheep were wont to wander, the only feature she could see were a pair of grey rocks, each about six or seven meters in height, that had been left there after the construction of the manor and had never been removed. Now, Ibronka, as a child with an unusually fertile imagination for a Dzurlord, had made believe that these rocks were people, the one named Herger and the other named Berger; and she had, in fact, built up in her mind an entire history for these imaginary people, and in this way she had pleasantly spent many hours. The reader will be aware of just how unusual this sort of mental activity is on the part of a Dzurlord; yet it is an indelible part of Ibronka's character, and therefore we feel obligated to bring it to the reader's attention.

On this occasion, while she was, indeed, looking out the window, her thoughts did not, in fact, involve her stone friends, but, rather, a living human being—to be precise, one who, mounted upon an old, broken-down horse of a shade of white in which an odd hint of red was mixed, she had seen cross upon the road that was clearly visible from her window. As the rider approached the manor, the bend in the road took him from her view, because her room, being in the back, didn't look out upon the path to the front of the manor, which was, evidently, the destination of the rider.

We would be remiss in our duty as historian if we failed to observe that at such times, during the Interregnum, any visitor was a cause for excitement; this visitor, complete with a horse—or, more precisely, a nag—that walked with its head nearly as low as its knees, was no exception. Ibronka, who was in a state of undress hardly suitable for meeting a stranger of any sort, hastened to dress herself without even waiting for her maid, after which she rushed through the manor until she came to the front door, which she flung open, only to discover to her astonishment, not to mention dismay, that there was no one there. Indeed, not only was there no one there, but there was nothing to be seen of either horse or rider as she looked out to the road. It was, she reflected, quite a pretty mystery: how could horse and rider vanish in such a short span of time in this age when, as she had been assured, there was little sorcery to be found, and that of the meanest, most paltry sort?

It is probable that she would have spent several minutes, perhaps even hours, considering this matter had she not been interrupted by the maid, who approached her with these words: "My lady, you have a visitor."

Ibronka turned and said, "I beg your pardon, Clari"—Clari was, the reader should understand, the maid's name—"but I fail to comprehend how I could have a visitor when it is clear that there is no one here at all. And yet, I fail to see how there could not be a visitor when I saw with these eyes a man approaching upon a horse, and saw it so clearly, in fact, that I could even describe the horse upon which he rode. You perceive, Clari, that I am confused."

"Well, my lady, I believe I can remove your confusion with two words."

"How, can you? I assure you, I should be ever so grateful if you could."

"Well, I will do so then."

"I am listening, Clari, but I beg you, speak at once, for I believe I will die if I do not understand soon."

"This is it, then: He is at the servants' door."

"How, the servants' door?"

"Exactly."

"But then, is he a Teckla?"

"Precisely, my lady. He is a Teckla."

"But then, why would a Teckla wish to see me?"

"He pretends, my lady, that he is a messenger."

"A messenger?"

"Yes, my lady."

"Then he has a message?"

"Your Ladyship has understood me exactly."

"Well, but who is this message from?"

"Oh, as to that —"

"Well?"

"I assure Your Ladyship, I have not the least idea in the world."

"Then," said Ibronka, suppressing her disappointment at not having a visitor after all, but hoping, at least, that the message was from some dashing prince, or perhaps kidnappers holding someone for ransom, or something interesting, "let the messenger be brought to me, and I, well, I will listen to his message."

"As Your Ladyship wishes."

Clari went off to fetch the messenger, and Ibronka, remembering as best she could how her mother would accept messages, set herself down in her mother's favorite chair, folded her hands in her lap, and, when the maid returned with the Teckla, nodded to him imperiously and said, "Well, my man? What is this famous message?"

The Teckla, a sandy-haired man of perhaps nine hundred years, bowed to her and said, "My lady, it is from your mother, and she says —"

"From my mother?"

"Yes, my lady."

"Very well, then. What does she say?"

"My lady, she says you are to pack a valise and prepare for a journey."

"How, a journey?" cried Ibronka, her heart suddenly beating faster.

The Teckla bowed his assent.

"But, a journey to where? And when am I to leave? And how am I to travel?"

"Oh, as to that —"

"Yes?"

"I assure Your Ladyship, I have not the least idea in the world."

"What is this? You don't know?"

"I am as ignorant as an Easterner, I promise you."

"But then, how am I to travel if I am unaware of these things?"

"If Your Ladyship would like my opinion—"

"Oh, if you have anything to say, well, I should like to hear it."

"This is it, then. I believe it possible that some of this might be contained in the letter I have been instructed to give you."

"You have a letter?"

"I have," said the Teckla, touching the pouch he wore over his shoulder and which, presumably, contained the letter.

"A letter from my mother?"

"Exactly."

"Well then, give it to me."

"I will do so at once, if you wish."

"Yes, at once!"

The Teckla bowed, opened his pouch, and removed a rolled-up piece of parchment, which was both sealed and tied up with a red ribbon. He handed this over with a bow, and Ibronka fairly snatched it from his hand, pulled off the ribbon, and broke the seal. As we have made it our custom, whenever possible, to give the text of such messages, we will take it upon ourselves to do so here: "My dear daughter," it read, "it has become necessary for you to travel. I wish you to take what you will require for a journey of some duration, and to wait for a caravan which will be passing through Lorimel in one or two days, from His Venerance the Duke of Kâna, who has agreed to permit you to travel with them. You must stay with this caravan until it reaches the coast, which will be near Hartre, after which you must search for another caravan and continue eastward until you come to the coastal city of Adrilankha. There, you must find my kinsman, Lord Shellar, Baron of Alban, who has been informed of your arrival, and will give you a place to live until such a time as I have more to communicate to you."

We cannot, however much we might wish to, make the reader fully understand the effect this letter had upon Ibronka; yet the reader should recall that the young girl had been born after Adron's Disaster, and that she had, during her short life, been raised with the expectation that there would be no opportunity for the sort of adventures of which the young Dzurlord dreams and upon which the older Dzurlord thrives. It is odd to consider that, to the reader of our own happy day, the years of the Interregnum appears rife with adventure; indeed, it seems to us now that it is the very end of the Interregnum that has put an end to the dangers and romance upon which dreams of action and excitement are fed; yet it is undeniable that to those who lived at the time, it seemed that it was the Empire itself that provided the structure and backdrop against which glory could be won, and that the dangers of the time were, though certainly threatening to life and limb, of a poor and miserable sort, there being no Imperium before which to stand and receive the rewards of gallantry. In other words, the dangers of the time were considered to be mundane and uninteresting dangers, which did nothing except to force one to stay at home to avoid an ignominious death which would contribute nothing to honor or prestige.

For Ibronka, then, to be given not only permission, but, indeed, orders to proceed out from her home and into the world was to tell her that, perhaps, she had been wrong, and that all hope of adventure was not lost to the world.

Some few moments passed in which Ibronka did nothing more than to give way to these happy reflections, at the end of which time she told the messenger, "Tell my mother I understand these instructions and will follow them to the letter. And you, Clari, go have the stable-boy prepare Tricky for a journey, and do you then pack my valise, for I must make my way to Lorimel and there await the caravan of which my mother speaks in this letter. Apropos, polish my boots as well."

"How, polish your boots, my lady?"

"Yes, exactly."

"Before beginning a journey?"

"Well, in all the stories I have read, the lackey was ordered to polish his master's boots before beginning an adventure, and so that is what we will do."

"As my lady wishes," said Clari, keeping her opinions to herself, as a good servant ought.

The Teckla, whose name, alas, does not appear in any record of the period, took his departure while Clari rushed off without a word to do as she was bidden. Ibronka, once alone, went to her wardrobe and found clothing that befit a Dzurlord setting out on her first adventure, and her sword along with a harness and scabbard, a travel cloak of black wool, and a sort of cap with a feather, after which she studied herself in the full-length glass in her room.

"Well, Ibronka," she told herself, "you are on your way, and, it is only fair to say it, you are looking quite well indeed." Still watching the glass, she flung her hair over her shoulder and set her hand upon the hilt of her sword in a gesture she had once seen her mother make when confronted with a neighbor using what Sennya called "inappropriate diction" regarding the straying of certain sheep. Ibronka decided she liked the gesture and would therefore keep it, and, this decision made, she turned away from the glass and went to see if Clari were ready with her valise.

In the event, Clari was more than ready. Not only was the valise packed, but the maid had changed into garb suitable for travel, and carried a small satchel which, like the valise, had hooks by which it could be attached to a saddle.

"What is this?" said Ibronka. "You are dressed for traveling, Clari."

"Yes, my lady. I am dressed for traveling."

"Well, but I wish to know *why* you are dressed for traveling."

"Why? Because I expect to travel, my lady."

"You? Travel? Where?"

"With Your Ladyship," said Clari simply.

"How, you pretend you will travel with me?"

"I confess, my lady, that was my thought."

"Your thought was that, when I left, you would come along?"

"Yes, my lady."

"But why?"

"Your Ladyship does the me the honor to ask why I expected to accompany you on your journey?"

"Yes, that is what I wish to know."

"Well, to serve Your Ladyship, as I've done these last sixty years."

"Well, but you are a maid, not a lackey!"

"And then?"

"Yet you pretend you can serve me while I travel?"

"If Your Ladyship pleases, I should like nothing better than to find out."

"But . . . what would Her Highness my mother say?"

"What would she say? Why, I believe Her Highness would be pleased."

"Feathers! You think so?"

"Nearly."

Ibronka considered this novel idea, then said, "I admit that I should be glad to see a familiar face on my travels, and, moreover, it would be good to have help from time to time in, well, I don't know, whatever one does between adventures." The reader should understand that Ibronka's comprehension of what an adventure consisted of was only of the vaguest, most incomplete variety; yet, in her defense, we must add that she was well aware of this, and didn't let it deter her in the least from setting forth.

The good Teckla, Clari, bowed at Ibronka's words, taking them as a sign that she could go; and she said, "I will go and saddle a pony, then. I was considering the little sorrel, Kork."

Ibronka nodded her agreement and said, "Well then, pick up my valise, and let us be on our way."

"How, without a meal first, my lady? Consider: It is some three or four hours to Lorimel, and there is nowhere to eat on the way. Moreover, it seems I ought to prepare sustenance for us on the journey, in case the caravan's victuals are not to our standards."

Ibronka, though anxious to be on the road, could not find any fault with this plan, and so she grudgingly said, "Very well, but I beg you to be quick."

"I will be like lightning, my lady."

"That is good, Clari, for if you are slow, I will be like thunder."

Clari smiled at the witticism her mistress did her the honor to share, and rushed off to complete the preparations for the journey.

Chapter the Twenty-Third

How Ibronka Met Röaana, and They Discussed Who Should Be Permitted to Fight Over Whom

W hile the worthy Clari prepares for the journey, we hope the reader will permit us to say two words about this maid who has so unexpectedly become part of our history. She had been born some hundred and fifty or hundred and sixty years before, far to the south, in what had, before Adron's Disaster, been the port city of Hartre, which we have already mentioned, but was now a tiny fishing village, and one, moreover, where it was becoming more difficult every year to fish effectively, owing to the gradual decay of the fine fishing vessels that had been built before the Disaster, and lack of technique in building new ones. When these factors combined to make life untenable for Clari's family, they—by which we mean the twenty-year-old Clari, her mother, her father, two older brothers, and one younger sister—all moved north in the hopes of finding some means of livelihood. By the time they arrived in the duchy of Blackbirdriver, Clari was thirty-five, and the family had been reduced to her mother and one older brother, all of whom were discovered by Sennya fishing the Blackbird River. The means of discovery had, in fact, been the aroma of cooking slipper fish, which Clari's mother had prepared according to the Southern style: filleting them, cutting them into strips, rolling them in flour, and sauteeing them in butter with the juice of tomatoes, salt, black pepper, and a few fresh greenbreads.

Sennya, upon tasting the fish, to which she had a right as they had been caught within her domain, had at once hired the woman as her cook, and the boy as stable-boy.

Some years later, Clari's remaining brother had succumbed to the same outbreak of plague that had taken Sennya's husband, and, some years after that, Clari had been given the responsibilities of maid, which also implied caring for the young Ibronka, although this had never been made explicit.

Having now given her history, we will, with the reader's permission, quickly sketch her appearance. She had, to begin with, the round face of the House of the Teckla; in her case in very pleasing form, with bright, intelligent eyes that were neither too round nor too widely spaced, and a high forehead for a Teckla. And, while she did not have the hands or feet of an aristocrat, she was, nevertheless, a not unattractive girl for one of her type.

In a very short time, the pony had been saddled, and Clari had prepared provisions—which provisioning, having brought her to the kitchens, had provided an opportunity for her to exchange farewell tears with her mother in a scene over which we will draw a veil out of respect for the sentiments with which a Teckla is as well supplied as anyone else.

These matters being attended to, they took their mounts—Clari directly into the saddle, Ibronka with the aid of a mounting post—and set off. It was only when they had followed the road around the manor and were passing the two stones, Herger and Berger, that Ibronka thought to wave farewell to her home, aware in the sense that the young are—that is, with her head, if not her heart—that she might never again see the place where she was raised. Then she turned her attention eagerly forward.

"My lady," said Clari.

Ibronka turned her head. "Well?"

"I beg leave to observe that, at this pace, you will kill your horse before we have made it halfway to Lorimel, not to mention Adrilankha which is, I believe, rather further."

Ibronka sighed and reined in her horse, after which they resumed the journey at a more reasonable rate, which brought them several hours later into Lorimel, a village that boasted three or four houses, one of them public, a market, a posting house, and, most important, a location along the Great Northwestern Road that had once run, unbroken, some six hundred leagues from the Kanefthali Mountains all the way to Adrilankha, and still ran unbroken for portions of this distance, although many of the bridges were now gone, and very little of the stone paving was still intact, so that it was difficult to make the journey along much of it during the rainy season.

Ibronka knew the public house, from having visited it in the company of her mother once or twice, but this was the first time she had gone there with the intention of letting a room—indeed, this would be the first night she had spent away from home, with the only exceptions being certain occasions she had spent on the mountain under the sky. The host recognized her at once, and insisted upon giving her the best room he boasted, which was, we are sorry to admit, nothing to boast of. Nevertheless, the excitement of the moment more than made up for damp walls, poor straw wrapped in moth-eaten mattress covers, and a certain amount of unwelcome insect life. In a word, Ibronka was enchanted. Clari, though not excited the way her mistress was, nevertheless accepted it with only an unexpressed wish that the time would be short before the caravan arrived. Having thus looked over the sleeping chamber, Ibronka hastened down to the jug-room, because she was well aware that adventures often began with chance meetings in the jug-room of a public house, and she was, as the reader has no doubt realized, more than just a little anxious to begin her adventure.

In this she was disappointed; the jug-room was entirely empty with the exception of a Teckla who was softly snoring in the corner, and two tradesmen who appeared to be Chreotha who were having a quiet discussion in another corner. Ibronka procured for herself a glass of wine, and, by the time she had finished it, had come to the conclusion that nothing of interest was going to happen, and she repaired to such comforts as her bed could supply, joining the worthy Clari, who was already sound asleep on the floor. We would not be faithful to our duty as historian if we did not point out that, once she was in bed, the combination of excitement and the discomfort of the bed prevented her from falling asleep for some few hours, yet eventually sleep claimed her, and, once asleep, she slept soundly and deeply until the next morning when she was awakened by a loud clamor that, as far as she could tell, came from the street directly below her window.

She sprang out of bed in an instant and, looking out of the window, saw at once that the clamor was caused by nothing less than the ringing of swords, as two men, both of whom appeared to be Dragonlords, circled each other and enthusiastically endeavored to dismember each other with swords of very good length, while a crowd, who also appeared to be Dragonlords, stood as near to the conflict as safety and the narrowness of the street permitted.

"Is it a duel?" said Clari, who had, evidently, been awakened as well.

"I can't tell," said Ibronka over her shoulder. "It is either a duel or simply a brawl."

"There is little enough difference," said the philosophical Teckla.

"Bah. Help me to dress; I must go down there."

"Very well," said Clari, who knew better than to attempt to dissuade the young Dzurlord.

Ibronka was quickly dressed and, still buckling on her weapon, went rushing down the stairs, but, alas, it was already too late: by the time she emerged from the front door of the hostelry, the steel no longer sang, and, indeed, she could see that one of the Dragonlords was stretched out full length upon the ground, while the other maintained a guard position, watching to be sure he didn't rise again.

"Bother," said Ibronka under her breath.

She turned to the man next to her, a Dragonlord with a dark complexion and very long arms, and said, "Tell me, my lord, what were they fighting about?"

The man shrugged his shoulders without looking at her and said, "A girl, of course. Why else should soldiers fight each other instead of a common enemy?"

"How, over a girl?"

The soldier grunted and glanced at her, and then looked at her again, this time more carefully, which raised upon Ibronka's countenance a certain flush, and sent her mind working in directions that, hitherto, it had never gone—that is, it had never occurred to Ibronka that girls might be fought over; indeed, she had considered that she might someday win a boy by laying the other pretenders to his affections upon the ground (by preference, having defeated all of them at once), but the idea of men fighting over her had never entered her remotest dreams. Yet, now that it did, well, it seemed, while not as pleasing as doing the fighting, to imply a compliment that, she decided, would not be entirely unwelcome.

"Well?" she said. "Who is this famous girl?"

The soldier with whom she was speaking grunted once more and made a gesture with his head. Ibronka, looking in the indicated direction, saw a slight girl with a pretty face dressed in the colors of the House of the Tiassa, and with an expression on her countenance of profound distress, even anguish.

"Well," she thought to herself, "if this girl is worth fighting over I must meet her." Having made this decision, she at once acted upon it by making her way past several soldiers who were now beginning to cluster around the victor to offer congratulations and the vanquished to offer assistance. Ibronka placed herself in front of the girl, who seemed to be her own age, and sketched a perfunctory bow, saying, "How are you called?"

The Tiassa hardly appeared to notice her—her eyes remained fixed upon the Dragonlord who still lay facedown, unmoving, and from beneath whom blood could now be seen to be flowing. Still, the girl was able to murmur, "Röaana of Three Seasons."

"Well then, Röaana of Three Seasons, I am Ibronka of Blackbird-river, and I wish to know if it is true that it was over you they were fighting."

The Tiassa now looked at her for the first time, and Ibronka could see that her eyes were very wide, as she—that is to say, Röaana—gave a quick nod, then turned her attention back to the fallen soldier.

"But," said Ibronka, "how did it happen?"

Röaana looked at her once more, then said, "You wish to know that?"

"I think I do. You perceive, I asked."

"Well, that is true."

"And then?"

"A soldier made certain suggestions that another found offensive, and so they had a discussion, the results of which you can even now observe."

"And did the insulter triumph, or the defender?"

"The defender."

"That is but just. And yet—"

"Yes? And yet?"

"You seem profoundly affected."

"Madam, I have never seen a man kill another."

"How, never?"

"Never. Have you?"

"Well," said Ibronka, "now that you mention it, I have not. Indeed, I didn't see it this time for I arrived too late. And yet, I do not believe it would affect me the way it has affected you."

"That is possible," said Röaana. "You are a Dzurlord, whereas you perceive I am a Tiassa."

"Yes, your observation is full of justice. But tell me, what is it like to have men fight over you?"

"I don't care for it," said the Tiassa promptly.

Ibronka nodded. "I had wondered. I believed it was better to do the fighting."

"I think that it would be."

At around this time, a Dragonlord with the markings of an officer upon her collar came riding up on a black horse, and, dismounting with practiced ease, said, "Some of you tell me what has occurred here."

The events were quickly explained to the officer, who shot poor Röaana an annoyed look, but then nodded and said, "How is Jorem?"

"I do not believe he will live out the hour, madam," said one of the soldiers.

The officer scowled. "Very well. Sergeant, see to his body."

"Yes, madam," said another soldier. "And as to submitting his name—"

"I will see to that," she snapped. She looked around, until her eyes came to rest upon Ibronka, whereupon she said, "Who are you?"

Ibronka, stung by the imperious tone of the officer's voice, said, "I? I am Ibronka of Blackbirdriver, and my mother is—"

"Princess Sennya," interrupted the officer. "Yes, I know of her, and we have been expecting you. Are you ready?"

In addition to being annoyed, Ibronka became confused. "How, ready?"

"Yes. We have been informed by His Venerance the Duke of Kâna that you are, by the wishes of Her Highness, to travel with us."

"And yet, madam," said Ibronka, "I had thought I was to await a caravan."

"Well, and that is what we are. The caravan is behind us, and we are part of its protection."

"Ah," said the Dzurlord. "I did not know there was to be protection. You perceive, I do not feel I require it."

A look of something like amusement passed over the officer's countenance. "Perhaps you do not," she said, "but, in any case, well, we are here, and if you are to travel with the caravan, we will necessarily be there as well."

Ibronka nodded and said, "Then in just a moment I will have my horse saddled and my servant ready."

"Very well," said the officer, and sighed, muttering under her breath about now having two of them to contend with.

Some few minutes later Ibronka, well seated upon Tricky with her packed valise hanging from her saddle and Clari riding by her left hand, found herself near the rear of the soldiers and toward the head of the caravan. She at once brought herself up next to Röaana, and said, "Come, what did the officer mean by saying she had to contend with two now?"

The Tiassa said, "You don't know?"

"Not the least in the world, I give you my word."

"Well, the officer pretends that I am pretty."

"Very well, and then?"

"So that now, she must contend with two pretty girls who are not under her command. She believes this will create more trouble for her of, well, of the sort that happened in that town through which we have lately passed."

"Lorimel."

"Yes."

"Well, I understand, and I believe I have been given a compliment, after a fashion."

"Yes, and do you like it?"

"You wish to know if I like it? Well, I believe I will have words with that officer before this journey is over."

"How, words?"

"Yes, the sort of words those two soldiers had over you."

"Please, I beg you not to remind me of that."

Ibronka shrugged. "Very well, then. Though I wonder why the presence of pretty boys does not have the same effect as the presence of pretty girls. They are, after all, equally in demand."

"Oh, it does, sometimes," said the Tiassa. "But consider—"

"Well?"

"While it would be pleasant to fight over a boy, would you have any interest in a boy who would enjoy being fought over?"

"Do you know, I had not considered it in that light."

"Nor had I, until just now."

"I should imagine boys wouldn't be interested in a girl who enjoys being fought over, either," said Ibronka after giving the matter some consideration.

"I think you may be right."

"Röaana, I will tell you a thing."

"Yes, Ibronka? What is it you wish to tell me?"

"Just this. Upon first seeing you, and seeing that you had been fought over, well, I thought I should dislike you. And yet—"

"Well, and yet?"

"I seem to feel a certain sympathy with you."

"I confess, I feel much the same toward you, Ibronka, if only because we are both in similar positions."

"Yes, that is true. Then, shall we be friends?"

"If you wish. Here is my hand."

"And here is mine."

"It is settled, then, we shall be friends, at least for so long as we travel together, and after that, who knows?"

"Apropos, whither are you bound?"

"Adrilankha. And you?"

"I? Feathers of the Phoenix! I am bound for adventure!"

Chapter the Twenty-Fourth

How the Mysterious Zerika
Is At Last Introduced;
Which Introduction Is Followed
By Much Discussion and
A Certain Amount of Planning

As daylight brightened the eastern face of Dzur Mountain, Piro awoke with the events of the last several days filling his thoughts, leaving him with some anticipation and a great deal of confusion. After spending some time attempting to understand all that he had learned, he came to the conclusion that it would be better to break his fast first and think later. This decision made, he rose, dressed, and made his way down the hall where, after a certain number of false turns and retracing of his steps, he came at last to the parlor where he had first met the Enchantress. Before he actually entered the room, however, he heard voices, and, being possessed of a great deal of that curiosity which is the birthright of any Tiassa, he paused for a moment to listen.

One voice he instantly recognized as belonging to the Teckla Mica, Tazendra's servant.

"You see this end," Mica was saying, "can be used to block or parry an opponent's attack; even a heavy sword cannot penetrate the wood nor break it—you see marks where some have tried. Of course, to defend against a rapier I prefer to turn it around, holding it in this fashion, because my enemy's blade can then be caught between the legs, after which, by the smallest twist, my opponent will be disarmed, or else his blade will snap; and, moreover, I am then able to instantly counter from that position simply by thrusting forward, especially into the face of my enemy."

"Well, I perceive there is a great deal to this art."

"Oh, there is, I assure you."

"And I freely confess that I admire your courage, which seems to be as great as that of a Dzurlord."

"Well, I admit that, serving my mistress, there are occasions when a good stock of courage is as necessary as knowing how to lace up a doublet."

"Yes, I understand that."

"And—but bide, I hear someone coming. I am certain of it, for you perceive, in the sorts of adventures upon which my mistress takes me, sometimes a sharp pair of ears is all that stands between you and a quick, unceremonious demise, and so I have trained my ears to respond to the least noise."

Of course, the sound he heard was Piro, who, having heard enough, had resumed his course toward the room in which Mica was holding forth. As he entered, Mica, who had been holding a bar-stool, set it down, rose to his feet, and bowed deeply, as did his companion, who was none other than Lar.

"What is this?" said Piro. "Are you instructing him?"

"Yes, my lord," said Mica. "That is, I was explaining to him the use of the bar-stool, a weapon with which I am not unacquainted."

"Yes, indeed," said Piro. "I know of the bar-stool from having heard my father speak of it."

Mica positively beamed at this evidence of Khaavren's memory and of his own exploits, and turned an eye upon Lar as if to say, "Here is the proof of all that I have told you."

"And is that," continued Piro, pointing to the object in question, "the very bar-stool of which I have heard such stories?"

"Alas, no," said Mica. "This is a replacement recently acquired."

"Ah," said the Viscount. "But I hope, at least, that your previous weapon was given an honorable retirement?"

"In a fashion," said the Teckla. "It was used to supply a replacement for the lower part of my left leg, which, alas, was lost in the service of my mistress."

"And of my father, as I recall the story," said Piro.

Mica bowed his acknowledgment.

Piro then addressed Lar, saying, "You should listen to all this worthy man tells you, Lar, for there is no doubt that my father and his friends should never have survived all of their adventures if they had not been served by clever and courageous lackeys such as our good Mica here."

Lar bowed, and vowed to himself that he would find an opportunity to display his courage before Piro at the first instant he could find to do so; Mica, at the same time, decided that he would permit himself to be burned alive for the young Tiassa as soon as it could be arranged. The quick-thinking Mica realized, however, that there was unlikely to be a chance for such an activity in the next few hours, whereas it was possible that he would be able to serve him in other ways, wherefore he said, "Would my lord care for klava this morning, as well as, perhaps, something with more substance?"

"Klava would make me the happiest of men, I assure you."

"Very well, then. Come along, Lar, and I will show you how to brew klava for the young gentleman."

"Ah," said Lar. "As far as klava goes, I well know how to brew it. Indeed, it is possible that I could show you one or two tricks regarding the art of which you are unaware."

"You think so? Well, come, let us see, then."

And the two Teckla left the room arm-in-arm, leaving an amused Piro to trudge down to the spring-room to wash his face, use his teeth-stick, and take care of certain other duties which everyone, from noble to common, must perform each day. It is just these sorts of matters which are customarily omitted from romances, and they are omitted for the reason that, quite simply, if everyone does them, there is little to be learned from even the most careful study, an opinion to which we fully subscribe. Indeed, we have only included the above passing reference to "morning matters" for the following reasons: first, to demonstrate our awareness that such matters exist and are performed by all human beings; next, to establish that it is not our fear of such discussions that prevents more reference to them, but, rather, our dispassionate judgment that nothing is to be gained by such references; and last, so that, with the above reasons in mind, we need never return to these issues again.

On the subject of returning, to which we just made reference in the previous sentence, young Piro returned to the sitting room to find a cup of perfectly prepared klava awaiting him, with not only heavy cream and honey, as he preferred it, but also a dash of vanilla, which he especially loved. In addition to the klava, there was as well a basket of steaming muffins, along with jars of butter, honey, and various sorts of preserves set out before him, leaving only the difficulty of deciding which of the delicacies to try, and which he would have to, with regret, leave unsampled, as his appetite, though as large as that of a youth should be, was not unlimited.

As he ate, he was joined by Tazendra herself, who called loudly for Mica, who had disappeared into the kitchens while Piro ate. The worthy servant emerged and quickly provided his mistress with klava and biscuits, upon which she gorged herself in such good style that for some time there was no conversation.

When Piro felt himself satisfied, he stretched out and gave a sigh. "Well," he remarked, "I believe that, with one more cup of klava, I shall be ready to restore the Empire."

"That is well," said Tazendra between mouthfuls. "As for me, well, I require a few more biscuits and, after that, by the Horse, I think I will be ready to assist you."

"Then, my good Dzur, after you have finished, we should set off and do so."

"How, do you think so?" said Tazendra seriously.

Piro, who had been attempting a jest, became confused when Tazendra failed to comprehend, and so he cleared his throat and said, "Well, perhaps we should await the others."

Tazendra nodded and said, "Yes, that would be best, I think, because in my opinion, well, Zerika would not wish to be left out."

"Ah, in that circumstance, we should wait by all means."

"I am glad that you think so."

Lar, proving his worth as a servant, appeared to see if anything was needed just as Piro finished his klava. Lar vanished and, for reasons of which the historian must confess his ignorance, Mica appeared a minute later with the requested drink, prepared exactly as Piro preferred it. It was soon after this that the Enchantress herself appeared. Piro and Tazendra rose and bowed to her. She acknowledged the salute and said, "Where is Kytraan?"

"Sleeping late," said Piro.

"Well, it is time he should be woken, there are plans to make today."

"Ah! Plans!" said Tazendra.

"Exactly."

Tukko appeared at the door and looked at Sethra, who gave a gesture with her eyes and head, to which Tukko responded with a nod and left again. A short time later, Kytraan joined them at exactly the instant that Lar appeared with his klava. The Dragonlord moaned softly, sipped his klava, and closed his eyes. Then he opened them, cleared his throat, and solemnly announced, "Good morning."

The others wished him a pleasant morning in turn and then Sethra rose and said, "Await me here, if you please," after which she made her way out of the room.

"Well," said Kytraan. "What are we doing today?"

"Making plans," said Tazendra.

Kytraan shrugged. "Well," he said.

"I wonder how soon we will leave," said Piro.

"Leave?" said Kytraan. "Pah, we just got here."

"That is true," said the Tiassa. "I was merely wondering."

"I have been known to wonder," said Tazendra.

There being nothing to say to this, they all fell silent and concentrated on klava and, in some cases, muffins, until the Enchantress returned. When she did, she paused in the doorway and said, "My friends, there is someone I wish you to meet."

Kytraan, Tazendra, and Piro all stood and waited. Sethra stepped aside and said, "Here is the Lady Zerika, of the House of the Phoenix."

As the named Zerika entered the room, two of the three bowed. That is to say, Tazendra gave her a bow as befit a Princess of the House of the Phoenix; Kytraan presented a courtesy as befit one who might well be the next Emperor; Piro began to bow, stopped, raised his head, and, with his mouth hanging open, cried out, "Zivra!"

The Phoenix in question gave Piro a shy smile and said, "Well."

The author hopes that he has, on this occasion, caught the reader off guard; that is, the notion of the reader being as astonished as, in fact, was Piro, would indicate that the narrative we have the honor of placing before the reader is, in at least this way, an accurate reflection of the events of history in their unfolding. We concede, however, that it is very possible that the reader has been in advance of us, and has known all along who was concealed behind the name Zerika. If this is the case, we must nevertheless insist that, if the reader knew who was about to appear under the mantle of the Phoenix Heir, then at least Piro did not.

In response to the exchange we have just mentioned, Tazendra turned to him and said, "How, do you know the lady?"

"And by a different name?" added Kytraan.

"The Horse! I nearly think I do," said Piro. "We grew up together, and were friends for most of my life, which life has, perhaps, been short by the standards of history, but it is the only life I have known."

"Well," said Kytraan, "this at least explains why you, of all people, should be summoned by this mysterious Phoenix."

"Yes, that is solved, but many other things are not."

Zivra—or, as we should properly call her, Zerika—said, "It is true. But come, embrace me, my friend. I have been anxious to greet you for some time, but have been kept busy by a stern taskmaster." These words were accompanied by a glace at the Enchantress, who acknowledged them by bowing her head.

Piro came forward and embraced his friend, saying, "Forgive my astonishment, but—you! A Phoenix! And a Princess!"

"Well," said Zerika, "I tell you plainly that it astonishes me as well. Indeed, I must remind myself of it each day, and still sometimes wonder if this last week has been a dream from which I might wake at any time."

"But tell me, if you would, how this happened? You perceive, the last time we spoke, there was some worry that you were to be sent off to be married."

"And so I was, my dear friend," said Zerika. "But married, not to a man, but rather to the Orb—if Fortune so favors us that we are able to retrieve it."

"Oh, as to Fortune, well, I have no opinion about her whims. But my friend Kytraan and I will do all we can, and I should be astonished if the Lady Tazendra were to do less. And yet, I should still like to know—"

"And you shall, my friend. Come, let us sit together, as we did in the old days with our other friends, and I will explain my history to you."

"That is exactly what I wish," said Piro, sitting down and giving her his full attention. The others also sat down, except for Sethra, who excused herself and promised to return in a short time. As Zerika sat, Tukko appeared beside her with a steaming mug of klava, after which the servant disappeared.

"To begin then," said Zerika.

"Yes, yes," said Piro. "By all means, begin!"

"The story is, my friend Piro, that it was your father who convinced my father to send my mother out of Dragaera City, and she only barely escaped the Disaster. As it was, she hardly survived my birth, although whether it was childbirth that took her, or plague, or brigands, or some other cause entirely, I don't know. But I know that Sethra Lavode was aware of me, and, although she will say nothing, I suspect it was by her hand that I eventually came to my foster parents in Adrilankha."

"Do they know who you are?"

"No," said Zerika. "Sethra tells me they are entirely ignorant, knowing only that I am an orphan, and that they were to surrender me to the Enchantress should she ever call for me."

"Very well, they were ignorant. What next?"

"Why, I was raised as their child until Sethra Lavode deemed the a place where you will find a road running through the jungle until you arrive at the market town of Wilder, and that will put you on the edge of the Pushta, where horses can travel in any direction without regard to roads."

"Well, and our direction?" said Tazendra.

"North and little east. You may meet a tribe of cat-centaurs near there, but they are rarely hostile unless given a reason to be."

"We will give them no reason," said Zerika.

"That is best," said the Enchantress. "You continue northward, then, until you get to the mountains, here."

Tazendra started to speak, but then shrugged. Sethra said, "Yes, I know, I am on the table once more. But this time, you perceive, I have another map."

"Ah!" said Tazendra. "Another map!"

"Exactly."

She rolled up the first map, and opened another, which was smaller and appeared to be older, but upon which the details were still clear and easily understood.

"As you can see," she said, "you will be skirting the Eastern Mountains, but not entering them. You must be especially careful in through here, for brigands in those mountains are particularly fierce."

"We will be careful," said Kytraan.

Tazendra shrugged, as if to say that the notion of confronting brigands did not bring thoughts of *care* to her mind.

"Here," continued the Enchantress, "you will once more pick up the Eastern River, and you will remain with it upon your left hand until here, where you will cross it once more."

"But, how will we cross it?" said Zerika.

"Oh, as to that, well, there was once a bridge, but it may now be gone."

"And then?"

"Well, in that case, you may need to find boats, or to fashion rafts. But you will then be near the lower slopes of Mount Klassor, which is heavily forested, and so you will have no trouble finding wood."

"Apropos," said Kytraan, "we ought to bring axes."

"Very well," said Piro. "I agree with the need for axes."

"What next?" said Zerika.

In answer, the Enchantress rolled up the map, and unrolled another, the largest of the three.

"Here," she said, "is where you yet again cross the Eastern River.

It is, you perceive, only a score of miles from there until you reach the feet of the Ash Mountains. You continue, then, until you reach this point, where you will ascend until you meet the Blood River, which you follow into Greymist Valley, and, thus, to Deathgate Falls."

"Well, and after that?" said Piro, who wished to speak to show that these names did not frighten him.

"After that, well, Zerika will descend and, we hope, emerge again with the Orb. You will then return to Dzur Mountain."

The Enchantress straightened her back and said, "That, then, is the route I propose. Do any of you have any questions?"

Piro cleared his throat and said, "Well, there is, in fact, one question that occurred to me while you were speaking."

"If you ask it, well, I will attempt to answer."

"This, then, is my question: In describing the route we are to take, you seemed to use the word *you* a great deal."

"Ah, you noticed that?"

"I more than noticed it, I remarked upon it."

"Do you know," said Tazendra, "I had observed this circumstance as well."

"But then," said the Enchantress, "that is merely an observation. Is there, then, a question as well?"

"Oh, certainly. And a most significant question at that."

"Well then, ask it."

"I am about to do so."

"Very well."

"Does this use of *you* indicate that you will not be accompanying us on our journey?"

"Yes, exactly," said the Enchantress. "You have understood precisely what it means."

"It is remarkable," observed Tazendra, "how much can be communicated by so small a word."

"Well, but," said Piro. "You perceive, your presence would be useful during our journey."

"Oh, I understand that," said Sethra.

"And then?"

"Alas, it is not possible."

"Not possible?"

"Or, rather, not advisable."

"And yet—"

"If you succeed—that is, if Zerika manages to acquire the Orb—there will be certain forces who will learn of it at once. Indeed, it has been only with complex and subtle illusions—and some amount of luck—that they have been held away to this point, and when the Orb is gone, these illusions will necessarily go with it. From Dzur Mountain, I may be able to thwart them."

"Ah," said Piro, who had the feeling that he would not be able to understand a more comprehensive explanation, and accordingly didn't ask for one.

"'May'?" said Zerika. "You say you *may* be able to thwart them?"

"Yes, exactly," said the Enchantress.

"Well, but—"

"Yes?"

"What if you fail?"

"Oh, if I fail—"

"Yes?"

"Then, no doubt, they will destroy you, take the Orb, and subjugate our world."

"And yet—"

"It is nothing to worry about, my dear Phoenix."

"How, nothing to worry about?"

"Not in the least."

"Well, but why should I not worry?"

"For the best reason in the world, my dear: because nothing can be done about it."

"Well, that is a reason, at all events. And yet—"

"Well?"

"I am not reassured."

The Enchantress shrugged.

"But after all," said Tazendra carelessly, "they can only kill you once or twice."

Zerika turned on her quickly, saying, "Madam, I beg you to believe that it is not my life that concerns me; thanks to Fortune I was not born entirely deficient in courage. What concerns me is my mission. You perceive, to me has been given the task of restoring the Empire—the *Empire*, do you understand me, madam? I think the task is of sufficient importance to be worth a few questions to see that it does not fail. If you disagree, well, say so plainly, and then we will consider what to do about it."

Tazendra, for her part, looked at the Phoenix with something like a glint in her eye, and said, "I hope to the gods I was not questioning your courage; do you be as kind in not questioning my loyalty. Therefore, if we have now reached an understanding, I beg you not to stare at me with those twin fires that are blazing behind your eyes, but show me a little kindness as befits one preparing to lay down her life for you as well as for the cause to which we are all dedicated."

Zerika rose and bowed to Tazendra, saying, "I'm sorry if I have misunderstood you, and, well, if I haven't, I cannot stay angry with you in any case; you know how grateful I am to have your strong arm for support."

"But then," said Kytraan, "if the Enchantress—" here he bowed to the lady thus indicated, "—is not to accompany us, well, perhaps it would be good to know who is."

Sethra Lavode nodded. "That is a good question," she said.

"Do you think so?" said Kytraan. "Well, then I am pleased."

"Yes," said the Enchantress. "It is so good a question, in fact, that I will answer it."

"Ah. Well, if you will answer it, I will listen, and I think my friends here will listen as well."

"I hope so. Here it is, then: In addition to Zerika, we will have you, Kytraan, and you, Piro, and Tazendra."

"Well, yes," said Piro. "But is that all?"

"By no means. You will also have your lackeys."

"Well, but no one else?"

The Enchantress shrugged and said, "If a Dragon, a Dzur, and a Tiassa cannot deliver a Phoenix to Deathgate Falls, then I fail to see how any others could help."

Kytraan said, "You believe, then, that more would not help?"

"More would be an army, and, as such, would call attention to itself."

"Attention?" said Zerika.

"There are a score of warlords who dream of re-creating the Empire with themselves as Emperor. Some of them would yield to Zerika, upon learning of her ancestry and goals. But others, perhaps, would not."

Zerika nodded and said, "Very well, I understand."

"Then," said Tazendra, "we have our troop, and we have our destination. What else remains?"

"Well, we must pick an auspicious time for a departure," said Sethra the Younger, who, according to her custom, had said little.

"That is always good when beginning a journey," agreed Tazendra.

"Well," continued Sethra, "I have done so. I cast the cards this morning."

"And?"

"The day after to-morrow, at the stroke of noon."

Zerika shrugged. "That is later than I should have liked to set out, but if is auspicious, then, well, it cannot harm us to have as much of Fortune working with us as we can."

"That is my opinion as well," said Tazendra.

"Then," said Kytraan, "we at least have plenty of time to prepare what we will need for our journey."

"And to rest before we begin," said Piro.

"And to study the maps," said Zerika.

"And to sharpen our swords," said Tazendra, "because I should be more than a little astonished if we do not need them."

How Tevna the Pyrologist
Came to Play a Small
Yet Crucial Rôle In History

It is well known that moments of historical drama cast people as well as situations into a new light—that is, the place of men in relation to circumstances is highlighted, changed, and, in general, clarified. This is true in general—that is, for the great masses of people; and also in particular—that is, for any individual upon whom we might choose to focus our attention. Many who seem important are shown, at such times, to be insignificant; while others, hitherto undistinguished, are pushed forward onto the stage of history to be tested in the most public of lights, where flaws and virtues are magnified as if seen through one of Baroness Holdra's glasses. Indeed, one might say that a crisis of historical magnitude is the best way known to determine the true character of those who wish to claim a place in the memory of the race. We will mention in passing that it is exactly for this reason that the historian as well as the writer of romance will devote his energies to situations of high drama and to characters who face mortal danger: while some critics decry the love of "adventure" on the part of the writer and of the reading public, yet at no other time can one see so clearly into the soul of a man or of historic circumstance; and if an historian or an artist cannot illuminate the soul, for what purpose does he wield a pen?

What then lies at the soul of those who deserve the attention of the historian? What can we find at the heart of those moments in history when accumulated tension meets intolerable pressure? To answer these question, we direct the reader's attention to the brave Khaavren, whom we left some time ago saying farewell to his old friend Pel, after already saying farewell to his only son, sent off to do that which the brave Tiassa was unable anymore to do himself.

Several days after Pel had left, Khaavren was watching the sea from the terrace on the south side of Whitecrest Manor—the sight of the ocean-sea, with her infinite variety of rhythmical, rolling, crashing sameness being always conducive to such moods as melancholia tinged with pride, and such being the flavor of Khaavren's recent thoughts. In the midst of these thoughts, which we hope the reader will permit us to leave with no more invasion than those generalities we have already perpetrated, Khaavren was interrupted by the cook, who was also doing service as doorman, wine servant, and several other domestic occupations.

"My lord?" began the servant hesitantly.

Khaavren slowly turned his head, showing no signs of having been startled. "What is it, then?" he said.

"My lord, there is someone who inquires if you are at home."

"Someone?" said Khaavren. "You perceive that to say 'someone' is to supply little information. So little, in fact, that I am unable to determine whether I wish you admit the inquirer into my presence, or, instead, to require you to tell one of those polite social lies—which you, as a Teckla, are permitted to tell—that will preserve my solitude." We would be remiss in our duty as historian if we failed to mention that Khaavren's tone of voice indicated a certain lassitude, as if he did not care very much what sort of answer he might receive to his question.

"And then, my lord, you wish me to provide more information about the caller?"

"You have divined my meaning exactly."

"I will tell you more, then."

"And this very moment, I hope."

"Yes, my lord, this very moment."

"Well, begin then."

"He wears clothing all of grey."

"How, grey?"

"Yes, my lord, as I have had the honor to tell you."

"He is, then, a Jhereg?"

"As to that—"

"Well?"

"There is a patch upon the right shoulder of his singlet which would indicate he is a Tiassa."

"Ah! Of my own House?"

"Exactly, my lord. And, if I may be permitted to express an opinion based on my own judgment—"

"Well?"

"His features seem to be those of a Tiassa as well."

"Indeed. But then, why would he wear grey?"

"His profession, my lord."

"His profession?"

"Exactly."

"And what profession is that?"

"He says that he is a pyrologist."

"Ah! Then he wears grey because that is the appropriate garb of a pyrologist."

"So he gave me to understand, my lord."

"Well then, all is answered."

"I am glad that it is, my lord."

Khaavren continued, "All, that is, except for one question."

"My lord, there is yet another question?"

"Only one."

"My lord, if you would do me the honor to ask it, I promise to answer if I can."

"Very well, here is the question: What is a pyrologist?"

"Oh, as to that . . ."

"Yes, as to that?"

"I must claim ignorance, my lord."

"I see," said Khaavren. "Well, then, has this pyrologist a name?"

"Oh, indeed he has, and a good one at that, my lord. He is called Tevna."

"Well, that seems to be a name less obscure, at any rate, than his occupation. And this Tevna, then, desires an audience with me?"

"With you, yes, or with the Countess."

"Ah. With either of us? Then why, pray, have you come to me, when you know that I have little interest in affairs of the county, and you must have known, or deduced, that such was his concern?"

"My lord, I beg you to believe that I went first to the Countess."

"And?"

"She is indisposed, my lord; or she was when I spoke to her, although in the time I have had the honor to be engaging in this conversation with Your Lordship, she may have become disposed again, and I should be happy to discover this, if you wish."

Khaavren sighed. "Let this Tevna be brought to me, then, and bring us refreshment as well, if you would. Something white, and not too strong. And some biscuits."

"I will see to it at once, my lord."

The cook left upon this errand, and returned shortly to announce, "Sir Tevna of Split Canyon."

Khaavren rose, bowed, and took a good look at the stranger—for if Khaavren's ardor had dampened and faded with the passing of the years, be assured that the sight with which he had been accustomed to assess anyone and everyone who might be received by the Emperor was as sharp and true as ever. He saw, then, a man of nearly two thousand years, with the narrow eyes and thin lips typical of a Tiassa, but dressed, as the cook had told him, all in grey; and dressed, moreover, in a certain dignity that nearly reminded Khaavren of his friend Aerich. It was this dignity, as much as the requirements of courtesy, that prompted Khaavren to rise with as much alacrity as he could muster in his depressed physical and spiritual condition, and, having risen, to perform a deep bow, after which he indicated a chair in which his guest might sit.

"Greetings, kinsman," he said. "Please be welcome at Whitecrest. Your family, if I heard correctly, comes from Split Canyon? I, myself, am from Castle Rock in the Sorannah, near the headwaters of the Yendi River."

"Ah, indeed? You must then be of the family of Shallowbanks."

"Shallowbanks, yes, and then Deguin."

"Ah, well, you perceive my father counts the Deguin clan among his cousins, and one of my mother's great uncles married a Sendu, who, as I am certain you are aware, are offsprings of the Shallowbanks."

"Yes, that is true. And you may also note that the Countess Whitecrest, who is my wife and who you will, no doubt, have the honor to meet in a short time, takes her given name, Daro, from a lesser daughter of a cousin of the Amzel clan, who are, if I am not in error, close relations to you, the first lord of Split Canyon having been a brother to the first Lady Amzel, they both being offspring of the Duchess of Fourpeaks."

"Why yes, that is true."

"Then, in consideration of how closely we are related, you are doubly welcome, and I hope you will enjoy your visit. Apropos—"

"Yes, kinsman?"

"Tell me, if you will, to what I owe the pleasure and honor of your visit."

Tevna raised his glass (which had arrived during the courtesies, but we chose to refrain from mentioning this fact because we did not wish to delay the reader's discovery of the information revealed in the conversation occurring at that time) and said, "I shall be glad to tell you the reason for my visit, but I must warn you first that my arrival is not occasioned by anything of a glad or frolicsome nature."

"It is, then, serious business?"

"I regret to say that it is."

"Well, so much the more, then, is my desire to make you comfortable, and thus relieve, in any way I can, the unpleasantness that must attend to serious matters."

"Believe me, the desire is appreciated."

"Tell me, then, what brings you to Whitecrest?"

"The plague," said Tevna.

Khaavren carefully set his wine glass down on the table near his right elbow. From this same table he drew a linen napkin, which he used to wipe his lips, after which he set the napkin down again and repeated, "The Plague."

Tevna nodded solemnly.

"You perceive," said Khaavren, "that when we speak of the Plague, there is no question of joking."

"I am glad that you understand that."

"I more than understand it, I have seen it: the swollen tongues, the listlessness in the eyes, the constant perspiration; the redness of the skin. I have seen it, for who could live in a large city in these times and not have seen it? Yet I had hoped it had passed its way forty years ago and would not trouble us again."

"It may be that it will not, and yet—"

"Well? And yet?"

"There have been signs."

"What signs?"

"The very ones you have described so well, only—"

"Yes?"

"Only they have not yet come to pass."

"You must explain," said Khaavren, "how it is that you have seen signs which have not yet occurred; you perceive that I find this unusual. In fact, more than unusual: strange."

"I can answer that in the simplest way, my dear kinsman."

"Well?"

"Here is the answer: I am prescient."

"How, prescient?"

"Exactly."

"Then, you can see the future?"

"At times."

"At what times?"

"On some of the occasions when I perform my trade. On this

occasion, I saw a vision of a place in Adrilankha, where a man had died showing certain symptoms of the plague."

"You see these visions when you practice your trade? That is, on the occasions when you act as a pyrologist?"

"You have understood me exactly."

"It may seem so, good Tevna, only—"

"Yes?"

"Only I have never until today had the honor to hear the word 'pyrologist,' so in consequence—"

"Yes? In consequence?"

"In consequence, I have no idea what it means."

"How, you don't know what 'pyrologist' means?"

"I have not the least idea in the world, I assure you."

"And so you don't know what a pyrologist does?"

"I am as ignorant as an Easterner."

"Well, but would you like me to tell you?"

"I would like nothing better."

"Shall I do so now?"

"Why, I believe that it is an hour since I asked for anything else."

"Here is the answer then: A pyrologist is one who burns the bodies of the dead."

"You burn the bodies of the dead?"

Tevna bowed his assent.

"But, forgive me, kinsman, why would one do that?"

"It has been found that the Plague will often travel from the dead body of one who fell victim to it to the living bodies of those around him. However, if the body is quickly burned, along with clothing, bedclothes, and any artifacts that were in close proximity—"

"Yes, if this is done?"

"Then the body can no longer spread the Plague. And, moreover—"

"Yes?"

"Sometimes I see visions in the flames."

"Are they true visions?"

Tevna did not answer this question at once; instead he stared at the floor, but it seemed to Khaavren that, instead of looking at the floor, he was seeing something far away. At last he looked up and said, "Sometimes they are misleading. But I once chose to believe the visions were not true."

"And?"

"And I did not go to the fishing village to which my vision had appointed me. There is no longer a village there; every merchant, peasant, midwife, and child died of the Plague."

Khaavren studied his guest for some few moments; then he said simply, "I was responsible for the safety of the last Emperor, he who was assassinated while I guarded him."

"Ah," said Tevna. "Then you understand."

"I believe that I do," said Khaavren.

"And you must, then, understand as well why, ever since that day—"

"Yes, ever since that day?"

"Ever since that day I have redoubled my efforts to be where I could be of use; to perform the task appointed for me, and to do everything within my power to prevent this from happening again. It is, you perceive, an atonement of sorts. No doubt you feel something similar."

"I might, only—"

"Yes?"

"There is no other Emperor."

"Ah. I had not thought of that circumstance."

"You perceive, it adds a certain difficulty."

"Well, yes," said the pyrologist.

Khaavren then cleared his throat and said, "But come, kinsman, you must have some reason for having come here; tell me what it is."

"But, your pardon, I believe I have done so."

"Not at all."

"Not at all?"

"Indeed not."

"And yet—"

"You have explained why you are in Adrilankha, but not why you have come, in particular, to Whitecrest Manor."

"Oh, as to that—"

"Well?"

"I can explain instantly."

"Well, if you do so, I will be grateful."

"Here it is, then."

"I am listening."

"I must have certain permissions of the Count in order to perform my function, as well as certain funds to carry out my work, and, in addition, not to be indelicate, the fee I require to maintain my existence."

"Ah! Well, now I understand."

"And then?"

"I will send for my lady wife, who is Countess of Whitecrest, and she will, I am certain, arrange all the details to your satisfaction."

As good as his word, Khaavren had Daro sent for, and she, now being disposed, soon arrived on the terrace, whereupon Khaavren kissed her hand and made the introductions proper among distant relations, in which he revealed to her the various levels of kinship among the three of them, after which he explained Tevna's mission. Upon Daro's learning this, her face became grave, and she said, "Well, certainly I will do whatever I can; I have seen what the Plague can do."

"Believe me, Countess," said Tevna, "I am grateful, and those whose lives you may save will be even more grateful." He drew from within his blouse several scrolls bound with blue silk ribbon. Then, after calling for and being supplied with quill, ink, blotter, and sand, undid the ribbon and selected some of the documents, and quickly wrote on them with a practiced hand, after which he presented them to Daro for her signature.

She studied these documents for some few moments. Tevna cleared his throat and said, "In effect, Countess, this gives to me some of your legal powers for the next month—in particular those powers regarding disposition of bodies. In addition, it says that you will pay fees and expenses, should my function be required."

She nodded, read the papers again, and then signed her name, after which she affixed her seal and lineage block; then she solemnly returned them to Tevna.

"And so," she said, "you will now go out into the city, and, with these papers giving you the right, claim the bodies of the dead from their loved ones, and burn them."

"I will look at these bodies, and determine if there is danger; only if there is will I commit the dead to the flame that cleans."

"Very well," she said. "I understand. It is sad, but necessary."

"That is exactly right," said Tevna. "To preserve the living, we use flame to purify the dead."

"And," said Daro, "it is right that we do so."

Tevna nodded, and said, "I should set about my task at once."

"On the contrary," said Daro, "I believe you ought to stay."

"How, you think so?"

"Yes, I am convinced of it."

"And yet—"

"Well?"

"In my work, well, minutes can, you perceive, make all the difference."

"Then perhaps you could return this evening."

"I should be glad to, Countess."

"We expect you, then, to dine with."

"I will be honored."

With this, the pyrologist took his leave.

Tevna, for his part, went out to the city, where he was pleased to discover that what he had seen as an of outbreak of the Plague was, in point of fact, nothing more than the death of a man who, due to intemperate consumption of wine, combined with an argument with a neighbor about who ought to be responsible for certain leaves that had blown from her tree to his yard, had died of apoplexy, with a bright red hue on his features. If Tevna's vision was influenced, more or less indirectly, by witchcraft, and by a certain Yendi of our acquaintance, well, he never learned of it. He returned to Whitecrest Manor with good news, some hours later.

From this, the reader may infer that, in fact, Tevna came to Adrilankha and left without performing his function—that is, without kindling a flame. We should say that this is true only if the reader were to make the mistake of thinking only in the most literal terms—a practice perhaps proper when reading law, but always suspect when reading history, and no less than foolish when reading romance. In point of fact, he did perform his function, though not in the manner that, before arriving in Adrilankha, he would have anticipated performing it.

The cook had prepared dinner for three, and in honor of the occasion, had procured three fat hens, which she prepared in a sauce of wine and white mushrooms, accompanied by certain vegetables quickly fried and seasoned with chives and other herbs. In short, it was a far better meal than Tevna had enjoyed in some few years, and he was not stinting in his praise of the food and the hospitality. When at last it was over, the three of them made their way into the parlor, where Cook served them candied cherries and an orange liqueur.

"My dear husband," remarked Daro as they sat, "do you not perceive a bit of a chill in the room?"

"In truth I do, my good wife," said Khaavren. "And that is not surprising, for you perceive there is an open window looking out on the ocean, and, as it is now quite dark, well, the night breeze from the sea is nearly always a chilly one, albeit one with a pleasant and refreshing smell, of which I have grown quite fond over the years."

"Well, but as we have a guest, we must not allow him to catch a chill."

"That is true, and yet you see we have logs laid for a fire; it requires but a moment's work to start the fire, and we shall then be warm."

"Then let us start it—ah, but wait. Perhaps our guest would care to do the honor of starting the fire?"

Tevna bowed. "I should be very happy to, Countess. Indeed, I should say that nothing could please me more than to visit this lovely city and to find no need to start any fire save this one."

The conversation during dinner had avoided any references to Tevna's work, but Tevna now having introduced the subject, Khaavren said, "Permit me, my dear kinsman, to say how happy we are to learn that, at least for this time, we have escaped a reappearance of the Plague."

Tevna quickly and efficiently ignited the fire, and with a few practiced breaths, made sure it was burning satisfactorily; after which he returned to his chair, brushed off his hands, and nodded to Khaavren. "It is a strange occupation I have, because I am never so happy as when I learn that I needn't practice it."

"Well, I understand that," said Khaavren. "Indeed, when I was Captain of His Majesty's guard, I was happiest when a watch would pass without the need for me to do anything at all."

At this, Daro smiled gently. "I think, my lord husband, that what you have said is not entirely accurate."

"You think it is not, my lady wife?"

"That is my opinion."

"Well, let us see, then. Why do you think so?"

"Because I have had the honor to see you at such times, and I have also seen you when you were in great danger, and in the midst of adventure."

"Well, and then?"

"It seemed to me that you were happiest when in danger."

"Cha! You think so?"

"I more than think so, my lord, I am convinced of it."

"And yet, it seems to me that I have no memory of being happy at such times."

"You do not? Think back to when the Reavers landed upon our shore, and you were everywhere at once, preparing the defenses, placing reserves, arranging signals."

"Well, I remember."

"I remember as well, my lord husband. I remember how the light seemed to shine from your face at such times, as if you were fully alive, and living each moment."

"Well, that is true."

"And then?"

"There may be something in what you say."

Daro smiled.

"But," added Khaavren, "it matters little now, wouldn't you say?"

"You think it matters little?" said the Countess.

"You disagree?"

"I nearly think I do."

"Well, and how does it matter?"

"In this way: I believe there are serious matters afoot."

"Serious matters?"

"Well, was not our son sent for?"

"That is undeniable."

"Well, I believe it is a portent."

"It is possible you are right."

"I am convinced of it."

"And then?"

"If there are serious matters afoot, then you must be involved in them."

Khaavren shook his head. "No, my dear Countess, I am afraid that my time for being involved in serious matters is long past."

"Ah, you think so!"

"I am certain of it."

Daro didn't answer him; she knew that further argument from her would do no good. Therefore, she did the one thing she could do: she gave an eloquent look to Tevna, the pyrologist. Tevna, for his part, saw at once that he was being looked at, and, moreover, understood that this glance was significant. To Tevna's credit, this glance, along with the conversation of the previous night, were sufficient for him to understand, at once, what was being asked of him.

"Well now," said Tevna, turning his eyes from the Countess and looking, not at the Count, but rather at the fire. He then seemed to address the fire, rather than Khaavren, as he said, "I hate to dispute with you, my dear kinsman, but I am not entirely certain that what you have said is correct."

"How, you think I have erred in some way?"

Tevna now looked away from the fire, as if he had seen what it had to show him, and turned to the Count, saying, "That is, there may be matters that you have not yet considered."

"Well, that is possible, because one cannot consider everything; the mind is unable to grasp everything."

"That is certainly true," said Tevna. "And so you will listen to what I have to say?"

"Of a certainty I will, for two reasons: In the first place, because what you say makes sense; and, in the second, because you are both a guest and a kinsman, and therefore I owe you the courtesy of listening to you in any case."

"Well, then, here is what I have to say."

"I assure you, you have my entire attention."

Tevna started to speak, then hesitated.

"Come, kinsman," said Khaavren. "Say what you wish."

"Well, but I'm afraid I may be overstepping the bounds of courtesy."

Khaavren shrugged. "Nevertheless, I wish to hear it."

"Very well, then: I tell you that you are in pain."

"In pain?"

"Yes, my dear host. Your soul has been hurt from what you perceive as a failure, and this causes you discomfort. I know this pain, because it is a twin of my own."

"I beg your pardon, but, even if what you say is true—and I don't deny it—I fail to see how this relates to our conversation."

"You do not?"

"Not in the least, I assure you."

"Well, I will explain it."

"Very well, I will continue to listen while you do so."

"Here it is, then: There is one thing that pain, whether of the body or the soul, always does."

"And that is?"

"It draws the sufferer's attention inward."

"You think so?"

"Believe me, Count; in my work, I have seen many people in pain, and the one thing they have in common is that it is very difficult for them to consider what is going on around them, because pain in the body or suffering in the soul invariably pulls the mind to itself; it is when we are not in pain that we are able to see clearly outside of ourselves."

Khaavren considered this carefully; Daro, we should add,

remained utterly silent, but listened to Tevna with her whole attention. At length, Khaavren said, "Well, you may be right."

"I am convinced that I am. And, if I am right—"

"Well, if you are?"

"Then you must permit me to continue."

"Very well, continue then."

"Here, then, is the rest: Because you are in pain, you are unable to look clearly at all that occurs around you, and, because of this, you have missed a vital fact."

"Ah! I have missed a fact?"

"I believe so."

"And a vital fact?"

"Exactly."

"Well, what is this vital fact that I have missed?"

"You wish me to tell you?"

"I should like nothing better."

"Here it is, then: The events that are happening in the world, if your wife the Countess is correct, are bigger than you."

"Well, but I do not disagree with that."

"You do not?"

"Not at all."

"But, you perceive, if they are bigger than you, than, my dear kinsman, your own pain, and your own desires, are suddenly less important than they were."

"How, less important?"

"Indeed. They matter to you, and those who love you, but go no further than that. You have been asking what you could do in the great events that are now stirring, and have found that you could do nothing. But that is because your suffering has caused you to phrase the question in the wrong way."

"I have phrased the question wrongly?"

"That is my opinion."

"By asking what I could do, I have asked the wrong question?"

"Entirely."

"But then, will you tell me what I ought to have asked?"

"I will do so this very instant, if you wish."

"I am most anxious to hear it."

"Then I will tell you."

"And you will be right to do so."

"Here it is then: Instead of asking what you could do, you ought to have been asking what needs to be done."

Khaavren considered this for a moment, then said, "The difference, you perceive, is very subtle."

"Perhaps it is subtle, but I believe it is important."

"You think so?"

"More than important, it is vital."

"You believe, then, that were I to look at matters differently, I would reach a different conclusion?"

"Well, but is that not often the case? Consider a man at some distance holding a sword. When looked at one way, you might perceive a sword, when looked at another way, you might see only a thin line, or perhaps not even that."

"Well, you are right about that."

"And yet, it remains a sword."

"The Horse! You are right again!"

"I am glad we agree, my dear kinsman."

"But what conclusion do you pretend I would reach, were I to see matters differently?"

"Oh, as to that —"

"Well?"

"I cannot say."

"Ah! That is too bad!"

"And yet —"

"Well?"

"I suspect —"

"You have, then a suspicion?"

"Exactly. I have a suspicion."

"Well?"

"I suspect that you would cease worrying about your infirmities, and, instead, you would set out to do what must be done."

"Cha! But then, I have never been good for much, save that my sword arm was tolerably steady."

"Well, that is not so little."

"Perhaps not, yet that, by itself, is no longer true."

"How, it is no longer true?"

"I give you my word, I can no longer lift my old sword, much less wield it in a manner to threaten another."

"Well, but have you considered exercise?"

"Exercise?"

"Yes. In order to rebuild your strength."

"Do you know, I had not thought of that."

"Well."

Khaavren turned Daro, a look of astonishment upon his countenance. "Do you think," he said, "that such a thing is possible?"

"My dear Count," she said, "I am convinced you can do whatever you set your mind to."

"Ah. But then, I was never much good without Aerich, Tazendra, and Pel."

"Pel can be found, I think, inasmuch as he left a means to reach him when he visited us."

"Well, that is true."

"And, as for your other friends—"

"Yes, as for them?"

"Once you have your strength back, well, you can send for them, or, if you do not know where they are, you can go and look for them."

"Yes, that is true as well."

Khaavren looked at his hand. He inspected both sides of it, as if wondering if there remained any strength within it upon which he might draw. Daro, as if reading his thoughts, laid her own hand on top of his, and, at the same time, smiled at Tevna.

"Let no one say," she told the pyrologist, "that you are not highly skilled at your profession."

Tevna rose to his feet and bowed to her.

Khaavren appeared not to have heard this remark, but stared into the fire, thinking, the flames reflecting in his eyes as if, indeed, the fire were coming from within him.

Chapter the Twenty-Sixth

How Piro and Company Traveled
Toward Deathgate Falls,
Passing Sites of Some
Historical Interest

It was on a Farmday in late winter of the 246th year of the Interregnum that Piro, Kytraan, Tazendra, and Zerika, accompanied by Mica and Lar, set out from Dzur Mountain, bound for Deathgate Falls and the Paths of the Dead. In addition to their horses, they brought a pack horse, upon which were blankets, axes, rope, whetstone, needle and thread, leather tools, and various other supplies deemed necessary or desirable for the journey.

Zerika insisted upon riding in front, and, because of this, Tazendra could not be prevented from riding with her. Piro and Kytraan came behind, and the two lackeys brought up the rear, leading the pack horse.

The first part of the journey was pleasant enough—they rode northeast toward their meeting with the Laughing River, through what had once been good farmland, although during the last two centuries the forests were beginning to reclaim it.

"Do you know," said Kytraan, "we have set out at a remarkably fortuitous time."

"How so?" said Piro.

"Well, you perceive that it is still winter."

"Well, that is true, but it never becomes cold in these latitudes."

"Exactly. And we are traveling north, are we not?"

"Well, and if we are?"

"Just this: By the time we reach the colder climes, well, it will be at least spring, if not full summer, and thus we will miss the worst of the cold as well as the worst of the heat."

"Yes, I understand."

"It is a stroke of fortune, is it not?"

"Well, if it is an omen, I think it is a good one."

"We cannot ask for more than that."

"Did we bring the maps?"

"All of them. Why do you ask?"

Kytraan turned around and gestured toward Dzur Mountain, which still loomed over them. "It is not yet too late to turn back, if we have forgotten anything."

"Ah. Well, we have the maps. And our swords. And, above all, we have Zivra, that is to say, Zerika."

"Then we have forgotten nothing important."

"That's my opinion."

Piro looked around. "This is all new to me. You perceive, on the way here we approached from the southwest. But this district I do not know."

Kytraan said, "It is the county of Southmoor, and was once a domain of the House of the Dragon dating back to the earliest days of the Empire."

"Well, it is very old then," observed Piro.

"It would have been grand to live then!"

"When? In days of the formation of the Empire?"

"Exactly! Every rock or bush, you perceive, might conceal an ambuscade. Every chance meeting might lead to mortal combat. Every —"

"But, that is exactly what we face today," observed Piro.

"Well, that is true. But then they were building an Empire."

"How, is that not what we are doing here?"

"Yes, but we have no army."

"It is true that we have no army. Yet —"

"Well?"

"Perhaps, before all is over, we will."

"That would be splendid!"

"You think so?"

"I am convinced of it. You see, if there is an army, there must necessarily be spectators to watch it."

"And then?"

"Well, some of them will certainly be girls."

"That is true," said Piro. "And we can watch to see which of the girls are the bravest, and pick them to have conversation with."

"Well, there is some justice in what you say, only I had thought of it more in the sense of the reverse."

"How, pick the least brave?"

"No, no. I had referred to permitting them to see us being brave, so they could choose to have conversations with us."

"I see, I see. Yes, that would be a fine thing as well."

"Then we are in agreement?"

"Perfectly, my dear Kytraan."

That night, they made camp still within sight of of Dzur Mountain. As Tazendra prepared to light the fire that they would use to cook (or, more precisely, to heat) their evening meal, Piro said, "Do we need a schedule of watches?"

"As it happens, we do not," said Tazendra.

"How, we do not?"

"Not in the least."

"And yet, is there no danger in this region?"

"There is some," said the Dzurlord.

"But then, should we not stay alert for this danger?"

"Oh, certainly, but no watch is required."

"And yet, my dear Tazendra, I fail to comprehend."

"Shall I explain?"

"Oh, if you should explain, well, I assure you I will be most grateful."

"Well, this is it, then: I have learned sufficient sorcery to be able to establish an enchantment around the area to alert us if anything larger than a norska approaches our camp."

"How, you can do this?"

"Of a certainty. And the proof is, it was Sethra Lavode who taught me the spell."

"Even without the Orb?"

"Even without the Orb."

"Well, my dear friend, I can only say that I am pleased you are here with us, and for more reasons than I had thought."

Tazendra bowed, and turned her attention back to the fire, over which, after preparing it in the usual way—with larger fagots on the bottom, interspersed with small twigs and such dried leaves as could still be found, as well as a good number of pine needles with which the area was abundantly supplied—she passed her hand several times, and, muttering certain enchantments under her breath, caused a small fire to begin.

Piro watched in awe, for he had never before actually witnessed sorcery. When the fire was going, she pulled from it a burning stick of medium length and with it walked in a circle about thirty feet in diameter, still muttering under her breath. When she had finished, she took in her a hand a long, pale staff with a small green jewel at its tip, and, with this, walked around the circle once more. When she had finished, she said, "Well, that should be sufficient."

"If you believe it is," said Kytraan, "than I, for one, am satisfied."

"As am I," said Zerika.

Tazendra bowed.

Whether the Dzurlord's enchantment was successful is something that we cannot know with any certainty, because it chanced that they were not disturbed that night.

Piro had not remained at Dzur Mountain long enough to have lost his acclimation to sleeping on the ground; therefore he slept well, and by the time ten or twelve days had passed, it seemed that he had spent his whole life in that way: riding and riding, stopping to eat and rest the horses, then more riding, a night's sleep, and back to riding. And yet, the company made for a time that was not unpleasant: Piro would discuss history with Kytraan, and reminisce with Zerika about their childhood, and speak with Tazendra about her adventures with his father, and jest with the two lackeys, and in this way the miles fell behind them.

"Do you know this region, my good Piro?" said Tazendra one day.

"I must confess that I do not."

"Well, you should, because we are now in the duchy called Luatha."

"Ah!" said Piro, looking around eagerly. "And the Sorannah?"

"Do you mean Sorannah the region, or Sorannah the county? You perceive, this entire province has the name as well as a county within the duchy of Two Rivers."

"I mean the county; because that county has a certain history for me."

"It is that way," said Tazendra, pointing with her left hand. "Across the Shallow River."

"The Shallow River?" said Piro. "And yet, I had thought it was the Laughing River."

"Oh, it is called that, too," put in Kytraan. "It is all a matter of who you ask."

"And so, where is Newmarket?"

"If it still exists," said Tazendra, "it is thirty or forty miles in that direction."

"Well, I should like to visit it, but perhaps we should postpone that journey for another occasion."

"That is my opinion," said Zerika.

"And then," said Piro, "the marquisate of Khaavren cannot be far."

"No, it cannot," said Tazendra, "and yet, I do not know precisely where it is. But then, were we to turn around and travel back downriver to the place where the Yendi River joins with the Shallow, and were we to wait there, well, even now we might see barges carrying that famous wine down to the delta."

Piro sighed. "Another journey we cannot make."

"That is too bad," said Kytraan.

"I believe," remarked Zerika, "that it is going to rain."

Tazendra said, "Well, I regret to say that I have learned no weather magic."

"In that case," said Zerika, shrugging, "well, we will get wet."

"It seems likely," agreed Kytraan. "Mica, did we remember tents?"

"My lord, we have oiled blankets, and we have poles, and we have rope, and we have spikes."

"Well, then it seems to me that we have tents."

And they did get wet, and, what is more, they stayed wet for several days, as spring in Luatha is not a dry season; yet they continued, and eventually the rains ceased.

"Eventually," said Zerika, "the rain will always cease."

"Well," said Tazendra, "but then, soon or late, there will be rain again."

"That is just as well," said Kytraan, "or the whole world would be a desert."

Mica turned to Lar and said, "They are becoming philosophical."

Lar nodded. "It may amuse you know that my master accused me of being a philosopher."

"How, he did?"

"I give you my word on it."

"Well, being a philosopher is not so bad."

"You think it is not?"

"At any rate, it keeps the mind active during drudgery."

"Well, I am acquainted with drudgery."

"Oh, as to drudgery, I could tell you stories."

"You will forgive me if I suggest that these stories might not be entertaining."

"Doubtless you are right, my friend, wherefore I will refrain."

"That is kind of you."

"Do you think so? Well—but what is that?"

"Horsemen, or I am blind."

"I agree."

"And a good number of them."

"At least ten, or I'm no arithmetist."

"And they seem to be approaching us."

"Well, I nearly think you are right."

"Brigands, do you think?"

"I have my bar-stool near to hand, if they are. And yet—"

"Well, and yet?"

"They appear to all be Dragonlords."

"Are there no brigands who are Dragonlords? I tell you plainly there must be, and the proof is that I knew some."

"And yet, I have never heard of an entire band of them."

"Well, that is true. Perhaps you are right."

"Nevertheless, as I have said, I have my bar-stool ready, and, you perceive, my mistress rolled her shoulders."

"Well, and is there meaning to this rolling of shoulders?"

"Oh, I give you my word, it is full of significance."

"But then, what does it mean?"

"It means, my dear Lar, that she wishes to be certain her sword is correctly hanging behind her back in a good position to be drawn quickly if it is required."

"Well, but then she fears we may be involved in a discussion?"

"Bah! What is it you say? My mistress fears nothing."

"No, no; I only meant—"

"Hush, they are speaking."

"Then let us listen."

To Piro's eye, the most remarkable aspect to the appearance of the knobby, sinewy, dark-complexioned Dragonlord before them was that, unlike Piro and his companions, he showed no signs of having been traveling: that is, his uniform was clean, and even showed signs of sharp creases, such as are made by a one who engages in cleaning and pressing of uniforms as a profession. When the Dragonlord spoke, it was to Tazendra, and he said, "I give you a good day, my lady."

Tazendra bowed from her horse, which horse, Piro noted, was rather larger than the Dragonlord's, and said, "And to you, my dear Dragonlord. I am called Tazendra Lavode. Have you observed that the rain has stopped?"

"Lavode?" said the Dragonlord.

Tazendra bowed.

"Well, Tazendra Lavode, I am Ryunac e'Terics, and this"—here he indicated the gentleman near her right hand—"is my sergeant, Magra e'Lanya. I am in command of this detachment of the Imperial

Army of His Majesty Kâna the First, Emperor of Dragaera, Prince of Kanefthali, Duke of Kâna, Count of Skinter, Whiteside, and—"

"Yes, yes," said Tazendra. "I do not doubt he has many titles. I, myself, am Baroness of Daavya, and, well, I have certain other titles as well. But I believe I asked you a question, my dear Ryunac."

"A question? Ah, well, to answer your question, yes, I have observed that it is no longer raining. But now, I would like to know who your companions are, and what are you doing here."

"In fact," said Zerika, "you have no interest in what we are doing here, my dear Ryunac. My name is Zerika, of the House of the Phoenix, and I claim no title whatsoever, and I believe your only interest is in knowing where we stand on Lord Skinter's pretensions. Come, is that not true?"

Ryunac frowned. "Which of you is in command?"

Zerika shrugged. "I should imagine I am, if anyone is. And, as to my question?"

Ryunac nodded, "Yes, you are perspicacious. That is what I wish to know."

"Then I will tell you."

"I will be most gratified if you do, my lady."

"The answer is, that we consider him an upstart warlord, like a thousand others, and we reject his claims utterly." Zerika accompanied these words with a bow of the utmost courtesy.

Ryunac, notwithstanding the bow, appeared unhappy with the answer. "You perceive," he said, "that this answer is not likely to make me love you."

"Well, but it is the truth, and I have been told that the truth has always some value."

"Indeed it has value. So much so, that it should not be squandered uselessly; especially when doing so can be dangerous."

He said this in a tone sufficiently full of menace, but Zerika said, "Dangerous? To us?" She looked around elaborately. "How, are there more of you that I cannot see?"

"Come," said Tazendra softly to Kytraan. "That was well spoken. There is something to be said for this little Phoenix."

Once again, Ryunac did not seem pleased with the answer. So unhappy was he, in fact, that he at once drew his sword and held it pointed at Zerika's breast. The other ten soldiers in his command, not to be outdone, also drew their weapons.

Piro felt his heart begin to hammer within his breast, yet, and we say this to his credit, even while he wondered how he would acquit himself in what looked to be his first fight, and hoped he would not prove craven in the event, his sword was already in his hand. It need hardly be added that Kytraan had also drawn his. Tazendra, for her part, had not drawn. Instead she turned to Zerika and said, "Have you any instructions?"

Now Zerika herself carried a blade that was, notwithstanding its slimness, of good steel, and of tolerable length. She drew in a smooth motion as of one who knows what she is doing and said, "Instructions?"

"Yes. That is to say, do you require any of them left alive as prisoners?"

"Ah. No, that will not be necessary."

"Very well," said Tazendra coolly, and reached over her shoulder for her sword, got a good grip on it, and drew it, with which motion she continued, and, at the same time spurred her horse forward in a cavalry maneuver that was as old as mounted warriors, so that with no warning she closed with Ryunac and she brought the edge of her blade straight down onto Ryunac's head. Ryunac, caught entirely unprepared, responded without an instant's hesitation by falling from his horse, stone dead.

"Would you care to order a charge?" said Tazendra.

"That would be useless," said Zerika.

Piro, we should say, had at first felt a strange sensation come over him. Strange, we add, because it was in not especially a concern for his own epidermis, but, rather, a sudden confusion regarding Zivra, or rather, Zerika. He had always felt a great affection for her, but had, somehow, never considered the possibility that, in a situation where steel was to be set against steel, she would be holding a weapon in her hand as if perfectly conversant with such arguments. It was as if she were suddenly a stranger, and this disconcerted him.

At the same time, the prospect of action—that is, of being involved in a conversation of steel against steel, with issues of mortality at stake—made the blood pound in his head and the fire of battle burn behind his eyes. Then, upon seeing Tazendra's action, Piro, without thinking, set his heels hard against the flank of his horse, which sent him forward at full speed. He was not, in point of fact, entirely certain what he should do, but he knew that going forward was the right way to begin; and when he saw an armed enemy in front of him, albeit one who was confused about what had just happened so quickly, Piro wasted no time in making a good cut, which happened to catch this individual on his right side. Piro was uncertain as to the effect this blow had had, but before he could learn, his horse had taken him entirely past the battle, and so he had to pull the beast up sharply and turn around in order to determine what he ought to do next.

As Piro had been making his gallant and not-uneffective charge, the others had not been idle. Tazendra, not satisfied with having dispatched Ryunac, spurred her horse toward the nearest soldier and treated him in a very similar manner, striking such a blow upon his neck that he was very nearly decapitated. Zerika, at the same time, urged her horse forward while holding her sword fully extended, using it, in fact, more as a lance than as a sabre, with the effect that the Dragonlord thus addressed, in his haste to avoid being spitted, tumbled from his saddle, after which he was trodden on by his own horse in the animal's sudden panic. Kytraan, who knew something of sword-work from a mounted position, and who, moreover, had the advantage of charging a foe who was caught off-guard, gave one of the enemy a good cut high upon her sword arm, and then turned and struck at another who, after a couple of passes, and seeing his comrades falling left and right, caused his horse to back up a couple of steps after which he turned and bolted out of the contest, riding west as fast as his horse could be convinced to carry him.

As for the lackeys, Mica charged as bravely as Kytraan, holding his trusty bar-stool by one leg and swinging it like a mad-man. It is true that this bar-stool came so close to Lar that only a quick duck by Piro's lackey saved him from a nasty head wound; but what is more important is that one of the soldiers failed to duck in time, and took a blow from this heavy piece of wood directly in the face, breaking his nose and several teeth, knocking him from his horse, and producing a copious amount of blood.

Lar, of them all, as he had no weapon, struck no blow; but at least charged through the melee in good style, giving out a high-pitched scream that he had learned of the band of brigands with whom he had been associated, and from whom he had learned the efficacy of such loud cries in frightening an enemy.

All of this, or, rather, the results of all of this, were what Piro saw when he turned around. More than this, however, he saw that those of the enemy who were unwounded and still mounted were utterly demoralized—so much so, in fact, that as if of one mind they turned and followed the late opponent of Kytraan who had left the engagement so precipitately, with the result that Piro and his friends were now in sole possession of the field of battle.

Tazendra guided her horse next to Zerika and said, "Shall we pursue?"

"No, my dear. Let them run."

"Very well," said the Dzurlord, who appeared disappointed by the answer. She then said, "What of the wounded?," by whom she meant Lar's opponent, who was rolling around on the ground holding his face, and Zerika's opponent, who was lying quite still, having been stepped on by a horse, but was still breathing.

Zerika said, "Let us set them on their horses and send them after the others."

"Very well," said Tazendra, and gestured to the two lackeys that they were to have the honor of carrying out this order. As this was being done, Tazendra turned to Kytraan and said, "Well done, my dear Dragon; you seem to have acquitted yourself very well."

Kytraan bowed to acknowledge the compliment.

"And you, my good Viscount," she continued. "Did you kill your man?"

"No," said Piro. "I wounded him, but I am certain I did not kill him."

"That is too bad," said Tazendra. "But do not let it disturb you; you will certainly have another chance."

"Well," said Piro.

"They know some of our names," observed Kytraan.

"And then?" said Tazendra.

"They know our names, and that we have killed some of their friends. They will be looking for us."

"So much the better," said Tazendra.

"We are not here to fight," said Zerika firmly. "Come, let us increase the pace. I do not wish to be delayed by more discussions."

To this they all agreed, and so they at once turned their horses toward the north again.

As they traveled, they began, now and then, to pass enclaves of Easterners, some clearly migratory, and having stopped for only a day or a week; whereas others had fashioned slovenly rows of hovels into a sort of village. As none of the Easterners appeared inclined to interfere with Zerika and her friends, the Easterners were ignored in their turn.

"I knew," said Kytraan, "that they had come west, but I did not know they were building cities."

"How, you didn't know that?" said Piro. "You didn't know that there are thousands of them in Adrilankha?"

"How, is that true?" said Tazendra. "Bah! It is insupportable! Easterners on Kieron's Watch!"

"Oh, as to that, you needn't worry," said Piro.

"Why is that?" said Tazendra. "You perceive, I am very curious."

"Because," said Piro, "though few knew it, it seems that Kieron's Watch—by which I refer to the shelf jutting out from the cliffs—required sorcery to preserve its stability, and so, at the time of Adron's Disaster—"

"The Horse!" cried Tazendra. "Do you mean that Kieron's Watch has collapsed?"

"Into the sea," said Piro. "In fact, before I was born. I know of it because my mother has often pointed out the place where it used to be. Therefore, you perceive, there will be no Easterners on Kieron's Watch."

"For my part," said Zerika, "I do not mind Easterners."

"How, you don't mind them?" said Kytraan.

"Not in the least," said Zerika. "I used to pass through their district when visiting Nine Stones, where I had certain acquaintances, and never had the least trouble, and, indeed, often had pleasant conversations."

Kytraan and Tazendra looked doubtful, but Piro, who had the greatest respect for Zerika, and who had, moreover, heard her say this sort of thing before, said nothing, but resolved that he would henceforth attempt to curb his prejudice. That he had made this resolution numerous times before and had failed in it did nothing to change this resolve.

Tazendra on the other hand, said, "You may believe what you like, my dear Phoenix, but it is well known that they are filthy, ignorant, clumsy—"

"Let us speak of something else," said Zerika.

"Very well," said Tazendra, shrugging.

In softer tones, so as not to be overheard by the Phoenix, Lar leaned over toward Mica and said, "And you, my friend? What is your opinion?"

"Of Easterners?"

"Yes, exactly."

"Well, that is an easy question to answer."

"Then you will answer it?"

"Yes, and at once."

"Do so, then, I am listening."

"My opinion is that, if there were no Easterners, you and I should have no one over whom to feel superior, and feeling superior to someone is, I believe, as necessary as breathing and eating."

"You think so?"

"I am convinced of it."

"Perhaps you are right."

"Certainly I am right. Why else would Fortune have created us to be so different were it not so that we could feel superior to one another? And that is the excellence of the Cycle, because each of the Noble Houses can, at one time or another, feel superior to the others, except for us, and we, well, we can feel superior to the Easterners."

"But, to whom can the Easterners feel superior?"

Mica frowned as he considered this question, and, after some thought, he said, "Perhaps the Serioli."

"Well, but then, to whom can the Serioli feel superior?"

"Oh, as to that, the Serioli feel they are superior to everyone."

"How, do they?"

"So I have heard, my dear Lar."

"Well, perhaps it is true, then, if you say so."

"I am convinced it is."

"And yet, there is another subject which concerns me even more than Easterners."

"Well, if there is a subject that concerns you, I should be only too glad to hear what it is."

"It is this: We have been making five leagues a day, have we not?"

"And if we have?"

"Only this: The Lady Zerika, who seems to be leading our expedition, pretends we can now make ten leagues a day."

"Yes, my friend, so I have understood."

"It seems like a great deal."

"Does it? Well, in the old days, we made ten leagues a day without fail; and, you perceive, that was without using the posts."

"So you believe we can do this without killing ourselves, or, at any rate, our horses?"

"Feathers! I am certain of it."

"Then I will say no more about it."

As to the question of the nature of the Easterners, and their status as a people, the historian will offer no opinion; but as to the good Mica's conviction that it was possible to travel ten leagues a day without injury to themselves or their horses, well, this was proved entirely correct, because they did, in fact, do just that as they passed through Luatha and continued northward, looking forward to their first sight of the Eastern Mountains, still far ahead; and, at their northern tip, some fifteen hundred miles away, Deathgate Falls and the Paths of the Dead.

Chapter the Twenty-Seventh

How Morrolan, Teldra, and Arra
Traveled South as Piro and Company
Traveled North, and Very Nearly
Met Each Other

Morrolan looked to the west and said, "Do you know, I begin to believe there will be no end to these mountains."

"As to that," said Teldra, "I have never taken this route, and so I cannot say, yet I am told that they end. And, indeed, they must, because it is well known that if one travels far enough south, one eventually reaches the sea."

"Perhaps the mountains continue all the way over the ocean, to whatever lands lie beyond it."

"If I may be permitted to say so, my lord, I find that unlikely."

"Well, no doubt you are correct." He then turned to his other traveling companion and said, "Do you realize, my dear Arra, that we are going about this exactly wrong?"

"How, wrong? In what way, my lord?"

"Well, it is winter, and thus quite cold."

"That much I had noticed, my lord, and it is why you are wearing your heavy cloak, and Lady Teldra and I are both wrapped in furs."

"Well, but we are traveling south. And so, you perceive, by the time it is summer, we will be too warm."

"There is some justice in what you say. And yet, well, no doubt we will have a pleasant enough springtime at some time during our journey."

"We ought to have timed our departure better," observed Morrolan.

"My lord," said Arra, "I must remind you that when we left, well over a year ago—indeed, closer to two years—we were in no small hurry. And, moreover, we had no way of knowing that we would be unable to cross the mountains, but rather should be forced around them."

Morrolan thought about the rains of spring, but instead of speaking of them, he said, "I beg your pardon, Arra, and yours as well, my dear Teldra. I have had a gloomy disposition of late, and I fear I have been but a poor traveling companion."

"Think nothing of it," said Teldra. "Long journeys, especially on foot, can turn anyone's disposition."

"Apropos," said Morrolan, "should we see about procuring horses, now that we have completely abandoned all thought of finding a pass?"

"That is not a bad idea," said Arra. "There are villages at the base of these mountains, and in many of them there may be horses with which someone is willing to part."

Teldra said, "I should not mind at all finding a good horse. As we are skirting the mountains, we should find no ground that will be too difficult for animals."

"It is decided then," said Morrolan. "Should anyone see signs of a village, well, say so, and we will go there directly."

"If I am not mistaken," said Arra, "you perceive that there is something like a road here, and there is a sign carved upon that stone that indicates a direction for something that is almost certain to be a village."

"Then let us go in that direction," said Morrolan.

"I have no objection to make," said Teldra.

They turned and made their way along the road, and it was, in fact, only a few hours before they arrived in Kliuev, a small village nestled into what here were called the Mountains of Faerie, although only fifty or sixty miles to the west they were part of that great chain called the Eastern Mountains. This village, though boasting a population of only thirty or forty, nevertheless maintained itself by raising goats along its upper slopes and growing rye along the lower, the whole augmented by giving aid and comfort to whatever highwaymen might be working along the nearby roads that connected to the waterways which, in turn, connected to what the Easterners called the River of Faerie, which eventually made its way to the Shallow Sea. That these roadways were well traveled was proven by the condition of Kliuev itself, which was in a far better state than it could have been merely depending upon an economy of goat's milk, goat's cheese, and rye.

It was late afternoon when Morrolan, Teldra, and Arra arrived along the dirt path that served as a main street of Kliuev, and the reader may well imagine that the trio attracted more than a little attention.

"There," said Arra. "Do you see? There are six or seven horses tied up outside of that house. It would therefore seem likely to be a public house, and, as I have not yet seen any signs of a livery stable, I would think this might be the place to begin."

"Let us go in, then," said Morrolan.

"Yes," said Teldra. "Let us do so."

They entered the house, and, in a very short time, came out again, unhitching and taking three of the horses that they had noticed earlier.

"Come," said Arra, "that didn't go so badly. We have horses, after all, and are none the worse."

"And yet," said Teldra, "I cannot help but wish —"

"Yes?" said Morrolan. "You wish?"

"I wish that we had understood their language."

"Understood their language?" said Morrolan. "Well, it seems clear enough what they were saying, even without speaking whatever barbarous tongue is used in this region. And, when they pulled those knives that gleamed so prettily in the lamplight, well, then they were speaking more clearly than ever."

"Well, that is true," said Arra. "And I must say, in that regard, I'm glad my sword is longer than the knife of that fellow with the beard because, I give my oath, I believe he was a better fighter than I."

"For my part," said Teldra, "I cannot help but wonder if, had we been able to communicate, they'd have sold us the horses."

Morrolan shrugged. "Well, it was a pretty enough little fight at all events, and I doubt this place will forget us soon."

"Oh," said Arra, "there is no doubt that you are right."

"Nor will I forget," said Morrolan. "After all, while I have, now and then, been involved in a scuffle, more or less serious, this is the first time I have bloodied my sword."

"Bloodied it?" said Arra. "I nearly think you did! You brought four of them to ground entirely on your own, and I should be astonished if there were not two of them who will never rise again."

"Well, but, as you have already observed, I have a sword, and they, well, they had only knives."

"Nevertheless, it was no mean feat."

"Well."

"And yet," said Teldra, "I do not understand why we were attacked."

"You do not?" said Arra. "Consider, my lady, that to a human, you and Morrolan are demons."

"Are we? That astonishes me."

"Does it? And yet, how are those like myself considered in lands inhabited by your folk?"

"Well, there is some justice in your observation."

"You think so? Then I am satisfied."

Morrolan turned around and observed, "They are not following us."

"That is well for us," said Arra, "and better for them."

"Yes," said Morrolan, "I nearly think you're right."

"And I," said Teldra, "believe that this is a far better way to travel than walking."

"Of that," said Morrolan, "there can be no doubt."

"Let us turn here," said Arra, "for if I do mistake the meaning of those wheel-tracks that are so abundant upon the ground, we will soon strike a road that will not only bring us south, but, moreover, will lead us to a bridge over whatever the next river is in these lands where it seems one crosses a river, or at least a deep stream, twice each day."

"Well," said Morrolan, "I agree with turning here, since you believe it is the best way."

"And tonight when we stop," said Arra, "you must not forget to offer up your thanks to the Demon Goddess, who must have had a hand in guiding your blade today."

"I will not fail to do so," said Morrolan.

They stopped that night, and had just spread their blankets on the ground—which was, we should add, pleasantly soft, they having crossed into grassland in the last few hours—when Morrolan felt a drop of rain upon his uncovered head.

"Bring out the equipment, Arra, and quickly," he said.

"Very well," said the Priestess, and hastened to bring out the supplies required by the heathen art practiced by Morrolan, which equipment involved braziers, candles, and other paraphernalia, all of which he hastened to use according to the system he had been taught, and, either his gestures, chants, and invocations had some effect, or the rain-cloud, for reasons of its own, passed them by, for they were spared being drenched.

"Well done," said Arra.

"I'll take the first watch," said Teldra.

Morrolan did not respond, because, after finishing his arcane activities, he at once fell into a deep sleep.

Among historians—who, as the reader may know, spend a great deal of time arguing amongst each other about issues that can have no interest except to other historians—there is an ongoing debate concerning a general question: Under what conditions can one travel more quickly by horse than by foot? It is, without doubt, a complex and difficult question, whether addressed by theory or through the use of historical examples. When addressed by theory there are so many aspects, or "variables" as the arithmetists say, as to provide an endless source of argument and counter-argument: the exact distance under discussion, the physical condition of the man, the nature of the ground, the breed of horse, the sorts of food consumed by the man, the sorts of fodder consumed by the horse, even the footgear or lack thereof on each of the contestants. Attempting to solve the problem by referring to history is no better, because there will always be enough differences in circumstance to render a precise comparison suspect.

Of course, one can set up extreme conditions: It is beyond argument that a rider will outpace a man on foot over a distance of half a mile of level ground; similarly, there can be no question that in a race of a thousand miles, an athletic man will handily and easily outpace the rider no matter what sort of horse or what sort of ground is considered.

The number that is most often used in casual discussion (and which, we admit, is the number that most often results in dissension) is something like three days. That is, should a mounted man set off in a straight line over a good road on a good horse, such as a Browncap, and should another man who is skilled at running over long distances chase him, and should these improbable conditions continue, the running man will catch the rider sometime on the third day. We should add that all attempts to test this have produced nothing but arguments over validity, as well, we should admit, as a great deal of money changing hands, because while historians may conduct tests for knowledge, there is no shortage of those who cannot see a race without placing a wager upon its result.

We have brought this up to point out that, in the event, there are very few cases of a man chasing a horse over long distances (although, to be sure, there is the incident that gave inspiration to the popular ballad "Lord Stonewright's Revenge"), rather, when comparing speed mounted to speed afoot in any practical situation, there are almost always determining factors beyond the simple issues of speed and endurance. In other words, the naive observer might believe that Morrolan, Teldra, and Arra would, in fact, slow down upon procuring mounts. Yet, in this situation, there was one factor that outweighed all others: This factor was nothing more or less than *comfort*.

To be precise, the fact that they were able to ride made the journey so much easier and more pleasant to the three of them—all three, we should add, being experienced riders—that instead of traveling ten or twelve hours a day, as they had been accustomed to do, they now began, without anyone making a decision to do so, to make stages of eighteen or nineteen hours a day, with the result that, though at no time did they consider themselves to be in a hurry, nevertheless they significantly increased the pace at which they made their way toward Morrolan's ancestral holdings—to be precise, toward the county of Southmoor.

After a good week of riding, Arra observed, "My lord Morrolan, it seems to me that we are nearing the end of our supply of food."

"Ah," said Morrolan. "In fact, I had noticed this very thing."

"And have you a plan?"

"It seems to me that this is a district full of wild norska, and moreover, it is one in which certain game-birds are available in abundance."

"And therefore?"

"Why, therefore I propose that we catch some of them, and, having caught them, eat them."

Arra nodded. "I think your plan a good one, and, for my part, I subscribe to it wholeheartedly."

"Well," said Morrolan, "but, do you hunt?"

"I?" said Arra. "Not the least in the world. I had hoped you did."

"No, I'm afraid I have never had to acquire this skill. Lady Teldra, do you, by any chance, have any abilities as a hunter?"

"No, I'm afraid I do not. Why, have we no food left?"

Morrolan shook his head. "Just a piece of hard rock candy. But—"

"Come then," said Arra. "There are villages nearby, and I think we have sufficient silver, and even a certain amount of gold, so that we can purchase what we require."

"Well, that is true," said Teldra. "And yet, if you recall the last time we came to a village—"

"I could go in by myself and purchase what we need," said Arra. "Apropos, we could use more fodder as well, as the grass is becoming thin."

"Bah!" said Morrolan. "How, am I to fear setting foot in a village because of absurd superstitions that may or may not be held by the populace?"

"Well then," said Teldra, "let us find a village and go there."

"Yes," said Arra, "let us do so."

In the event, it was some few hours of riding before they saw signs of habitation, by which time they were all more than a little hungry.

The village of Keybrook was entirely different from Kliuev. It was, for one thing, rather lower in the mountains, and thus was less of a freehold for highwaymen. Next, instead of goats and rye, the economy was based on beef, chicken, and maize. It was also rather larger, and substantially more prosperous. Yet the most significant difference was simply that, as the mountains were lower here, and contained many passes and valleys, it was hardly a barrier, and hence, like Mount Bli'aard far to the north, there was more commerce than is usual between human and Easterner. The result, therefore, was that, though they were treated in a way that was only barely cordial, they were nevertheless able to purchase those items they needed without difficulty.

"Well," said Arra, "what do we have, then?"

"Let us see," said Morrolan. "Two sacks of corn meal, ten pounds of jerked beef, some sort of cheese that crumbles before it can be cut but is not bad for all of that, three loaves of soft bread, plenty of hard-bread, several smoked bowfins, which will be wonderful if they are half as good as our hosts claimed, and a whetstone of which I, at least, stood badly in need, and four sacks of fodder for the horses. What else?"

"Plenty of ediberries," said Teldra.

"How, ediberries? I do not recall buying those."

"You did not, my lord. But, if you look ahead, you will see them growing wild along the path, so that we can pick as many as we like."

"Well," said Arra, "I see nothing wrong with this plan."

"Nor I," said Morrolan, "though we should not eat too many, as they serve to drive away sleep."

"How, do they?" said Teldra. "I had not known this fact."

"It is known by those who study the Art."

"How," said a stranger. "You study the Art?"

Morrolan turned, and found himself confronting a small, swarthy Easterner whom he had not seen before, and who had evidently been resting by the side of the road near the edge of the village. At the

Easterner's side was a medium-sized dog colored a sort of dirty white, and between his feet was a black cat.

"Well," said Morrolan, "I give you good day, sir. I had not heard you approach. I am called Morrolan e'Drien. This is the Lady Teldra, and Arra, the Priestess."

The other bowed, "May I present my friends, Awtlá and Sireng," he said, indicating the dog and the cat. As for myself, alas, I cannot give you a name, as I am searching for it."

"How," said Morrolan, "you are searching for your name?"

"Exactly."

"Then you are a practitioner of the Art?"

The other bowed.

"Well, I know of these things. It does not seem so long ago that I was also searching for my name, only I came across a coachman who seemed to have a good supply of them, and gave me one."

"Well, then perhaps I should search for a coachman. You perceive, I have been looking for my name since I was twelve years old, and, as I am now, well, considerably older, I would just as soon find it and be done."

"Well, I understand that. Have you had your journey yet?"

The warlock nodded. "Many years ago."

"And you have found a soul-mate?"

"Two of them," he said, indicating the animals at his feet.

"So that all you require is a name?"

"You have understood me exactly."

"Well, I wish you well."

"Thank you, Morrolan."

"Do you know, warlock, it has just occurred to me that you speak the language of Faerie."

"Well, it seemed useful to know."

We should mention that Morrolan, Teldra, and Arra had been speaking only the language of the Empire since they set out, because Teldra pretended such practice would help Morrolan and Arra become more fluent.

"Well, it will be if you journey across the mountains. Or even around them, as we are now doing."

"How, you are going to the land of Faerie? Ah, but then, why should you not? For a moment, I had forgotten I was speaking to elfs. You perceive, it is not usual in this district."

Teldra smiled. "We are not so bad, you know, once you become acquainted with us."

"Oh, I have spoken with elfs before, I assure you."

"And?"

"As you say, my lady."

Teldra bowed, and the warlock, turning to Morrolan, said, "What of you?"

"Oh, I? Well, you perceive I have my name. Moreover, I have journeyed to a place where I learned many things not available to plain sight. And, as to my soul-mate, well—"

"Yes?"

"At first I thought it was Arra."

"At first?"

"Yes, but then I came to believe it was the Lady Teldra."

"And yet, you were uncertain."

"Oh, but I am certain now."

"Are you?"

"Yes. I am utterly convinced."

"That it is Teldra?"

"No, that it is the Demon Goddess."

"What do you tell me?" cried the warlock.

"The goddess, herself, is my soul-mate."

"Bah!"

"It is," said Arra, "exactly as he says."

"Well," said the warlock. "I must tell you I have heard of nothing like this. Do you not think it, well—"

"Presumptuous?"

"Exactly. The very word."

"Yes, I think it is."

"And so?"

"It is the truth, nevertheless."

"In that case, well—"

"Yes?"

"Have you any objection if my friends and I accompany you?"

"Not the least objection in the world," said Morrolan. He looked quickly at Arra and Teldra, both of whom signified that the warlock's company would be welcome. The dog wagged its shaggy tail. The warlock, putting a thumb and finger into his mouth, gave off a loud, piercing whistle, after which a black horse trotted up, snorted, and shook its head.

"How," said Morrolan, "you have your horse trained to come when you whistle?"

The warlock smiled. "In fact, I do not."

"You do not? And yet—"

"Much is illusion, my brother in the Art, is it not?"

Morrolan bowed. "Perhaps you are right, and yet, if I do not err, your horse is not an illusion, and I have never seen one so strong."

"You have a good eye for horses, my friend."

"Tell me, of what breed is it?"

"Oh, as to that, well, I couldn't say. But, believe me, he has a certain lineage."

"Oh, I do not doubt that in the least. What is his name?"

"Duke."

"Well, I should think at least Prince for a horse like that."

"He is not presumptuous."

"That is good," said Morrolan, smiling.

After a few miles, the warlock said, "Tell me one thing."

"One thing? Ah, having gotten our fill of supplies, and the day being so pleasant, well, I would answer three questions."

"But I only have one, so I hope you will be content."

"Entirely, my good warlock. So come, ask your question."

"This is it: Exactly where are we going?"

"Oh, you wish to know that?"

"Awtlá, the dog, well, he is curious."

"Ah, I understand that. Well, the answer is, we are bound for my ancestral homelands, a county called Southmoor."

"Southmoor? Well, but that is near Adrilankha, is it not?"

Teldra answered him, saying, "Perhaps fifty leagues from Covered Springs, in the southwest corner. But wait, you know Adrilankha?"

"Know it? I nearly think so."

"How, you have been there?" said Morrolan.

"Oh, indeed. I lived there for some time."

"The trey!"

"It is true. And you, have you been there?"

"Never. I have only heard of it from Lady Teldra."

"Well, perhaps we will go there, and I will show you some of the places of interest."

"I should like that."

That night, Morrolan asked the warlock which watch he preferred.

"Oh, I have my choice?" he said.

"And why should you not?"

"And yet, are you certain you trust me?"

"I do," said Arra, with no hesitation.

Morrolan shrugged. "If Arra trusts you, well, that is sufficient for me."

"And for me as well," said Teldra.

The warlock bowed. "Well then, if I can choose my watch, I should like to select —"

"Well?"

"All of them."

"All of them?"

"Yes, if that is acceptable."

"And yet —"

"Well?"

"Will you not require sleep at some point on the journey?"

"No, for I shall sleep while I am on watch."

"How, that is your intention?"

"More than my intention, my dear elf, it is my plan."

"And yet, it seems to me —"

"Come, I know what you are thinking. I believe I can convince you."

"Do you think so?"

"I am certain of it."

"Very well, then, I am prepared to be convinced."

As darkness fell and they made their camp with the practiced ease of old campaigners, the warlock walked out of the camp along with his two companions, and, some few minutes later, came back without them.

Morrolan said, "Your friends, then, are on watch?"

"Exactly."

"And they are trustworthy?"

"Without meaning to give offense, my good Dragonlord, I aver that they are more reliable than any of the rest of us."

"Very well, then," said Morrolan. "I have said I trust you, and, therefore, I do."

"That is best, believe me."

That night, Morrolan found that, as he lay wrapped in his blankets, his head was near Arra's, and he said very softly, "Do you know, it almost seems as if, in the flickering of the fire, I saw a large, grey wolf circling about our camp? And it was, moreover, an extraordinarily large wolf, if I am not deceived."

"And I," whispered Arra, "am convinced that I have a seen a dzur padding about at the very edge of the light."

"Well?"

"Well, I think he is more accomplished in the Art than he pretends."

"I nearly think you are right."

"Let us sleep then."

"Yes, let us do so."

The next morning, as they were preparing to break their fast, Morrolan saw the dog curled up next to the fire. It saw Morrolan looking at it and thumped its tail once. The cat lay next to the dog, cleaning itself. Morrolan shrugged.

They traveled in this way as the days and weeks wore on, and the mountains, which were ever upon their right hand, began to seem lower and lower, until one day, very near noon, Morrolan remarked, "Do you know, I am beginning to wish that it would either rain, or clear up, but this threatening sky is beginning to wear on me."

"I'm afraid, my lord," said Teldra, "that it will not clear."

"How, never?"

"No, this is the Enclouding of which you have heard."

"How, the Hand of Faerie, as it is called in the lands where I was raised?"

"Yes, exactly."

"Well," said Morrolan, "I hope I shall become used to it."

"I believe you will, after a time," said Teldra.

"Well, let us go on."

It was eight or nine days later that they awoke to discover that the Mountains of Faerie, as they were called in the East, or the Eastern Mountains, were no longer upon their right hand, replaced with only the most harmless-looking hills. Morrolan and his friends looked back to the north, and saw, as it were, the trailing edges of the mountains.

"Well," said Morrolan. "I never thought to see them end."

"I admit," said Arra, "that I, too, was beginning to despair of seeing their end."

"I nearly imagine," said Teldra, "that I can smell the sea, although it is yet more than fifty leagues distant."

"Come, look there," said Morrolan.

"Where?" said the warlock.

"There, between those hills. Do you see?"

"It looks," said Teldra, "to be a small troop of horsemen."

"Yes," said Morrolan. "I cannot make out their number. Four? Six?"

The dog looked in the indicated direction, and began pointing, front paw up, tail straight.

"They are elfs," said the warlock.

Teldra nodded. "They do not appear to be coming in our direction, however."

"No, they are going north, as near as I can make out."

"Well?"

Morrolan shrugged. "Let them alone, then."

"I concur," said Arra.

Morrolan watched them a bit longer, then, after packing up, mounted once more.

"Southward," he said. "And a bit to the west. The homeland of my ancestors lies ahead."

"And much else as well," said Arra.

"Of that," said Morrolan, "I have no doubt."

Chapter the Twenty-Eighth

How Various Others Are Spending
Their Time While Our Friends
Are Traveling

S hould the reader be at all curious about what has been happening with Wadre and his highwaymen, not to mention the sinister sorceress who calls herself Orlaan, we now propose to satisfy this curiosity. She was sitting, to all appearances as imperturbable as an Athyra monk, when Mora approached her and delicately cleared her throat.

Orlaan opened her eyes and looked up at the bandit. "Well?" she said.

Mora bowed with utmost respect, and said, "I am bidden to inform you that they have left Dzur Mountain."

"Ah! Have they, then?"

Mora bowed her assent.

"Well, and in what direction have they set off?"

"North."

"North?"

"It is as I have the honor to inform you."

"Well. I wonder what business they have to the north. You perceive, I had been prepared for them to travel back southwest toward Adrilankha, or west toward Adron's Disaster, or south toward the Coast, or even east as a means of escape. But I cannot imagine what might take them north."

Mora, having nothing to add to these reflections, and being, moreover, a little uncertain in the presence of the sorceress, said nothing, but rather waited.

"Well," said Orlaan after a moment. "Let us follow them and find out."

"As you say, madam," said Mora.

"Send Wadre to me."

Mora bowed, departed, and, a few minutes later the bandit chief was standing in the very spot she had but lately vacated.

"You wished to see me, madam?"

Orlaan nodded. "As you know, our quarry is running."

"Well, and?"

"We will follow them at a good distance. It is my desire to see whither they are bound, but not yet to interfere with them."

"Very well."

"Apropos, we must not permit them to see us."

"Very well."

"But neither must we fall too far behind them, because I may choose to attack them at a moment's notice."

"Very well."

"When will we be ready to set out?"

"Well, we must saddle our horses."

"Yes, I understand that."

"And then, our gear must be packed."

"I agree that you should have your gear."

"And then, our food and other supplies must be put into our saddle-pockets."

"Certainly we must all have food for the journey. And then?"

"Five minutes."

"Ah. You move quickly."

Wadre shrugged. "We are bandits. We have become accustomed to the need to be on the road with little delay."

"That is good then. See to it."

"At once," said Wadre.

The brigand was as good as his word; five minutes later the entire band, with the addition of Orlaan, were mounted and moving north. They skirted Dzur Mountain, and, brave though they no doubt were, many of the brigands gave the mountain covert glances, or made superstitious gestures in its direction as their route brought them to their closest approach.

"Do you think she is watching us?" asked Orlaan, with an expression of irony on her countenance.

"No," said Wadre.

"Well, and why do you believe she is not?"

"Because if I thought she were, well, I should be forced to scream and then, turning my horse, to run from here as quickly as possible. This would be inconsistent with my dignity as a bandit leader. Therefore, you perceive, I must believe she is not watching us."

"Ah! You are a pragmatist."

Wadre shrugged. "It is the only philosophy suitable to a brigand, don't you think?"

"Well, that, or perhaps fatalism."

"Bah! I am of too optimistic a nature to be a fatalist."

"You must be very optimistic, my good Wadre, to maintain your optimism in the very lap of Seth—"

"Now please," said Wadre. "Whatever your own beliefs, please do me the courtesy of respecting my own, and do not name her, especially while we are within the shadow of her home."

"As you wish," said Orlaan, shrugging.

That evening, they stopped and made camp, and, as they were cooking up a sort of stew, Wadre said, "I wonder how far ahead of us they are?"

"Eleven and a half miles," said Orlaan.

"Bah!" said Wadre. "How—" Then he stopped in mid-sentence, shrugged, and continued stirring.

"I wonder where they're going?" said Orlaan quietly, speaking to herself.

We are not going to detail yet another in what, we confess, is in danger of becoming an endless sequence of wearying episodes of travel. When we portray these episodes, we do so with regret, and only because the history we have taken it upon ourselves to relate absolutely requires it; thus when we are able to pass them by, as we do now, we readily take the opportunity to do so.

The reader may, then, rest assured that, for several weeks, and even months, they continued in the trail of Piro and his friends, and that, at the expiration of that time, Orlaan was quietly asking herself the same question, and, as of that time, had not arrived at an answer.

It was during that time—that is, during these weeks and months—that there came a visitor to Dzur Mountain, and a visitor, moreover, with whom the reader is already acquainted, that being our old friend Pel, who was, as the reader may recall, given the task by Kâna himself to treat with the Enchantress.

The entrance Pel found was, typically, one of the lesser-known doorways into the strange keep of Sethra Lavode—in particular, it involved climbing to the very top of the mountain, slipping between two large boulders which did not appear to have any space between them, moving aside a doorway that appeared to be a stingerbush, and climbing down a ladder into a sort of entry-way made of brown rock.

Once down, he waited, assuming his entry would be noted. In this, he was not disappointed; it was the Sorceress in Green who appeared on this occasion, a sword in her hand. Pel did not draw a weapon, but instead made a bow and said, "I am the Duke of Galstan. Do I have honor of addressing Sethra the Younger, of whom I have heard so much?"

"No," said the Sorceress, "you do not. Is it your custom to enter homes unannounced?"

"Not in the least," said Pel. "On the contrary, I would have wrung the clapper, were it not for the fact that I didn't see one. Moreover, I would have entered by the front door, if I knew where it was. I am an emissary of his Imperial Majesty Kâna, of the House of the Dragon, and I request an audience with Sethra Lavode."

The Sorceress studied him, then abruptly sheathed her sword and made a certain motion with the fingers of her left hand. Upon seeing this, Pel, his eyes widening slightly, made a similar yet different motion with the fingers of his left hand, after which the Sorceress said, "Follow me, then, my lord Galstan."

Pel bowed and followed her.

Soon Pel was in the room our friends had occupied some weeks previously. The Enchantress entered, and said, "Well, it is Pel, isn't it?"

"How," said the Sorceress. "You know him?"

"On, indeed," said the Enchantress. "He is the Duke of Galstan, of the House of the Yendi, but he styles himself Pel, after a small river in the northwest."

"And you were aware that he is a Yendi?" said the Sorceress.

"Oh, certainly."

"Well."

"It has been some time," said Pel.

"Indeed. And word has reached me that you are here on behalf of Skinter."

Pel bowed.

The Enchantress studied him for some time, at last saying, "You perceive, I do not ask you to sit."

"This fact had not escaped me."

"Well then, is our business concluded?"

"To my regret, madam, I must confess that it is."

"Well. The Sorceress will see you out by the same way you entered."

Pel bowed once more, and, following the Sorceress in Green, left Dzur Mountain, after which he made his way to a near-by posting house, some twenty or thirty miles away, from which he contrived to have this message dispatched back to Mount Kâna:

Your Majesty, I have the honor to report that I have met with the Enchantress of Dzur Mountain. We discussed those issues with which I was charged, and I regret to report that I was told, in terms that can leave no room for confusion, that the Enchantress intends to oppose us with all of the forces at her disposal, and even with all of those which, not being presently at her disposal, she can contrive to assemble for the purpose of thwarting our intentions. She is, in other words, an implacable enemy. She went so far as to insist, using language that was unmistakable, that she questioned even Your Majesty's right to the duchy of Kâna. Other than this, I was able to learn little, except that she is engaged in a project of some sort that is working directly counter to our aims; but she was too cautious and too clever to give me so much as an opportunity to learn anything about it.

Your Majesty, I feel it vital to learn what this project is as soon as possible and will therefore be engaged in this task. Your Majesty may be assured that I will communicate as soon as possible, and that until then I remain Your Majesty's obedient servant, Galstan.

The district in which the posting house was located, a part of the county of Southmoor, was characterized by its proximity to the home of Sethra Lavode; that is, to the peasantry, every aspect of life was defined by the mountain and the Enchantress. In addition to certain sorghums, the region produced sugarcane, groundnuts, and wetcorn, as well as an endless crop of legends, myths, stretchers, and outright lies. It should hardly surprise the reader to learn that the life of the region was overshadowed—literally and figuratively—by the omnipresent peak. It has been said by a noted historian* that every superstition found anywhere in the world eventually ended up in the counties south of Arylle, where they were all fervently believed, whether they contradicted one another or not.

A stranger would find himself regarded with the highest suspicion; but were the stranger a clever Yendi such as Pel, he would find few peoples more subject to the particular machinations at which he was so skilled. For this reason, then, we can find him at this same house after merely a week or six days, and it should come as no surprise that in this time he has learned of whom to ask questions, and where to place inquiries, and, availing himself of these matters, has had a watch set upon Dzur Mountain itself.

---

*As far as I can determine, the "noted historian" in question is Paarfi himself. —SB

He has learned, then, of all the significant comings and goings, and these, in turn, have led him to make other inquiries, for which he finds himself required to wait.

His waiting ended one day, as we have said, something like a week after his visit to the Enchantress. On this day there came a clap outside of his room. Upon his command, the curtain was moved aside, and there entered a Teckla of five hundred or five hundred and fifty years, who bowed to him as to one of exceedingly high rank, a salute to which Pel responded as if it were his due.

"What is it, Tem?" asked the Yendi.

"My lord, word has come back from my cousin."

"Ah!" said Pel. "Well, it has been a long wait."

"My lord, you have my deepest apologies for that."

"Well, it is all the same, if the information is reliable."

"Oh, as to that—"

"Well?"

"I assure Your Lordship I would stake my life upon it."

"Not only would you, my dear Tem, but you are doing so. With this in mind, let us hear what your cousin has learned."

"My lord, a large tribe of Easterners has crossed the mountain."

"Well, what of it? There have been many."

"Yes, my lord. But this is larger than most. Several hundred at the least."

"Well, but you perceive, this still does not interest me. What is it about this tribe that is remarkable?"

"They have come, my lord, from the passes of Mount Bli'aard."

"Have they indeed? Well, but there are many Easterners beyond this pass."

"And the Easterners spoke of a band of humans they passed."

"Humans?"

"Exactly. And they were able to describe them remarkably well."

"Then let us hear these famous descriptions."

"Two women and four men, all mounted, plus a pack animal. One of the women carried a large sword strapped across her back, and one of the men wore blue and white, whereas the two who always rode in back were dressed in yellow and brown."

"Very well, then, I agree, that is our quarry."

"That was my cousin's opinion, my lord."

"When were they seen?"

"Three days ago, if Your Lordship pleases."

"How, three days ago?"

"Yes, my lord."

"Impossible!"

"My lord?"

"Consider, Mount Bli'aard is five hundred leagues from here if it's a mile. How could word reach us so quickly?"

"Oh, as to that—"

"Well?"

"I cannot say, my lord?"

"How, you cannot say?"

"I'm sorry, my lord."

"Sorry!"

"That is to say, I regret—"

"You know, but will not tell me?"

"I regret to inform Your Lordship—"

"This is insupportable."

We should say that Tem was, by now, noticeably trembling, and to such a degree that Pel became, rather than angry, curious about who or what could have made such an impression on the Teckla that he refused to answer the Yendi's question. With unusual directness, then, Pel asked, "But, why can you not say?"

"My lord, I have taken an oath."

"How, an oath?"

"Yes, Your Lordship, and a most binding oath."

"But to whom have you taken this oath?"

"Your Lordship must understand that to answer that question would violate the oath quite as much, and in the same way, as answering the question Your Lordship has already done me the honor to ask."

Pel frowned, and was suddenly struck by an idea. He said, "Tell me, my dear Teckla, if you have not heard of something called the 'wire,' which consists of many persons of your House, all of whom have eyes and ears, and all of whom are paid certain moneys to use these eyes and ears, and to relay messages as quickly as possible."

Tem's mouth came open, and he said, "Your Lordship knows of the wire?"

In answer, Pel smiled, and, reaching under his cloak, pulled forth a certain signet, which he showed to the astounded Teckla, who at once dropped upon his knees and said, "I should have known, my lord."

"Not at all. You have done well, and said no more than you should."

Tem bowed profoundly. Pel, now that he understood that the information had come through the very network that he, himself, had set up, returned to considering the information itself.

"And so," he mused aloud, "they have gone to Mount Bli'aard? Toward Redface, perhaps, or —"

"No, my lord."

"How, they have not gone to Redface?"

"They have not gone to Mount Bli'aard."

"And yet, did you not just tell they were seen there?"

"They were seen there, but they did not travel to the mountain, my lord."

"But then, where did they go?"

"North, my lord."

"North? North from Mount Bli'aard?"

Tem bowed his assent.

Pel frowned. "But north of Mount Bli'aard there is nothing except . . ." His voice trailed off as he considered. After a moment he said, "Could there possibly have been a corpse with them?"

"How, a corpse?"

"Yes, a corpse. A dead body."

"I am convinced there was not, Lordship."

"That is very interesting indeed, Tem."

The Teckla bowed.

Pel was silent for a long time, considering everything he knew, all that he suspected, and much that he guessed, and at last he said, "Have the host prepare my bill, then return and assist me to pack. I will require my horse to be prepared as well. I will be leaving tonight."

"Yes, my lord. And may I be permitted to hope Your Lordship will return someday?"

"Yes," said Pel. "You may hope."

As for what Pel intended to do, as this does not enter our story for some time yet, we must, regretfully, delay the revelation until a more appropriate moment. For now, we will return once more to the point in time when Orlaan was asking herself where Piro and his friends were going; yet it is not Orlaan on whom we look, nor is it our friend the Viscount, but, instead, we will observe a place many long miles to the west and south where, sitting on the ground in another campsite, Ibronka asked Röaana, "Is that not the ocean-sea I am smelling?"

"As to that," said Röaana, "I believe it may very well be. Or, at any rate, if it is not, well, I am imagining the same thing."

"Then, if we can smell the sea, we must be nearing the coast."

"That is my opinion as well."

"And, moreover—"

"How, there is more?"

"Nearly. Moreover, when the reach the coast—"

"Yes?"

"We say farewell to the caravan of handsome Dragonlords."

"Ah!"

"You say, 'ah'?"

"Yes, my dear Ibronka."

"But what do you mean?"

"I mean, my love, that upon saying farewell to the caravan, well, you must also say farewell to that handsome corporal who has been paying you such attention for the last hundred leagues."

"Why, Röaana, upon my word, I have no idea what you mean."

"How, you don't know why he has been dropping back to see to his rear echelons twenty or thirty times a day?"

"My love, there is a certain emphasis in how you say 'rear echelons' that causes me some distress."

"Is that why you are blushing?"

"Bah. I could make you blush as well, if I wished."

"Could you? I cannot think how."

"Well, my dear Röaana, I might mention a certain subaltern with extraordinarily long and flowing hair who fixes saddle cinches so well. Or perhaps he does not fix them so well after all, for if he did, he would not need to check his work at least once each hour."

"Oh, that means nothing."

"I beg your pardon, but it must mean something, or else—"

"Yes, or else?"

"Or else you would not be blushing."

"Well, you perceive that at least we match."

"Yes, that is true, at any rate."

"And, as for the subaltern, I will tell you something."

"Well, I am listening."

"He kisses well."

"How, you permitted him to kiss you?"

"And, if I did?"

"Well, and how was it?"

"I assure you, my dear Ibronka, I could come to enjoy this pastime."

"Well, but when did you find time to kiss him?"

"Do you recall a time two nights ago when there was a disturbance among the horses, so that half the caravan was alerted?"

"Why yes, my dear, I do remember it."

"After it was over, I happened to be standing near those horses, and it chanced that Saynac—"

"That is the subaltern?"

"Exactly."

"Well, go on."

"It happened that Saynac came by after seeing to the horses, and, well, we went for a short walk."

"I never knew!"

"Well, but have you never had the chance to kiss your corporal?"

"How, you pretend I would let him kiss me?"

"My dear Ibronka, if you wouldn't, then, well, I tell you plainly you are missing out."

"Well then, I am not missing out."

"Ah! Well, but when did you kiss?"

"You were just speaking of the evening when the horses were disturbed?"

"Why yes, in fact, I was."

"Well, that is to say, it was Dortmond and I who disturbed the horses."

"You shameless thing!"

"Well, and what of yourself?"

"Oh, I am equally shameless, I promise you. Your corporal's name, then, is Dortmond?"

"Yes, that is his name, and his kisses are superb."

"Well then, as I said, you shall miss him."

"It is true what you say, as, no doubt, you shall miss your subaltern."

"But, leaving dalliance aside, my friend, we must consider what we are to do when we reach Hartre, which is the end of the caravan, but not of our own journey."

"Well, to continue together would be safer than for each of us to continue alone."

"With this I agree. And more pleasant as well, for I tell you plainly that I enjoy your company so much that I consider us friends."

"Well, and I agree entirely, my dear Röaana. Here is my hand."

"And here is mine."

"Then it is settled. When we reach Hartre, we will continue

together along the coast, and if there are dangers, well, we each have good steel, and a good friend."

"That is my opinion exactly."

At this point Clari approached them and said, "Excuse me, my ladies."

"Yes, Clari?" said Ibronka.

"I have just learned that we arrive in Hartre to-morrow, my lady, and I thought you should know."

"Yes, that was well thought. Thank you, Clari."

"You are welcome, my lady."

The maid bowed, and prepared to depart, but Röaana said, "One moment, my good Clari."

"Yes, my lady?"

"I am curious as to how you came by this information."

"How I came by the information?" asked the maid, appearing slightly uneasy.

"Yes, Clari, if you don't mind telling me. And, moreover—"

"There is more, my lady?"

"Well, I wonder where you have been this last hour since we made camp."

"Oh, madam, if you or my mistress required me—"

"Not at all," said Röaana. "As I said, I am merely curious."

"Come to that," said Ibronka, "well, I am too. How is it you have learned that we will arrive to-morrow when neither I nor my friend Röaana have come by this information?"

"Oh, well—"

"Yes?"

"That is to say—"

"Come, come, Clari. What is it?"

"Well, there is this Captain—"

"How!" cried Ibronka.

"A Captain?" said Röaana.

"That is to say—"

"No, no," said Ibronka. "You have said quite enough."

And the poor maid was required to stand and listening to the Dzurlord and the Tiassa laughing like children for quite five minutes before she was dismissed and permitted to return to her Captain and resume their interrupted conversation.

Early the next day, the caravan arrived outside of Hartre, which, as we have already had the honor to mention, was a once-thriving port city as well a center of fishing, though its prosperity had fallen off considerably since Adron's Disaster. It was Kâna's plan to rebuild this city both as a defensive bastion against Elde Island (he considered Rundeel too close, and Adrilankha too far), and, simultaneously, to establish regular shipping between it and Northport, the latter of which was well located for his home in the Kanefthali Mountains. It was to this end that he had caused a caravan full of trade goods and accompanied by a small part of his army to be sent to Hartre. His intention was to arrange for a ship to be built, refurbished, or commandeered, depending on circumstances, then filled with goods and sent to Candletown, where other goods might be traded for, and to sail from there "around the corner" (as sailors call it) to Northport.

It was, in the opinion of this historian, a good plan, and one that showed that Kâna, or, at any rate, his cousin, had that ability to see into the future in some degree that marks a true leader. Indeed, it would be instructive to follow this expedition, with all its unexpected turns and repercussions; yet as it only occasionally and indirectly intersects with the history we have chosen to relate, we cannot permit ourselves more than a brief summary of its goals, as we allow it to pass us by while we follow those persons who were as incidental to Kâna's mission as this mission is incidental to our history. What is more significant to our history, then, is the fact that a day after their last conversation, the Tiassa, the Dzurlord, and the maid met at the rapidly dwindling encampment to discuss their plans for the next day.

"Well," said Ibronka, "we must leave early in the morning, and get a good start."

"Yes," said Röaana, "to this I agree."

"I will be ready, my lady," added Clari.

"But," said Röaana, "apropos, have we supplies for traveling?"

"Oh," said Ibronka, "as to supplies, well, I am on tolerably good terms with one of the quartermasters, and so we can get all we need."

"Well, that is good then. And as to fodder, there will, I believe, be grass all of the way, and I can procure for us a certain amount of oats, as one of the grooms has been showing me some attention."

"And I," said Clari, "have found a merchant who pretends to have more canvas than he requires, and has made me an offer of some of it when he learned we would be traveling."

"Bah," said Ibronka. "My dear Röaana, this girl will show us both up."

"That is true, my dear Ibronka, yet we will have our revenge, for each time she does—"

"Yes, each time she does?"

"Well, we will make her blush."

"Ah, that is a good revenge."

"Well, there is no more to say about that, then."

Needless to say, the matter of revenge was entirely successful, as the poor Teckla was fully flushed.

Röaana then said, much to the relief of Clari, "On another subject entirely, I have something to say."

"Well?"

"I am not ashamed to admit to you that, well, I have some concerns."

"How, concerns?"

"Yes. We have more than five hundred kilometers to travel, and that is if we go in a straight line; you perceive it is even longer if follow the coast."

"Well, and then?"

"There are only two of us and the pretty Clari, and I know little enough of the lands through which we will be traveling, and, to be honest—"

"Yes, yes. Be honest, by all means."

"Well, I should be sorry to meet an ignominious end before ever reaching our destination. That is to say, the sort of adventures I anticipate do not involve being waylaid by highwaymen in a lonely jungle in the dead of night. It does not seem to be a very romantic way to die."

"Do you know," said Ibronka, "there is a great deal of justice in what you say. But then, can you think of anything to do about it?"

"Oh, you wish for an idea?"

"Yes, exactly. An idea. Do you have one?"

"Well, I admit I have sometimes had ideas."

"That is but natural; you are a Tiassa."

"Oh, I don't deny that."

"Have you an idea now?"

"Your pardon, my ladies, but may I speak?"

"Certainly, Clari, if you can be spared from the attentions of your Captain, well, we should adore hearing what you have to say."

Clari blushed and said, "Oh, my lady, he has already said farewell and gone about his business."

"I hope," said Röaana, "that he said farewell with more than words."

"Oh, my lady!"

"Well, but," said Ibronka, "what is it you have to say?"

"My lady, my family is from Hartre."

"Well, and?"

"There are certain clans of Teckla in the district who, I think, retain some affection for my family."

"Go on, Clari. You perceive this conversation interests me exceedingly."

"It seems to me, my lady, that if I should speak with them, I might learn something of the safest routes to travel, and perhaps how to avoid whatever dangers there might be, and, if Fortune smiles, we will even be able to find maps."

"For my part," said Röaana, "I think this an excellent plan."

"Yes, indeed," said Ibronka. "It is very well thought of, Clari. Go and see to it."

"I will do so this very instant."

Clari was, we should say, so successful in her mission that when the three of them set out at dawn of the next day it was with a certain confidence that they would, indeed, arrive in due course in the city of Adrilankha, and, not withstanding the lack of escort or caravan, without any of the more unpleasant sorts of adventures.

Having now looked in upon Ibronka and her friend, we will continue our steady progress in time (if saltatory in space) by looking in on Brachington's Moor, where our old friend Aerich, sitting at a sort of secretary, has just pulled upon a certain bell-rope.

In a very short time, a frail-looking, grey-haired Teckla, who, for all of his apparent age, nevertheless stood straight as a bar of iron, came into the room and gave Aerich a courtesy. Aerich acknowledged the salute, and carefully set down the paper upon which he had been writing, as well as the long feathered quill he had been writing with. He looked at the paper, which but awaited his signature, as if he didn't recognize it; then he turned his attention once more to the Teckla who stood patiently waiting before him.

"Well, Steward," said the worthy Lyorn. "How did the winter stores of fodder hold out?"

"Your Venerance," said Steward, "we had a bin that had only just been broached."

"Good," said Aerich. "Then we will plan on the same levels for next year. Make a note of it."

Steward bowed.

"Next," said the Duke, "how is the water?"

"Your Venerance, it was last tested at the beginning of winter, and found to be pure enough."

"See that it is tested again."

"Yes, Venerance."

"Finally," said Aerich, "how progress the plans for the restoration of the smokehouse?"

"The carpenters pretend they have to send away for the sort of lumber Your Venerance has requested."

"And then?"

"They do not expect to be able to begin for ten or twelve days, Venerance."

"Very well, that is acceptable."

Steward bowed. "Is that all Your Venerance requires?"

"No."

Steward waited.

"You are familiar with the southwest room on the third story."

"Yes, Your Venerance. And the proof is: It is an empty room that is never used, and it has a wooden floor that is swept twice a week."

"Yes, and there is a closet in that room. The closet is locked. Here is the key. You will unlock the closet, remove what is within, and arrange it. Fawnd will help you; he is aware of how the equipment works. You will attach the climb ropes, set up the striking board, place the targets, and lay out the mat."

"Yes, Venerance."

"It will be ready by morning to-morrow."

Steward bowed.

"You will have Fawnd awaken me one hour earlier each morning from now on, but my breakfast will be ready at the usual time."

"As Your Venerance wishes."

Aerich nodded, and looked once more at the letter he had just written. The text upon it was as follows:

> *My Dear Galstan*, it read, *I hope this letter finds you well. I hope, moreover, that your mission was successful. I have heard nothing from you or from our brave Tiassa, yet I imagine it is too soon for the results, if any, to be known, and even too soon for me to write to him. Nevertheless, if you have learned anything, I should be most glad to hear of it.*
>
> *As for other matters*, it continued, *I confess that I worry about you. A certain delicacy prevented my interrogating you while you were here, yet I begin to believe that I should have. Word reaches my ears of stirrings to the west that are stretching out in our direction. The encroachment of Easterners in this district increases, and more of them are moving west. Tazendra, who left some years ago upon what she*

called a "quest," has not returned, nor have I heard word of her. A certain oracle who lives in the district and passes by once or twice a year, speaks of occurrences in Dzur Mountain and pretends that great events are afoot.

And in all of this, I think of you, my dear friend, and am taken with a fear that matters will put us upon opposite sides. This would be a great sadness to me. For this reason, I wish to know something of your plans, your intentions, and, especially, whom you are now serving, and in what capacity. Believe me when I say that my only reason for this request is the desire to avoid crossing blades with you. Of the things I treasure in this life, there is nothing to which I attach more value than my friendship with you, Tazendra, and Khaavren; and if anything I can do might serve to prevent a rupture of that friendship, I should like to know what it is, because you must believe that, if it lies within my power, I will do it.

I remain, my dear friend.
Your affectionate
Aerich.

Aerich picked this letter up, quickly signed it, spread the sand, and brushed it off, after which he handed it to Steward, who accepted it with a bow.

"To what address does Your Venerance wish it sent?" he asked.

Aerich considered for a long moment, then finally said, "None. Throw it into the fire on your way out."

Steward bowed, and, without expression, carried out his master's orders.

Chapter the Twenty-Ninth

How Our Friends Arrived
At Deathgate Falls, and
What They Did There

The months between Zerika's departure from Dzur Mountain and and her approach to Deathgate Falls have been the subject of countless romances and numberless ballads, none of them agreeing with any of the others in important details, except for those occasions when some especially inspired incident, such as the supposed "debate with the dragon," are copied by all of those who follow. In fact, none of those on the journey have spoken of anything save its remarkable end, wherefore, however, much the historian wishes to, he can say nothing useful on this long and, we may assume, arduous journey until the point in time when, nearly a full year after setting off on their mission, Piro looked around and said, "How high up are we?"

Kytraan said, "It feels to be the same height as North Pinewood Hold, which has been measured as nearly half a league higher than the sea."

"Bah. North Pinewood Hold is a thousand miles from the sea; how can they know that?"

"As to that, I cannot say."

"In any case," broke in Zerika, "if Sethra's maps continue to be as true as they have been, then we are going no higher."

"How, no higher?" said Piro. "And yet, we can plainly see peaks above us."

"That is true, but we should soon run into the Blood River, which we will follow into the Greymist Valley. And, as we will be following a river, well, you perceive we must therefore go down."

"Cha!" said Piro. "In this place, well, if the river were to flow up I should not be astonished."

"For my part," said Kytraan, "neither would I."

Zerika smiled, "Well, nevertheless, it behaves as other rivers do, at least in such mundane matters as choosing a direction in which to flow. However, do not drink the water."

"I shall not, I assure you," said Piro.

"Nor will I," said Kytraan.

Tazendra, in the meantime, had been studying the area carefully. She turned back, frowning.

"Your pardon, my dear Dzurlord," said Zerika, "but it seems to me that you are frowning."

"Am I?" said Tazendra. "Well, I am not astonished at that."

"How, are you perturbed?"

"A little."

"Then, have you failed to find the trail?"

"Oh, no, the trail is exactly where it should be."

"And then, what is the trouble?"

"Exactly that."

"I beg your pardon, my dear Tazendra, but I do not understand what you do me the honor to tell me."

"We have found everything too easily, precisely where the map says it is, and, furthermore, with no opposition, either natural or human. We have only twice had to dismount to guide our horses up slopes, and only once has the weather been sufficiently inclement that we were forced to seek shelter, which shelter, you may remember, we found at once. We have not seen a single dragon in the mountains, nor have we heard the call of the dzur, nor even met a darr, though all of these beasts live here. Three times we passed what could have been bands of brigands, but they avoided us. We even saw an army of Easterners, but, as you recall, even they didn't come near us. I tell you plainly it worries me. A quest such as ours should not come so easily."

Kytraan and Piro considered this remarkable reasoning, but Zerika only shrugged. "I think you have nothing to worry about, my friend. I am certain that, if everything is easy now, well, soon enough we will have enough opposition to satisfy even you."

"How, you think so?"

"I am convinced of it."

"Well, I am satisfied, then. The trail will take us around that boulder, and I can even see the glint of water just beyond it."

"And so you think — ?"

"That we have found the Blood River."

"Then we are very nearly there."

"Well," said Tazendra.

Zerika urged her horse forward and others followed.

It has been suggested that the Blood River got its name because of its reddish tint; an absurd notion when one considers that all bodies of water beneath the Enclouding have, to one degree or another, a reddish tint. Others have claimed that it is, in fact, a river of blood: that somehow the blood from those who pass over the falls finds its way, perhaps through hidden springs, back up into the Ash Mountains. While this has never been proven or disproven by investigation, this historian begs leave to doubt it. In this case, as in so many others, the simplest explanation is probably the truth: The Blood River is an obvious, if fanciful, name for the body of water that passes through the Greymist Valley and flows over Deathgate Falls to the Paths of the Dead.

The Greymist Valley itself stretches some twenty or twenty-five miles, beginning next to Hanging Mountain, and continuing past the next of the three peaks that, still part of the Eastern Mountains, are together called the Ash Mountains. This next mountain is called Gyffer's Peak, and it, of the three, is the one beside which the greatest channel has been cut by the fast-flowing Blood River. The valley has never been inhabited save by various vegetation and the meaner sorts of wildlife, yet it is a picturesque enough setting, with the dark mountains looming above on both sides, the snowy caps of Gyffer's Peak behind, and the soft green of Round Mountain before.

Gyffer's Peak, in general, has rather gentle slopes, and, unlike the others, is even populated upon some of its lower slopes, though not, as we said, in the valley itself. But there are several villages on the west side where coffee beans are grown. In the days of the Empire, these beans were often brought overland to the Eastern River or to the Spearhead Channel and thus to the Kieron's Sea. Needless to say, this economy has collapsed with Adron's Disaster, and so the villages were, at this time, all but deserted, which led Tazendra to remark, "Perhaps, on our return journey, we can stop and gather some coffee beans, for I am told the very best beans come from this district."

"Perhaps," said Zerika. "Yet it seems you are likely to be too busy on the return for such excursions."

"Then you think there will be trouble."

"It seems likely enough."

"Then I am satisfied."

"I beg your pardon," said Piro to Zerika, "but it seems to me that you have said, 'you.'"

"Well, and is it not a perfectly good word?"

"Oh, as to that, I say nothing against the word."

"And then?"

"But I worry about implications."

"Ah! Implications!"

"Yes. That is to say, it would seem as if you imply that you will not be with us on the return."

"How, had you thought I would be?"

"I must admit, that was my assumption."

"And mine," said Kytraan.

"And mine," said Tazendra.

"Well," said Zerika, "but, while it may be possible to descend Deathgate Falls, it is not possible to return by climbing up it again."

"It is not?" said Piro.

"So I am informed by Sethra Lavode, who should know, I think."

"Well, but then," said Kytraan, "where will you be?"

"Oh, as to that, I have not the least idea in the world, I assure you."

"You don't know where you will be?" said Kytraan.

Zerika shrugged. "Sethra has told me that, if I succeed and am permitted to leave the Halls of Judgment, I could emerge anywhere. There is no way to predict."

Tazendra, Kytraan, and Piro all looked at each other. Piro then cleared has throat and said, "So you will appear somewhere, and be entirely on your own?"

"Yes," said Zerika.

"In that case," said Piro, "I shall descend the Falls with you."

"As will I," said Tazendra.

"And I," said Kytraan.

"No," said Zerika, "you will not."

Piro said, "And yet —"

"I may," said Zerika, "or may not be able to emerge from the Halls of Judgment with the Orb. But it is certain you will not."

Kytraan said, "But —"

"You will die," said Zerika. "Sethra knows that as certainly as she knows anything."

"Oh," said Tazendra, "that is of no concern."

"And yet," said Zerika, "should you die, and be held in the Paths of the Dead, well, you will be able to do me no good in any case."

"That is true," said Piro. "Nevertheless —"

"There is no nevertheless," said Zerika. "I have decided."

"And yet —"

"The matter is settled," said the Phoenix.

None of them had heard Zerika speak in such a tone before; especially to Piro, who had known her the longest. It startled him in no small degree to hear his old friend, who had always been of a quiet and retiring nature, speak with such finality and certainty, as if her word were law, and a final decision was made simply because she declared it so. Piro stared at her, Kytraan nodded dumbly, and Tazendra sighed and shrugged, and so the matter was settled. Behind them, Mica and Lar exchanged looks, but, of course, neither dared to enter into the conversation.

There was then little sound as they rode, though the Blood River, making its swift way over rocks and boulders, created its own sort of ceaseless music that was not unpleasant.

Some hours later they heard a steady crashing sound that Piro recognized as coming from a waterfall. "Is that it?" he said, straining to look forward in the growing dusk.

Zerika frowned. "It shouldn't be. If the map tells the truth, we have yet another ten or twelve miles before we reach it."

In fact, they soon reached a waterfall, in which the Blood River went crashing over the lip in a great torrent to land amid spray and fine mist some hundred feet below. They stopped and admired it from an overhanging cliff for some time, then turned to continue on the path. As they did so, Mica said, "Hello."

Tazendra turned to him. "What is it, Mica? For I perceive you have spoken."

In answer, the lackey pointed behind them. They all looked in the indicated direction.

"What is it?" said Tazendra after a moment. "I see nothing."

"Mistress, I saw what seemed to be several horsemen in the valley behind us."

"How many?" said Zerika.

"I am uncertain, my lady."

"How far behind?" said Tazendra.

"I am a poor judge of distances, mistress, yet it was a long way; I could not make out figures clearly, only that, for a moment, it seemed that there were several horses and riders silhouetted upon that ridge."

Zerika turned to the Dzurlord. "Well?"

Tazendra shrugged. "If he says he saw them, well, I, for one, believe him."

"Very well," said Zerika. "Then we will leave the path, and will rest without a fire tonight."

To this, the others agreed without complaint, though it was a trial, especially on Lar, who had been taking a certain pleasure in preparing simple yet tasteful meals as they traveled.

They left the path, then, and dismounted, leading their horses some hundred meters up into the mountains, and, eschewing Tazendra's sorcerous abilities, they arranged for each of them to spend an hour on watch, looking to see if anyone came near them during the night. While they didn't see anyone, Kytraan, during his watch, fancied he heard, very faintly, the sound of horses' hooves. While he did not wake up the camp, he mentioned it the next morning as they prepared to resume their journey.

"Well," said Piro, shrugging. "There is nothing to do but go on."

"With this I agree," said Zerika.

Returning to the trail once more, they looked carefully, but saw nothing. Zerika pulled her cloak more closely around her against the morning chill, then glanced up at the heavy Enclouding. "The wind is from the west," she remarked.

"Is that an omen, do you think?" asked Tazendra.

Zerika shrugged.

They discovered as they rode that, some time after passing the waterfall, they had, in fact, left Gyffer's Peak, and were now on Round Mountain. The Blood River, once more flowing on their right, was slower and wider, as if gathering itself for the great plunge that it knew was coming.

"Do you know," remarked Tazendra as they rode, "from a distance, the mountain appears quite green; yet I see nothing here except grey rocks."

"Well," said Kytraan, "perhaps we are above the greenery."

"Look up there," said Piro. "What is that?"

"It is not green," said Tazendra.

"It appears," said Kytraan, "to be either a particularly odd formation of stone, or else a sculpture, though of what I cannot say."

"It is a phoenix," said Zerika coolly.

They came closer and found that it was, indeed, a sculpture of a phoenix, and one, moreover, that appeared to have survived the ages with no wearing away whatsoever. Zerika stopped and dismounted, then knelt before it, her head bowed; and she spoke very quietly, as if addressing it. The others remained mounted, back a certain distance, and silent.

When Zerika had finished, and was climbing onto her horse

(unaided, we should add, except for a convenient rock lying near to the path), Tazendra said, "Do you hear something?"

Piro nodded. "I believe it may be the sound of a waterfall up ahead."

Kytraan said, "Would that be—?"

"Yes," said Zerika. "We have arrived."

They urged their horses forward, and soon reached another statue, this one showing a jhegaala in its wingèd form, just taking to the air.

They passed more statuary. When they reached the tiassa, which was poised upon its hind legs, wings outspread, Piro wondered if he were supposed make a sort of obeisance; but not knowing, he contented himself with removing his hat as he passed by it. Shortly thereafter they passed the sculpture of the dragon, showing only its head; Kytraan bowed to it as they moved on. They passed the marker of a hawk, not caught in flight, as was its depiction in the Cycle, but standing, posed, looking back toward Deathgate Falls, which was now clearly audible, though still muffled.

They followed the river through a curve, the sound of the Falls becoming ever louder, and soon passed a larger-than-life sculpture of a man, standing naked, sword in hand, looking back away from the Falls.

"Kieron the Conqueror," said Zerika. "The first human to pass this way. Sethra says he still remains in the Paths, waiting for his time."

Kytraan removed his hat and solemnly saluted the statue. Piro said, "With the Empire fallen, well, I wonder what better time there would be."

Zerika shrugged.

The river seemed to be picking up speed now, as if suddenly in a hurry to reach the Falls and be done with its journey at last. Nearby was the dzur, which, like the dragon, showed only the head of the beast, mouth open as if to tear at the observer's throat. Just beyond it was the lip of Deathgate Falls. Seen from the top, it appeared, as a waterfall often will, to be utterly harmless, just a place where the water picked up speed, broke into occasional frothy whitecaps, and disappeared out of sight, without the least indication of the distance it would fall, nor what waited beneath. The west bank of the lip, dominated by the dzur's head, was a semicircular clearing of around forty or fifty feet in diameter; it almost seemed to have been carved out of the rock to provide a place for any last rituals before the body of a departed friend or family member was given to the Falls. And, indeed, perhaps this was the case, for there are mysteries surrounding Deathgate Falls that the historian will make no claims to have solved.

The travelers approached the lip and looked over it, seeing nothing below except thick mist.

"How far down is it?" asked Piro.

"No one knows," said Zerika.

"Well," said Kytraan. "What now?"

"I must consider," said Zerika, "the best way to descend."

As they considered, they were startled by loud cries, like screams or screeches. All of them looked around, until at last Tazendra said, "Above us."

They looked up, and saw four or five shapes circling overhead.

"Jhereg," said Zerika.

"Has something died?" said Tazendra.

"When they see activity here, they know there is usually a corpse nearby," said Zerika.

"And yet," said Kytraan, "it would seem that they would hesitate to attempt to feed upon a corpse when it is surrounded by men."

"These are not the jhereg of the jungles or the cities," said Zerika. "They are much higher up, and, consequently, larger, than they seem."

"Oh," said Piro. "Should we be worried?"

"No," said Zerika. "Soon they will realize that there is no scent of a corpse, and they will not bother us. They will not attack a living man."

"In fact," said Kytraan, "I am just as glad that they will not."

"Well," said Tazendra, shrugging.

Zerika turned her attention back to Deathgate Falls.

"How will you get down?" said Piro.

"I am considering that very question," said Zerika.

"How, did you not discuss it with Sethra?"

"Well, we did discuss it, only—"

"Yes?"

"We did not arrive at a conclusion."

"A conclusion," pronounced Tazendra, "would be good."

"We have rope," said Zerika. "We could tie it to one of the sculptures and I could lower myself that way."

"Have you sufficient rope?" said Piro.

"Two thousand feet," said Zerika. "If that isn't enough, well, then I can always let go. Jumping was an option we considered."

"Not seriously, I hope," said Kytraan.

"Entirely seriously. It is placing myself in the hands of the gods."

"And yet—"

"It was not," said Zerika, "our first choice."

"Well," said Piro. "I, for one, am glad that it was not."

"I agree," said Kytraan, "because if you jump—oh."

Piro looked at him. "Oh?"

Rather than giving him an answer, Kytraan pointed back the way they had come.

"Horsemen," said Tazendra.

"Several of them," agreed Piro.

Mica, with the attitude of a man who had been in such situations many times, coolly untied his bar-stool from his saddle and held it ready in his hand.

"You think there will be trouble?" said Lar.

"It is possible," said Mica, doing his best to imitate his mistress's manner at such times, and, we must admit, making an entirely credible job of it.

"Well," said Lar, and, taking a deep breath, began to dig around in his saddle-pockets.

Zerika said, "How many of them are there?"

Tazendra stood up in her stirrups, as if a little additional height would give her better vision. "Perhaps a dozen," she said.

"Do you think they wish to stop us?" said Kytraan.

"As to that," said Piro, "who can say?"

"Soon we will know," said Tazendra, and gently rolled her shoulders, the significance of which we trust the reader remembers.

"The question," said Zerika, "is whether we ought to wait and find out."

"I believe," said Piro, "that the question is, have we any other choice?"

"That, too, is a good question," said Kytraan.

"If we charge them," said Tazendra, "then, well, all will soon be settled."

"That is true," said Zerika. "And yet, what if their intentions toward us are friendly?"

"Or their presence could be entirely unrelated to us," said Kytraan. "Consider that we are at Deathgate Falls, where for millennia bodies have been brought to attempt passage to the Halls of Judgment."

"Perhaps," said Zerika. "But how many expeditions to Deathgate have you heard of since Adron's Disaster?"

"Well, it is true that there have not been many, but nevertheless—"

"I believe," said Zerika, "that we are safe in making the assumption that their presence here is related, in some manner, to our own."

"Let us charge them," said Tazendra.

"But," said Piro, "how could they know about us?"

"In many ways," said Zerika. "The simplest divination could answer a question to anyone who knows enough to ask. Or they could have spied us as we rode, and be following us for some reason. They could have been sent by Sethra with aid for us. They could have been sent by the gods to stop us. They—"

"Let us charge them," said Tazendra.

"On my word of honor," said Kytraan, "I am not far from agreeing with Tazendra."

"We cannot attack them," said Zerika, "until we know if they are hostile, indifferent, or friendly toward us."

"Nevertheless," said Tazendra, "I believe—"

"The matter is settled," said Zerika.

Tazendra sighed.

"But in case they are hostile," added the Phoenix, "let us remain mounted."

"With this I agree," said Tazendra.

Kytraan urged his horse forward until he was shoulder-to-shoulder with Tazendra; Piro, for his part, came forward to the Dzurlord's other side. In this position they waited.

"Do you know," said Kytraan after a moment, "I believe I recognize the fellow in front."

"Yes," said Piro. "If I am not mistaken, it is the charming bandit whom we met on the way. Wadre, was that not his name?"

"Indeed," said Kytraan. "That is it exactly. And that seems to be the sorceress we met. What was her name?"

"Orlaan. But what could they wish? We have no more wealth than we did the last time we met."

"That is true," said Piro. "And yet, I do not like it that they are together. I believe that their intentions toward us are not friendly."

Tazendra shrugged. "Then so much the worse for them."

"Your mistress is not lacking in confidence," remarked Lar.

"She has reason," said Mica smugly.

"You perceive," said Kytraan, "that the sorcerer, Orlaan, has drawn her weapon."

"Well," said Zerika. "Then let us show her equal courtesy."

"With this plan, I agree," said Tazendra, at once drawing her over-sized blade, which she contrived to hold with one hand as if it were a rapier. It was, we should say, what is called a hand-and-a-half sword, and rather bedecked with jewels, most of them rubies upon the hilt and even inside the bell; yet it was by no means a "dress sword," but, rather, one intended for business.

Kytraan drew his much more modest, though still entirely serviceable, blade, which was of the type most favored by soldiers, having enough weight to protect one's self against the heaviest blade, enough length to permit a good thrust when it was called for, but being mostly designed for cutting, being sharp on both edges for its entire length, rather wide, and with a hilt long enough to accommodate two hands for those situations where brute strength, and nothing but brute strength, would do the job.

Piro, not to be left out, drew his own sword, which was considerably the smallest of the three, at least in thickness, though it was of good length, and made of fine steel, dating back to the Sixteenth Cycle, and never having required more than the touch of a whetstone to restore a razor's edge to it. Piro's mother had discovered it in the armory of Whitecrest Manor and, though she pretended ignorance of its history, recognized it at once as a well-constructed and versatile weapon.

Zerika had a dueler's blade—thin, light, and flexible—the sort of weapon one would not expect to encounter in general combat, and which looked as if it would break easily if asked to parry too heavy a stroke, yet she drew it and held it as if she was well acquainted with its length.

Soon Wadre and Orlaan, followed by the rest of the band, came up before them and held there. Orlaan gave them a bow that seemed to Piro to contain a good measure of irony, and she said, "Greetings to you, fellow travelers. I am called Orlaan, and I have met some of you before."

Kytraan and Piro returned her greeting, and Zerika said, "I am Zerika, and this is Tazendra, and I wish you a good day."

"A good day?" said Orlaan. "Well, you wish me a good day. You hope my day is good. And yet, my dear Zerika, as you style yourself, I have cause to believe that for my day to be good requires yours to be less than good. What then?"

"Oh, then?" said Zerika, shrugging. "Then I no longer wish you a good day. You perceive I am a very changeable person."

"And I," said Orlaan, "admit to a curiosity, which I hope you will do me the kindness to satisfy."

"And yet, madam, if a good day for you requires a bad day for me, I fail to see why I should satisfy your curiosity or anything else."

"That is entirely just."

"And then?"

Orlaan shrugged. "You must have a question or two of me. Come. A bargain. If you will answer a question for me, well, then I will answer a question for you."

"In fact," said Zerika, "I do have a question for you, and that is, do you intend to attempt to thwart my mission?"

"Ah, but how can I answer that before I know what your mission is? And that, you perceive, is exactly my question."

"You know well enough what we are doing here, madam," said Piro suddenly.

"How, you think so?" said Orlaan.

"I am entirely convinced of it."

"Well," said Orlaan. "If the lady who has done me the honor to introduce herself as Zerika is, as she seems to be, of the House of the Phoenix, than, well, I believe I can make a guess as to her mission."

"And then?" said Zerika.

"I regret to say that I cannot permit it to continue."

"Well, that is right and correct," said Zerika, returning irony for irony.

"And what of you?" said Piro, addressing Wadre.

The brigand shrugged and said, "As for us, well, we must do something."

"But do you know of our mission?"

"I? Not the least in the world, I assure you."

"And if I were to tell you that we hope to do nothing less than to restore the Empire, well, what then?"

Wadre shrugged. "I should then say that you are not alone. Indeed, I have met forces from as far away as the Kanefthali Mountains who have come east with that intention."

"And yet," said Piro, "we have—"

"No," said Zerika. "We will not engage in arguments with brigands. Or, at any rate, we will not argue with words."

"Come," said Tazendra, "I like the sound of that." She flexed her sword, displaying how easily it moved in her hand, while sketching a sort of salute ending with the the weapon pointing at the eye of Mora, who was directly opposite her. Now Mora, who was Wadre's lieutenant, was not one to let a compliment like this pass without response; she immediately spurred her horse, yet the horse had hardly moved when Wadre moved his arm in an indication that she was not to advance beyond him, wherefore she drew rein, her sword, and the conclusion that the time was not yet quite at hand to charge. Those behind her, seeing the weapon in her hand, made haste to arm themselves as well.

"If you are determined to play," said Wadre, taking his own weapon into his hand, "I give you my word we will accommodate you."

"Shards!" said Tazendra. "I hope I will not need to beg!"

Piro felt his heart leap as the moment for action seemed veritably at hand. He gripped his sword tighter, then, remembering his lessons, made his hand relax, so his grip was "firm enough to withstand a shock, but never so tight as to inhibit the flow of blood to the hand," as his father had said. Kytraan, likewise, drew himself up in preparation for exchanging blows.

"Steady," said Zerika in a sharp tone.

Piro, for his part, froze in place. Kytraan shifted in his saddle, but otherwise held himself still. Tazendra turned her head, looked back at the Phoenix, and said, "Well?"

"We are not here," said Zerika coolly, "to dispute with these persons, but for a purpose which you know as well as I. I suggest that we give them the opportunity to leave peacefully, and let us do what we came to do."

"That," said Orlaan, "is unlikely."

"Then you intend to dispute with us."

"That is precisely our intention."

"Then I must reflect."

"Reflect?" said Tazendra.

"Reflect?" said Orlaan.

"Reflect?" said Piro.

"Reflect?" said Wadre.

"Exactly," said Zerika. "You perceive, I am not here to be a hero, but to accomplish a purpose, and I must consider the best way to do so."

"Well," said Orlaan, "I give you my word, I intend to stop you."

"Madam," said Zerika, "I do not doubt your word."

"That's lucky," said Orlaan.

For a moment no one moved, and then Zerika abruptly sheathed her sword.

"How," said Tazendra. "You cannot mean to surrender!"

"Surrender is," said Orlaan, "a wise choice."

"As for surrender, well, I'm afraid I must leave you, my friends, to make that decision on your own. Tazendra, I leave you with command, do as you think best."

"How," said Tazendra. "You leave me?"

"I do."

"That is, you leave?"

"Precisely."

"But, where are you going?"

"Where I am required to go."

"But you can't —"

"Good luck, my dear Viscount, and I hope Fortune permits us to meet again."

Piro said, "Zivra —"

This was, however, all the Phoenix had to say. Without another word, then, she turned her horse, and, applying her heels to its flanks, charged forward — that is, directly over the edge of Deathgate Falls, and so down to the Paths of the Dead waiting far below.

Chapter the Thirtieth

How They Battled Above
Deathgate Falls

T he reader, who is certainly aware that not everyone who plummets a great distance into a landscape full of the mystical and the arcane is gone forever, must bear in mind that those who found themselves atop Deathgate Falls having seen the Phoenix ride off the cliff had no such awareness at all, but, rather the opposite: the certainty that they had seen the last of Zerika. We must therefore ask the reader, who knows the outcome of Zerika's action, to remember that those who lived through the experience had neither the foreknowledge of the oracle, nor the hindsight of the historian, but knew only what they could see: Zerika had just ridden straight off Deathgate Falls. Indeed, even Zerika's own remarks upon the subject, which the reader might think should have given them a clue, were lost in the suddenness of the event.

For a moment, no one stirred—everyone astonished by Zerika's precipitous action. Piro, who had been watching her, continued to stare at the place from which she had jumped, as if he expected her to emerge from the Falls in the exact spot from which she had departed. While, to the right, he knew that his friend was dead, yet, to the left, he was unable to truly accept it. The others, though shocked, managed to recover more quickly. It was Kytraan who spoke first, saying, "My dear Orlaan, and you, my good Wadre, it seems that your reason for being here has just, well, vanished."

"That is true," said Tazendra. "But I hope if you were, as I believe, about to do us the honor of charging us, well, the mere fact that there is now no reason to do so will not be sufficient to dissuade you."

"I must admit," said Wadre, "that it is very near to doing so."

Orlaan did not reply, but contented herself with staring at the place from which Zerika had jumped, as if she, like Piro, expected to see the Phoenix return from over the thundering waterfall.

"Bah," said Tazendra. "We cannot have you come here, threaten

us, prepare for violence, excite us, intrigue us, make us ready ourselves for mortal combat, and then have you simply turn and ride
away. It would be, well, it would not be right. I say so. Upon my
word, if you will not charge us, well, we will charge you."

"It is useless," said Wadre, shrugging.

Orlaan slowly brought her eyes up to meet Tazendra's. After giving the Dzurlord a look of hatred, she turned away once more.
Tazendra, for her part, frowned and said, "There is something familiar about you."

Orlaan shrugged.

Piro was finally able to pull his eyes and his attention away from
Deathgate Falls, and return it to those in front of him. Using only his
knees, he brought his horse forward until he was shoulder-to-
shoulder with Tazendra and Kytraan.

Wadre, meanwhile, said, "Are you certain you will have it so? As
you have said, there is no longer a reason —"

"Certainly," said Tazendra.

"No," said Piro.

Tazendra looked at him. "I beg your pardon, young man, but —"

"We have come here for a purpose. Our purpose has failed. To
take out our frustration by bloodletting is, well—what would your
friend Aerich say? Or my father, Khaavren?"

"Oh, as to that —"

"Well?"

Tazendra sighed. "Yes, you are right, Viscount. I concede the
argument. And yet —"

"Yes?"

"There is something about that woman."

"Who, Orlaan?"

"Yes. She made a gesture that seemed familiar to me, and, moreover, did you notice how, when you mentioned the name of your
father and of Aerich, her eyes gleamed, as if with hatred?"

"I noticed," said Kytraan.

Orlaan scowled, and lifted her hand, palm out. Tazendra, for her
part, matched this gesture by quickly raising the staff that had been
hanging from her saddle. Orlaan scowled and, evidently not prepared to face a sorcerous duel with someone who was obviously a
wizard, lowered her hand. Tazendra lowered her staff and shrugged.

Orlaan turned to Wadre and said, "Kill them."

"Very well, then," said Wadre, who then turned to Mora and
said, "Kill them."

"That's better," said Tazendra.

Now our friends were positioned, at this time, on the west bank of the Blood River, and those in back (by which we mean the lackeys, Mica and Lar) were only ten or fifteen feet from the waterfall itself, so they had very little room to retreat. Not that Tazendra had a moment's thought of retreating—on the contrary, she at once spurred her horse forward, giving a loud cry rather like the screech of the creekowl, and began swinging her sword in what appeared to be wild, uncontrolled motions over her head. In reality, these motions were neither wild nor uncontrolled, but, rather, precisely calculated to inflict as much damage as possible upon her enemy—that being, in fact, Mora herself—while making it appear that the Dzurlord had less skill as a swordsman than she had; and, simultaneously, doing everything she could to startle and perhaps even frighten the enemy. The efficacy of these tactics we shall prove at once.

In addition to Orlaan, who was standing aside from the fight, and Wadre, who was, although commanding it, not yet directly participating, there were ten of the brigands. Now, it is well known that in a fight on horseback, the initiative belongs to those who are moving; that is, the usual laws of military science that make the defender stronger than the attacker are overridden, if the reader will excuse the unintentional play on words, by the inherent strength of a mounted attack and the inherent weakness of a mounted defense. This was one advantage our friends had, which helped make up for the disparity of numbers. Another advantage occurred almost at once when Tazendra's blade snaked its way under Mora's guard and cut her solidly in the side, breaking two of her ribs as well as knocking her onto the ground.

At the same time, Piro, who had now experienced his first battle, was taking no chances with his own skin, but allowed his horse to carry him forward while maintaining a good guard position until he saw that he had an opening, where one of the brigands, thrown off balance by an instinctive response to Piro's rapidly charging horse, left his sword too far out of line, a mistake for which he paid dearly, as the point of Piro's sword took him in the side of his neck, giving him a deep puncture that was not easily mended, and even less easily ignored.

Kytraan lost no time in upholding his end. He at once charged directly at Wadre, reasoning that the brigands would be less inclined to fight if their leader were dead. The reasoning was good, but made without Wadre, who objected to the idea of permitting his skin to be punctured, and who registered this objection by turning his horse's head and taking himself out of combat, whereupon Kytraan turned his attention to another rider, with whom he dueled in splendid, and, one might even say, classic style for two or three passes before giving his enemy a cut in the shoulder that caused him to drop his weapon.

By this time, we should say that the enemy, by which we refer to Wadre's band, was well scattered; this scattering being augmented by Mica, who though he had not hit anyone with his famous bar-stool, had at least made several of them duck as he rode directly through the middle of the melee, swinging wildly. Moreover, Lar had made his presence felt, which was proved by the pale expression upon the Teckla's face, and by a brigand who was stretched out insensible full length upon the ground.

"Now that was well done," said Mica admiringly.

Lar did not answer, being too overcome by his first taste of combat; but he did manage to make a small bow to acknowledge the compliment.

"But tell me," said Mica. "What did you hit him with that laid him upon the ground so effectually?"

For answer, Lar held up a large pan made entirely of cast iron.

"Well," said Mica. "That seems to be a strong argument."

Lar gestured back toward the man lying on the ground, as if to say, "He thinks so, at any rate."

In the meantime, our friends turned their horses, prepared to receive a countercharge as best they could, pleased that they had evened up the numbers somewhat, and even more pleased that they no longer had the waterfall at their back. However, there was no countercharge. Indeed, there was no one to make a countercharge. The one called Orlaan was nowhere to be seen, and, except for those who were wounded or insensible, the brigands had scattered to the winds; indeed, Wadre could be seen and even heard trying to call them together.

"What," said Tazendra. "Have we won so easily?"

"I think we have," said Piro.

"Their heart was not in the fight," said Kytraan.

"Neither was mine, come to that," said Piro, looking at the top of the cliff. Indeed, if we have failed to reveal what was passing in Piro's heart during the moments of battle, it was, in part, because his own confusion provided little room for any other emotion. The reader, we believe, can understand readily enough: a friend with whom he had grown up was now, so he believed, lost. He recalled his delight upon meeting her at Dzur Mountain, and how he had spoken with pleasure of setting out with her on an "adventure." He had been aware that adventure means danger, and it had even occurred to him that he could die in the course of carrying out his duty; he had never considered that he might have to watch his friend die, and that in his duty he would utterly fail.

Now, for the first time, he had some understanding of the remorse that dominated his father's life: the sense of having committed himself to a cause, and to fall short in the test. Though still stunned by the suddenness of what had happened, he also tasted bitterness. Piro had been prepared for hardship, for pain, even for death; he had not been prepared for failure and the loss of a friend.

And yet, we must remind the reader that Piro came of strong stock, and that he was, moreover, young. And so for this reason, the bitterness to which we have just alluded, while there, did not overwhelm him. As he stood upon the cliff, staring out over Deathgate Falls, he set his jaw, and he clasped the hilt of his sword.

"Well, but what do we do now?" said Tazendra.

"To remain here is useless," said Kytraan.

"Well, but then? If our mission has failed—"

"Yes?" said Kytraan. "If it has?"

"Well, then at least we can gain satisfaction."

"How, satisfaction? What sort of satisfaction do you speak of?"

"What else, but the satisfaction of tracking down the rest of those brigands?"

"Ah," said Kytraan. "Yes, I can understand that. For my part, I think it an excellent plan."

"Do you?" said Tazendra. "That is splendid. And you, Piro?"

"No," said Piro, turning from the cliff to look at his companions.

"No?"

"No, we return to Dzur Mountain."

"And yet—"

"Above all, we must speak with Sethra Lavode. It was she who gave us this mission, and to her we must report on its results."

"And yet," said Tazendra. "To permit those brigands to escape—"

"They are nothing. They are beneath our notice."

"Well, but what about that Orlaan?"

Piro frowned. "Well, as to Orlaan, there is something there."

"Yes. I wish I could remember . . . ah! I have it!"

"Well?"

"She is Greycat's daughter."

"How, Greycat? Garland? Who hurt my father's hand, assassinated several nobles, and was the cause of so much trouble at the end of the last Phoenix Reign?"

"The very one. His daughter ran from the fight, and must have escaped the Disaster, though it could not have been by much. Now, what was her name?"

"Grita," said Piro, who, perhaps because of how rarely his father was willing to speak of the past, was all the more certain to remember every detail when he did.

"That is it," said Tazendra.

"Grita," repeated Piro, as if to himself.

"What then?" said Kytraan.

Piro considered for several minutes; then at last he said, "We return to Dzur Mountain. And as for Grita, well, we need not worry about finding her; she will find us. And I think it may be that our friend Wadre will find us as well. We must not relax our vigilance for an instant."

"We will not relax our vigilance," said Tazendra, who, the reader may note, at this moment surrendered to Piro the command entrusted to her by Zerika. We hope the reader will not judge her too harshly for this. In any case, so far as we know, the Empress at no time uttered a word of criticism on the subject.

"And what of the wounded?" said Kytraan.

Piro looked at the brigands, one insensible, others wounded and striving to stanch their bleeding. "Leave them," he said. Let us go."

Piro gave a last look at Deathgate Falls, then turned and led his friends in retracing their steps, less than an hour in time from when they had reached that place. No one spoke as they made their way slowly back up the Blood River.

Chapter the Thirty-First

How Sethra Lavode Received a Visitor

As our friends rode, there was a very remarkable sight some five hundred leagues away—indeed, one very worthy of remark, had there been anyone there to see it. Of course, it is an oft-debated question as to whether there is such a thing as a sight without an observer, a sound without a hearer, or a flavor without a taster. This debate, we should point out, occurs mostly among philosophers of the House of the Athyra, rarely among historians of the House of the Hawk. The reason for this is simple enough: An event happens, and it produces an effect. Both the event and its effect are part of history whether they are known at once, learned of centuries later, or never discovered at all. To put it another way, the historian must take history as it actually occurred, and has not the freedom (or, rather, the apparent freedom) to consider whether or not something that happened has a metaphysical unreality, any more than a Dragonlord in the midst of battle has the luxury to consider whether enemy soldiers are mere phantasms conjured by his imagination for the playing out of tactical scenarios. The reader might argue that there are, indeed, certain persons who are both mystics and historians; to this, we can only suggest the reader take for himself the trouble to read what such persons produce, after which the reader is invited to draw his own conclusions as to the result of such unnatural combinations.

This settled, then, we repeat that, though there was no one to see, there was a remarkable sight some five hundred leagues to the south and a little west. An observer would have seen, in a grove of trees in a small wooded area in the western part of the duchy of Arylle, a peculiar shimmering in the air, similar to the distortion that can be caused by particularly warm air, although confined to a narrow space. This shimmering gradually intensified, and took on a golden, glittering quality, as if the sparks of a fire were swirling about in a minuscule cyclone. Over the course of just a few seconds, these sparks coalesced until they came to resemble the outline of a human body standing upright. The sparks became more solid until it was, indeed, a human body, in particular one resembling a lady of the House of the Dragon, standing there—although whether it enveloped a human soul is a question we will leave to those Athyra philosophers with whom we dispensed in the preceding paragraph.

She stood still for a moment, her eyes closed, then opened them and looked around with the curiosity of a baby; or, at any rate, of something newly born into the world. She showed no fear; indeed, other than a mild curiosity, she displayed upon her countenance no emotion of any kind. After looking around for some few moments, she began moving. We will not say "walking" because what she did was not precisely walking, although her feet moved back and forth in much the manner of someone walking. Nor did she appear to be fly-ing, because she never rose in altitude. It was, perhaps, not unlike floating, except that she remained in an upright position and, as we have said, her feet continued to move.

We must say that, in all of history, and in all of the natural and magical sciences, we have never heard, before or since, of anyone traveling in this manner, and, what is more, we must regretfully admit that we do not know how it was accomplished, yet there is no question that it happened, because the traveler was witnessed repeat-edly during the journey; and it should come as no surprise to the reader that to the simplehearted peasants along the traveler's route, the sight was a cause of fear and awe; and stories are still told of the ghost, or the ghoul, or the demon, or the evil wizard, who walks through the fields at night and eats babies, or steals cattle, or does whatever else monsters are supposed to do for the entertainment and terrorizing of children.

Needless to say, none of these things happened. All that hap-pened was that the traveler continued, and at great speed—indeed, whatever else can be said for her method of locomotion, it was cer-tainly the quickest that had ever been seen in those regions, save for the occasional glimpses of cat-centaurs—so quick, in fact, that she had covered twenty leagues before three hours had elapsed from her mysterious appearance. Now, we should add that these were not any twenty leagues—that is, not twenty leagues in general, but a very specific twenty leagues; to be precise, the twenty leagues between where she arrived upon the world and Dzur Mountain, which was her immediate destination. In other words, three hours after she had arrived she was upon the slopes of Dzur Mountain, where she slowed down, and began walking in a more typical manner, perhaps because she did not wish her peculiar means of travel to be observed, or perhaps because that means of travel could not be used except on level ground, or perhaps for some other reason unknown to this historian.

She came to Dzur Mountain from the north and the east, which permitted a more gentle, gradual ascent up that part of the mountain that resembled the tail of the great cat, and then along its back until, reaching its head, she came around to the west in order to climb that which can be called its face for two different yet related reasons.

There are many entrances to Dzur Mountain, some open, some concealed, and some (many, perhaps) known to the Enchantress and never discovered by anyone else. The one the traveler came to was as much of a "front door" as Dzur Mountain boasted; that is, it was a large, plainly visible—that is to say, undisguised—door, facing west and near the northern edge of what, seen from a distance, would appear to be the left ear. The traveler climbed up easily, without any apparent difficulty, even where she was required to pull herself up using only rocks as handholds. To an observer, it would have appeared that she only touched the rocks, and then, with the least effort, floated up until, in a very short time, she stood before the doorway we have just had occasion to mention.

The door itself was solid iron, which iron was wrought with the symbol of a dzur. Upon reaching it, the traveler stopped, considering, as if for the first time uncertain how to proceed. Her dilemma, if, indeed, she had one, was solved by the door itself opening inward to reveal a Teckla whom we have already met, and whom we know as Tukko. This worthy poked his head out of the door, gave the traveler a quick look, and said, "Go away," upon which he shut the door. Or, to be more precise, he *endeavored* to shut the door; the intention being foiled by the traveler, who prevented him from carrying out his plan in the simplest possible way—by placing a hand upon the door, stopping it, and then pushing it back with a strength that caused Tukko to be propelled backward at a great speed and to land unceremoniously on his back a considerable distance down the hallway.

After taking a moment to regain his feet, his composure, and his memory of his duties, by which time the traveler had fully entered the hallway, Tukko turned and pulled upon a bell-rope that was hanging a few feet behind him. Having accomplished this, he backed away, as if afraid he was about to be attacked. The traveler, however, made no hostile move, but, on the contrary, raised up both of her hands, palm out, as if to show that she was unarmed. And, indeed, it was only at this point that Tukko realized that the strange visitor did not, in fact, appear to be carrying a weapon of any sort. Now, as this was unusual, even to say unprecedented in Tukko's experience — particularly from someone who, by countenance and garb, appeared to be a Dragonlord—he suddenly became unsure of how to proceed. He looked at the visitor, his head tilted to the side like a bewildered dog's.

The visitor, now that she was inside, stood still, as if waiting for something or someone. If she was, in fact, waiting for the Enchantress, she was not disappointed; Sethra Lavode appeared in two minutes, looked over the situation, spoke briefly with Tukko, and frowned.

"Who are you?" she said.

"A friend."

"A friend? Well, that is good. Were you aware that it is not usual for a friend to enter a friend's home by force?"

"No."

"No? You were not aware of this fact?"

"I was not."

"You pretend you did not know that you should not force your way into the home of someone you call a friend?"

"I give you my word, I was never informed of this circumstance."

At this moment, the Enchantress was joined by Sethra the Younger, who appeared in response to the alarm Tukko had raised, and now rested her hand upon her sword, which was a heavy weapon of tolerable length. She said, "Who is this?"

"I am uncertain," said the Enchantress. "Yet, she claims to be a friend."

"If she is a friend, why did Tukko raise the alarm?"

"There may have been a misunderstanding on some level."

"Ah," said Sethra the Younger, continuing to gaze upon the stranger with a suspicious eye.

"What is your name?" said the Enchantress.

"Name?" said the stranger. "Oh, as to my name, well, what do you wish it to be?"

The Enchantress frowned. "You are a demon," she stated.

The visitor bowed.

"Who sent you to me?"

"The gods."

"How, the gods?"

The demon bowed once more.

The Enchantress looked at her apprentice. "We have been sent a demon," she said.

"So it seems. But to aid us, or to hinder us?"

"Oh, to aid us."

"You think so?"

"I am convinced of it." Then, turning back to the demon, she said, "Please come in. Follow me, we will sit and speak, one with the other."

"Very well," said the demon.

The Enchantress led them within, and, when they were all seated (the author cannot, in all honestly, say comfortably seated, because the demon did not appear comfortable, but, rather, appeared stiff and even rigid as she sat), she offered wine, which was politely refused.

"Well then," said the Enchantress, "let us have conversation."

"Very well," said the demon. "To this I agree. We will have conversation."

"Good. Then tell me, if you will—"

"Oh, I will, I assure you. You need have no fear that I will not answer any question you do me the honor to ask to the best of my ability."

"—why have the gods sent you to me?"

"As to that, well, I cannot speak for the gods, because they are ineffable."

Sethra the Younger made a sort of sound, earning her a glance from the Enchantress, who then cleared her throat and said, "I do not mean their motives, my dear."

"You do not?"

"Not the least in the world. I mean, what have you been sent to do?"

"Ah. Well, you perceive that is a different question entirely."

"And one that you can answer, I hope."

"Certainly, and the proof is that I am about to do so."

"And this instant, I hope."

"Yes, indeed, this very instant."

"Then I am listening."

"Here it is, then: I have been sent to aid you."

"To aid us?"

"Exactly."

"But, to aid us in what particular?"

"Oh, against the Jenoine, of course."

"Ah. Then the gods believe we could have trouble on that score?"

"Exactly."

"That is well, because I am of the same opinion. And you have some skill that could be useful against them?"

"I believe so."

"But tell me, what skill is this?"

"I know something of how to open and shut the holes that exist between the worlds."

"You are, then, a necromancer?"

"Exactly. That is the very word the gods used in describing my skills when they did me the honor to teach me your language."

"I begin to understand," said the Sethra the Younger.

"As do I," said the Enchantress.

"It is good that you understand," said the necromancer.

"So then," said Sethra the Younger, "the gods believe, as do you, that the Jenoine are liable to interfere with Zerika's effort to retrieve the Orb."

"It is good," said the Enchantress, "to find one's self in agreement with the gods."

"Is it?"

"Yes. It shows that the gods have some wisdom."

"Well."

The Enchantress addressed the necromancer, saying, "What then, do you require in the way of preparation or material?"

"As to that, I am here to aid you in any way you require."

"So then, I am to make my own preparations, and you will assist?"

"You have understood me exactly."

"Well, I am, unfortunately, in a position that no general ever wishes to be in."

"What position is that?" asked Sethra the Younger.

"Conceding the initiative. That is, I am unable to act, but am forced to respond."

"But," said Sethra the Younger, "have you not often said that you prefer the defensive?"

"I prefer the tactical defensive but the strategic offensive."

"Well, I understand that. But then, what are we to do?"

"We have no choice about what we do: we must wait."

"I mislike waiting," said Sethra the Younger.

"I know," said the Enchantress.

"For myself, I don't mind," said the necromancer.

"How, do you not?"

"Not the least in the world, I assure you."

"You do not grow impatient?"

"Well, but to wait is to hold one's self still in a place."

"And then?"

"There are other places, where one need not hold one's self still."

"Other places?"

"One place is the same as another. You perceive, the mind moves where it will, and if the body is to wait in one place, well, the mind can be busy in another."

"By the Mountain," said the Enchantress. "You *are* a necromancer."

"Well."

"What do you mean?" asked Sethra the Younger.

"I mean that our friend," here she indicated the necromancer, "treats as matters of simple practicality what others consider as most abstruse theory."

"I do not understand what you do me the honor to tell me, Sethra."

"Well then, Sethra, permit me to explain."

"I will be delighted if you would do so."

"I am about to."

"I am listening."

The Enchantress then turned to the necromancer and said, "Have you observed that I am undead?"

The necromancer shrugged as if it was of no importance, and said, "Of course."

"Well, what then is your opinion of death?"

"It is the limitation of one's ability to reach certain phases of reality."

"And then?"

"It can sometimes be inconvenient."

The Enchantress nodded, and turned to her apprentice, saying, "Well?"

Sethra the Younger nodded. "I comprehend."

"And then?"

She bowed to their guest saying, "My friend, for so I hope I may call you, you are not simply a necromancer. As far as I am concerned, you are *the* necromancer. If I have the chance, well, I hope to learn a great deal from you."

The necromancer bowed.

"And then?" said the Enchantress.

"Well," said Sethra the Younger, "it is my hope that I will learn at least enough so that—"

"Yes? So that?"

"The Gods! So that I won't mind waiting so much!"

Chapter the Thirty-Second

How Röaana and Ibronka Arrived
In Adrilankha, and the
Greetings They Received There.

Ibronka, Röaana, and their servant, guided by maps and information supplied by the worthy Clari, arrived in Adrilankha early in the morning, as the port city was just beginning to stir. None of them had ever been in a city of such size, and so a great deal of time was spent doing nothing more than looking around: In one direction was the West Market, that large circle filled with stalls and places for carts and even a few brick buildings, as well as the Port Exchange Building, which market, by itself, was the size of any of the villages they had passed through (if the reader will remember that they did not actually pass through Hartre, rather stopping on its edge). In the other, they observed the majesty of the Six Domes along Cliff Road, sparkling of silver, and looming over them the Imperial Customs House, its distinctive red paint having long ago faded to a sort of pale orange, but still impressive for its octagonal shape and its magnificent bell tower. Then, the Pavilions of the Gods, the tops of which, red, green, yellow, and blue, could be seen in all their elegant sweep over the more humble dwellings—which dwellings themselves were of greater grandeur than any the Tiassa or the Dzur had seen upon their journey. And then the Port Authority, all of white, with its watchtower like a golden needle looking out over the sea, the port, and the city.

Soon, in fact, they found themselves standing still in the middle of Lower Kieron Road, simply looking around in awe, and pointing out sights to each other while Clari, equally awe-struck, looked about with her eyes wide and her mouth open. Fortunately for the three girls, it was as yet early in the morning, for otherwise they would have been easy prey for the monstrous horse-carts and buggies which prowled the streets once business began.

Eventually they noticed, high up on the cliff, a large manor house, constructed all of white stone. As they studied it, they asked a passing Chreotha what it might be.

"That is Whitecrest Manor, where lives the Countess of White-crest" was the reply.

"How, the Countess lives there?" said Röaana.

The Chreotha bowed.

"Well then, that is my destination. Somewhere will be a road that leads up to those heights which, I have no doubt, look upon the sea."

"It is good you have found it," said Ibronka.

"Well, but what of your own destination?"

"As to that, well, I think it will be somewhat harder to find."

"Then let us search."

"You will, then, help me?"

"Naturally."

"It is kind of you."

"It is nothing."

"I beg your pardon, but it is a great deal."

"Well, if you insist upon it."

"I do."

"Then, who is it you are to see?"

"A certain Lord Shellar, Baron of Alban."

"A Dzurlord, I presume?"

"Oh, yes."

"A kinsman?"

"I know nothing about it. My mother directed me to him, and that is all I know."

"Do you think she contemplates marriage for you?"

"Not the least in the world. She pretends I am too young to think of such things, and that, moreover—"

"Yes, moreover?"

"—that I will be unable to find a proper husband before I have proven myself in a score or so of good fights."

"And yet, where are there good fights to be found in this day and age?"

"Well, I hope here in Adrilankha!"

"For your sake, I hope that is true."

"Thank you, Röaana."

"You are welcome, my dear Ibronka. But, as to this Shellar—"

"Yes?"

"If you also know he lives in Adrilankha, well, that is a good start in finding him, I think."

"Well then, how do we begin looking?"

"We could ask the Chreotha who was so knowledgeable about Whitecrest Manor."

"But, you perceive, he went on his way after answering our question."

"Ah, did he? I had not made this observation."

"But perhaps there is someone else to ask."

"That is a good thought."

"Do you think so?"

"I am convinced of it."

"Well, but then, let us find someone."

"Yes, let us do so. Come along, Clari."

This being agreed upon, they took but a moment to find someone of whom to ask directions. This individual, an elderly lady of the House of the Vallista, had, by chance, heard of Lord Shellar, and spoke of his home being in the hills on the north side of the city, though she was unable to be more precise than this.

After they had thanked her and bid her a good day, Röaana remarked, "Do you know, it is possible that we ought to have asked her how to get there."

"Well, that is true. But, in the meantime, let us go north and see what we find."

"Very well."

As the reader has perhaps guessed, or even expected following such a decision, our friends became quite lost in the confusion of streets that ended unexpectedly, or became other streets without warning, or changed direction for no apparent reason. Even the clever Clari was unable to help them make sense of the geography of Adrilankha. In fact, it took them less than an hour to discover that they were utterly bewildered, and were not only unable to find the north side of the city, but were also unable to return to where they had been. In all of this confusion, however, they were fortunate to discover an open-air market that included seafood that was not only brought directly from the boats, but, moreover, prepared "on the spot" by quickly searing it in a light oil with ginger and certain vegetables and seasoning it in a particularly pleasing way, so that, although lost, they were at least able to enjoy a pleasant meal while considering their dilemma. Now this market was supplied with benches that permitted them to sit while eating, and it was while they were thus engaged that they spoke of their predicament, Ibronka being the first to state it clearly, by saying, "You perceive, do you not, that we are lost?"

"Oh yes," said Röaana, "I am perfectly aware of that."

"That is good," said Ibronka, "for it is best to be aware of one's situation in exact and precise terms so that there can be no confusion."

"My dear, I agree entirely."

"In that case, the next step is to see if we can learn where we are."

"Once again, my dear Ibronka, you show wisdom beyond your years."

"As to how—but to whom is Clari speaking?"

"It seems to be a Teckla."

"Well, that is but natural."

"True, and yet I am curious about their conversation."

"Are you? Well, let us then listen and see if we can determine the subject upon which they discourse."

"With this plan I agree."

In fact, Clari, after finishing the leavings from Röaana's and Ibronka's meals, had observed a Teckla walking through the crowd as if he knew where he was going, and made the deduction that a man who knew where he was going probably knew where he was, and that, knowing where he was, he might be able to communicate it. Acting at once upon this chain of logic, she had hailed the Teckla, and, arresting his progress, was proceeding to question him.

"All of this," the worthy Clari was saying, "is entirely clear, and I thank you for taking the trouble to explain it to me. And yet, I fail to see how we can arrive in the north part of the city, which, as I have said, is our destination, by proceeding first east, and then south."

"But, what direction would you imagine you should travel?"

"What direction? Why, where I am from, if one wishes to arrive in the north, well, one goes north. Then, sooner or later, one arrives."

"Well, perhaps that works in the duchies. But here—"

"Yes, here?"

"Here, you must sometimes go south to arrive north."

"Well, but if you would explain why this is, perhaps it will make the journey less irksome."

"It is because, in the first place, the north side does not refer to the north side of the city, but, rather, the north bank of the river."

"How, the north bank of the river?"

"Yes, exactly."

"The Adrilankha River?"

"That is the very one."

"But, the Adrilankha River flows from the north and travels south."

ell."

e Teckla pondered for some little time, then finally said, "The
ing to do is to get somewhere from which you can reach the
idge."

ery well, I accept that."

he best place to reach the Iron Bridge from is Kieron Road,
e the bridge is easily seen from the road, and there is an
that runs directly to the bridge from the road."

ery well, then how do we reach Kieron Road?"

mply follow Lower Kieron Road east."

nd to reach Lower Kieron Road?"

hat is harder."

nd then?"

ell, it would be easy if you were at the Iron Bridge."

ari frowned.

e Teckla continued, saying, "You might get there by way of the

ell, and what else might happen?"

h, as to that, well, you might become lost."

s we are already lost, you perceive that this possibility does not
me exceedingly."

that case, I would suggest finding the canal, and from there,
you can, the Street of the Keysmith, which runs into the canal,
low that south until you come to Lower Kieron Road."

nd to find the canal?"

ou don't know how to find the canal?"

ot the least in the world, I assure you."

ell, but, are you a stranger to Adrilankha?"

ow, I have been asking you these things for an hour and you
know I was a stranger?"

ell, I confess that I had begun to suspect."

hooey," said Clari, or something very like it.

that case," continued the Teckla, "if you wish to find the
you should go north along the Avenue of the Vintners until you
he Circle of the Fountain of the Dzur, and from there find the
Road, which you will take you north until you strike the

t then, I must find the Avenue of the Vintners."

h, but that is the easiest thing in the world, for it runs into this
arket in which we sit, and, in fact, if you follow my finger, I am
g to it now."

"Well, and if it does?"

"Then, you perceive, there can be no nort
east and a west bank, which I believe is the cu
end of the world to the other."

"As to the custom of rivers, well, I do no
perceive, the Adrilankha River makes a curve
beneath the High Bridge, so that, at that poin
city, it runs from west to east. By custom, th
curves once more, we refer to the north bank
the river."

"It is not right for you to do so," said Clar
it is confusing to travelers."

"Well," said the Teckla, shrugging. "You
powerless to change this custom, it having
time, and I not having sufficient authority."

"Humph," said Clari, as if this excuse wa
justify the crime under discussion.

The Teckla shrugged and spread his han
lessness. "Well," said Clari, "I concede that i
then, let us review: What is called the north p
the part on what is called the north bank of th
the east. We must, therefore, go east until we
to arrive at the north."

"You have understood exactly."

"Well, but, how do we cross this famous
"In the simplest manner: by crossing the
"Well, that is good, I agree with crossing
"Yes?"
"How do we reach the Iron Bridge?"
"Oh, as to that—"
"Well?"

The Teckla frowned. "I do not believe
here."

"Well, but then, how am I to reach the no
"Well, if you wish my advice—"
"I do, I promise you."
"Well, from here, I should recommend g
will be far easier."

"I'm afraid," said Clari, "that my mistress
determined upon north Adrilankha, and so n

"Ah, that is too bad, then."

"Very well," said Clari. "I believe I can follow these directions."

"Can you? Then I think you must be a most remarkable girl."

Clari shrugged.

At this point Ibronka broke in, and said, "In thanks for your directions, my friend, I should buy you a glass of wine. But in fact, well, I think I will buy you an ale."

"Ah, that is best, because I prefer ale."

"Then here it is, and may you enjoy it."

"I thank you."

By some chance, though it took them several hours, they did, by following the Teckla's instructions, eventually reach the Iron Bridge, which took them into that part of the city that was referred to as the "north side," even though it was directly adjacent to the district called "South Adrilankha," which was, in fact, in the easternmost part of the city. From there they managed to learn the location of Lord Shellar's manor, which was called Nine Stones, and proved to be a tall structure made of stone and sealed within a large estate, surrounded by a wall, with an iron gate. Inside the gate, they could see three large stones, and assumed (correctly, in the event) that there were six more elsewhere on the grounds.

They stood outside of this gate for some few minutes before noticing a pull-rope, which they made use of, and soon a servant appeared and inquired as to their business.

"My name is Ibronka, and this is my friend Röaana. We, along with our servant, have come, at the wishes of my mother, the Princess Sennya, to visit the Lord Shellar of Alban."

"Shellar?" asked the servant, frowning.

"Why yes. Is this Shellar's manor?"

"It is," admitted the servant. "Or, rather, it was."

"How, it was?"

"My lady, I must inform you Lord Shellar passed away two years ago, and his son is now Baron of Alban."

"How, Shellar is dead?"

"I regret to admit it, my lady."

"But then, whose home is this now?"

"His son's."

"His son's?"

"Exactly."

"Well, but may I request the honor of an audience with him?"

"Of a certainty, my lady. I will cause the gate to be opened, and if you and your friend and your servant will be good enough to follow the path directly ahead of you, you will be met and your horses tended to. While this is done, I will inform His Lordship of your presence, and he will then decide if and when to grant you an audience."

Ibronka nodded and said, "We will do exactly as you have said."

By this means, then, in only a few minutes, Ibronka and Röaana stood in the fireplace room of the manor (Clari had been shown to the kitchens), where they were greeted by a Dzurlord and an Issola.

"Greetings," said the Dzur. "And welcome to Nine Stones. I am the son of the late Lord Shellar. I am called Shant, and this is my friend Lewchin."

For it was, indeed, none other than fiery Shant and graceful Lewchin, Piro's old friends from the Society of the Porker Poker, who were now greeting the pretty Ibronka and her attractive friend Röaana. The Dzur and the Tiassa—that is to say, Ibronka and Röaana—made polite salutes to the Dzur and the Issola—that is to say, Shant and Lewchin—after which Lewchin said, "We welcome you to our home, and as you have been promised hospitality of my lord's father, and as he is, alas, no longer with us, well, we hope you will be good enough to accept from the son what was promised of the father."

"I give you my word," said Ibronka. "Nothing would make me happier, although as for my friend," here she indicated Röaana, "she has promised to accept the hospitality of her kinsman, the Countess of Whitecrest."

"Ah," said Shant. "Well, in that case, as it is late, we hope you," here he indicated the Tiassa, "will at least consent to share a meal with us, after which you may use our coach to reach Whitecrest Manor, for you perceive it has become late, and the streets are, alas, not safe at night between here and your destination."

"I should like it of all things," said Röaana, bowing.

"Then it is settled," said Lewchin, smiling.

The fare was plain but good—what Shant called an "omelet" and actually consisted of a combination of eggs, potatoes, fieldrice, and a bit of kethna, all of it from the area near Adrilankha. Ibronka remarked, "I had thought you only ate seafood in this city."

Lewchin smiled gently. "In the old days, I am told, there was very little seafood eaten here; it was too valuable for trade."

"And now?"

"There is some fishing now," said Shant. "The catch is mostly sold in the local markets. But as for us, well, we have land not far from the city, and bring in what we need."

"That is good, then," said Ibronka. "It is, in fact, much the same as the Princess my mother does, although she says that in the days of the Empire the land produced more, which is something that confuses me."

"Does it?" said Lewchin. "And yet, is it not possible that sorcery was used to aid in growing?"

"Do you know, I had not thought of that!"

"Lewchin," said Shant, smiling, "reasons like an Athyra."

"It is sad," said Ibronka, "that sorcery is now so much more difficult."

"And there are no good fights anymore, either," said Shant.

"I know," said Ibronka sadly.

Röaana caught Lewchin's eye for just a moment, then looked away, each of them suppressing a smile.

When the meal was over, Shant proved as good as his word, summoning a servant to drive Röaana to Whitecrest Manor. The coach was brought up, Röaana's horse tied behind, and the Tiassa bid Shant and Lewchin thanks and farewell, while warmly embracing Ibronka. "We will meet again, I think" said Röaana.

"Well, I am convinced of it."

"Until then, embrace me."

"Gladly."

After a warm embrace, the Tiassa climbed into the coach, which, at a word of command, rattled away through the gathering dusk. While in the coach, Röaana closed her eyes, and let the motion of the coach, which had a certain regularity to its bounces and jostling, lull her into a sort of sleep, for which reason she wasn't certain how long they were traveling before the coach at last came to a stop. The door opened, and Röaana looked out.

"But this is not Whitecrest Manor," she said.

The answer came, "It is, nevertheless, your destination."

These words, which appear so ominous on the page, were delivered in a tone of kindness, or, at any rate, with no menace, so that the Tiassa took no threat from them.

"But where are we? I see two roads meeting, and both continue, forward and backward, left and right."

"You are, then, where you need to be to go anywhere."

"Who are you? You are certainly not the servant I remember when leaving Nine Stones."

"I am the coachman."

"I don't understand."

"A coachman is a man who drives a coach."

"No, I don't understand what has happened to me."

"Ah, it is nothing. You are dreaming, that is all."

"Dreaming? Now?"

"Certainly."

"Then why can I not awake?"

"Because you are in my dream, and so it ends when I wake."

"Oh. Well, I must be dreaming, because that very nearly made sense."

"Well."

"But what am I doing here?"

"Making a choice."

"Ah. Well, but is it an important choice?"

"For you? It may be."

"Well, but I do not feel ready to make an important choice."

"To put off choosing is to choose."

"Is it?"

"Sometimes. At other times, well, it is merely to put off choosing."

"I beg your pardon, Coachman, but, do you know, you are not helpful."

"I am not helpful? But you must understand that I am not here to help. I am here to bring you to a place."

"Well, yes, but what place?"

"Oh, as to that, sometimes it is where you tell me to bring you. Sometimes it is where you wish me to bring you. Sometimes it is where you require me to bring you. Sometimes it is to a crossroads."

Ibronka considered. Then she said, "I am not certain what I am being asked to choose."

The coachman nodded. "That makes it more difficult, does it not?"

"But—"

"Well, consider that you are choosing your future. Does that help?"

"The Gods! It is worse than I had thought!"

"Well."

"What if I continue on? What will I find?"

"Who knows? Most likely love and contentment, or something else as worthless."

"How, you pretend these things are worthless?"

"I don't know, I've never had them."

"And if I turn back?"

"There are too many directions to discuss them all, my dear."

"And yet, you say I must choose."

"At any rate, you may choose."

"I can have what I wish?"

"Whatever choice you make."

"But then, I could ask for love, and adventure, and wealth, and happiness, like those tales of helping a spirit to Deathgate Falls, and his demon appears and grants one whatever—"

"It is not a wish I offer, merely a choice."

"Well, I do not understand."

"I promise nothing. I give nothing. You may chose a path, that is all."

"Well, then I choose adventure, danger, and to risk all in pursuit of fortune and glory."

"You choose that? And yet, it is your friend who is the Dzur."

"Well, and why should she have all the fun? She can have the love and contentment."

"Very well. That, then, is your choice."

"Do you think it a good one?"

"It is not my place to judge."

"Well, but I still do not understand."

"That is natural."

"But can you tell me why was I given this choice?"

"Why? Perhaps it is a stroke of Fortune, good or ill. Perhaps you have pleased or displeased some fate, because of your looks, or your manner—"

"Manner?"

"Manner. Whitecrest Manor."

"I fail to comprehend."

"Whitecrest Manor, madam. We have arrived."

Röaana opened her eyes, and saw that she was, indeed, outside of the very manor which we have already had the honor of visiting. Röaana glanced quickly at the manor, and then looked hard at the servant who held the door for her, but he seemed to be the same servant with whom she had left Nine Stones some few hours before.

After some hesitation, she permitted the servant to assist her from the coach. By this time, the night-groom had become aware of something occurring, and had come out to meet the coach. After acquiring Röaana's name and errand, he escorted her to the door, promising to attend to her horse as soon as possible. This established, the coach drove off, leaving Röaana's horse tied to the rail. And only a few minutes later, Röaana found herself in the presence of Daro, the Countess of Whitecrest.

Röaana gave her a courtesy and said, "I present to you the respectful greetings of my father, Lord Röaanac, and my mother, the Lady Malypon."

"Well," said Daro, "you must tell us of them, after you have refreshed yourself. You understand, I hope, that you are welcome here for as long as you wish."

"You are very gracious."

"Not at all. Was the journey difficult?"

"No, my lady, merely long."

"The longer the journey, the more pleasure in the rest at the end."

"I had not heard that before, my lady, yet I testify to its veracity. But, if I may ask, I had heard that the Count, Lord Khaavren, was here as well."

"He is here, but is resting at the moment; no doubt you will meet him to-morrow."

"I shall look forward to that very much."

"Well, but in the meantime, have you eaten?"

"The Lord Shant and his friend Lewchin were kind enough to feed my friend Ibronka and I."

"Shant? The Dzurlord?"

"Why yes, my lady. Do you know him?"

"He is a close friend of my son, Piro, the Viscount."

"Ah. I had not known you had a son."

"Indeed, my dear, and very much your own age. But he has been on an errand these past several months, and I cannot say how long it will be until he returns."

"Well, I shall very much look forward to meeting him, my lady."

"And he you, as well," said Daro with a knowing smile, after she had made a quick calculation, as will all mothers under such circumstances, as to the closeness or distance in relationship between an attractive and interesting young woman of the proper House and her own son. Needless to say, Daro, after making this calculation, found it to be of sufficient distance. As for Röaana, well, the idea of a young man of her own House, and one, moreover, who was engaged on an "errand" of some months' duration (which to Röaana could only mean an adventure), this idea could not help but meet a response in her imagination. Yet, the young gentleman not being present, she did not spend a great deal of time considering the matter, but permitted her active mind to leap on to other matters at once.

And whither did it leap? Well, from the young gentleman, it went at once to his mission, wherefore, with that directness that so characteristic of the Tiassa, she said, "What is this mission upon which the young gentleman has left?"

"As to that," said Daro, "I have no knowledge, save that it involves the Enchantress of Dzur Mountain, and that Sethra Lavode considers it important."

"The Enchantress of Dzur Mountain!" cried Röaana, astonished.

Daro smiled. "She was acquainted with my lord the Count before the Interregnum, and even, I believe, considered him a friend."

Röaana gasped, dumbfounded. In the meantime, the cook appeared, bringing a bottle of wine, which Daro caused to be opened and poured, after which she held up her glass and said, "Welcome, my dear."

Röaana managed to drink the wine, and to mumble a thank-you, though she had not quite recovered her composure from the shock of discovering that Sethra Lavode was not only real, but, moreover, was known to the very people with whom Röaana was now staying. At length, Röaana managed, "Did you ever meet her yourself, my lady?"

"The Enchantress? Well, I was at court then, and Sethra was there also, and so our paths crossed briefly once or twice, but that is all."

"Upon my word, that is sufficient!"

"You think so?" said Daro, smiling.

"You must forgive me, madam, but, you perceive, this is outside of my experience, for I am from the duchies, where the Enchantress is a legend, not a reality."

"Yes, I understand that well enough. Think nothing of it."

At this time, the night-groom entered said, "My lady, our guest's horse has been stabled, brushed, and fed. But what am I to do with her valise?"

"Put it in the western-most of the rooms set aside for guests," said Daro, "for the young lady will be giving us the pleasure of her company for some time."

"Yes, my lady. And, if I am permitted, I should like to extend my welcome to the lady who has done us the honor to visit us."

Röaana smiled a thanks at the servant, who bowed and departed.

"To-morrow," said Daro, "you will meet my lord Khaavren. Until then, as you say you are not hungry, perhaps you would care to rest."

"Indeed, my lady, I cannot deny that I long, above all, to sleep in a real bed."

"And so you shall, my dear. The cook will show you to your room, and I bid you a good night."

Chapter the Thirty-Third

How Zerika Negotiated
The Paths of the Dead

We will now, at last, return to the noble Phoenix, Zerika, whom we last saw having jumped, horse and all, from Deathgate Falls. The reader may have observed that some time has passed; that is, we have brought our history forward since Zerika made what has been called "the Great Leap Into History." During this time, it may be correct to say that Zerika was suspended, but it would be just as accurate to say that she has fallen behind, because it is well known that *time*, ordinarily so well behaved, moving forward at a rate of something like sixty seconds for each minute, sixty minutes for each hour, and thirty hours for each day, becomes bewildered in the strange region below Deathgate Falls, and begins to behave in a manner that defies all common sense, so that we would require it to come forward with an explanation for this behavior were there any practical means of enforcing such a decree.

Put in simpler terms, this is what the reader ought to understand: Time behaves differently in the Paths of the Dead, and, as time is the mode in which history occurs (let the reader try for himself to imagine history without time if he wishes to understand this), there is, in the narration of events that occur within the Paths and have an effect outside of them, a necessary confusion that mirrors this peculiarity of time. We assure the reader that we will do our best to keep this confusion to a minimum, in the first place by not bringing up the matter again during the remainder of this chapter, as it has no effect on the matters we are presently endeavoring to describe.

This understood, we will discover Zerika at the bottom of the waterfall, which towered above her for a distance she was unable to determine for the simple reason that the mist and the spray from the crashing waterfall clouded her vision. It was while she was considering this, and also attempting to wipe from her eyes the droplets that continued to fall into them, that it occurred to her that she had lived through the fall. Her next thought was, in fact, to wonder if she had lived through it; it was certainly possible that she was dead, and had come, as a dead person, to just the place that the dead go.

"I feel as if I were alive," she remarked to herself. "But then, having never been dead, I do not know what that feels like, and am thus unable to make a fair comparison. Well, we will make certain tests, so that at the end of them I will know that I am alive, or I will know that I am dead, or, in the worst (and, I must admit, most likely) case, I will be unable to tell and be forced to conclude that it doesn't matter."

This decision taken, she made her first test by the simple expedient of standing up, only coming to the realization in this way that she had been lying in shallow water. Her next discovery was that, as a result, she was wet, not to mention cold. "Were I a disembodied soul," she said to herself, "would I feel wet? It seems unlikely. But then, perhaps I would—the mind is capable of lying to itself to a remarkable degree, such as when we fancy we have observed an interested glance on the part of a young man we find attractive, or when we believe that our opponent in some game must have violated the rules, for otherwise we would have won. Well then, do I have a pulse? Yes, it seems that I do, inside of my elbow where it always resides. And, moreover, a remarkably rapid pulse at that. Once more, it is hardly conclusive, but an indication nevertheless."

It was only then that she noticed her horse, lying in the stream, and obviously quite dead. "Ah, poor Sparrow!" she sighed. "You were a good friend. Who knows, perhaps you saved me at the end; as I have no memory of my fall, and still less of the sudden stop that always follows a rapid descent, it is possible that I survived because you absorbed the impact for me." Although, as she thought about it, it seemed unlikely that, even with her fall broken by the horse, she would have emerged without at least a certain number of bruises.

With a last fond glance at her horse, she continued her inspection of the area. It did not take her long to discover that everywhere, on both banks, all up and down the river, were bones, all of them bare and white, and all of them scattered about, so that none could be seen to be the complete remains of anyone. It took Zerika no time at all to understand what they were or how they had come to this state. She glanced upward to see the giant jhereg circling overhead, and addressed them, saying, "Well, I hope I am truly alive, because to have my body eaten by you would be undignified, although it has been the fate of many who were better than I."

With this thought she shrugged, and said, "Now, to remember all of the lessons I was given. It would be a pity to have come all of this distance and through all of these trials only to have my mission fail when I became lost in the Paths simply because my memory did not perform as it should. Let us, then, concentrate, and try to remember."

With these stern instructions to herself given, she set to work to follow them, recalling everything the *Book of the Phoenix* had told her about the proper trails to follow, the dangers to avoid, and the obstacles to overcome. Her sharp, quick eyes looked around for the first landmark, and at once spotted a tree that grew *as if it had been bent around a corner, with branches tapering away, save the topmost, which points in the direction to follow*, as the book said. And, indeed, there it was; rather smaller than she had expected, but undeniably the tree, and there was no question of where it pointed. The edition of the book she had was amended with cautions that the leaves of the trees could be distracting, but not, evidently, in this season, as the branches were quite bare.

Zerika wasted no time in setting her feet upon the path appointed. To be sure, it was not much of a path; she had not gone three steps before she found that she could not go forward because of the thickness of the foliage that sprang up in front of her as if out of nowhere. "Well, it is certainly too soon to be stopped, I have hardly begun. Let us see how deep this is." With these words, she plunged forward directly through the brush, which was difficult, but not impossible. For some time, the Phoenix was forced to continue on faith, hoping that she was continuing in the same direction as she had set out while looking for the next landmark. As she continued, wishing the book had been more precise about how long it was between signs, she quite naturally slowed her pace, worrying more with each step that she had gone in the wrong direction.

At length, however, the dense brush cleared, and she discovered that she had come to a small brook, which she could have crossed in three steps without getting her ankles wet, and, with some relief, she stopped momentarily, before starting again abruptly upon recalling that stopping unnecessarily within the Paths was—at the very least—unlucky. *Do not drink of the water, else your soul will slip into the brook and be carried away*, she had been cautioned. She followed the advice without difficulty, but it did remind her that she was becoming thirsty. "Well, there is nothing to be done now," she remarked to herself. The stone sticking up from the brook *like a poniard menacing the sky* was directly in front of her, just as it should have been. She crossed behind it. Then, looking back at the stream, she saw how the flow of the water past the obstruction created two branches, one of which indicated her next direction. She spent some time making certain she was properly in line with it, fixed her eye upon a landmark some distance ahead of her, and set off once more.

For a while it was tricky, as the marks she had memorized came almost too quickly for her to remember: Step over the stone shaped like a terrapin; make for the place where the brush forms a vee; double back upon your own steps when you see blue flowers in your path, then look for a place where two animal tracks diverge, and cut between them, and so on. It was an exercise in memory, and, moreover, in precision, but it was what she had prepared for.

She came to a pond, which was roughly circular, and a good thirty or thirty-five feet in diameter. The water was black and very still, and there she stopped, considering it. The book had said only, *pass the pond neither to the right nor to the left, touching none of the water, and at no time stray from your path.* "Well," she said to herself. "Here is a pretty little problem. If I go around it, I will be straying from my path, and I can hardly go directly through it without getting at least my feet wet, and perhaps much more, for it looks like it may be deep. If I could leap thirty feet it would solve the problem, and certainly if I could fly I would at once do so. And yet, lacking both wings and material to create a bridge, I—but what is that? A vine? It is above me; can I swing over on it, trusting it not to break? And yet, it does not seem that the vine will reach sufficiently far, it merely goes up to—but stay, to that very branch that stretches over the pond. And on the other side, is there a way down? Well, yes, if I can negotiate from the end of that branch to the one of that tree upon the other side, well, it might be done, and that will certainly put me upon the other side of the pond without straying either to the right or the left, and without touching the water. It looks as if it might be possible. Come, let us attempt it at once."

Zerika took into her hand the vine, and, grasping it firmly, began to climb. While she had never before attempted such a maneuver, with vine or even with rope, she found it easy enough to achieve, owing, perhaps, to certain irregularities on the vine itself that provided purchase for her boots. Having arrived at the branch, some five or six feet over her head, she straddled it, and then made her precarious way across by shifting herself along it, until she found that her boot touched the lower branch of a tree upon the other side. The transfer to this branch was easy enough, and, once she was fully upon it, she contrived to hang from it with both hands so that, upon letting go, she had only a drop of four or five feet, which drop she managed without any harm.

"Well," she said, catching her breath. "That could have been worse. What will come next? I am now to listen, rather than watch, and, in doing so, I am to continue in the direction in which I was walking before the pond. Very well, we will walk, and we will listen."

She set off, and had hardly taken ten steps before she heard a scream, fat off to her right. *Do not let the cries of lost souls take you from your path, nor the sight of those who suffer cause your eyes to stray.* "Well," she said. "All right, then." She held herself still until she was confident she knew from what directions the cries came, then set off in the opposite direction. A little later, she caught fleeting glimpses of figures waving to her, or attempting to find their way through the Paths, but, as she was told, she ignored them. Some, she knew, would eventually reach the Halls of Judgment, others never would; but everyone's path within the Paths was his own and she could not help them. She wondered how it was that any soul who came to these Paths without preparation ever reached the Halls of Judgment. Yet it was certain that many did. "Well," she decided, "but they have eternity to make the attempt, and that is certainly a very long time. Indeed, from what I know, eternity is even longer than the amount of time it takes a servant to prepare one's morning klava in a morning where one is forced to rise early after a night's excess; and that is the longest time I know."

From this point, she continued for some distance in a straight line, her eyes fixed upon a spot in the distance in order to be certain she did not deviate from her path, which path, we should say, was as straight, clear, and as easy as any in that strange landscape where the bizarre was created out of improbable combinations of the mundane. As she walked, some of this appeared: it seemed that far ahead of her, directly on her route, something was stirring. She strained her eyes attempting to determine what it was, reminding herself that there should be nothing that directly threatened her, both because she was on her proper path, and, moreover, because she was living (she had, the reader may perceive, gradually come to the conclusion that she was, in fact, still alive, and proposed to operate under that assumption until she had good reason to reconsider it).

She frowned, continued walking, and watched. It appeared to her that there were black specks on her path, and that, though she was still unable to determine precisely what they were, they were becoming larger. "Well now," she said. "As I do not know what those specks represent, well, I cannot say if it is something that ought not to be growing larger. Yet it seems to me that it is just as likely, or, in fact, more likely, that they are remaining exactly the same size, but coming closer. But larger or closer, I certainly wish the book had thought to warn me about this; it seems to be a sufficiently significant event as to be worth two words. But then, if no action is called for, the book would say nothing; it is certainly as practical as a recipe book, and a touch of poetry would have done it no harm whatsoever."

The objects continued to grow, or to approach; Zerika continued to walk toward them because she had not yet found the next landmark which was to indicate that she should turn. In a short time, two things became apparent: first that the objects were weapons—in particular, swords and spears, which were all aimed at her; and second that they were, indeed, approaching, and at a furious speed. When she realized this, she very nearly ducked out of their way, and, upon realizing that this would be a mistake, very nearly stopped. "But," she reflected, "I have been assured by Sethra Lavode that nothing within the Paths can harm me so long as I remain on the proper path, and, moreover, I am told that I must continue to move forward. Well, I will continue to move forward, and if I am punctured, well then—but there they are gone, and while it *looked* as if several of them pierced me, at least it didn't *feel* as if any of them did.

"But I wonder what these Paths will throw at me next? I wonder as well when I will find the trees that form an arch, which is my next landmark. Now what is that? Another pond like the last one, only without a convenient vine laid out for me. Ah, but is that a bridge across it? It seems to be very like a bridge, only thinner. What, now the Paths wish to know if I can walk across a two-inch wide plank without falling in? This place is insupportable. I will walk it then, holding my head steady and keeping my back straight, for that, along with slightly bent knees and arms slightly out from the body, is the secret to balance. There, I have walked across it. What next? It doesn't matter, I will face it and overcome it with as much grace as I can muster."

She continued on, still with no sign of the arch she was looking for. The ground dropped slowly, and she was afraid she'd meet a swamp or a bog, but it continued to be dry enough, appearing to be a sort of valley, full of grass. "Well, it is easy enough to walk, at any rate. But I have never walked through so many different landscapes in such a short time. I cannot have gone two leagues, and I have seen jungle, forest, chaparral, marsh, rocky desert, and grassland. If I did not know this region was magical, well, I should at once deduce that it was enchanted. I wonder at who designed it. It must have been the gods. They sit upon their thrones, laughing and drinking wine, or whatever it is the gods drink, and planning out how to torment the poor souls who want nothing more than to reach the Halls of Judgment where, pah! where most of them are given purple robes anyway, and made to serve the dwellers for some period of time more or less prolonged. I think when my time comes I will leave instructions to permit my body to decay where it is, or be burned, and let my soul fly free into its next life. Yes, that is what I will do, or—what now? Are those trees I see ahead of me? Perhaps there will be two that form an arch, for, whatever direction this is—the directions I know are meaningless here—I am tired of it."

She took another step, and the ground shook beneath her feet. She stumbled, but did not fall from the path. "What was that?" she said to herself. "I was never told this would happen." Another tremor quite nearly knock her from her feet, but she maintained her balance. "I wish," she said, "that there were someone to glare at." She took a few more tentative steps, and, as the ground remained firm, was beginning to feel confident once more when a pit, perhaps four feet wide and of unknown depth, opened up directly before her feet.

Zerika made one of those decisions that is half instinct, and half thought out, as a result of which decision she took one more step and allowed her knees to buckle, after which she leapt into the air, her leap taking her across the pit, and landed upon the other side hardly breaking step. After this feat, she still had the presence of mind, after careful consideration, to curse, which she did once, with considerable emotion.

She resumed her walk, then, glaring about her. "If I were in charge," she remarked, "I should think it was enough to ask the poor soul to stand before me and be judged. I should not require it to go through such peregrinations to even arrive at the place of judgment. And suppose I were some poor pilgrim who managed to pass all of these absurd obstacles and tests and false trails, and then the gods were to judge me as unfit for any advancement, and they should sentence me to life as a norska or a kethna. How unfair! If they presume to judge, they ought to have a least built this place so that one can simply walk to the Halls of Judgment. It is a shame that my Empire, if it is established, does not extend to this region, or I swear by the gods who live here that I should tear it down and start over within a year of the beginning of my reign. There. I have said it, and if the gods should hear me, well, so much the better."

Having expressed her displeasure with the universe, she turned her mind once more to her path, which led her to the very arch of trees she had been looking for, which discovery pleased her so much she nearly forgot that she was supposed to change direction before it, rather than after passing through it. She remembered in time, however, turned to the right, and continued on her way. It was not long before she found her way blocked again, this time by what seemed to be a boulder, at least twice her height, and laid directly across her path.

No matter that she didn't wish to, she was forced to stop; and more than stop, to reflect. As she reflected, she observed; and observing, she saw; and seeing, she considered; and, after considering, she planned; and after planning, she moved several small stones in front of the boulder, and laid a log on top of these stones, which permitted her to ascend to the top of the boulder. Once there, she considered once more: this time, the question under consideration was how to get back down without injury.

"Well," she decided, "I cannot safely jump, but perhaps I can slide." She did this, and found herself in undignified safety on the path below the boulder. This was followed by a loud *crack* and the boulder split exactly in half, each part rolling away from the path behind her.

"Useless," she muttered, "although, no doubt, significant in a mystical way that is beyond my mortal comprehension. Bah."

She began walking once more, this time taking herself as far as a wide stream, almost a river, which did not, however, appear very deep. She glanced at is suspiciously, but, as she had not been given any other direction, resolved to pass directly through it, hoping to emerge with nothing more than wet feet.

She was brought up sharply by a second look at the river, which revealed two things to her quick eyes and agile mind: the first was that this was the Blood River, and that all of her laborious walking and ducking and jumping and climbing and twisting and turning had done nothing more than to bring her back to the river from which she had begun her walk, albeit some distance downriver, which fact could be deduced by the fact that Deathgate Falls was no longer in sight. The second was that this part of the river was full of corpses, in various states of decay.

It is not our intention, as will some of our brother historians, to dwell upon these decaying corpses, delighting in a discussion of grotesqueries; we are certain our readers can imagine the appearance, not to mention the odor of these bodies; and can imagine as well the effect upon our young Phoenix. By this time, however, she had no inclination to permit anything to interfere with her purpose; she took a deep breath through her mouth, held this breath within her lungs, and walked across the river, which was, in fact, at no time more than knee deep, though it was bitter cold. If her path took her over rotting corpses, well, soon enough she was upon the other side, breathing again, and there were only a few bleached bones there, which were quickly behind her.

"What next?" she said to herself. "Let us attempt to remember. Perhaps the greatest danger lies in all of the distractions causing one to forget what one has learned." She set this thought firmly aside, and concentrated on recalling everything that the book had taught her was to come next.

The ground rose slightly as she walked away from the Blood River, and soon she was on bare dirt, stone, and a few patches of weeds or grass scattered about like flecks of foam upon a brown ocean. She came to a sequence of three narrow ditches, and, upon reaching the third, turned left to walk in it, following it as it curved back, bringing her to where, it seemed, she ought to have met the Blood River yet again, only she did not; instead the ditch gradually ended and the ground became rockier, until, after some time, she found that she was walking between walls of granite so close together that she barely had room to pass between them. When the wall on her left suddenly appeared to collapse onto her, her reaction, which was to interpose her left hand between the granite and her face, was so instinctive that she could no more have stopped it than she could have prevented herself from falling had she stepped off a cliff. Her difficulty was only increased when, an instant later, the other wall did the same thing, and so she found herself unable to move, each hand engaged in holding back a mass of granite that took nearly all of her strength to keep from falling onto her.

For a moment she held herself very still, but then she remembered that one was never to stop in the Paths, or if one did stop, one should begin moving again as soon as possible. She swallowed, and took a small step forward, adjusting her grip on each side by the smallest amount. As she did, the wall crashed in behind her. Zerika noted it, and continued, moving forward just a little, and carefully adjusting each hand together, and wondering if were true that nothing could actually hurt her. Well, she decided, even if it didn't hurt her, it would almost certainly slow her down.

She continued as she had, making certain above all that neither her feet nor her hands ever got too far ahead, until finally the wall tapered down to the point where she could simply step forward beyond it. She took a moment to glance back, and there was no trace of where she had gone, only crumbled rock over the path. She wondered what would happen to the next Phoenix to come this way. Did it repair itself? Or was it nothing but illusion in the first place? She shrugged and continued on her way.

The ground climbed a little, the rocks becoming fewer, to be replaced by thin grass and occasional shrubs, after which the ground climbed a little, the rocks becoming fewer, to be replaced by thin grass and occasional shrubs, after which the ground climbed—

"I have been here before," said Zerika, continuing to walk. A little later she said, "I have been here too many times.

"Well now," she reflected. "This isn't right. This was not supposed to happen. I am actually caught. It isn't illusion—or, if it is, it is a very convincing one. And it suddenly occurs to me that, for all I know, the gods are watching me and laughing even as I go around and around. If I were not a Phoenix, and thus above such mundane emotions, well, I should begin to become not only annoyed, but frustrated, perhaps even to the point where I should weep with anger. It is fortunate that I am above such things."

She wiped her cheeks and continued both walking and reflecting. After some time, unable to come up with any other idea, she closed her eyes. She opened them after ten or twelve paces, to find that nothing had changed. She closed them again, this time keeping them closed rather longer, until, in fact, she tripped and landed on the ground, which was, fortunately, rather soft. Her eyes naturally opened as she stumbled, and she was delighted to find that she was now in a more jungle-like region than hitherto.

She got to her feet, took a deep breath, and continued. "Well, that wasn't so bad after all. I should be all right now, as long as I didn't go off in the wrong direction, or miss a landmark, or, by closing my eyes, violate some arcane rule of which I was unaware. So, we will continue hopefully forward, and, why, there it is! A small pile of rocks, arranged in a pyramid, which I am to step over and then, fixing my eyes upon the tallest of the evergreens before me, continue until I reach a place where I am at the bottom of three hills. This should be easy enough, as long as the hills are hills in fact, and neither mountains nor piles of dirt. If I get back, I will attempt to clarify some of these matters for those who follow. It is the least I can do."

In fact, she found the hills without undue difficulty, and turned as she was directed, feeling more confident now; beginning to think that this was a task that was, after all, within her abilities, and she did not forget, even as she concentrated on looking for the next landmark, to think kind thoughts of Sethra Lavode, who had been so insistent upon her memorizing very nearly the entire *Book of the Phoenix.*

We should hasten to add that, although confident, she was not *over*-confident; that is, she maintained a keen awareness that she could take nothing for granted, but, on the contrary, remembered that she required all of her faculties and must remain extraordinarily alert for whatever the Paths might next place before her. And yet, even with this alertness, she very nearly missed what happened next.

The book had said she was to *look for the place a cliff no higher than your head stands upon your left, and upon this cliff seek a bush of flowers of the brightest red.* This pretended cliff, which was in the event no more than a mound of dirt with, apparently, the front face cut away as if by a shovel, did, indeed, have a bush upon it, and the flowers of this bush were blooming like the reddest of geraniums. That part of her instructions was simple enough, but what followed was the command to turn her back upon the bush, and set her foot onto the animal trail that led directly away. She did this, and, just as her foot was about to descend upon the trail, realized that there were *two* animal tracks leading away: one seemed to have been made by the passing of medium-sized animals with cloven feet, such as deer or brownstag; but there was another, considerably smaller, which might have been made by many norska. It was this second that led more directly away from the diminutive cliff and the bush, although the difference in direction between the two was hardly noticeable.

Zerika hesitated only an instant before changing her direction and following the smaller of the trails. Once more, she was unsure of her decision, but, having made it, she continued, her eyes sharp for the next landmark, refusing to acknowledge her doubts. "All may yet be very well," she reminded herself sternly, this having been a favorite remark of her ancestor's in times of trial.

The animal path widened, until it became fully a trail, which

Zerika knew was either a sign that her choice was right, or else meant nothing at all. The next landmark she sought was a brook *where the water tumbles down three small steps, none higher than your ankle. There you will step upon the highest of these, stepping off with your right foot and then —* "What is that?" She frowned, staring ahead.

Before her, directly in the trail, was a bush of some sort, on the top of which was a nest, and in the nest was a small white bird, evidently sitting on eggs. She considered the shrub, deciding it was too tall to leap over, and too wide to go around. "On the other hand, it is not terribly thick.

"It is interesting," she continued, "that that bird is the first living thing I have seen here. Well, but of course one cannot expect to find many living things in the Paths. It is something of a blessing that I have seen this bird." Without breaking stride, she walked through the bush. The bird flew off, screeching, while the nest and the eggs fell to the ground; Zerika only acquiring a few small scratches. "It is sad that it was in my way," she reflected.

She found the brook with the three stones, and followed the instructions from the book. This brought her, presently, into what appeared to be a large, prepared, tended garden. There were a few flowers, some of them blooming white or blue or yellow; but there were also rows of maize, wheat, and various legumes and tubers, as well as paddies of rice and orchards of plums, olives, rednuts, walnuts, and snowgreens. Had Zerika been more familiar with agriculture (which, in fact, she was to become in the centuries that followed), she would have been aware of the utter impossibility of finding any soil or climate which would permit these disparate items to grow within a stone's throw of each other; but as she was unaware of this fact, she did not take a moment to consider the peculiarity, but simply made her way past trees and among rows until, after some time, she found her next landmark, and continued.

"I am becoming weary," she admitted to herself. "More than weary, in fact, I am becoming exhausted. How long have I been walking? Certainly more than a day and a night, as time is normally measured, and far enough to have reached the coast as distance is normally measured—not that any of these measurement apply here. But still, I am not made of iron, or even of hardwood, and there are limits to how long I can remain awake and how many leagues I can travel. If these Paths think to defeat me by nothing more than wearying me, well, they may succeed.

"But then," she continued, "I shall at least not make it easy for them to do. As long as the landscape itself does not contrive to confuse me, I believe I can continue for some time yet." Of course, these words were hardly formed before the landscape began to show every sign of attempting to confuse her. With one step, she was high upon a mountain; the next step brought her to the shore of a sea, and before she had adjusted she was deep within a jungle, after which she was trampling through a stream or brook in a deep forest, until it was all she could do to concentrate on looking for the next landmark, which, eventually, she identified as a petrified tree with branches reaching out as if to embrace her. She recalled her instructions and passed it on the right.

The instant she did, the alterations in the landscape ceased, leaving her following what seemed to be an animal trail that led upward to a small hillock, and one that was almost free of vegetation, save for grasses that reached as high as her knees. For the first time, she was able to get something of a view of her surroundings, and, ironically, once there, she could see nothing except a landscape shrouded in mist.

"Well," she remarked, "it is what I should have expected, that the Paths are best viewed from within, and attempting to observe them from above merely obscures them. It is just the sort of thing that would happen. But it doesn't seem right that I should be punished for the attempt, as appears to be the case with my foot somehow trapped by a sort of vine or some other piece of vegetation that has wrapped itself around my ankle."

She considered her predicament. Whatever had grasped her did not appear to be getting any tighter as time went on, but neither was it loosening. She recalled what she had been taught about obstacles in the Paths of the Dead and reflected. "If this is an effort by the Paths, or the gods, to tell me something, well, I wish the statement were a little more clear. If it is something obtuse and metaphorical, such as that the attempt to view the world as if one were outside of it is a philosophical trap, well, I must say that I have never believed that, and so the lesson is wasted and the trap has been sprung upon the wrong person. To the left, if it is a warning about making superficial examinations, I can only comment that I am hardly old enough to have had time to make any examinations of anything that are more than superficial, and I will protest that, once again, the trap has been sprung upon the wrong person.

"Let us consider other possibilities, then. If this is a warning about the dangers of holding ontology in contempt, then perhaps there is some justification for it, because I have never given this study, and its twin companion epistemology, the attention they truly deserve. Yet I recognize that to leave one's own method of thought unexamined is to be held captive by the workings of one's own mind, and that it is by subjecting one's thought processes to the same criticism to which we subject the subjects themselves that we are able to escape the restraints that hold so many thinkers prisoner of their own prejudices and shallowness. Yes, I am aware of this, and I freely confess that, especially if I am to rule, it is incumbent on me to make this study, and I resolve to do so. Yet, it seems trivially obvious that I will be unable to make this study if I am forever trapped in the Paths of the Dead by whatever has gripped my ankle, wherefore, with the limited understanding I now possess, I will take action, both to accomplish my purpose, and to deepen my understanding of the processes by which I am surrounded."

This said, she drew her poniard, which was fortunately sharpened for some portion of the edge, and cut at the thick root that had snared her. It permitted itself to be cut easily enough, and so, once free, she wasted no time in continuing her walk in the direction she had been going, a path which now took her down into what appeared to be a valley.

"Of course," she said to herself, "it might have been simply pointing out to me that one ought to stop as little as possible while negotiating the Paths. One must not forget the mundane explanations, which, after all, are the reflection of the profundities, and are what give them reality."

She made this observation as she walked, attempting to remember what she ought to look for next, and was suddenly struck by the realization that, try as she might, she could not recall what she ought to be looking for. This thought brought her a certain amount of trepidation, that might have continued for some time had she not at just that moment emerged into a clearing which was dominated by a massive stone archway, on top of which was a gargantuan carving of a phoenix, rising as if about to take flight; and beneath the archway figures moved, some of them in purple robes, some naked, others dressed more normally, all of which she recognized from story, myth, and legend, as well as the words of the *Book of the Phoenix*, as marking the entrance to the Halls of Judgment.

Then she did stop, and turned around, making a glance at her path, which appeared to be nothing more than a simple trail through a typical jungle.

"Well," she remarked, "all in all, that wasn't so bad."

She turned and, passing through the archway, entered the dominion of the gods.

Chapter the Thirty-Fourth

How Zerika Spoke to the Gods
About Certain Issues of Grave
Concern to Each of Them

Upon passing into the domain of the gods, Zerika became convinced for all time that she was, in fact, alive; for there was no other way to account for the pounding of her heart. And yet, afterward, she was never able to say precisely where she went; as she had had to pay close attention to everything around her in order to reach that point, now, feeling that she was in a place of comparative safety, she was able to continue without close observation, and so, not noticing at the time, she was, consequently, never able to recall it. We should add that this is an unfortunate event for latter historians, always curious about details of that strange and mystical place, but was unimportant to Zerika herself.

And so she passed on, passing by sights and sounds—and perhaps personalities—about which history must remain curious, eventually reaching a place which the reader will recognize from the last time we were here: the Halls of Judgment, the abode of the gods. She was, to be sure, still in a confused state of mind, unable to carefully note what she saw, and her memories were never completely clear. But she made her way around turnings in a path she followed with only the dimmest of awareness, through pavilions she could never recall, over bridges that bridged she knew not what, and at last through a very high archway, and then into the center of the large circular area that we are convinced the reader will recall. We should add that she was never aware of entering the circle itself; to her, it seemed that she stepped through the archway, and was suddenly surrounded by those she knew to be the gods. And, in that instant, where she had been walking as if half-awake, exhausted from her ordeal in traversing the Paths, now she was fully alert again—indeed, she felt her heart hammering in her breast, and was aware of the sharp taste of the air, of the faint, sweet smell of lilac overlaying a tang as of the sea.

She turned in a slow circle, trying to grasp, as well as she could, where she was, and what, and whom she was confronting. It must be admitted by us—because Zerika, herself, has insisted it is true—that the image of her as confident, as full of conviction, and as ready to face her ordeal is utterly untrue. Indeed, she has said on more than one occasion that being there she felt overtaken by a fate over which she had no control, that she was alone as she had never been alone, and that she was more surrounded by a hostile environment, and less able to confront it, than she had been while negotiating the Paths. She has spoken of a numbness in her feet, and of the effort it took to keep her terror and sense of hopelessness off her countenance, and of believing that she was utterly powerless in the hands of a fate that seemed determined to crush her.

If this is true—and we will not do ourselves the honor of doubting Her Majesty's own words—then permit us to suggest that it is to her greater honor that she comported herself as she did; in other words, that she willingly defied what she saw as her fate, and did the very thing that in our opinion defines a hero: She struggled against the greatest of all obstacles, her own doubts, and did, quite simply, what she needed to do.

So then, as we have said, she looked around carefully, seeing what she could (and, indeed, comprehending what she could) of the Lords of Judgment, until, at last, her eyes came to rest on one she recognized from certain icons and engravings as being Verra, who has been known—or, at any rate, reputed—to concern herself with the Empire; and to her Zerika made something like an obeisance. As she did so, by the peculiarities of that place, she found herself, at least in appearance, standing directly before her.

The goddess looked at the Phoenix, and permitted her face to relax into something like a smile as she said, "We have been expecting you, little one."

Zerika, still at a loss for words, could only bow her head.

"We know why you have come, little Phoenix," said the goddess, "yet we nevertheless require you to state your mission plainly, and in words that will leave no room for confusion."

"Very well," said Zerika, managing at length to find her voice. "If that is your command, well, then that is what I will do." She was, we should say, a little startled to hear how calm her voice sounded, and how clear, when in fact she was more deeply and thoroughly terrified than she had ever imagined she could be.

Verra nodded to indicate that this, indeed, was her command.

Zerika took a deep breath in an effort to steady herself. She hesitated, ran her tongue around her lips, swallowed, took another breath, and opened her mouth. From somewhere—for it was no plan of hers—the words came from her mouth: "Well then, what I wish is easily enough stated. I wish for the Orb to be given to me, and that I may be granted passage from this place, that I may bring the Orb back to the Empire."

"What Empire?" came a sudden voice from somewhere behind her.

She turned, and at first she was unable to identify the speaker, but then it seemed that she was looking directly into a great fire; a fire that burned with nothing to consume, that left no ash, and that had no shape, form, or direction. She did not know how she had suddenly come so close to this entity (nor, indeed, why she felt no heat radiating from it, much less why she wasn't burned alive) without any sensation of motion; but she attempted to answer the question without permitting this peculiarity to fluster her any more than she was already flustered by the circumstances of her interrogation.

She said, "The Empire that once existed, and shall exist again when I return from this place with the Orb."

"Then you believe," said the being, and only then did the Phoenix realize that it was not exactly "speaking" as the term is usually used, and that Verra had not been either, "that only the Orb is required for the Empire to exist again?"

Zerika bowed. "That is precisely my contention."

We should add that Zerika, before making this statement, had considered what form of address to use to the god or goddess (who, as the reader no doubt has realized, is Ordwynac), but, having been unable to determine a suitable form, had settled on none at all.

"It requires no armies? No navy? No intelligence? No taxes? No communication among its branches and to its far-flung duchies and principalities? No arrangements for transportation? No intendants? No judiciary? No Council of Princes? None of these things are necessary, but only the Orb?"

Zerika bowed her head as he spoke, as if each scornful phrase were a lash. When he finished, she remained there with her eyes down. But if her spirit were crushed, at least momentarily, her mind continued to work. After a moment, she raised her eyes and said, "Yes, that is what I believe. All of those other things will come with time, and effort—or, in the worst case, can be done without. Only two things are necessary."

"Two things?" said Ordwynac. "Come, then, tell us clearly what these two things are."

"The first," said Zerika, now speaking with no hesitation, "is the Orb."

"Very well," said Ordwynac. "We understand that the Orb is required. But what is the second, out of all those items I did you the honor to list?"

"The second," said Zerika, "is my will."

A moment of silence greeted this remark by the young Phoenix, and it seemed to Zerika that she had startled them. At last, Ordwynac said, "Your will? You believe that all that is needed is the Orb and—your will?"

"Yes, that is what I believe," said Zerika.

"And," said another of the gods, this one somewhere to her right, "what of those who attempt to build their own Empire? What of the impoverishment, the lack of transportation? The plagues? The incursions by barbarians, from the Islanders, and from the East?"

She turned and found that she was facing a goddess who looked, in some ways, not unlike Verra, though with a more pale complexion and features not quite so sharp—and more than facing this goddess, she seemed, indeed, to be standing directly before her. She found this, we should add, more than a little disconcerting, particularly as she realized that this would re-occur each time one of her questioners did her the honor of addressing her. This realization caused her some disturbance, and thus, in turn, some hesitation. However, it must be allowed that she was permitted time to recover her faculties; that is to say, the gods once again waited patiently while she organized her thoughts.

Gods, as is well known, are nothing if not patient, unless provoked.

This time she was given was, we must add, what is called a "two-edged sword," meaning that it had elements that were both good and bad. That is, she not only had time to prepare an answer, but, in addition, time to reflect upon just how frightened she was. This was, in the opinion of the author, perhaps the most difficult moment of the ordeal that began at the top of Deathgate Falls, because at this moment her nerve very nearly failed her. It came thundering upon her consciousness that she was, indeed, surrounded by the Lords of Judgment, and that one wrong word could mean the end of all she had worked for, all Sethra Lavode had trained her for, all that, insofar as she understood the workings of Fortune and Fate—the two siblings who continually vie with each other for control of Destiny, and against which and for which each human consciousness must struggle or to which each must surrender—she had been born for. Her fear of failure rendered her incapable of speech, incapable of thought, and for a moment she stood, as helpless as Reega before the onslaught at the gates of Thuvin.

She had been extensively prepared for the ordeal of walking the Paths of the Dead; and, indeed, had this preparation been any less rigorous, she might well have perished there, or become lost. But how can one prepare to meet the Lords of Judgment? What could Sethra Lavode have told her to make this ordeal easier? What preparation would have helped her to bear up under the weight of the combined scrutiny of the Guardians of the World? The author would never suggest that there are not matters—many of them—where success is determined by skill, by practice, by training; yet it cannot be denied that, from time to time, there arises a situation where success or failure is determined by one's character—either something that cannot be learned, or, perhaps, something that is learned unintentionally during the process of undergoing all of one's life experiences. Zerika was in just such a situation, and as she understood it, nothing less than the fate of the Empire now rested upon what sort of inner strength she had.

And it was at just this moment that, not only was she able to call upon those strengths of character that lay latent within her, but moreover, that her strength was forged. That is, not only was the question answered of whether there would be an empire, but the question of what sort of Empress Zerika would make was, at that instant, decided.

Some questions, as is well known, cannot be answered by any historian, be he of a scientific or mystical bent. We cannot know precisely the chain of events that led to the creation of the Great Sea of Amorphia; we cannot know how the Serioli stumbled upon the process that led them to create the first Morganti weapons; and we cannot know from where, ultimately, Zerika found the strength to confront the goddess before her, and through this goddess, all of the Lords of Judgment. But, perhaps, when all is over, it doesn't matter whence came this strength, only that it was there, and that Zerika found it; for she lifted her head (which she had allowed to drop down as she shook and trembled) and said, "All of these matters will be attended to, by the Empire."

"By the Empire?" said Ordwynac again, and, as Zerika turned

her head, she found that she was directly in his fiery presence once more. "My little pet, you cannot both create the Empire, and use the Empire to defend it, all at the same time."

Zerika looked into the heart of the flame and said, "That is precisely what I am going to do, however."

"How?" said another of the gods, and she was now in a new direction, and looking at one she recognized from his green, scaly skin as Barlen.

Zerika spoke to him, the words now coming more easily. "The Orb will help. And I have the assistance of Sethra Lavode, which counts for something, I believe. And there are still many who wish for nothing so much as to bring the Empire back. With the Orb, I will summon to me the forces necessary, and do what I must do."

"And have you," said Ordwynac, causing Zerika to stand before him once more, "what it takes to do these things?"

"Yes," said the Phoenix, looking directly into the flames.

"Why should I believe that?"

Zerika felt her eyes narrow slightly, and a certain annoyance begin to grow within her. "Why should you doubt me? And, moreover, of what use is the Orb to you, here?"

"That is not your concern, my dear," said Verra.

Zerika looked at the goddess—whom she was now facing—and refrained from arguing, because it seemed to her that Verra was kindly disposed to her, or, at any rate, to her mission, and she saw nothing to be gained in such an argument. Instead she said, "Very well, then, it is not my concern. And yet—?"

"Well?" said the goddess, not unkindly.

"I am the Heir. By rights, it is mine, and I can do what is needed. If it has no purpose here, then, well, why not permit me to take it where it belongs?"

"It is not so simple, little Phoenix," said one of the gods, and Zerika found that she was now facing the one we know as Moranthë. Zerika looked at the goddess—similar in some ways to Verra, yet different—and waited. The goddess said, "We have one valuable thing that you do not, little Phoenix: we have time."

"I am not certain that is true," said another.

"Whereas," said yet a third, "I am convinced it is entirely incorrect. While we have time, we also know others who have time."

"Yes," came from another. "If we delay, they will not. And what then?"

"Nevertheless," said Ordwynac. "If she is not able to do what she must do, then by putting this artifact in her hands, we are not only leaving their world defenseless, but ourselves, as well."

"Why do you believe," said Verra, "that she will not be able to do what she must?"

"Why do you believe she will?" replied Ordwynac.

Zerika found herself again facing Verra, who looked at her closely, as if, indeed, attempting to see through her. The Demon Goddess then spoke, saying, "She has said she will."

"Then," said Ordwynac, "you will place the fate of the world, and our own fate, on what this human chooses to say of herself?"

"Well, my dear Phoenix," said Verra, addressing Zerika again. "Tell us, if you will, why we should believe you can do what you say."

"Because," Zerika replied with no trace of hesitation, the words spilling forth before she had time to consider them, "I am far too frightened at this moment to prevaricate."

There were various sounds from around her, and it came to Zerika that the gods were laughing. She felt her face become red, but held her ground and continued to meet Verra's eyes. After a moment, Vera nodded slightly, still smiling a little, and said, "I, for one, believe you." Zerika had the feeling that this remark was directed less to her than to the other gods. She remained still, and waited.

"That is all very well," said someone who had not yet spoken. Zerika abruptly found herself listening to a feminine voice and facing what at first she thought was nothing at all until she became aware that there was, perhaps, a certain vague discoloration before her; as if something were almost but not quite there. As she was attempting to decide if something were wrong with her eyes, or if there was, indeed, a goddess before her, she heard the voice again. "But I should very much like to know if you have a plan for how to face these difficulties. That is, a specific plan."

"I do not," said Zerika at once. "I have no plan. I do, however, have resources that I believe will be adequate to the task, and I will, in the first place, marshal these resources. Then I will determine what sort of problems confront the Empire, and I will attack each in its proper place."

"That is not a bad answer, little one," said the goddess whom, by the now, the reader has identified as Nyssa.

"Yes," said Ordwynac. "She is, without question, good with answers."

Zerika looked up at this god, feeling her eyes narrow, and she said, "Words represent thoughts, and I am sharing my thoughts, because they are all I have to hand at present. Give me something stronger than words to wield, and I will gladly do so."

"Indeed?" said Ordwynac. "Little human, do you think to threaten me?"

"Not at all," said Zerika coolly.

"That is good. I am glad to see that at least you do not think to match your strength and resources against the Guardians of the World."

"I certainly do not," said Zerika, and added, "not unless I must."

This remark was greeted by unanimous silence among the gods—a silence that lasted for what seemed to Zerika to be some few minutes. Then, once more, there was the sound of laughter—this time a veritable cacophony of all different sounds of mirth. Zerika maintained her poise like an Issola and waited until the laughter had died away. When, at last, it had, Verra raised her head to address all of the Lords of Judgment. "Are there any other questions from any of you?"

For a moment there was silence, and Zerika dared to hope that, whatever the outcome, her ordeal was over.

But it was not.

Barlen spoke—not to Zerika, however, but to Verra. "You believe her," he said. "Do you think she has the mettle to see it through?"

"I know one thing for certain," said the Demon Goddess. "One thing that cannot be argued with."

"And that is?" said Barlen.

"She has arrived here, over Deathgate Falls, and through the Paths of the Dead."

"Pah," said Ordwynac, or something very like it. "What is involved in that? A few tricks of memory, no more."

Zerika did not permit herself to become angry at this unkind and untrue—or, at the very least, oversimplified—denigrating of her task. Rather she let the anger wash over and past her, knowing that she could not be at her best if in the grip of anger, any more than she could were she in the grip of fear.

Verra said, "Tell me something, my dear little Zerika. How did you traverse the Falls?"

"The Falls themselves? Why, I jumped from them."

Verra quickly glanced across the way toward Ordwynac, and said, "How, you jumped?"

"I did, Goddess."

"But then, why would you have done that?"

"For the simple reason that, as my escort and I were under attack at the time, there was no other choice."

Verra nodded to Zerika, then looked up and directed a complacent smile at Ordwynac.

At length Ordwynac addressed Verra. "Well then, she has courage. This is not something I have doubted. But courage, by itself, is hardly sufficient, is it?"

Zerika turned and addressed the god directly, saying, "I believe I have more to offer than mere courage."

"Perhaps," said Ordwynac. "But is what you have sufficient? That is what we must decide."

"I have already decided," said Verra.

"Well, that doesn't startle me," said Ordwynac.

"For my part," said Barlen, "I am not far from agreeing with Verra on this occasion."

"Well," said Ordwynac. And then, to Zerika, "What is it you have to offer, that is more than courage?"

"As I have had the honor to tell you, I am Heir to the throne, that is, the only remaining Phoenix. And I have the wit to have arrived here through the Paths of the Dead while yet living. And I have the aid of the Enchantress of Dzur Mountain. And I have the will to do what I have to. All of this you know. What more is needed?"

"I will tell you what is needed—" began Ordwynac, but, by this time, Zerika had had enough.

"Nonsense," she said.

She remained still, feeling the weight upon her of the scrutiny of the gods, and aware of their surprise at the word she had dared to utter.

When none of the gods spoke, Zerika began to do so once more, in this fashion: "I do not know what you are doing, but it is not determining if I should take the Orb. You know—all of you—that I must take the Orb from this place, and that I must—that I am destined to—reawaken the Empire, or to try until I am slain in the effort. You pretend to be evaluating my worthiness, but you are doing nothing of the kind, because I know and each of you knows that there is no other choice."

Zerika paused for a breath.

"So I must ask myself just what you *are* doing?"

She allowed her glance to cover the entire circle, looking at them all with an unwavering glance.

"I have an answer," she said. "I believe that you not only want me to leave with the Orb, but you—or at least some of you—want me so intimidated that I will put together the Empire as you see it, in the way you wish it, to serve your ends."

She paused.

"This will not be.

"You are the Guardians of the World, and the Lords of Judgment. But I will be the Empress. If there is a thing you wish of my Empire, you may ask me for it, as it always has been, and I will decide, as the Emperor always has. That is how it will be."

She paused, then said, "Now give the Orb into my hands. I have spent too much time here, and I must reach a place of safety beyond this realm before I sleep, and I am very weary."

There was a considerable silence that followed this declamation. So long was it, in fact, that Zerika had time to realize that, in fact, she was every bit as weary as she had said; she was wondering if she would be able to remain on her feet. At that instant, she found that she was looking at one of the gods she had not hitherto confronted. This one appeared to her as a being not unlike a Serioli, a very old Serioli—one with wrinkles and splotches of great age, and whose gnarled hands rested palms up upon thin knees the outlines of which were visible beneath a frail garment of dark blue. And in these hands and upon these knees was an object that Zerika knew at once, though she had never seen it, nor, indeed, heard more than the most cursory description of it.

It was a sphere about eight or nine inches in diameter, and of a grey so dark it was almost black, yet she fancied she could see the faintest sparkles from various points on its surface, as if certain jewels were inside it, their color breaking through here and there. The god spoke softly, saying, "Zerika of the House of the Phoenix, here is what you have come for. Bear it to good fortune." With this, the ancient god extended the Orb, and Zerika took it into her hands, feeling its weight gradually settle. It did not seem especially heavy to her; she judged that it could not weigh more than ten or fifteen pounds. She stared at the god, uncertain of what to do or to say. It seemed to her that he smiled a little, and she found that she had dropped her eyes, bashful as a girl, and given him a bow.

When she raised her head again, she was no longer in the circle where she had been, but now stood directly before the Cycle itself, which realizing caused in her such astonishment that she nearly dropped the Orb.

When she had recovered a little, she stared at the Cycle, the most ancient and sacred of all artifacts. It was larger in diameter than two men, made of a stone that does not erode, and, perhaps, older than Time. It was close enough to reach—indeed, the symbol of the Vallista was directly before her face—but she dared not touch it. She looked up toward the top, her neck straining, and she saw that, indeed, the symbol of her House, the Imperial Phoenix, was still at the pinnacle, flanked by the Athyra retiring and the Dragon advancing. Here was most mystical of the forces of the universe made tangible. All of the responsibilities of rulership, and all of her connections with other Emperors dating back to her ancestor, Zerika the First, suddenly seemed real and present to her as she studied the massive stone artifact.

We cannot, however we may try, communicate to the reader the emotion experienced by Zerika at this moment. Indeed, we cannot imagine how she must have felt: overwhelmingly weary, ultimately triumphant, tightly holding the Orb and now facing the Cycle itself, that most ancient of artifacts which brought forth all the humbleness and pride that is the birthright of any legitimate Emperor.

Soon, as she stood there, she realized that she was not alone. She turned her head, and saw a man dressed in the purple robes of the servants of the dead. Zerika turned to him and waited. The Purple Robe bowed, and indicated with a slow, graceful gesture that she was to follow him. She took a last look at the Cycle, blinking back tears, and set off after him.

She found that they were waking downward along a path of flat stones set into a grassy hillside. The path continued up another hill, this one topped with deciduous trees of some sort she didn't recognize, and also thick with bushes. The Purple Robe remained with her as they reached the bottom of the hill and began climbing. Zerika looked up at what, in fact, was a rather small hill and wondered if she would be able to climb it without assistance. But, she reflected, to receive aid in climbing from a Purple Robe would be, well, it wouldn't be right.

She fixed her eyes at the top of the hill, set her countenance in an expression of determination, and began walking. She felt her hands, holding the Orb, begin to tremble, and clutched it more tightly to her, holding it against her body. She began to take smaller steps as the path rose more steeply, and as she felt her strength deserting her. She glanced over at the Purple Robe who walked next to her, and thought again about leaning against him, but set her teeth and simply continued walking.

Eventually, she reached the trees, and observed that the stones of the path were now set more deeply into the ground, and seemed older. With each step now, it seemed, the forest grew thicker, the path narrower, the stones even older, and she had the sense she was walking backward in time.

The stones at her feet were now cracked. In a few more steps, they were broken, with weeds and grass growing up among them. In not much longer she was walking upon soft grass. At around that same time, she realized that she was alone; the Purple Robe had, somehow, been left behind.

At about this same time, she became aware that the Orb was no longer a burden her hands—indeed, it seemed that it weighed nothing at all. She glanced down at it, and realized that it was emitting a very soft, pale yellow glow. Without breaking stride, she opened her hands. The Orb floated into the air, and began slowly and gracefully circling her head.

At this time she realized with momentary confusion that, not only was there no longer a covering of tree branches over her head, but neither was there a sky; instead, it was as if she stood under a roof of stone. At the same time she detected a musty odor, and overlaying it, familiar scents: grass, pine needles, and wildflowers.

This confusion was, however, as we have said, momentary—she quickly realized exactly where she was. She wondered where Piro and his friends were, and then knew that, too. She became aware of the Enchantress, in her lair at Dzur Mountain, and now she understood much of that most peculiar of abodes as well. And, as she concentrated upon the Enchantress, it seemed to her as if the two of them were looking at each other from only a few meters apart, and it seemed that Sethra Lavode looked into her eyes.

Zerika spoke to her, saying, "It is done."

"Yes," said the Enchantress, permitting herself a small smile. "Now matters become difficult."

"Of course," said the Empress Zerika. "We must move at once. There is no time to delay."

Then the Empress turned her attention to other matters, and Sethra was gone.

Zerika the Fourth, Empress of Dragaera, realized that she was no longer tired.

Some Notes Toward Two Analyses of Auctorial Method and Voice

By C. Sophronia Cleebers
Resident Special Faculty,
Dragaeran Studies

How to Write Like Paarfi of Roundwood

1. Always refer to yourself as "we." It is unclear why Paarfi prefers to use the first person plural. He doesn't seem to be speaking jointly for himself and his patron of the moment; neither is he speaking jointly on behalf of himself and Steven Brust. His true camaraderie is reserved for himself and his manuscript, but that doesn't usually prompt a writer to speak in the plural. It may be that he's using the editorial "we." Alternately, he may just have a mouse in his pocket.

2. Do not use "he or she" or "his or her" constructions. The Dragaeran language uses *gya* to refer to someone of indeterminate sex, thus avoiding these difficulties. Steven Brust has chosen to translate this as "he," "his," and "him," to Paarfi's everlasting dismay.

3. It appears that Dragaeran, like some languages in our own world, grammatically distinguishes statements of observed fact from guesses, inferences, and unsupported allegations. To illustrate this, compare English, which allows the same verb to be used for all those senses—both *I see it is red* and *I see it is new*—with the Hopi language, which requires the speaker to distinguish them: *I see it is red*, but *I infer that it is new*.

In Brust's translation, this distinction is conveyed by the verb "to pretend." It takes the place of such words as *feign, guess, allege, assert, imagine, claim, believe, say* (without further substantiation), *theorize, think, be under the impression that, represent as being*, and *pretend* (in its usual sense), as well as the interrogative, *do (you) wish to make me believe*; that is, in statements unsupported by material observation.

It is clear, from Brust's translations of Paarfi's pre-Interregnum works, that at that time the Dragaeran language also distinguished states of imperfect knowledge on the part of the speaker, a distinction that Brust most commonly translates as "to almost think." For whatever reason—the linguistic evolution of Dragaeran is beyond the scope of this essay—it appears that by the time of the events described in the present volume, everyday speech had dispensed with this distinction concerning one's own state of knowledge.

4. When "nearly" is not used to express a quantity, it is used as a somewhat ironic intensifier or as confirmation. Saying *I nearly think so* in answer to a question roughly translates as "I do indeed think so." Using it as your sole response—"Is it cold outside?" "Nearly."—is more like replying "You'd better believe it is."

5. Many English speakers have one or several habitual phrases with which they fill hesitant pauses in their conversation. A few of these phrases retain some slight meaning; others come close to being neutral noise. To approximate the effect of Paarfi as translated by Brust, these should be replaced by "well." Among the phrases thus replaced: *you know; let's just say that; could be; I guess; yeah; I suppose; I can see that; if you say so; whatever; maybe so; I've heard that said; you could say that; in that case; if that's how you feel about it;* and *that may be so, but.*

Judging from the different circumstances in which we see it used, "well" is one of those words, like "right" or "nu," that are capable of conveying a broad and subtle range of meaning, depending on the inflection the speaker gives them.

"Well" is always followed by a comma. The only exception is when it's used as a one-word sentence, which usage is approximately the equivalent of saying "If you say so" in a dubious tone of voice.

6. Some useful and characteristic phrases you may wish to cultivate include: *It is to be hoped; we wish to express the earnest wish; I do myself the honor to suggest; who have done us the kindness; about which* (or *whom*) *we have the honor to write; to lay before the reader; as we will endeavor to show; as we will take it upon ourselves to demonstrate; as the reader is now aware; with our readers' kind indulgence; and consequently; with regard to; concerning the matter of;* and *we are at a loss to understand.*

A sentence such as "We will omit the list entirely, confident that the reader is missing nothing of any importance by the omission" can't really be cultivated, being entirely too particular and memorable to be used more than once in the same lifetime; but if you reach the point where you can construct equivalent sentences of your own, you may with some justice consider yourself to have achieved a certain degree of mastery.

7. A turn of phrase that must be used judiciously:

the reader will undoubtedly have noticed
the astute reader will have observed, no doubt,
as the reader will, no doubt, have deduced,
as the reader has no doubt surmised,
as the reader no doubt realized some time ago,
although the reader can, no doubt, form whatever conclusions he wishes.

There are of course other variants. Generally speaking, when Paarfi says the reader will undoubtedly have noticed something, it's either because he's about to repeat some piece of information which was mentioned earlier, or because he wishes to draw attention to some implication or consequence that the reader would doubtless have noticed on his own if he'd thought about it, but then again might have missed, which would be a pity.

Some of the more captious and demanding critics might deplore these small reminders as superfluous or excessively obvious; but in truth they are a great help to readers who are trying to follow such a lively and complicated story, and who would rather concentrate on the interesting events going on, than soberly store up each small fact against possible future need, and dutifully examine each sentence for all its possible implications.

8. Only Khaavren, and later his son Piro, use "Cha!" as an exclamation. Any characters may say "Bah!" on occasion, but Tazendra says it oftener. "Blood of the horse!" is an oath properly used only by those present for the stirring events at the non-battle of Pepperfields.

9. Another phrase that requires special handling is, *The reader will permit us to say two words about —*. The convention to be observed here is that neither Paarfi nor anyone else ever stops at two, though most speakers come closer to that modest number than Paarfi does.

Say two words about is a Dragaeran idiom, equivalent to our "say a few words about." Note that this is slightly different from the equally idiomatic *two words* and *say two words to*, which are better understood to mean what we would express as "(I would like to) have a word with (you/him/them)," sometimes shading over into what we would refer to as "my two cents' worth."

10. It is not enough to use run-on sentences; they must also parse. Consider this 138-word three-sentence specimen from Paarfi's preface to *The Phoenix Guards*:

> But should he who holds the present sketchpad of
> words in his hands wonder how it came to occupy such
> a place, we should explain that it was one of our note-
> books while we were preparing for the longer work
> mentioned above. Yet Master Vrei, who happened to
> see the notebook one day while we discussed the vol-
> umes in question, and read it on the spot, announced
> that, by itself, it would, if not provide an accurate look
> at certain aspects of court life before the Interregnum,
> at least be a possible source of, in his words, "enlight-
> ened entertainment." It was with this in mind that, for
> the past twenty-one years, we have had the honor of
> refining, or, if we are permitted, "honing" the notebook,
> and preparing it for the publication we humbly hope it
> merits.

You have to be orderly when you pile up that many clauses at once; otherwise they'll fall over.

11. If you are in doubt as to the appropriate tone, politeness and grati- tude for past favors are always a good fallback position. This should not be mistaken for natural humility of character. Neither should Paarfi's absence of levity be mistaken for the lack of a sense of humor. Consider his description of a swordmaker's cellar shop as ". . . a small, stuffy base- ment, which would have been damp, smelly, close, and dark, were it not, in fact, well-lit, which prevented it from being dark."

12. Bear in mind, at all times and in all circumstances, whatever the sub- ject under discussion—be it never so dear to your heart, and worthy of thoughtful consideration at far greater length than that to which you are regretfully obliged to constrain it—that conciseness is a virtue of such paramount importance that neither Paarfi nor the present writer would ever dream of relinquishing it, even for a moment; bearing in mind as well, that the related and yet not wholly identical temptation to entangle both the narrative and the reader in a thousand branching paths of digression, from which initially attractive yet ultimately fruitless byways (like those deceptively promising mountain trails which, when followed, gradually diminish to faint and narrow tracks and thence to mere noth- ingness, leaving the traveler stranded at some spot deserted by humanity

not through whim or chance, but justly, on account of its intrinsic lack of any interest whatsoever) one may only with great difficulty find one's way back to the main thread, must also be sternly avoided.

Every time you explain this point to the reader, follow it with a firmly worded assurance that that is exactly what you intend to do. Believe yourself when you say it.

13. We have by now passed out of the territory of simple linguistics, and into the art of thinking like a Paarfi. The single most significant fact about him is that he set out to be a historian, not a novelist, but his milieu has little use for historians as such. It is therefore not an unmixed blessing for him that his patroness, publisher, translator, and enthusiastic readers are all fans of historical romance; but writers as a class get few enough blessings of any sort, and are inclined to take what they can get.

What we take to be his books — *The Phoenix Guards, Five Hundred Years After,* and *The Viscount of Adrilankha,* in the first volume of which, *The Paths of the Dead,* this essay has the honor to be included — should be understood to be mere notebooks, sketches for the much longer and much more serious work of real history he has in contemplation. Thus, to Paarfi's way of thinking, he has left out 90% of the details: a veritable saint of brevity.

14. Paarfi's background as a historian, as opposed to a writer of entertaining romances, may also explain why he periodically, and laboriously, feels obliged to explain matters any novelist would take for granted. See, for example, the opening section of Chapter the Sixth of the very volume which you now hold in your hands, and which we therefore need not quote.

15. An underappreciated point, which was ably discussed in the Dean of Pamlar University's preface to *Five Hundred Years After,* is that Paarfi's rendering and Steven Brust's translation of Dragaeran speech is actually shorter, faster-moving, and less archaic than the language spoken by the characters. As the estimable Dean put it:

> In the interest of accuracy it must be admitted that one aspect of our author's depiction of these events is not, in fact, strictly in accordance with the actual practice of the times. The mode of speech employed by those at court, and by Khaavren and his friends as well, in casual discussions or when leading up to speeches actually recorded in history, does not represent, so far as can be determined, any actual mode of speech, past or present. It

is taken from a popular anonymous play of the period, *Redwreath and Goldstar Have Traveled to Deathsgate*, where it is found in a game played by the principals to ward off unwanted inquiries. The proof of this is the exclamation of one of their executioners at the end of the play, "The Dog! I think I have been asking for nothing else for an hour!" This, or similar exclamations, are used several times in *The Phoenix Guards*, and more often in the book you now hold, to indicate that the time for empty courtesy is over.

But in the subtleties of its employment, the gradations of consciousness with which it is used, the precise timing of its terminations, this mode of speech does in fact give very much the flavor of the old court talk without that speech's tediousness or outmoded expressions: it is a successful translation that does not distort anything of significance to anybody except a linguist.

Once again, we must understand that when Paarfi proclaims his undying commitment to brevity in prose, he is telling the truth. Those inclined to doubt this are invited to examine references in the text which mention the amount of time consumed by a given conversation. Note that in some instances the allotted time is far longer than can be accounted for by the words on the page.

16. Be aware that what may appear to be errors are almost certainly intentional, the result of Paarfi and Brust trying to cope with nearly untranslatable circumstance. For instance, the mixing of feet, inches, yards, miles, meters, centimeters, kilometers, leagues, and furlongs is an attempt to convey the complexity of an Empire in which six different systems of measurement were used simultaneously.

17. Finally, in order to write like Paarfi, or for that matter like any other Dragaeran, you have to *thoroughly* internalize the Cycle, the Houses, and the number 17.

How to Write Like Steven Brust

Basics: Steven Brust's ethnic background is Hungarian Trotskyist labor organizer. He's from Minnesota, but right now is living in Las Vegas, where he plays a lot of poker. He's also a guitarist, banjo player, and drummer. He owns a parrot named Doc, and answers the phone by saying "I'm your huckleberry"—unless you manage to wake him before noon, in which case he says "This had better be good." *The Paths of the Dead* is either his nineteenth book, or *The Viscount of Adrilankha* is his nineteenth book and *The Paths of the Dead* is the first third of it.

Steve has two theories about literature, and one set of instructions on how to write it.

First theory: "The Cool Stuff Theory of Literature is as follows: All literature consists of whatever the writer thinks is cool. The reader will like the book to the degree that he agrees with the writer about what's cool. And that works all the way from the external trappings to the level of metaphor, subtext, and the way one uses words. In other words, I happen not to think that full-plate armor and great big honking greatswords are cool. I don't like 'em. I like cloaks and rapiers. So I write stories with a lot of cloaks and rapiers in 'em, 'cause that's cool."

Second theory: "The novel should be understood as a structure built to accommodate the greatest possible amount of cool stuff."

How to write like Steven Brust: "It's really simple. What you do is put up a sign on whatever wall you face when you're writing. The sign says: *And now, I'm going to tell you something really cool.*"*

Steve says it works for him.

---

* Steve adds that he got that last one from Gene Wolfe. As a perusal of Wolfe's many fine works will demonstrate, this method works for him, too. You may therefore be confident that you now know how to write like all three of these excellent authors, Paarfi and Brust and Wolfe as well; so if it happens that your ambitions lie in that direction, you must concede that purchasing and reading this book was a sound investment of your time and money.